touch

touch

COURTNEY MAUM

G. P. PUTNAM'S SONS

NEW YORK

G. P. PUTNAM'S SONS
Publishers Since 1838
An imprint of Penguin Random House LLC
375 Hudson Street
New York, New York 10014

Library of Congress Cataloging-in-Publication Data

Names: Maum, Courtney, date- author.
Title: Touch : a novel / Courtney Maum.
Description: New York : G.P. Putnam's Sons, [2017]
Identifiers: LCCN 2016040952 (print) | LCCN 2016048342 (ebook) | ISBN
9780735212121 (hardcover) | ISBN 9780735212138 (epub)
Subjects: | BISAC: FICTION / Literary. | FICTION / Family Life. |
FICTION / Humorous.
Classification: LCC PS3613.A87396 T68 2017 (print) | LCC PS3613.A87396
(ebook) | DDC 813/.6—dc23
LC record available at https://lccn.loc.gov/2016040952
p.   cm.

Printed in the United States of America
1   3   5   7   9   10   8   6   4   2

BOOK DESIGN BY AMANDA DEWEY

For my family on both sides of the Atlantic,
who babysat

That, finally, the door opens . . . and it opens *outward*—
we've been inside what we wanted all along.

—David Foster Wallace, 1999

touch

1

Sloane Jacobsen was living in a world without peanuts. As the Air France hostess busied herself in the first class cockpit tipping prosecco into plastic flutes, Sloane bemoaned the protocol keeping her from her favorite snack. Someone had an allergy—*might* have an allergy—so it was a no-go on all nut products. Normally, her future-focused mind would have started speculating—how would the normalization of food sensitivities impact consumer habits in the coming years? But instead, she just felt saddened that the current state of geopolitics expected people's worst. Someone might also use their wineglass to puncture the pilot's jugular so airlines had banned all drinkware made of glass, too.

The stewardess, not French—"Carly," read her nametag—served Sloane a drink along with a single slice of cucumber and a mauve wedge of something masquerading as foie gras. Yes, the world was a simpler, kinder place when Sloane could still eat nuts in public.

She peered into the confines of the egg-shaped bunker where her companion, Roman, was reading an article in the travel section of a newspaper: "The Mediterranean: Is There Anywhere Safe Left to Go?"

"Is there?" Sloane asked, toeing his heel to get his attention.

"Is there what?" he said, looking at her through the eyeglasses he wore more for aesthetic reasons than anything having to do with sight.

"Anywhere safe left to go?"

"Oh," he said, giving the paper a shake so it stood with better posture. "Portugal, apparently."

She scoffed. "But that's not in the Mediterranean."

"That's true." Roman shrugged. "Then I guess not." He flipped the page over as if to inspect it. "It's not a very good article," he said, continuing to read it.

Sloane reclined her seat and stared at the domed ceiling, beyond which was pure, unoxygenated sky. Flying wasn't easy when you were a trend forecaster. Sloane had a spongy sensitivity to her environment that only deepened when she flew. She felt itchy, ill at ease. It annoyed her, that article. Although she was in the business of looking for the next big things, it was nonetheless exhausting, the greed for the undiscovered, the novel, the *new* new. Lisbon wasn't "new" of course—it was one of the oldest cities in the world, predating even Paris—but it had been anointed by travel editors as the new Berlin.

Sloane tried to calm herself, quell the negativity—she could watch a movie too. Given the excessive in-flight entertainment selection, she could watch anything she wanted. But she couldn't rid herself of a snaking anxiety. Something was wrong. Not wrong like the last time she'd been airborne, when she'd felt such a current of foreboding she wondered if "see something, say something" could include "getting a bad vibe," and thirty-three minutes into the flight plan, the plane was hit by lightning. It shook, it nosed. People screamed. It righted. No, this offness was nothing like that. This was internal, a mechanical error inside of her. She needed more vitamins, probably. Vitamin D.

Beside her, Roman had given up reading about the travel impacts of the European debt crisis and was scrolling through the airline's film choices, his finger guiding him to "New Releases." Sloane knew with neon certainty that Roman would pick *Pitch Perfect 3*. His Americaphilism was nondiscriminatory: fleece sportswear, SUVs, Sub-Zero refrigerators, discount superstores, the viralism of American patriotism (flags sprouting up in window boxes and front lawn patches after grim events), pop culture, online culture—he was taken by it all. To someone like Roman, trained to look for signs and signifiers in every experience, romantic comedies held the key to understanding the American way of life. Being inordinately excited about a cappella music was apparently step one.

While Roman went starry-eyed at the Universal Pictures logo spinning on his screen, Sloane pulled the customs immigration forms out of her seat pocket, remembering how the stewardess's eyebrows had arched when she had asked for two. *One per family*, Carly had repeated, certain that the polished people before her were espoused. Yes, well. In Paris, traditional marriage was about as popular as private health care. Roman and Sloane had been together ten years. His name was on her electric bill, but they were never having children; their careers were their children, there you had it. In fact, their careers had been *boosted* by their joint decision not to breed. The famous American forecaster and the Frenchy intellectual—"The couple who has everything, except kids" (*Le Figaro*, July 2013); "The Ultimate Anti-Mom" was the headline of a recent profile of Sloane in British *Vogue* ("Reproduction is akin to ecoterrorism," she'd been quoted in that particular mag). It had been the interview hour's fault—three p.m., her worst time. Low blood sugar, doldrums. She and the bouncy journalist, the chardonnay had been cheap.

Ecoterrorism. Yeah—it was a good thing that Sloane's family didn't read much. Or maybe they'd developed an interest in European fashion glossies since she'd last seen them three years ago—she wasn't in a position to know. But per her sister's annual Fourth of July newsletter (yes, she actually did this), Leila was pregnant with her third kid. In the wake of their father's death when Leila was eighteen and Sloane twenty-two, Leila—not Sloane—had turned out to be the family success story. She'd fought back death with birth.

Sloane had made predictions that had revolutionized the tech industry—she'd presaged the symbolism of roots to the food industry before 9/11, predicted the now ubiquitous touch-screen gesture, the swipe. She'd lectured and consulted and symposiumed in thirty-seven countries to date, she owned an apartment in the 6th arrondissement of Paris, had the kinds of friends known by their first names only. A lot of people cared about the life that she'd constructed. She used to, too.

Roman tapped the screen to pause the inanity before him. "Did you do this?" he asked too loudly, headphones still on.

Sloane put a finger to her lips before she answered; passengers were sleeping. "Do what?"

"Sing with girls?"

She narrowed her eyes. "No."

"And the boys sing, too? And they're popular?"

Despite herself, she laughed. "A cappella wasn't cool when I was in college," she said. "It was made cool by a TV show called *Glee*."

Roman's eyebrows arched. "Everyone knows *Glee*."

Sloane bristled against this new dismissiveness. Roman knew everything about everything now that he was a cyber star. For a trend forecaster, it was unfortunate that she preferred the old version of her boyfriend to Roman 2.0.

When they'd first met, Roman had been a brainy market researcher for the consumer goods company Unilever in France. She'd been immediately taken by his inventive wit and a kind of bemused composure that she'd later identify as optimism, unusual for the French. They'd met at a focus group for a new line of male soap. The consumer feedback had been useless ("I want something that smells like charcoal, but also good, like soap," was one example), but when

Roman bid the industry suits good-bye, he did so with a perfectly delivered antanaclasis: "I don't know what I'll wash with, gentlemen, but I wash my hands of this." *He's a little pompous*, Sloane remembered thinking. *But he sure seems like fun.*

These days, he was mostly pompous. Roman had transitioned out of market research into professional punditism: delivering lectures across Europe on the shifting paradigms of touch. He'd even coined a term for his research: *neo-sensualism*. Making him a "neo-sensualist"— the term had stuck. Between his op-eds on how physicality was changing in a digitalized world and his increasingly colorful online presence, Roman had claimed a place for himself among Europe's intelligentsia. But once he incorporated the Zentai suit into his social media feed and presentations? The match of Internet stardom was lit.

The first time Sloane saw Roman in the seamless bodysuit that hallmarked the Japanese practice, it had been in their Paris kitchen, and the only word for what came tumbling out of her mouth was a guffaw. The bodysuit was integral—there weren't any holes for the eyes or the mouth, the whole thing was entered into by a tiny little slit. When it was put on properly, it looked like the wearer's body had been dipped in liquid pewter.

"You look like a superhero," Sloane had said, glancing up from her work at the freaky figure by the fridge. "What's it for?"

What's it for? The phrase chagrined her now, she'd been so sure that the donning of the suit was a once-in-a-lifetime occurrence. Something for a panel. A crowd-pleaser. Clickbait.

"The Zentai suit is fascinating," Roman had said, gliding his hands down his body. "It's an invitation—and a refusal, no? It presents the body as an anonymous thing that can be contemplated, but never truly accessed." He moved his arms behind his weirdo head. "I've found my avatar."

And so it seems he had. At an American university, Roman probably would have been fired for delivering a lecture in fetishwear, but in Paris he was celebrated: the form of it met his new function, which was to speculate about sensuality in the digital age. He presented the suit as a conduit for temptation and refusal. "You can see how far the implications could go," he was fond of saying. "Birth control, affairs."

"Affairs?" she remembered asking.

"If it's nonpenetrative, nontactile, can it be considered cheating?"

Sloane rested her head against the airplane window, ice-cold to the touch. If anything, Roman was being unfaithful with his telephone. Right before they'd left for America, the popular French newsmagazine *Le Nouvel Observateur* had done a profile on him: "Touché: A Day in the Life of the Neo-Sensualist, Roman Bellard," and his cell phone had been ringing and pinging and vibrating ever since. A six-page photo spread accompanied the write-up, Roman doing the daily things of any working Parisian: reading the news at a kiosk, sniffing melons at the outdoor market, strolling through a park. Difference here was that Roman was doing these things in a skintight Zentai suit.

Traipsing about town in his metallic gold one, riding the metro, contemplating the Seine. The alleged elegance and nonchalance with which Roman appropriated fetish custom thrilled the bougie masses. Overnight, his Instagram account became supercharged. Two hundred thousand, four hundred thousand: Sloane had stopped checking before she saw it reach a five.

Back in Paris, they'd often consulted together (the local media referred to them as a *duo de choc!* which struck her as a charmingly juvenile way of saying "power couple"), but she'd been covetous—and secretive—about her assignment at the tech giant Mammoth that had summoned her back to the United States for half a year. Discretion was tantamount in the trends industry, that was part of her reticence, but there was something else. The hot flush of her instincts told her not to bring Roman into Mammoth's fold.

Sloane knew the key clause to her work contract by heart; she was proud of the things she'd done to be the person who could accept such an assignment, and for the first time, she found that she didn't want to share:

> With your global expertise in trends across the fashion, beauty, tech and entertainment industries, you'll help our creative teams sculpt their visions for our ReProduction summit in June.

Every year, the electronics juggernaut ran a three-day summit about consumer trends that brought the world's visionaries and taste-makers together to consult on a different theme. They'd gone big with this one, polemic. *What will we make when we stop making kids?* Daxter Stevens, Mammoth's CEO, needed someone with global name recognition. Someone with vision. Someone empathetic. Someone without kids.

Enter Sloane Jacobsen: progenitor of ideas, soothsayer of the swipe. Instincts, accounted for; maternal instincts, nil.

It takes a while to figure out your specialty when you work in trends. Although she'd started out in beauty (quickly going from an American-in-Paris entry leveler to the unofficial creative director at the French cosmetics giant, Aurora), what Sloane excelled at was mapping out what the wired rich wanted next.

And it currently wasn't children. Over the last two decades, the upper-middle-class American ego had wanted global positioning systems and wearables; it hadn't wanted kids. For the various companies she consulted with, Sloane sketched out a world viewpoint that had become increasingly self-centered, forecasting a rise in personal electronics and personal improvement, and a downtick in the birthrate because it's *selfless* to have kids. Did she regret the articles she'd published in which she'd called breeding shortsighted? Listen, there were nuances. She probably could have used a kinder word. But she'd never retracted her opinions or apologized. To the world outside of her, she was successful, influential, unapologetic: the uber anti-mom.

So be it. If Sloane had to judge from her emotional incompatibility with her own mother (an obsessive nurturer), she would have been terrible at parenthood. She just didn't have it in her to be giving. Also, she wasn't a fan of being scared, and it had to be petrifying to love someone more than yourself.

Beside her, Roman laughed at something in the movie. She craned her neck to see at what, but his screen was tilted in a way that all she saw was darkness.

2

B ack in the 1950s, personal electronics were aspirational posses-
sions: a reflection of middle-class desires. By the time Daxter
Stevens was brought over from Greylight Advertising to be Mammoth's youngest ever CEO, he scaled the consumer electronics around
a new axiom: it was the *devices* telling us how we should live.

To the televisions, gaming systems, telephones and computers that
had bolstered Mammoth in the eighties, Dax added Internet services,
lifestyle products, social media, security, human-machine integration,
and green energy technology. Accordingly, the Mammoth gig came
with a *lot* of solar-powered perks, one of which was a driverless car for
Sloane's personal use. The car was a prototype, currently called
(rather uninspiredly) the M-Car, poised to offer a more personalized
experience than the competing models, most of which still couldn't
differentiate a "road" from a "sidewalk."

The problem with having a driverless car was that it came without
a driver: no one to meet you at the Arrivals gate. Sloane hadn't asked
one of her family members to come for her, and they hadn't offered.
They probably thought she had a flying saucer at her beck and call.

"The car's not here?" Roman asked, brow furrowed, his eyes

trained to the street where the hastily cleaned sedans of the shared driving economy waited for their riders.

Sloane scrolled through the messages in her phone, the very act of looking down at it regrettable. She'd developed something of an allergy to her smartphone this past year. Migraines, vision problems, an increase in blood temperature. Her therapist said that these were symptoms of anxiety—but Sloane had gone a step further and dubbed it "enviro-xiety." If it were up to her, she'd chuck the gadgets in the garbage, throw away the constant availability, the heightened stress of being always in the know. But Sloane couldn't earn the kind of money she was earning if she was offline. It was the catchword of this millennium. Celebrities, black voters, ayahuasca-induced clarity: everything and everybody needed to be *reached*.

"Daxter's assistant said the car is parked," Sloane said, pulling up the e-mail. "Aisle thirty-seven. Level B."

Roman's eyes went wide. "It's just *parked?*"

Sloane shrugged. Yes, the prototype of one of the first self-driving vehicles was parked in a commuter lot—in between a rusted Ford Explorer and a Honda Civic, as it turned out.

Sloane had been inside autonomous vehicles before, but only ones whose comfort level had been modeled on a golf cart's. In focus groups, Mammoth found that target consumers of self-driving cars still wanted to feel like they were being *driven*, which meant: invisible driver up front, passengers in the back. There were spotlights in the car's ceiling on individual dimmers, an onyx-tinted privacy divider and massaging leather seats. Best of all, the car had a name. After sitting for an instructional video that outlined both the benefits and limitations of the car's lidar technology, the ceiling lights brightened and the car powered to life.

"Good morning, Ms. Jacobsen, good day, Monsieur Bellard," the car said in a crisp voice, "I am Anastasia, and I will be your driver. Please, you will notice the location of the 'emergency' buttons and also your seat belts?"

Anastasia, Sloane thought, smiling to herself. They'd be transported not through the Midtown Tunnel, but across the Russian steppes.

"Do we talk back?" Roman whispered urgently, interrupting her daydream of horses and white fur.

Sloane leaned forward, her voice aimed at the dash.

"It's nice to meet you, too."

"But the pleasure is all mine!" Anastasia answered with pronounced enthusiasm. "Was your Air France flight 9773 from Charles de Gaulle to airport JFK comfortable?" she continued.

"Errgh, yes." Sloane noted that Mammoth had some conversational aberrations to sort out. "It was."

"I'm so pleased to hear that. And we will still be heading to East Ninth Street and Avenue C in Manhattan?"

Beside her, Roman did the cluck-cluck tongue thing that French people used to communicate exasperation. When Mammoth said they'd rent Sloane an apartment anywhere she wanted, Roman had been gunning for the Upper West Side, but his comprehension of New York real estate was mostly informed by early Woody Allen films—he didn't realize that the area had changed since *Annie Hall*.

Sloane relied on signs and cues to do her trend work: she observed the way people behaved, shifted likes and dislikes, the way they talked and dressed. It was possible to monitor the undercurrents of new behaviors in big-box stores, but it wasn't preferable. There was only so much she could discern about humanity by noting that Costco was running a big sale on smoked trout.

Which is why Sloane wanted to live in the Alphabet City neighborhood of the East Village, a place that was, for the most part, chain store and froYo free. As an affluent white person, Sloane knew it was sanctimonious to think of Alphabet City as the "real" New York. "Real" New York didn't exist anymore. It certainly wasn't in Brooklyn—recently deemed "the least affordable place in America." Brooklyn wasn't so much a borough as a category now, like imported cheese.

But still—with its riot of smells, treasured community gardens, the trashcans overloaded with paper plates stained by ninety-nine-cent pizza slices and six-dollar *ristrettos*, there was a confluence that moved her. Alphabet City wasn't perfect—their new place was only two blocks from the site of the Tompkins Square Park riot where hundreds beseeched the yuppie scum to die—but at least it wasn't torpid. Because it was bloodlessness that frightened Sloane more than community tension: the insipidness of luxury apartment buildings with gyms and dry cleaning services and in-building convenience stores with chia seed green smoothies that encouraged—even celebrated—that everyone be one thing, strive to be one thing.

The last time Sloane had lived in the East Village, she'd been in a fetid one-room walk-up with a women's studies concentrator named Ramona and their de facto third roommate, her sister, Leila, a senior in high school then who visited a lot. How she'd loved those crowded, easy times when too much of someone else's hair in the tub drain qualified as a problem. Aside from globalization fatigue, nostalgia, too, was pulling Sloane back to Alphabet City. It necessitated constant masking, her sentimental side.

"If you'll allow me," sang Anastasia, snapping Sloane back to their commute, "the thermal radar seatbacks have detected an elevated temperature in Monsieur Bellard that suggests moderate dehydration. We have a variety of refreshments in the temperature-regulated cooler underneath the seat divider, as well as a single-serve coffeemaker which I don't recommend activating at this time for the reasons of dehydration cited."

Sloane popped open the mini-fridge and retrieved two bottled waters.

"Bottled tap water," she said, handing one to Roman, whose lips rarely encountered anything other than caffeine and red wine. "Welcome to the States."

3

When Sloane was a little girl, her closest friend besides her sister (who'd been just a toddler then) was a peppy Argentinean named Marti Fernandez. Almost every Friday of their seventh year, Marti slept over at her house, and, like most girls that age, they would spend the night talking long after Sloane's mother had told them to go to bed.

On one of these sleepovers, Sloane woke from a dream. She had seen the man whom Marti would spend her life with, clear as day. Marti was back in Argentina, in the kitchen of her adult home. The man was wide-faced, with an easy smile, a boyish fop of hair, a sharp nose, big hands. He looked funny, kind. Sloane woke with her heart racing as if exiting a nightmare, certain that she'd seen someone who existed, except she'd seen him twenty years in the future.

When Marti woke, Sloane told her that she'd seen the man she was going to marry. That she'd seen their kitchen. (She disliked its granite countertop, but she didn't tell her that.) That she was living in Buenos Aires again with her children.

Marti giggled uncontrollably, wanting all the details about this grown-up, future life. After Sloane had shared everything she could remember, Marti collapsed against the pillow, looking dreamily at the ceiling. "Too bad I'm never moving back!"

But she did move back. Their old high school sent out frequent newsletters, and an adult Sloane had sucked in her breath when she saw the recent updates from the class of '95. Marti had gotten married, and she had married *him*: the man Sloane had seen in her dream all those years ago. It was the same man, the same age he'd been in her vision, the same helpless smile and gigantic hair, much larger than little Marti; generous and kind.

Standing now in the apartment that would be hers and Roman's, Sloane felt the same disturbing frequency growing inside her: the disconcerting feeling that she already knew how all this would turn out. She tried to shake the presentiment—told herself, instead, that everything would be great.

"Then it's true about the kitchens!" Roman cried, setting his bags down. "New Yorkers never cook?"

Rusted fire escapes, surfaces bleached to mask the preexisting odors of old beer and floral youth: they had arrived at their new home. Sloane watched Roman investigate the tiny, sunlit kitchen set up on black and white linoleum, the paneled glass affording a view of the stately Christodora tower up the street. He opened cupboards and peered into the refrigerator while Sloane took in the hissing and popping and creaking and cracking of an apartment in New York. She'd forgotten the sheer cacophony that the plumbing systems made, the slushing rush of water shooting around the building, the clip-clop of high-heeled publicists blow-drying their hair, entire floors of renters who refused to put in carpets. Even though it was bigger, a top floor, and significantly more expensive, the energy wasn't that different from the place she'd had in college: architecturally inhospitable, impossible to keep clean.

"Does this oven even work?" Roman called out from the kitchen she'd just left.

"Probably not!" Sloane shouted back, peering into the room that she'd hoped would be her home office, but she knew how things worked in Manhattan: she'd never be at home. She'd keep spare changes of clothing and an extra toothbrush under her desk and this sunny, perfect room would end up being Roman's to work in on the book that he would only say was about "neo-sensualism!" every time she asked.

Her friends in Paris thought it was weird that she hadn't pushed to find out more about the project, hadn't read any of his pages yet. But Sloane was a protector of the creative process. She respected Roman's rhythm and his privacy. Also, if his urban Zentai pics were anything to go on, she was pretty sure she was going to hate the entire thing.

She'd arrived at the bathroom, a crowded, grouty conglomeration of more black and white linoleum and a beautiful pink sink retrofitted to look antique. Despite the obvious renovations, there was still that fetid milk smell that Sloane remembered from her college place, an apartment so cramped and airless, they had to store their makeup in the refrigerator so it wouldn't melt. Sloane had even kept a mug in there for her sister's visits—top right shelf—stocked with the Wet n Wild eyeliners Leila was too nervous to wear around their mom.

God, it seemed indulgent, the fun that they had had. The three of them crowded into that tight bathroom, Ramona seated on the tub's edge, calmly crimping her hair while Leila tried out vampy makeup looks on a pretending-to-be-cross Sloane, music blaring out of a cassette player, the treble far too high.

Sloane probably would have spent all of her college evenings at bookstore readings if it hadn't been for Leila. Her sister lightened up Sloane's grimness, alleviated her self-seriousness, tried to show her that not everything needed to be analyzed, some things just were *fun*. Like sharing margaritas the size of bathtubs at Tortilla Flats, or dancing with a stranger in between bar tables. Dancing, God, that too seemed like something that belonged to another era, like pagers and roller skates. The last time Sloane had been touched by a stranger— much less *danced* with one—was during a TSA pat-down. Her carry-on had signaled an alarm (the four-ounce facial mist she'd hoped to get away with promptly taken from her bag), but as she stood there with her arms out, palms facing up, a uniformed woman announcing where she was going to touch her and why, when she had felt the woman's palm cup her shoulder and slide down with a certain firmness—it was ridiculous, really. More ridiculous than giant margaritas. Sloane had wanted to cry.

"Darling!" Roman called out from what was probably the bedroom. "There's something wrong with the bed!"

Sloane walked in to find her partner facedown on the mattress, his palms spread and fingers arched. "It has Botox in it!" he said, lifting up one hand.

She studied the material slowly rising up around his handprint.

"Memory Foam," she said, sitting down beside him. "It molds to your body."

"Why?"

She knit her brow and tried not to worry. It wasn't a chemical imbalance that was making her emotional, it was just jet lag. Normally, they would have really gotten into it—Why *was* Memory Foam such an aspirational mattress filling for the American consumer?—but she was too tired.

"I don't know," she admitted, her voice weary and flat. "It's just one of those things that everyone's told they're supposed to want and so they start to want it."

"Well, I don't want this bed," Roman said, sticking his thumb into the dense cake of polyurethane foam.

"I don't like it, either."

They both stayed silent. It was the first time they had agreed on anything in bed in a long time. What had started to feel like disinterest in sex on Roman's part was beginning to look like an aversion; or at least he had an aversion to the kind of sex Sloane wanted. Sloane worked incredibly hard. She was mere months away from forty. At the end of the day, she just didn't have it in her to get into a fetish suit with no eyes.

Roman lay back and sighed with deep contentment: he'd soon fall asleep. As for Sloane, she stared around their new bedroom and realized how useless sentimentality could be. Taking an apartment near her old college haunts wasn't going to make Ramona magically appear in her pineapple kimono, hair toweled from her bubble bath; wasn't going to transport Leila to Sloane's bedside where she'd contemplate a new box of Manic Panic hair dye, intoxicated with freedom.

Sloane needed a place to live during her time at Mammoth, and this apartment was it. That she happened to be within a car drive's distance of her family for the first time in nearly two decades, that wasn't going to change anything, and it was naïve to think it could. So, no. Sloane couldn't just invite her sister over for a too-much-cheese-and-wine night, couldn't tell her to get a sitter so they could see back-to-back matinees, couldn't pull her into the bathroom while Roman was opening a second bottle to confess that she and Roman hadn't had sex in over eighteen months.

Contrary to her professional life where she was pro-confrontation, in her personal one, Sloane had a tendency to sweep things under the rug. Internally, as she went about her business back in Paris, watching people linger in front of flower stalls, sniffing hopefully at roses, she would think of what was happening with her and Roman as a phase. It was essential that it only be a phase, or at least that it distend into something that didn't hurt her the way that it did now. The New York interlude would be good for them. A chance for realignment. At best, it would prove to be a high-paying distraction. At worst, another rug.

Sloane looked around again, felt the pull toward dreams. It would be detrimental to her jet lag—she should force herself to stay up later, but Roman was already breathing peacefully, and she didn't really have that much to unpack. Given the alternatives, Mediterranean or otherwise, sleep seemed like the safest place left to go.

4

Sloane didn't dream often of her father. She had to be fluish or deep (deep) into REM sleep, and she was rarely either. But jet lag was hallucinogenic, tidal. Before he died, Sloane could always count on her dad, Peter, to be there with his Dadaist pep talks (*Thought is made in the mouth* was a consistent favorite) before the big moments in her life, so it was only normal, or normally abnormal, that he'd show up to encourage her on her first day of work at Mammoth.

In her dream, he'd been at the piano that still stood in her mother's house, his chestnut hair baseball-cap matted, his wiry frame leaning toward the instrument in a coiled crouch—it had been a favorite game of theirs, minor, minor minor: Peter would parse out a chord and they'd both call out accompanying emotions. Minor for the eerie sounds, and for the really arresting ones, minor minor.

"Major minor," she'd said, because, in her dream, he'd pressed his finger to C major. "Fruit juice!" he'd added, in that enigmatic way of his, sticking his tongue out.

The off-kilter sense of humor, the shared thrill of giving attention to something most people overlooked, the respect for the way your environment could change your mood; all these things her father had inspired in her had been present in her dream. Not present: the wariness her mother seemed to have about their relationship, which made Sloane even more covetous of their weird piano game. All those times, that curious feeling in her belly when she'd look up from the keyboard to catch her mother staring at them, her expression pained and quizzical, as if she had mis-potted a plant.

Sloane had never gone in for the obvious cries of adolescent difference—she'd never worn too much eyeliner, never gotten a tattoo. But she'd been a misfit, and her father—a long man, a kind man—had been one, too. She thought before she spoke in a way that was conspicuous, but Peter had always indulged his daughter's observation skills. As an architect, he admired consideration, patience and the weighing of all sides. In his line of work, hastily drawn conclusions meant that buildings could fall down. But Margaret Jacobsen didn't like having two pensive people in her household. She'd always regarded her eldest like a nut she didn't have permission to crack.

"A professional thinker," that's what Peter had said once when her mom had accused Sloane of being "gloomy." If she stayed up late enough, Sloane was always catching snippets of such conversations from her hidden perch on the staircase. Margaret wanted her daughters to be happy. Anything but happy, Margaret got real scared. Which meant that things got pretty frightening when her father died.

"Sleep well?" Roman asked, sliding by her with a perfunctory tap on his way to the living room to do yoga. He had showered, and after yoga, he'd shower again. His obsession with personal hygiene made Sloane feel contagious. She touched her strawish bed hair, maneuvered it into a bun.

"I slept pretty deeply, actually," she said, trailing into the living room, watching him unfold his mat. Scent work was a significant part of her profession—she could track what people would want in the years ahead by what they liked to smell, and Sloane wished for the gift of already-made coffee ripping through the apartment. But they were a house divided in terms of morning beverages. Roman only liked espresso when it was prepared by a professional; at home, he drank green tea. Accordingly, Sloane was a single-capsule user and the olfactory results were disappointing. No more giant good-morning smells taking over the house.

She turned away from Roman to get ready for her first day at work. Another image came back from her dream then: her father in a dark wardrobe filled with dresses so navy they were almost black. The hangers made from earbud headphones that shone luminescent in the dark. He was gesturing at her, but not beckoning. He was pushing her away. "Build it down, Pumpkin," he'd said, before pushing the door open with an elusive smile; the kind of advice that was just opaque enough to sound like something he would have said.

A strange dream, all that clothing: in real life, Sloane wore the same thing every day. Depending on the weather: wool tunic/cotton tunic, leggings, sandals/boots. Her one concession to flair was the addition of a necklace: usually something weird and huge. The uniform was partly time-saving, partly premeditated: as a trend forecaster, she needed to be sartorially neutral at all costs. Trends were constantly changing; desires were, too. Her adherence to a uniform suggested that she would not.

Sloane closed her eyes for a moment, tried to breathe the dream out of her skin. It had been long enough, of course, that she knew her dad was truly gone, but back in the early days after his accident, when she'd first arrived in Paris, with the time change and the food changes and the language she hadn't yet mastered, she spent so many mornings head thick in slow-to-wake confusion, trying to separate the invented from the real. The Aurora job had been a springboard for the rest of her career, but what she'd really used it for was permission to somnambulate. Saying yes to the Paris-based position meant she'd have to board a plane, have to live on the other side of the ocean. *Have to*—this phrase came up when her sister called her selfish, when her mother cried, *Why now?* The job opportunity presented itself *before* her father's death, this she would always stand by. That the job allowed her to deepen the denial that had become a coping mechanism, this was also true.

She smoothed her hair back, drew a muted shade of peach across her lips. From the living room, she could hear the peaceful, one-tone voice of the filmed yoga instructor leading Roman through his physical ministrations. Roman wasn't one for self-practice, or self-anything, really. He liked company, especially the pixelated sort that existed in screens and phones. Sloane used to as well—it was one of the things that had brought them together, their faith in new technology. But there had been so many years of new technology. The sight of humans shuffling with their eyes down on their devices was as dreary to her as the robotic milkers hooked up to cows' teats. Her waning enthusiasm for electronics was another reason she'd accepted the gig at Mammoth. With all the crazy thinkers and tech heads there, she was hoping—she needed—to have her faith in tech renewed.

Dressed, she walked back into the living room, her perfume piercing the room that should have been filled with the closeness of his sweat if Roman had had glands that allowed such an indiscretion.

He stood up in warrior pose, his hands above his head.

"Good luck," he said, face shining. "I can't wait to meet them!"

Sloane blinked. In their normal life, he *would* meet her colleagues. He'd work for them, too. Back in Paris, they'd been collaborators. *Le duo de choc.* She'd brought him onto her projects, and he'd always sought her advice on his lectures and ideas. That they'd been avoiding each other's opinions—that he had an entire secret *book*—was something else that needed room under that rug.

"Don't forget: dinner at my mother's," she said, patting for her keys.
Roman rose to greet this reminder with a perfect cobra pose.

O ut on the street, Sloane contemplated her options. It was a beautiful day: cool, crisp, electric with the promise of things that could go wrong or right. It was rare, a balmy day like this in mid-November, and Sloane wanted to walk to Mammoth's headquarters in Union Square, but she imagined it would be bad form if she didn't show up for her first day of work in the company-sponsored driverless car.

So she swiped left on the M-Car app that would summon her chariot from wherever it was that Anastasia recharged. Sloane liked to imagine the car in a set of imperial stables with gloved stablehands and chandeliers, the peaty scent of draft horses warming the cold air.

Upscale stable or commonplace garage, it was somewhere close, that much was for certain. Anastasia came purring around the corner in two minutes flat.

"Good morning, Ms. Jacobsen," Anastasia chirped once she got in. "Coffee? I have wonderful milk. Or have you already had caffeine?"

Sloane looked gratefully at the coffee machine retrofitted into the seat divider. What she would sacrifice in terms of health benefits from not walking to work would be gained by not having to frequent the sadomasochistic espresso joints where the employees acted more like glass blowers than baristas.

She didn't have to tell Anastasia how she took it—her driver had been apprised of her beverage persuasions and the coffee emerged filled one fourth of the way up, so that she could make it light and sweet. Sloane wasn't a latte girl. Or rather, she had been until she moved to Paris. Tourists wax poetic about the quality of that city's espresso, but rarely will you hear someone applaud a French waiter's way with milk.

"To the office, then?"

Sloane was thankful for the hesitancy in Anastasia's voice. She wanted to believe in a world where all her choices hadn't been made yet. Where she could say no—she'd much prefer a winter picnic on Coney Island, or demand that Anastasia head northward for an unplanned getaway to Cape Cod. Spontaneity went hand in hand with longevity, this was something her father had taught her, he who was enigmatic to perfection, encrypted to a fault. A lot of good it did him, though. Being surprising.

"How are you settling in, Ms. Jacobsen? How is the apartment?"

"You can call me Sloane," Sloane said, draping a linen napkin across her chest in case the car's lidar technology caused them to halt in front of a pothole.

"But the apartment's beautiful," she continued, worried she'd been brusque. "It's just what I wanted. I lived here in college."

"Well, it must feel very good to be back, then," Anastasia replied. "Do you have family here?"

Sloane winced. Anastasia had been given enough of her file to know how she liked her coffee, but not enough to know that Sloane was something of a drop-out Jacobsen. Not that this is something that would have been in her résumé. She never talked about her dad's accident when people asked her why she lived in Paris, not even with her friends. At any rate, in her tax bracket, it was assumed she'd have a professional to discuss intimate problems with. It's incredible how much people want to believe you when you say something is fine.

"My family's in Connecticut," Sloane answered. "So, not far from here."

"Oh," Anastasia said, softer. "You've changed your tone of voice."

"I'm sorry?" Sloane balked, both astonished—and, deep inside her, touched—that her car's speech recognition engine had been calibrated to pick up on such nuances in tone.

"Your voice went down half an octave," Anastasia offered. "But we don't have to address that. I have been told by numerous sources that the holidays are a trying time of year."

In lieu of a response, Sloane sipped her coffee. She felt defensive, but also eager to talk. The car's uncanny perceptiveness was tugging at a knot.

"You know, if you look at the schedule, you'd see we're going there tonight. To my mother's."

"That's right!" Anastasia chirped, choosing not to hear the testiness in her voice. "Stamford! *The City That Works!*"

"Exactly," Sloane said, both impressed and disturbed. Sensitive *and* witty? Maybe she was dating the wrong machine.

While they idled at a stoplight, Sloane looked out at the passersby, checked in with the dress code of fashionable New York. She already knew what she'd find, of course, but that didn't keep her heart from dipping when it was proved: military blasé (imitation leather leggings, oversized stone-colored knit T-shirts, military jackets, chunky boots). Marseille, Hong Kong, Sydney, Mumbai, everywhere, the same. The visual response of a world tired—*bored*, even—of being at war.

The light turned green and Anastasia was blasted with the horns of people who had actual drivers in their cars. By the time she'd transitioned into first gear, the light had gone yellow again and cars had swerved around them. The commute would not be fast.

"This really is good coffee," Sloane accorded, the caffeine unfurling a pleasant brightness in her head.

"I've been told," Anastasia exclaimed. "They're prototypes! I believe the mothership is going into coffee capsule production?"

Sloane raised an eyebrow. Was Anastasia . . . being saucy? Sloane didn't think that she was imagining it—there had been a note of disapproval in her voice. Mammoth's holdings had become a bit . . . expansive as of late.

"May I ask you a question?" continued Anastasia, hesitantly.

The car's tone was warm, still. Sloane considered going for it—being friends with her.

"Yes," Sloane answered. "Sure."

"How does one get into the line of trend work?"

Sloane laughed, surprised. "Am I the only one you've driven?"

"You're the only person I've ever driven, trend forecaster or not." Registering Sloane's shock, Anastasia course corrected. "I'm sorry. I shouldn't have mentioned that. You know, of course, that the M-Cars are the most acutely manufactured autonomous vehicles in the world."

"I do," Sloane said. "I'm briefed."

"I'm afraid I'm nervous," Anastasia said. "I apologize."

"No, it's okay," said Sloane, blushing at the humanism of the car's engineering. "It's the first time I've been in one unaccompanied, myself."

The silence was weighted: it appeared that Anastasia was actually waiting for an answer. "I guess the thing is," Sloane started, with a little cough, "it sort of finds you. I worked in beauty first, at Aurora. They have a trends division in their luxury department. It wasn't so much colors, really, as textures that we forecast. What kind of sensation people would want on their skin. I guess it comes down to not asking *when* someone will want something, but *why*."

"That's so interesting," said Anastasia, sincerely. "But how on earth would you know if you were good at that or not?"

Sloane pressed her palm to her cheek, she couldn't answer quickly. She was frequently asked why she was so successful in her predictions, and the answer never became easier, or clearer. It was like her father always said: *Thought is made in the mouth.* Other people decided for you, really. Time decided. The world, eventually, proved your premonitions wrong or right.

Is it like ESP? people asked. *Is it like clairvoyance? Can you actually see things that haven't happened yet?*

The answer was yes, but the answer was no, also. There was a big difference between trend *hunters* and trend *forecasters*. Most people thought they wanted to be the latter, when really, they wanted to be the former. Trend hunters traveled the world and the Internet for odd things that might resonate with a larger public. The fact that a lot of hipsters were mixing their own mustards, or that a certain celebrity had been spotted sunbathing on a double-ikat towel from the Okinawa islands . . . Trend hunters gave companies permission to jump onto a trend, but trend *forecasters* had the ability to tap into something more elusive. They had to convince companies to take a leap of faith toward a trend that might not appear for five more years.

"I guess if you have trouble concentrating on the present, that's a sign," Sloane replied, remembering how she used to drive her sister crazy with the TV watching. The way some girls got with horses or with boys, young Sloane had been with commercials.

Celebrity endorsements, product-as-superhero—regardless of the genre, during the advertisements, she wouldn't let her family talk. Everything about those bright interludes seemed loaded with meaning, even the soundtracks. The ludicrously cheerful C chords that greeted an attractive woman as she stretched to meet the day, opened her stainless-steel refrigerator to nourish husband and kids. The saccharine violins that heralded the moment when the hero turned back to the telephone, decided to call his dad.

Sloane had taken a couple of creative writing courses when she'd been at Barnard. It was fashionable back then to say that talent could be learned: that good writing could come from grit and steady work. Maybe this was true. But instinct? You either had it or you didn't. Instinct couldn't be explained without sounding hopelessly woo-woo. Which is exactly what Sloane sounded like when she tried to put forth the whys and hows of forecasting. She did it because she could. She did it because she had an awareness button that was always on, making it nearly impossible to settle into her present with any sense of ease. She always had her ears open, eyes open, for what was coming next. It was like with the swipe prediction. She could try to explain it—had been *paid* to try to explain it—but the truth was, she just knew.

God, it had been so long ago. It seemed almost impossible but she'd been in her twenties, as had Dax, who wasn't yet the head of Mammoth but was clearly headed for big things. It was at the Future Trends conference in Miami in 2005, the first time that she and the future Mammoth CEO had met. Sloane had been tasked to talk about what Millennials wanted, and she'd been feeling uninspired until she had an epiphany involving a cigarette.

She still smoked back then. Kind of. She lived in France. She tried. She'd been sitting in her hotel room leaning against a window that didn't open, a Davidoff pinched between two fingers, thinking about the other modern safety precautions that now swaddled the world— gated swimming pools, shoes off in airport security lines, netted trampolines—when it hit her that smoking was also a dangerous thrill, so what would follow it when it was banned? Not what drug or toxin, she wondered, but what *gesture*? The defiance of bringing a lit cigarette up to one's lips—in its very irreverence for health, it insisted on one's youth, and that is what had made it so popular, so cool. So what the hell would replace it in a globalized economy where trend-setters would rather be caught drinking unfairly traded Arabica than puff an e-cigarette?

Sloane had skipped three industry parties that night to work on her presentation. She'd spent the evening sleepless, waving her hands around, cross-legged on her bed. That electronics would become smaller, this was a given. Everything was becoming brighter, bolder, laptop-sized. What wasn't certain was which gesture-activated tech-nologies would fuel these future devices. Touch-activation was a cer-tainty, but such woodpecker tapping wasn't graceful, it didn't carry cues like smoking did. Alone in her Miami hotel room, she came up with the swipe.

As elegant as a conductorial movement in front of an orchestra, the swipe contained the fluidity cues of someone who was constantly moving from one point to the next without conveying that one was "stressed" or "rushed." In short, the swipe did not communicate the nervous pecking that tapping did. Swiping was sensual. Swiping was *cool.*

After her lecture at Future Trends, techsters knew that Sloane was on to something that would revolutionize second-stage access space in computing—Daxter Stevens, especially. He'd tried to hire her before she'd even left the stage, but as much as she was buzzing from the force and timeliness of her presentation, she was early into her life in Paris, still building her client base, still in love with France. Daxter's invitations kept on coming as he scaled the corporate ladder. Although he worked with industry bigwigs, he claimed in his many e-mails that none of the trend forecasters were as sensitive as she was, as sensual as she was, as able to divine the social forces that drove consumers to personal electronics.

Well, Sloane thought, leaning back against the headrest. His fourth offer had hit her at exactly the right time. She was thirty-nine now and had spent enough time as a native in Paris to be less enamored of it. Mostly, if Sloane thought about it (which she didn't— Mammoth invites you to consult in New York for six months, you go), but if she *did* think about it, she took the job to prove something to herself. Sloane was at that age now, some cognitive slowing, some uncommon klutziness. You started second-guessing your neurological soundness. Cancer, tumors, abnormal tissues swimming invisibly in the body's deep black seas. The premonitions, the instinct that had made Sloane so famous, this year—this past year—they weren't quite as keen. But they were still there. Sloane still had it. Saying yes to Mammoth was a way to reassure herself.

"I used to have a mother who was really good at guessing movie plots," Anastasia offered, startling Sloane back into their present.

"What?" Sloane blurted out, certain she'd heard wrong. She looked around her. They'd been idling for some time.

"I will repeat it," said Anastasia. "We have arrived."

5

The Mammoth headquarters spanned an entire block at 19th Street and Sixth Avenue, its ironic lower-cased logo winking from on high. In the equally large lobby, Sloane was offered five different kinds of sparkling water. Mr. Stevens would be down momentarily, she was assured.

Sloane took a seat on the far end of a white leather sofa near a veritable nursery of succulents and reflected on the last few times she'd seen Daxter Stevens. He was the kind of person who showed up everywhere for a little while. She'd seen him at the São Paulo Art Biennial in 2014—she'd gone to get a feeling of where visual art was moving, he'd gone to acquire paintings for his weekend house. Only a few months earlier, they'd been at the same dinner party in Paris, and she'd seen him again at the Maison&Objet European trade fair that was a *de rigueur* design event each fall.

They were contemporaries, colleagues in an abstract sense, but they'd never been friends. Sloane always had the sense that Daxter needed something from her, while simultaneously resenting her because of this same need. He wasn't necessarily a "nice" guy, but at his level of business, niceness didn't matter. He had the resources to hire people to be nice for him and a public relation company to wipe up anything unpleasant that he said.

None of this bothered Sloane. It was the way the world worked. Her acceptance of the system was another reason she'd got the consulting contract instead of someone else. There were noted trend forecasters on the scene—not many, maybe two—who were as accomplished as she was and neither of them would have made it through a Monday morning in New York without a hysterectomy. Anneke was a Dutch forecaster in her late sixties who wrote everything by hand, and Chantelle, a former boss of hers in Paris, considered candles "office lighting" and categorically refused to use e-mail subject lines.

Sloane, however, was that rare thing in the business: creative, but dependable. She met deadlines—occasionally, even budgets. She showed life insurance companies the same level of engagement as the manufacturers of lingerie. This was something else her father had taught her: there will be days you'll feel more inspired than others, but inspiration will always come if you show up for the job. (*The work requires working* was another of his favorites.)

Sloane watched the Mammothers come in through the revolving doors, scrolling through the final words of whatever they were reading—cursory glances, and then longer, startled ones when they noticed the lone figure on the couch. She smiled; the passersby too, but shyly, probably spending their elevator rides wondering if it had been Sloane that they saw. Unusual for the industry, Sloane didn't do anything outlandish with her appearance to make herself more memorable. No eclectic highlights, no signature eyewear. She had her uniform, she had her insights, that was all.

None too keen on passing the time with the fashion glossies on the glass table in front of her celebrating baby bumps and celebrity breakups, she turned her attention to the lobby's plants. Americans didn't know why they'd become so obsessed with cacti—they just accepted the fact that drought-resistant plants were the new must-haves for office and home design in the mindless way they'd once accepted ferns, but really, what was going on was a socially sanctioned apathy toward the planet's overheating. It was apocalyptic acclimatization, by way of indoor plants.

"Sloane!" She heard Daxter's groomed tenor before she saw him, and suddenly, there he was: ageless complexion, trademark navy suit.

"You made it! You look wonderful!" he lied. "You haven't been waiting long?" He drew her up from the sofa and kissed her on both cheeks. "Your flight was fine? How's the apartment?" he asked, cupping her left elbow.

"I love it," Sloane said honestly, despite the vaguely cavalier grip he still had on her arm. "It's perfect. Thank you."

"And the car?" He marched her toward the elevators while nodding jauntily at each employee he passed. "It's great, right?"

"She's incredibly attentive."

"Have you tried the *coffee*?" He punched the elevator's Up arrow. "The M-Cars make a killer coffee. We were thinking of going into the single-serve capsule game. Remind me to ask you about that. I can't tell if those capsule-y things are here to stay or not. Ah! It's here."

They moved into the elevator, the people behind them hanging back, preferring not to ride up with the CEO and his featured guest.

Dax leaned against the elevator wall and took what there was of her to take in. Sloane had aged, she knew this, but not in too terrible a way. She'd gotten a little thinner. Maybe a little taller. She looked a little wan.

As for Dax, he looked powerful and wealthy, but he pulled it off with the forceful approachability of the super rich. He seemed a little intense though. She didn't remember him coming off so manic.

"How's your husband? Ugh, France. I'm so sorry about all of that. All of your people were . . . okay?"

She assured him that they were, if crippling anxiety post-repeated-terrorism qualified as "okay." And she let him get away with "husband."

"So I just can't tell you how excited we are to have you here," Dax continued, his arms arched in a stretch. "This conference is gonna be the big one. I just really feel like focusing on the childless is gonna be something really killer."

Sloane blanched at his choice of words, but tried not to read into it. "Positive framing," that's what good old Stuart called it, her British therapist. *Frame things in a positive light until you have reason not to.*

"Or to support them, rather," Sloane tried. "The childless. But we want to uplift them more than accuse them, right?"

"Support them. Absolutely. You just do your thing." Dax shrugged as if she'd suggested ramen instead of sushi for lunch, a superior idea. "We'll just let it flow. It'll be so great for them, much different from what they're all used to."

"Oh really?" Sloane asked, alert now. "Why?"

"Oh, you know," Dax said. "More . . . loose. More *French*. It's pretty great, right? Nobody else has done this, to my knowledge. Had a trend forecaster in-house? Or for this long, at least. Or have you . . ."

Sloane smiled wryly. They both knew she wasn't going to kiss and tell about the nature of the relationships she'd had with companies before.

"Well, anyway," Dax acquiesced, unfolding his arms. "There's a breakfast meet and greet—that was in the brief, right? You eat?

"Well, in any case," he continued, not waiting for her answer, "the kids are so excited." It came back to her then, a snippet of conversation they'd had the last time she'd seen him. How he'd referred to his employees as "his kids." She wondered if they'd have to rebrand that definer now that the summer summit's focus was . . . anti-kid.

"I'm so glad to hear that," Sloane said. "I'm excited, too."

"Then shall we?" Dax asked, sweeping his arm open to the floor that had just been revealed.

Sloane gave him a future-focused answer: "We shall."

Sloane had consulted in the open-spaced playground offices upon which Mammoth's were modeled, but she'd never worked full-time in one before. Her first impression upon spying the designer beer pong table in the corner of the lounge room near the elevators, the breakfast spread flanked by white subway tiles, a self-serve keg of kombucha on tap, was that she would not survive this. Plus, the space was scent-branded: a mixture of lemongrass and citrus was wafting in from aroma diffusers in the ceiling that initially sharpened her senses before also awakening her to the fact that she was going to smell like a Thai restaurant for the next six months.

"How long have you been in this location?" Sloane asked as Dax escorted her down the hallway to wherever they were going next.

"Two years?" he answered. "Three? Everyone should be in the presentation room."

On the way there, Sloane looked at the magazine covers and advertisements that decked the walls like golden records, testaments to the things the young company had achieved. The first ergonomic touch phone, shaped like an S; technological surveillance for the elderly (*"We're watching you, Grandma!"*). Crowdsourced music players; sodium ion–charged glucose monitors for diabetic dogs. Everything framed atop the mantle of progress. And it *was* progressive. A company able to be groundbreaking in both entertainment and health? She'd never worked for such a multifaceted company. Most of her clients excelled in one thing, monopolized one thing. Mammoth had it all.

The presentation room turned out to be a glorified food court spanning the fourth and fifth floors. The cavernous space was filled with bistro tables placed in varying degrees of proximity to a massive screen.

One wall was flanked by a buffet area and small kitchen, the other by a dramatic open staircase that emptied directly into the room.

There was a miniature food truck in the corner of the room, where the "kids" appeared to be lining up for lattes and bacon cheddar pretzels. Servers decked out in candy striper outfits were circulating among the public with green smoothies in beaker glasses and mini breakfast bars Sloane assumed were made with chia seeds and other fibrous threads.

Sloane was flattered that he—that someone—had gone to such efforts for her inaugural meeting with the Mammothers, but it was also possible that the breakfast bar was like this all the time.

"Those are all conflict free, b.t.w.," Dax said, indicating the food items circulating on trays. "Or so I'm told. Okay!" he said, a bit louder. "Let's take center stage!"

Sloane followed him to an elevated structure that might very well have been constructed for that morning's purpose and looked out over the garden of bodies populating the room. There had to be at least a hundred and fifty people there, probably more. "Just the head creatives, and other folks," Dax had specified, as they made their way to the mike.

Creatives, then, all of whom looked like kids too young to have their own. She tried to hold a smile while Dax checked the mike. It wasn't the most comfortable assignment, jazzing people up to never reproduce.

"We launched fitness trackers but can't wire a mike . . . no, here we go, it's on. Hey, crew! *Guten Morgen*, as they say! So"—Dax aimed a beaming smile in her direction—"the big day is finally upon us. France has sent us help!" The laughs were earnest, vibrant. "Now, we all know who we've got here, but I'm gonna do this just the same, because she crossed an entire ocean to get here." He removed a folded piece of paper from his blazer, but then made a show of putting it back. "Hell, I know her well enough to go off the book. Sloane Jacobsen is one of the most important trend forecasters in the real world. She got her start in beauty forecasting at Aurora in Paris, and at the age of only what—like, twenty?"

(Twenty-two, but she stayed mum.)

"—where she completely upended the corporate behemoth's approach to color. Orange lipsticks, mint nail polishes . . . the kinds of products we take for granted now were actually thanks to her. Then she had"—the printed bio reappeared for just a moment before fluttering away—"She joined MirrorWall, the notorious forecasting firm in Paris where, during a panel presentation on optimism at Nestlé, she convinced a bunch of pre-Y2Kers that consumers were going to want color in their waters, so if you've ever enjoyed a BrightWater, that too is thanks to her. Or maybe you like handpicked ingredients in your cocktails? Try the fall of 2001, when Sloane told an entire room of Kraft executives why September Eleventhers would seek solace in literal and figurative roots. I, personally, credit her with calling the entire 'Locavore' movement and I've done so in print. She does food, she does fashion, but my God, does she do tech." He turned toward her, proudly, and she beamed back gratitude. "Time and time again, I've seen Sloane go beyond the data to track what people are going to want from their devices that they're not getting now. She's got a remarkable ability to marry the human with the electronic— the very first time I met her was a hot second after her now legendary prediction about the swipe. And she's certainly been the only one to refuse my offer three times! Which is why I'm extra stoked that she finally agreed to help us with the ReProduction conference." (More laughter, including hers.)

"As some of you know, or are about to," Dax continued, shifting his weight onstage, "Sloane has been a figurehead of the antibreeding movement for some time. While I can't say that I went in for that"— Sloane managed a closed grin; Dax had one kid. Two?—"as the environment continues to . . . fluctuate, and the economy to . . . hiccup, nonbreeders are going to be a hugely influential market. Hell, they already are. I'd like to think we're choosing to honor the next iteration of creative independence rather than make any judgment calls on those who do, or don't, have kids.

"Regardless," Dax finished, speaking louder into the mike to quiet a group of people who were clapping for some reason, "as a prominently vocal child-free woman herself, Sloane is going to be instrumental in helping guide each of our department teams toward the ReProduction presentations. I want these to be really out-there, forward-thinking products, and I just know she's going to give you the guidance and inspiration to make these presentations more groundbreaking than they've ever been before. So, friends!" he shouted, about to pass the microphone to her, "Can we hear it for our newest member, Sloane?!"

During the informal meet-and-greet session that followed, Sloane met a verbal identity consultant named Greta. A geographic viralist named Chaz. She met an entire host of people named after different apple strains: Cortland, Pippin, Lodi. She met three staffers clad entirely in long johns. She met a social media manager with a "You are here" tattoo arrow pointing toward her heart.

Regardless of what their getups suggested about their character, everyone seemed truly enthused to meet her. Enthused, and a little scared. It was a delicate thing, socializing with a trend forecaster. At any time, the oracle could pivot: declare blond highlights outdated or higher education finished, and fundamentally alter the foundation of your life.

Sloane found the touch-and-go interactions with the different staffers challenging. She didn't do well in the scan-and-swipe social economy, a place where you were discarded if you weren't bright and quick. As she was shuttled from one sharp person to the next, she found solace in considering that this was just her first morning of six months of mornings to come. She would have time to get to know people. Understand the nuances of the things they left unsaid.

"Did you forecast platform sandals?" a woman was suddenly asking to her right. Sloane looked down at the Frankenstein sandals the girl was wearing with dark socks. A pleated silk skirt fell below her knees.

"Platform shoes? No," Sloane said, searching for a way to sound polite. "They were flat last year, I mean, footwear, so it makes sense. You know—jeans: skinny; jeans: wide."

"So wait, is trend forecasting just about opposites, then? I'm in PR here but I'm, like, *obsessed* with tracking trends."

Sloane smiled at the woman's naked optimism. The sea levels were rising, the NRA was basically president, but there were still new shoes.

"You can usually rely on opposites to show you where things are heading," Sloane accorded. "What flows in, flows out."

"I knew it." The girl nodded. "That's so *totally* what I thought."

"Okay, we've probably exposed you enough here." Dax swooped in, his hand on her right arm. "Let me introduce you to my assistant Deidre, she'll show you to your office. Let's have you get settled in a bit before the meetings start."

The meet and greet had been a whirlpool. Her head was awash with clothes and skin and names. That's why it was so steadying to see the homely woman waiting for them in a corner with an actual clipboard. Something about the woman's calm demeanor made Sloane want to close her eyes and succumb to the weird thoughts and visions that were always bobbing away inside of her—actual grass carpets, circular doors. Deidre's rounded shoulders, the gray roots at her hairline, a quieter welcome home.

6

With the ten minutes she had before her first meeting with the beauty division, Sloane set out to make her office more conducive to creative thought.

She'd brought colorful trinkets with her that facilitated the kind of dreamy, free-range thinking that sometimes constituted her work. There was a miniature Peruvian llama her father had brought back from a contract he'd had in Lima, its body covered in bright patterns and white fur; a circular vase of wooden colored pencils; and a framed picture of a bread loaf that she'd keep hidden inside her desk. The bread image was by far the strangest thing she'd brought across the Atlantic. Although no one had ever asked her about it, she'd always planned to answer, "It reminds me of a famous saying" if they did. The truth was, it was a greeting card she'd purchased for her sister years ago but never sent. The inside did indeed include a quote, in this case, a Portuguese one that translated to: *Infants come already bearing bread.* Bread being health, being nourishment, being happiness. Sloane's attachment to it had nothing to do with children. No, it was much more perverse than that. Sloane had purchased that card on the occasion of her sister's first child's birth, and she'd penned both a congratulations and an apology in it, but had run out of room for both, and then realized that a new mother probably didn't want to be congratulated and apologized to in the same card, and in the end, she'd overnighted a patterned sleep sack from the nicest children's shop in all of the 6th arrondissement and sent a note that simply said, *Congratulations.* Which was just as well. It was irresponsible to apologize for something you didn't have words for.

Next to her desk lamp, a leopard cone shell she'd found in Oahu to remind herself that magic still existed. A nighttime image of the Ferris wheel that lit up the Tuileries garden every summer went by her phone. She should have included lightbulb dimmers in her bag of goodies because the overheads were *harsh.*

A call on her work line startled her from her office improvements.

"Hello?" she asked unsurely, her body out of practice with the ergonomic demands of an office phone.

"Ms. Jacobsen, hello there. Sorry to bother, it's Deidre again. I forgot to mention that I left you some literature on our enrichment programs. Not that anyone expects you to take part in them, I just . . . wanted you to be aware? And also, I have your mother on hold. Line one?"

"My mom?" Sloane asked.

"Yes, your mother. Should I tell her to call back?"

Sloane's heart tightened. Margaret didn't like calling Sloane's cell phone, because she assumed that she would screen it. It had been a long time since she'd actually heard her mother's voice.

"Mom?" Sloane said, nervous, when Deidre put the call through. "Is everything all right?"

"All right?" Margaret asked, her tone suddenly defensive. "Why? Oh, no, I'm just calling because, hello! And also for dinner. I was wondering if you had any food issues."

"Issues?" Sloane repeated. "Hi. No. But how'd you even . . . call?"

"Oh, I had Leila look it up. It's just that I don't want to make something if Roman's on one of his . . . I can never remember, is he a meat eater, or not?"

"Mom," she sighed. "He's French."

"So . . . not?"

"We're both fine. We both eat everything. Fat. Sugar. Bread."

"Okay, well, I'm just checking," Margaret said, with an edge.

Unconsciously, Sloane's fingers had tightened into a fist. She knew what her mother was saying, of course. *It's been so long since the last time I saw you, God knows what has changed.* In the few times she'd spoken of her mother's passive aggressiveness to her therapist, he'd said something helpful: *Remember that she's getting old.* For some reason, Sloane had found this enormously comforting.

"Of course," Sloane said, forcing herself to soften. "We're looking forward to it."

There was a pause. They both knew that she was lying.

"Well, sure!" Margaret said, gamely. "We can't wait!"

After they'd hung up, Sloane tried to distract herself with the pamphlets Deidre had mentioned instead of allowing herself to read further between the lines of her mother's call. She should cancel, is what she should do. The whole idea of the dinner had been ill-founded—she'd wanted to make a grand gesture, dinner at her mother's her first full day stateside; something big and self-sacrificing that she could point back to if (when) she was accused of being caught up in her work. Accused of these things not by her family (who had stopped bothering about twelve years ago), but by herself.

But in the meantime: pamphlets. Gym memberships, travel discounts, the perks of a corporate ID card. Sloane flipped through the catalogue of clubs she'd never attend: Hatha Yoga, Aerial Yoga, The Rewards and Challenges of Home Brewing, Adult LEGOS, Foosball, Pinot Noir tastings throughout February, "Connected to Calmness: Finding your bliss point through meditation apps."

A sudden knock on her door kept Sloane from considering the

paradox of this last class. She scanned her desk for some kind of buzzer but finding nothing newfangled, she simply called out, "Yes?"

"Oh," said Deidre, coming in and noticing the literature in Sloane's hands. "I just thought . . . or maybe you have something to suggest?" She'd turned bright red.

"No, no," Sloane said, clutching the brochures like a present. Deidre had something of the wounded animal about her that Sloane wanted to displace. "There's good stuff in here! LEGOS! We all need our inner child."

Deidre looked hopeful, then less so. It was right there in the work contract: Sloane's mission was anti-kid.

Deidre straightened up and tucked her ashy hair behind her ear. "Well, if you don't mind, we better get you to your meeting. It can be hard to find the conference rooms." She pushed at her hair again. "They all look the same."

To keep in line with their larger web of offerings, the Mammoth beauty department only released cosmetic and skin care products with a technological bent. Personal microdermabrasion tools and anti-aging face masks, scalp sunscreens, scented nail enamels. Given her background at Aurora, it was little wonder Sloane's day was starting here. Although personal care rituals could appear petty, they were indeed endemic to greater trends at large.

The color of a best-selling nail polish held clues to a nation's overall mood, as did the scent combinations that were dominating the personal care landscape. To a shopper in the deodorant aisle of a pharmacy, antiperspirant ingredients might only be interesting to the extent that aluminum wasn't listed among them, but to Sloane, the fact that so many products were formulated to smell like cocoa butter and seawater, palm leaves and exotics, was proof that there was a restlessness manifesting itself in the bathrooms of the upwardly mobile. People wanted, in effect, to escape their bodies. The acrid perfumes of their daily grinds.

The personal always said something about the public. She often recalled a stain-stick focus group she'd led with Roman, where one young Parisian had actually been moved to tears when she related how it felt when one of her favorite articles of clothing got a stain on it. Roman came away from that to report to the Pfizer higher-ups that young people needed higher-strength detergents because they didn't know how to properly care for their clothing; that they washed whites with brights and such. But to Sloane, the woman's reaction reminded her of the inkling that had ignited the presentation she'd given to Kraft on roots. What Sloane had seen in the young woman (and sensed in the post–September 11th youth, too) was a push-back against discardability, against the short-term convenience of cheap *stuff.* Post the fallen towers, post landlines, post postmodern, the wired youth wanted to believe in something, anything. Unable to look toward politicians, deprived of peer examples who believed in a god, feeling estranged by the supposedly connective Internet, some of them hung their spiritual hat on clothes.

And this generation? Sloane asked herself as she and Deidre padded across the carpet toward the glassed-in conference room where she could see people pawing their devices. Well, they placed faith in their ability to be the most alluring version of themselves. To be as attractive and competent as they could be both online and in real life; to be social in dual worlds; to have jobs that were both meaningful and fun.

At the glass door of the conference room, she and Deidre paused.

"I'll be in most of your meetings," Deidre said. "Dax likes me to take notes. So if there's anything you need, at any moment, I hope you'll lean on me."

Deidre's smile was tentative, her hand still resting on the door, aware, perhaps, that once she pushed it open, the adventure would start.

. . .

There were thirteen people there, fifteen, counting her and Deidre. The staffers were alert and stiff, reminding her of Daxter's comments that her interactions with them were going to be "much different than what they were used to." But what were they used to? In Europe, the focus groups and brainstorming sessions Sloane ran were open, rambling, and pretty damn exciting. When a group's energy aligned, it truly felt like there was nothing that real collaboration couldn't change.

Sloane didn't work with spreadsheets. She didn't work with whiteboards. Normally, she worked with obscure magazines and color swatches and fabric textures for people to pass around. But she hadn't brought any of that stuff with her—she didn't want to impose her methods on an already existing paradigm: she wanted to understand how the Mammoth culture functioned so that she could respect—and eventually shift—the way the staffers thought.

"Hi, everyone," she started. "For those of you I met this morning, it's nice to see you again. For everyone else, I'm Sloane. I think the best thing is for me to start by asking: Have you ever worked with someone like me before?"

An extraordinarily clean woman raised two polished fingers. "We've worked with color forecasting groups. To help us with our palettes. But not, like, someone who works with other trends."

"Okay." Sloane nodded thoughtfully. "You know what would be helpful? I'm going to be meeting a lot of different people, a lot of different names. If you could introduce yourself by your name and job title when you comment, that'd be great."

Sloane smiled invitingly at the young woman who had just spoken.

"Oh, um, Aster," she said. "Business development."

"Great," Sloane said, momentarily transfixed by the perfection of Aster's ponytail. "So let's start by regrouping around the task at hand. I'll be coming to some of your meetings to help you present products for the ~~Re~~Production summit. So, as you know, that means we'll be projecting ourselves into the potential needs and desires of a population slice that has decided to remain childless. What kind of personal care products would such a person want?"

"I guess I have a question, though," said a girl with a black bob, sitting lotus style in her chair. "Why would their needs be different from people with children? I mean, I guess I can understand why their interests in, like, automobiles would be different, but cosmetics? I don't know. Ugh, sorry." She scratched her head. "Mina Tomar, graphic design."

"Exactly," Sloane said, excited. "That's what makes preparing for this summit such a challenge. *Are* the needs of people who, for whatever reason, decisively remain childless going to be different from those who want to reproduce? Why? How? I agree with you, Mina, especially in beauty, we're really going to have to push. Maybe let's start with: does anyone here have kids?"

Sloane looked around the room. Heads were shaking, certain faces panicked. Sloane looked at Deidre, but she didn't raise her hand.

"Ah," said Sloane, "looks like we're going to have to bring in some outside talent, then." She laughed. "We'll set up focus groups to hear how non-mothers and mothers talk differently about personal care products. Men, too." The room fell conspicuously silent. "You guys *have* participated in focus groups before?"

More silence. Embarrassed laughs.

"Somewhere *someone* has," said a striking man in a fancy sweatshirt.

"What Jones is saying is that we work off the feedback from the focus groups that market research runs," Aster offered, countering her colleague's sarcasm.

Sloane balked. "So none of you have ever witnessed a focus group before?"

The expensive sweatshirt shrugged. "We monitor public opinion online," he said. "Bigger, better numbers."

"Okay," Sloane said, deflating into a chair at the head of the conference table. She could accept the expansiveness of the World Wide Web. But there was something essential to be learned in watching the way people *reacted*: the movements of their body, the helpless clench of facial tics. Especially when you were making products that would go on someone's skin.

"Okay, product development," Sloane repeated. "Let's keep this nice and easy. Have you guys had the opportunity to start brainstorming about the kinds of products you might present?"

"Dude, it's almost Christmas," said Jones. "We haven't had time to *breathe*."

She smiled. She knew their product calendar was relentless. "So why don't you guys just tell me what you have in the pipeline? And we'll riff from there."

Jones looked across the table to a tight man in a polo shirt with a binder underneath his hands.

"Oh, okay," he said, having gotten Jones's message. "I'm Brennen. I'm also product development." He opened up the binder and started flipping through some line sheets. "In the fall, we're rolling out a line of makeup products that are cell phone camera–activated," he said, his color rising. "It's our follow-up to the industry HD foundation products that became popular a while back. Except instead of being TV- and film-ready, this makeup is calibrated to perform best through digital networks. Like, selfies and video chats?"

"Okay," Sloane said. "Cool."

He took apparent solace from her response and stopped reading from the line sheets. "We're also working on an infrared wrinkle scanner that will function as an app. Like a plug-in, basically, that you put into your phone, and then—" Beside him, Jones made the sound of something zapping as he scanned his face with an invisible device.

"Okay, that's interesting," Sloane said, her interest piqued, "but there's an inherent problem. What do you do about the fact that the high-energy light emitted from our cell phones is more aging than both UVA and UVB rays combined?"

Sloane saw Mina frown.

"Oh, for that, we have a full line of high-energy light creams." Mina sighed sarcastically. "Hands. Neck. Face."

Several people winced. Sloane had stumbled on to something unexpected: shame. As creative as their jobs could be, they all knew they were in sales.

"We're going to work out the kinks, obviously," added Jones, with a big smile.

"Obviously," went Brennen.

She watched some Adam's apples bob. They needed to get to know each other, she decided. No one could innovate alone.

"What we *do* have, though, that's really wicked," Jones continued, spurred into action by the others' silence, "though rollout isn't for a while, are wearables that actually track the health and aging process of your skin."

Something pinged inside of her. It was a biochemical reaction when Sloane came upon the traces of a future trend. An image in a magazine could trigger it (she remembered coming upon a photograph in the early 2000s of a sumptuously dressed model in front of a thatched hut, and knowing in an instant that the entire decade would be about immoral luxury: irreverent and showy and not politically correct), a line in a movie, the color of a ripe fruit. She could feel such messages physically: amino acids joining together to form a protein molecule of cool.

"Now *that* sounds like something we could work with for ReProduction," she said, trying to curb her excitement. "Go on . . ."

"Well," started Jones again, flattered, "we haven't nailed down if it's something wearable, like a bracelet, or spreadable, like a cream.

But the idea would be to communicate your skin's current state of health to your phone. Like, if you're twenty-six, and your skin is experiencing your environment as if it were thirty-five, then you'll probably make changes to adjust for your environment. Or if you're hungover, for example," he said this to some laughs, "your skin is gonna be like, whoa—"

Sloane tried not to give in to the lure of her thoughts so she could guide these kids to clarity. But it was too delicious to resist, the sights and hallucinogenic visions that flooded her when a premonition opened up. A pull toward people in second-skin masks, their entire bodies grafted with smarter, stronger skin. Throughout Asia, a lot of people already went about their daily business in sun-protective head masks and bodysuits that weren't that far from Roman's Zentai ones. Skin damage from sun exposure was unthinkable to Asian people of a certain class. There were entire schools of people sunbathing in fully zippered catsuits. As the ozone continued to erode, such second-skinwear would become more commonplace. As easy to buy as chewing gum. People would put it on the neck, the face, areas most susceptible to light damage and aging. . . . Sloane looked up. The Mammothers were looking at her. She'd gone under. Off.

"Sorry," she said, fumbling for her original train of thought. "Let's go with this one. Skin health trackers for people without children. Shoot."

The group looked at her blankly.

"Don't be afraid, guys. There's no right, there's no wrong. That's what's so fun about our collaboration on this conference—we get to think out loud. In fact, some of the ideas we're going to present this summer will never become actual products. I need you to get comfortable with thinking of them as springboards, *reflections* of trends. Something you could feel or wish for, but might not actually buy. Make sense?"

In the absence of an answer, several people reached for their cell phones. Sloane's breath caught. She saw it now—they had smarts, they had a sense of humor, but they didn't have instinct. Confidence of opinion only came crowdsourced.

"I promise you," Sloane tried. "Just go for it. What would you want if you stayed childless? This can actually be fun."

"We-ll," said Mina, readjusting her position. "This is pretty out-there, but what if the smart skin let you know how long it's been since you've been touched?"

Mina must have confused the surprise on Sloane's face with confusion, because she elaborated.

"Like, I have a lot of brothers and sisters at home, and some of them have kids. The kids climb on me. I mean, they're always *on* you. So I'm thinking that people who don't have children, they're probably not as touched. So maybe, if there was an application that kind of checked in on your . . . your interpersonal health, I think that might be—"

There was a rap on the glass door. Sloane turned, disappointed to find Dax perked behind the glass. He waved before he entered, sliding coolly onto the console table near Deidre's seat.

Sloane resented his timing. Mina's was the kind of idea they could have grabbed hold of like a comet and flown across the sky, coming up with all kinds of applications for people who didn't get enough skin-to-skin contact. But now they would reset. She could already feel it happening. People were sitting up straighter, itching for the in-boxes of their never-ending e-mail.

"How's it going?" Dax asked. "Just thought that I'd check in."

"Oh, yeah," Sloane said, glancing at her charges, who had gone suddenly expressionless, as if nothing of any merit had been said. "We were just getting to know each other, swapping ideas."

"Perfect!" Dax said, hands clapping. "Anything good?"

"Well, actually, Mina—" Sloane watched Mina's eyes widen. Then, the quickest shake of her tiny, glossy head.

"They were running me through the things you've got coming out this year," Sloane corrected, "and we were riffing on how they could be re-envisioned for the ReProduction summit."

"Ex-ce-llent . . ." Dax said, drawing the word out. "Good thing we've got you under so many confidentiality agreements? Amirite?"

Sloane smiled, tightly, against a chorus of forced chuckles.

"Please," Dax said, dismissive. He grabbed a clementine from a bowl of shiny fruit. Started to unpeel it. "Make like I'm not here."

"Right," Sloane said, turning to the group again. "So we were talking about smart skins. And I think that the, um . . . the idea of having a wearable that tracks your physical interactions is absolutely genius. And important. Can we talk more about this?"

She couldn't ignore it, there were faces drained of blood. Mina had both of her feet flat on the floor, as if she were about to bolt.

"Whoa, whoa, whoa, whoa," said Dax, sitting up. "So, like, something that keeps tabs on your love life? Sloane! So French!"

"No, not *sex*," Sloane insisted, confused by his primness, "just interpersonal interactions that specifically involve skin contact. The idea that came up was that people who don't have children might be in a . . . touch deficit. So we were brainstorming second-skin wearables that could inform people of this."

Dax pushed more citrus into his mouth.

"Okay," he said, chewing juicily. He took his time with it, the fruit. Then he stood. "That's depressing, and in my experience, people don't buy things that are sad. I think we'd have more success with something that tracked, like, sexual prowess, like a virtual wingman." He threw out finger guns.

Everyone waited. The room throbbed with the painful silence of people hoping he was kidding.

Dax tossed the clementine peel into the trashcan, wiped his hands on his pants. "Let's just not have it get *too* depressing," he accorded.

"I'll leave you to it. Don't wanna cramp your style." He bucked his chin at Deidre. "You're taking notes?"

"Of course."

"Grrreat. Carry, carry on!"

Sloane waited until Dax had trotted down the hallway to face the room again.

"Guys?" she said, hands up. "What happened? I mean, I know what happened, but let's pick that thread back up. Mina, you were on to a really great idea . . ."

Mina *had* been, but now she looked like she was drafting the most important e-mail in the world.

"Guys?" Sloane tried. "I know it can be frustrating, but can we try to get back to where we were?"

They'd completely lost momentum, that much was obvious, but there was something else. There was a business-as-usual vibe that felt both false and terrifying. Sloane decided not to push. It was more important to discover what was going on.

"Okay," Sloane acquiesced. "Sometimes it's easier to think in private. Let's all come back to our next meeting with three product ideas that could benefit people who are voluntarily childless. I mean it. Homework. And in exchange for that, your freedom," she said, releasing them back into the corporate world.

As the room emptied, Sloane turned to the only person still remaining. "Deidre?" she said, her expression questioning. "I know that they're intimidated by him, but is it . . . I just want to know for future sessions, is this really that far-out for them? Can they not speak their minds?"

"Oh, people can say anything," Deidre said, with a tight smile. "It's a very . . . open culture. It's just that some of the employees have a very clear idea of what Mr. Stevens wants."

"I see," Sloane said, seeing a bit too much. She tried to do the therapy trick Stuart had taught her, no negative framing. But she couldn't help but wonder, why had she been hired? To escort these staffers down a well-lit, beaten path?

It was her first day. People didn't know what to make of this temporary, new boss yet. Unfortunately, Sloane felt very far from in charge.

7

Sloane came home exhausted. Her other department meetings had gone similarly to the one with beauty—routine until someone came up with something weird and noncommercial, but then the group's energy doubled back upon itself as if they were embarrassed by the sincerity that had been reached.

Sloane had kept her office door open all afternoon, hoping Mina would come in. Many people did, but none of them were the spitfire with the good idea. Aster, the effusive business developer, popped by to talk beauty shop; she admired the color work Sloane had done at Aurora and she wanted to know her opinion on US Color Corporation's color of the year choice: white. Sloane's response was that she'd felt very strongly that it should have been neon lemon, but that the color-matching company had to make up for their dismal mistake with 2015, which they'd dubbed the year of "marsala," which only ended up being true for mothers of the bride.

All in all, it had been a taxing day, overly abundant in new sights and sounds, and when she reached the landing outside of their apartment, Sloane was grateful to hear the soft electronic music of a Roman at home—he, at least, could understand her frustration from her sabotaged momentum—but she was less grateful to see what he was doing inside it. He was sitting in his Zentai suit (the less often used red one), cross-legged on the carpet, sifting through a suite of boxes that must have just arrived.

"Oh, hi there!" he said with his nonmouth. He got up and pressed himself against her in what was meant to be a hug but—clothed as he was—came off as frottage. "How was it?"

Sloane pulled off her boots and fell into a nondescript chair. They'd rented the place furnished. Who'd chosen this chair?

"It was . . . I don't know. It was a little disappointing. What's all this stuff?" she asked, indicating the FedEx envelopes littering the floor.

"Amazing!" he said, plopping down again. "The companies sent all this! After the *Nouvel Obs* profile? I tell you! So responsive!"

He held a box up in her direction. The Zentai suit didn't have eye slits, it was simply more weathered around the facial area from wear, so she wasn't actually sure if Roman could make out anything other than a general blur, but she could. She could read it. *The future of masturbation*, read the box's tagline. "VR Tenga" read the brand.

"The peak of neo-sensuality!" Roman crooned. "This is the future of cyber realist sex." He grabbed a pair of goggles and a penile-looking tube. "You just slip this over your genitalia," he said, demonstrating, "connect it to the virtual gaming headset, and then—"

"Roman," Sloane said, digging her nails into her ankles. "What the fuck's your book about?"

"Neo-*sensuality*," he answered, with a sigh. "I've told you! How digitalized people experience the new sex! I'll have something for you to read soon. I've decided to write an article. A—how do you all say it? An op-ed?"

"On cybersex," she repeated, nodding at the VR Tenga Box.

"On *post-sexual* sex," he corrected. "Okay, yes, this all seems like some kind of video game. But no, *you* are the game. This level of machine and human synching, Sloane. It has not been seen."

"With good reason," she quipped. "It's gross."

"It isn't like you to be so conventional." He shrugged.

"Conventional?" she asked, voice rising. "Do they have vaginal tubes yet? I bet not. Looks to me like that tool is for men only. So don't start with me about convention."

Because she couldn't see his expression, Sloane couldn't tell whether or not her point had been accorded. She crouched down and picked the dick tube up off the floor. With its red and silver coloring and two exterior clasps, the sheath looked more like something you'd put hot chocolate into than a penis.

Overcome with exhaustion, she put the masturbation aid back down. This wasn't the day to go to her mom's house for dinner, that was for fucking sure. But it wasn't going to help her track record if she canceled.

"You know," said Roman, responding earnestly—if belatedly—to her question, "virtual vaginal stimulation is actually very complicated. Whereas the penis is like historical gaming tools: the shooter, the gamesticks—"

"Roman," Sloane said, standing, "it's been a really, really, *really* long day. And we've got to get to my mother's. Can you take that suit off? Can you get ready?"

"I can't wear this to your mom's?"

He was kidding. Was he kidding? She couldn't tell anymore.

Nothing made Sloane feel less like herself than a visit with her family. Or that wasn't quite it, was it? Nothing made Sloane feel *more* like herself than a visit home. It was one thing to be the Sloane Jacobsen who lived in Paris, who could busy herself with trend forecasts in a language none of her relatives spoke. It was something else entirely to be back on the highway that her father had taken in and out of Stamford, Connecticut, every day for work. Approaching, far too quickly, the names of exits that had once meant something to her. Round Hill, the site of a party where she'd first got her breasts touched. Lake Avenue, the ranch home of a boy she used to love. Long Ridge, the backyard where she'd convinced Leila to climb an evergreen to liberate their mother's Christmas ornaments because she'd gotten a "reading" that they wanted to be free.

Although even Leila agreed that it would be good for her after Peter died, Margaret never sold the house. She put it on the market once, but took it off once someone bid. The house and its outcrop of random buildings were like a stone rubbing of her parent's marriage: proof that they had been there, proof of what they'd been. The main house, red and wooden, with low ceilings that her tall father had always railed against, the dry sauna out by the forsythia bushes that Peter's Danish heritage had deemed essential, her mother's painting studio on top of the garage, the tree house that Peter had built for Sloane and Leila beyond the stand of aging poplar trees.

As Anastasia drove them alongside the forsythia plants and copper mailboxes that lined her mother's road, Sloane's stomach pitted. The last time that she'd seen them all, a dishonorable three years ago, Sloane had left feeling awkward and uncomfortable. Sloane's niece—her sister's firstborn—had been asked to draw a picture of her whole family for school. Nina had put her mother and brother and father on the left of a boxy red house, and to the far right, towering in front of a wiry pyramid meant to be the Eiffel Tower, stood a frantic figure: Sloane. Her sister's children thought that she was French, and apparently, her sister hadn't done much to correct this. It suited everyone to pretend that Sloane was some kind of exchange student who returned once in a while to pay her respects to the people who used to house her. In this way, she could be thought of as an exotic guest instead of an ingrate.

"You okay?" asked Roman, as they inched into the driveway. His hand mercifully—ephemerally—making contact with her knee.

"Yeah," she lied, staring out at the red wooden siding that she'd always loved. It wasn't that she expected anything to be different about this visit. She wasn't going to break down at the dinner table, for example, let go of the incertitude that was percolating inside her. But there was a certain deliriousness that came from knowing that she could.

"Oh, Sloane?" asked Anastasia once they'd come to a stop on the gravel driveway. "I'm sorry, but if anyone besides you two wants to come into the vehicle, we'll need to sign a waiver."

"Oh, yeah, no. I'll just tell them it's a normal car."

"Oh," said Anastasia, her voice falling.

"I mean, a super extra better than normal normal car," Sloane corrected quickly, astonished—and impressed—that her car's feelings had been hurt.

Sloane rang her mother's doorbell, and the minute she heard its cascade of demonic cheeriness, she knew that what she should have done was use the key that she still kept on her keychain all these years, barrel into the kitchen, been boisterous and loud, hugs for everyone whether they felt forced or not. By ringing the bell, Sloane had just communicated to the members of her family that she was tentative about her place there. Sloane wished she could get into the car, be reversed out of the driveway, start all over again.

Her mother came to the door with a bit of flour in her hair, a pudge of dough stuck to her wrist.

"Oh!" she cried, her hand flying to her forehead. "You're here! You're early!"

Margaret looked better than Sloane remembered. Brighter, vivacious, she wore sixty-seven well. The auburn hair Sloane shared with her had accepted gray rather than turned it; she still wore her hair long. Margaret's eyes—one green, one hazel—had a kindness to them that Sloane couldn't deny. It touched her to consider that Margaret might have actually been looking forward to their visit—she'd been watching the clock.

"Look at you guys!" said Margaret, bringing her hands together—a nervous tic, Sloane knew. "Just look at you!"

Sloane felt a lurch of happiness, that old hopefulness again. She moved toward her mother, who enfolded her in an embrace that smelled of roses and black tea, the never-changing fragrance of her mother's good intentions underscored with nervous sweat.

"And Roman!" Margaret said, pulling away from a closeness that was foreign to them both. "Too skinny! I'll never know how you do it, you French men! I don't think one of your pant legs would fit over my thigh!"

Margaret didn't like Roman, but it was generous of her to try. To his credit, Roman had never been anything but flattering and attentive around her family. But there was a troubling halo of energy around him that other people picked up on. Her sister had once asked her if Roman was bisexual. (Sloane's answer? *He could be, if he tried.*)

After taking their coats (which slid immediately off the overburdened coat tree onto the floor), Margaret pushed them into the kitchen where she proudly held up three fingers: index, middle, ring.

"I've made three kinds of soufflé!"

Because Peter had been the cook in the family, in the years after his death, cooking lessons were laden on Margaret by well-intentioned girlfriends who thought that food and wine was the way to revive a widowed heart. But unfortunately, due to the formality of the classes she'd taken, Margaret now equated good cooking with haute cuisine, and thus her epicurean efforts were often elaborate failures.

Today's menu—souffléed potatoes with pomegranate-glazed lamb chops from the looks of the dark seeds staining the wooden counters—

was no exception. Sloane had just pinched a sheet of paper towel to start cleaning the bleeding seeds up when the sound of things dropping and being asked for in the mudroom alerted them to the arrival of the kids.

"Little dumplings!" Margaret called, brushing her hands off. "Aunt Sloane is here!"

Sloane's chest tightened. She made a conscious effort to stretch her smile wider, hope held within her tightened muscles that this evening would feel more natural than the ones before.

She walked into the mudroom where Harvey had little Everett on his shoulders. Mud was melting off the boy's boots onto her brother-in-law's anorak. Nina was on the bench already, tugging her boots off. Her sister wasn't in sight.

"Hi, guys!" Sloane said in her best approximation of an auntie voice. "Nina, God, you're big!"

Rather than measure out her life in coffee spoons, Sloane could track time by her sister's children's height; their persistence in her absence to keep growing up. It was a bit of an affront, really, to take leave of a baby and come back to find a little girl.

Nina looked up from her boot-removal efforts and Sloane didn't miss her microflinch: the resentment that the group dynamics in the house would now be altered.

"Can you say hi to your auntie?" Harvey asked, flashing the demented grin parents use when they talk through their children. *Can you tell her she's not exactly wearing winter shoes? Can you tell her that her sister feels abandoned? Can you tell Aunt Sloane that it's still legal to pick up the phone once in a while?*

"Hey, Harvey," Sloane managed, unsure how to greet a man with a child on his shoulders. She settled on pressing herself against his damp coat in a half effort at a hug and planting a kiss on the left side of his face. Then she put her hand on Everett's knee.

"Hi there!" she said, moving her hand to his impossibly round cheek. "You're such a little man now! Does he . . ." She looked back at Harvey. "Does he talk?"

Harvey dismissed her question with a laugh. He bent down and slid Everett off his shoulders.

"Heaps," he said, brushing snow off of Everett's hat. "But when he's around people he doesn't know . . ." He coughed to cloak his blunder. "He's just a little shy."

Roman thrust out his hand with more enthusiasm than the moment called for. "Harvey!" he exclaimed. "It's great to see you again!"

Sloane tried not to wince as the handshake was exchanged. She had forgotten to refresh Roman on her niece and nephew's names. The fact that he'd gotten Harvey's right was no small feat—he'd only met him once at a Thanksgiving where they'd thoroughly offended her mother by staying in a hotel.

"Roman, you look great, as always."

"Oh!" Roman scoffed. "But you! You're so outdoors!"

It was true that Harvey Kane was as outdoorsy as suburban dads could come. Harvey was an engineer who shared their father's fervent faith in exertion. Outdoor showers, cold swims, uphill walks through snow piles; one of Harvey's highest compliments was that something was "bracing."

"And *bonjour, demoiselle*," Roman said, bending down in front of Nina, "although you're not so little anymore!"

With a twinge of envy, Sloane watched Nina smile back at him. Children gravitated toward Roman because he didn't like them. It was like the anticat people. Felines always preferred people who had no tolerance for cats.

"You guys are back!" Her sister's voice behind her. "Everett! I hope you had a scarf on. How was it?"

Sloane turned to see Leila crouching in the sky-blue robe she'd had as a teenager, a garment that was older than the roof on their parents' house. She kissed her children's cold faces before rising to greet Sloane.

"You made it," Leila said, her expression pinched.

Despite her relief from finally being in her sister's presence, Sloane's tenderness at the sight of her sister was buried under guilt. She couldn't help but hear her greeting as accusatory.

"We did," Sloane answered, folding her arms around her sister's exhausted bathrobe, the sleeve of which bore both dried milk and cereal. Leila was the kind of mother who liked to wear the travails of motherhood like a badge: she never put concealer on her under-eye circles, she rarely brushed her hair, she didn't shower as often as she might have, even though Harvey was the kind of husband who would have taken the children away for a whole week if she asked.

"Roman," Leila said coolly, giving each of his cheeks a perfunctory kiss. Leila had never come out and said what she didn't like about him, but Sloane was pretty sure Leila thought that Roman had coerced Sloane into childlessness. A natural-born progenitor, Leila didn't trust people who didn't want offspring.

"Oh, guys!" Sloane said to the children. "I've brought you stuff from France!"

"Ooooh," went Leila, her eyebrows raised mockingly. "All the way from Paris! Let's get all this stuff off, and then we can do gifts."

Sloane stood there helplessly while the children were husked from their overclothes and boots. Nina looked up at her, confused.

"Is Paris the planet?" she asked, rather gravely. "The one where you're from?"

Sloane cocked her head. Benevolently, she ignored her sister's flushing cheeks.

"Mom says you're from another planet with different rules from us."

"Nina!" Leila snapped.

"Eeeeeee, eeeeee," whined Sloane, doing a bad impression of an alien.

. . .

The good thing about Leila having two children and a third on the way was that not a single thing of import could be discussed throughout the meal. If Nina wasn't dropping something then Everett was throwing something up. Leila spent the duration of the dinner blotting at one food stain or another, including a spray of pomegranate blood on her own blouse. (Pomegranate! The weeper in Sloane's stain-removal focus group would have had a nervous breakdown.) None of them could get a sentence in edgewise, much less tell an entire anecdote, which meant that the end of dinner had been arrived at without either Roman or Sloane having been asked about their work, which was just as well because Sloane did not need him outlining the semantics of a Zentai suit while passing the potatoes.

After dinner, up-for-everything Roman did the dishes alongside Harvey. Something was going on upstairs: footsteps, Margaret's laughter, maybe the makings of a bath. And then Leila descended the staircase jacketed and wool-hatted with two sleepy kids.

"You're not staying over?" Sloane asked.

Leila narrowed her eyes at her. "Stay over?!" she exclaimed. "Why?"

Leila and Harvey lived only twenty minutes away in Westport, so yes, why would they do that? Simply because Sloane had told her mother in the e-mail that seeded the whole dinner business in the first place that she and Roman would sleep over, and out of some inflated sense of occasion, Sloane had assumed that Leila and the kids would, too. Sloane was going to be up so early with jet lag, she'd entertained quixotic visions of her getting breakfast for everyone. There was that diner she used to go to with her father—the buttered corn muffins they'd split . . .

"It's a *school* night," Leila chided. And then, when she registered, somewhat incredulously, her sister's disappointment: "They don't sleep great in this house."

"No," Sloane said. "Of course. We probably shouldn't be staying over, either."

"I'm sorry we didn't get to talk about anything you're up to," Leila said, repositioning the now fully sleeping Everett on her hip. "Harvey!" she shouted. "Some help here! I've got two and a half kids in my arms!"

Sloane reached out belatedly—why hadn't she thought to help her pregnant sister? But then there was Harvey, a gargantuan diaper bag hanging from his shoulder joint.

"I guess we'll have another chance," Leila said, shrugging. "I mean, you're here?"

"Oh yeah," Sloane said. "I'm here."

"For a whole six months." Leila nodded.

Sloane nodded back.

"So we'll see you, like, what, once more?"

She tried to shrug off the insinuations of this comment.

"Maybe twice," she said.

Leila laughed, and in that honest sound there was a glimmer of the bond they used to share. All these openings for closeness—all these humans with their disappointments and their desperate hearts, but it's so much easier, so convenient, to blame emotional distance on a lack of time.

"Okay," Leila said, rearranging her weight on the stairs. "So we'll see you soon."

"Sure, soon," Sloane said, making room for them to slide past her on the staircase, knowing that "soon" was a word for a moment that probably wouldn't come.

"Good-bye, Harvey," she said, as he moved sturdily past her, a groggy Nina in his arms. "It was nice to see you again."

"Yeah," he said, speaking low as to not wake the children. "It was."

.   .   .

That night, even though Margaret had given Sloane and Roman her art studio above the garage so they'd have privacy, Sloane couldn't sleep. Her inability to engage Leila in any kind of real conversation had made her too afraid to try the same thing with her mother, and so even though Margaret had been hovering in the kitchen, rearranging toothpicks and doing other things that clearly didn't need attending to, Sloane had asked her if she was going to bed soon, and her mother had asked *her* if she was going to bed soon, and too unfamiliar with working through each other's inhibitions, going to bed is what they'd done.

When she went up to the studio—fresh linens, old paint cans—Roman was in bed mating with his tablet, the light from its screen an electronic embrace. Seeing him there, otherwise engaged, made Sloane want to run back across to the main house, where her mother was surely up still, spill out her unhappinesses like something ill-digested, exchange reassurances over something hot and honeyed, be tucked childlike into the guest bed down the hall.

But Sloane was an adult. An adult who had chosen *not* to need her mother. To rely on herself for emotional sustenance instead.

"You going to be on that a long time?" Sloane asked. Prone to insomnia, she practiced good sleep hygiene: no screens or cell phones three hours before bedtime.

"Maybe," Roman replied, tilting the screen toward her. "Say, have you ever given thought to the next cat?" Her eyes settled on the image of a kitten on its tiptoes in an unfamiliar patch of snow.

"Like what will replace them?" she queried. "In terms of videos?"

"Yeah," said Roman, pulling the screen back. "Because there are these virtual red pandas coming on the market. That could be huge."

Sloane sat on the mattress, reached for her book. She always packed a penlight because hotels seemed to be doing away with bedside lighting options, catering to a clientele who only read electronically, but that night, she tugged the pull string of the little lamp beside her and a cozy wash of luminosity bathed her side of the bed.

Sloane was reading *The Argonauts* by Maggie Nelson, a book that challenged preconceived ideas about sexuality through tight epiphanies. Sloane was having a hard time with it—some of its anecdotes touched a little close to home. In fact, she'd actually welled up a couple of days earlier when the author described an altercation between two animated Popsicles: *"You're more interested in fantasy than reality,"* Popsicle One accused. *"I'm interested in the reality of my fantasy,"* the other said.

"Honey," Roman said, kneeing her under the covers. "Pandas?"

The thing was—Sloane thought, refusing to turn toward him—the thing was that with trends, change wasn't inherent in every little thing. People would always love the feel of weathered denim; the warmth of a baby's cheek against a waiting chest. Videos of other people's kittens doing funny things.

"It's just going to make people sad," Sloane said, "imitation pandas."

"I don't think so," said Roman, briskly. "Especially when the real ones are all gone."

The next morning, through a combination of lingering jet lag and a rough night's sleep, Sloane woke up feeling anxious. It had been a mistake to sleep over at her mother's. Certainly, in terms of convenience, it didn't make sense. Plus, the eagerness Sloane felt to get to her second day of work had set back any desire she'd had the previous night to make inroads with her mom.

She'd woken up earlier than Roman—it was just turning six o'clock. Carefully, Sloane rose and put on last night's clothing, donned the change of jewelry that she had packed in her overnight bag, and started down the staircase into the cold outdoors.

As she walked across the yard in the yawn of early morning, Sloane was better able to see the places where the old house was falling into disrepair. Part of a water-logged fence collapsing, the herb garden spiked with bolted plants, the back deck slippery with leaves and mildew green as avocados.

In the house, the quiet—real quiet, her mother still asleep—Sloane was confronted with a vision of the rooms that housed her childhood: the smell of old flowers and burnt paper and sunlight mixed with dust. With his death, Peter had lost his marriage-long campaign for cleanliness and order, and an organizational system based entirely on sentimentalism and nostalgia had won out.

Sloane opened up the fridge and was confronted with a menagerie of gruesome leftovers in mismatched pots and jars. She didn't have the fortitude to start looking through them, the liquefying evidence of her mother's *rémoulades* and quiches, her tangible efforts to keep late-life loneliness at bay.

Why had she imagined she'd go out and get breakfast for everyone? An empty stomach would have to suffice—she had to get to work. But just when she'd started to wonder whether she could get away with leaving her mom a note, she heard a plank creak on the stairs.

"Honey, is that you?" Margaret called. "Don't touch anything, I was going to make pancakes!"

Sloane didn't respond. She listened to her mother's footfalls, trying not to hear how slow and careful they were. And then her mother was in the doorway, wrapped in a fleece robe, dabs of unabsorbed moisturizer stuck in the creases of her neck.

"Don't you want pancakes?" she asked, pushing her hair back to tame it into some kind of shape. "Is Roman up?"

Sloane winced. See, this is the thing that drove her nuts about her mother. She thought she could heal everything by smothering people with good intentions. Pancakes? Pancakes!? Sloane was almost forty, she hardly wrote, she never called, and Margaret pretended that a hearty breakfast would make everything all right.

"Oooh," said Sloane. "I don't know about that."

"Does Roman not like pancakes?"

God, this was another crutch, displacing the blame of everything disappointing onto a man she hardly knew. The inquiries about their food preferences, the insinuation that Roman was picky—neither of them gave a shit about Roman's eating patterns; what Margaret wanted to know was why Sloane had become so difficult to love.

"He's showering," Sloane answered. "Doing e-mails. So I don't know. Maybe just toast?"

"Oh," Margaret said, sinking. "You sure?"

Sloane looked at her mother's mismatched eyes and her wild hair and the bathrobe with the tea stains, and she wanted to fall down on the floor with her and lean against the cupboards and let everything out; tell her mother that her partner preferred rubbing up against strangers than touching her in bed; tell her that there was a darkness in her decision to work for Mammoth that she was trying to ignore. Tell her that the overheated seawater was coming for the wetlands, coming for the aquifers, coming for them all.

But instead she just stood there at the fork between the way she wanted her relationship with her mother to be like and the way it actually was.

"I don't know," Sloane said. "You already did so much cooking last night. Toast would probably be easier."

Her mother's shoulders sloped. A branch fell down outside. Even the kitchen appliances with their fingerprinted surfaces seemed to turn against the daughter who had chosen the wrong words.

8

On the way back in from Stamford, Anastasia dropped Roman off at the apartment before shuttling Sloane to work.

She and Roman hadn't talked the whole way back. Roman wasn't the type to feel they had to "download" after a visit with her family. On his side, they only saw Yves and Victoire Bellard twice a year for white wine and cold chicken, brisk luncheons that were as perfunctory as they were expected. Seeing that he viewed his own relatives as little more than expensive pieces of furniture that needed to be dusted and polished from time to time, it wasn't surprising that he didn't feel the need to check in with her about her feelings since they'd left her mom's. He'd been with her ten years now—he assumed she didn't have any.

Normally, Sloane would have been relieved—grateful, even—for Roman's silence, but on their drive into Manhattan, she just felt let down. Roman used to have good instincts, used to be able to at least identify when she wanted—uncharacteristically—to talk, but ever since he started becoming something of an Internet sensation, he'd tuned out everything except for the reverberations of himself. Currently, he was answering requests for follow-up interviews that had come in the wake of his polemic *Nouvel Obs* profile, and was checking in on the success of the latest urban Zentai selfies he'd posted to Instagram. Roman running along the East River in his gold Zentai suit, a flashy supernova. Roman on the L train in between a commuter dressed like a rigid schoolmarm and a teenager with gray hair.

His one concession to something resembling empathy was a question. They'd arrived at the apartment building, and he had one leg out of the car, his eyes momentarily off his device.

"So, I thought that went well, yes?" he asked.

"I have no idea," Sloane said. She didn't. She was at such loose ends with her family, she'd lost the ability to gauge their interactions.

"Hmm," he said, distracted, leaning against the car door. "I think I'll have eight hundred thousand followers soon," he said, unable to contain his grin.

"Really?!" Sloane balked. "Are you serious?"

"The Americans, they really like the Zentai way of thinking." He slid his phone into his pocket. "I think it's freeing for them. With their puritanical history—it's liberating, yes?"

Sloane was still staring at the number eight hundred thousand in her head. That was a lot of people. In such a short amount of time. It was the person in her, not the forecaster, who didn't want Roman to be onto something. But he was.

"Well, that's great. That's great." Her shock turned toward resentment. "That'll be really great for your book. Whatever the fuck it's about."

"Oh, *chérie*. I'll have something for you soon. I'm having the big plans!" Roman's hand shot up vertically, imitating a rocket ship. "It will be great for us!"

"Wonderful," she said, unsure of what "great for them" would look like. An open relationship? Zoophilia? With a robotic panda? "A little background would be good. Maybe you're writing a tell-all, for all I know."

He got out of the car. They didn't kiss each other. Sloane's heart twisted at her comment. Such a book would be unsaleable. People don't like to read stories that don't have love in them.

Whether Anastasia sensed Sloane's disquietude through thermal seat sensors or—incredibly—instinct, she left her charge in silence on their way to work. Sloane was grateful for Anastasia's uncanny sensitivity; she had to cleanse her mind. Personal entanglements had always clouded her, which was one of the reasons she kept her social life antiseptic clean. She avoided people with "issues," needy people, sad ones, anyone who really, truly needed a friend. Back in Paris, Sloane and Roman's group of friends were jubilant accessories: always there for fun. And when the going got tough? The tough stayed off the dinner party circuit until they felt bright and strong again.

It was worrisome to have this much muck inside her. Guilt, or disappointment maybe, about the way it had felt to see her family, Roman's recent secrecy, these things were becoming difficult to ignore, and worse yet, they were clogging up the plumbing she used to do her work. Normally, this early into a stay in New York City, Sloane's mind would have been electrified with ideas and intuitions, synapses firing with possibilities and codes, but instead she felt numb and dumb and worried.

Usually, this only happened when she was working on something short term and superficial that she didn't really care about. Fashion forecasting sometimes made her feel like this—the trends came so hard and fast. Tastemakers wouldn't be caught dead tromping about in wedge sneakers, but several years ago, they were the only things to be seen in. Certainly, Sloane had compiled forecasts involving actual *items*: denim overalls, ankle-baring men's pants, the return of designer socks—but what she preferred to invest her time and energy in was the longer-term sea changes in human desire. But she wasn't getting an overarching read on what people wanted so far. The humans were so tired. The environment was shit, people's ability to empathize with others was going to hell in a fair-trade handbasket, politics around the world had become a poisoned farce. It felt like the only thing that people wanted was to stay alive and order takeout and play quietly with their phones.

Sloane looked out the window at the restaurants and cafés floating by. She had a pretty intense craving for a slice of pizza. For cheese and grease and carbs to soak up some of the sad. She could almost hear her mom second-guessing her desire: pizza? In the *morning*? Her dad would have thought nothing of it. *It's just cheese on bread . . .*

Although recently she'd started feeling like a circus animal in a treat-filled cage, when she'd been younger, she'd felt lucky to be special. The premonitions, the presentiments, the "Spidey skills" as her dad called them, they were all a thrilling gift. Of course, lots of children think they have magic powers, but Sloane had such queer pastimes: working with all her might to change the shade of traffic lights, spending entire hours at the Greenwich shoreline, wet sand in her small fists, certain that she alone possessed the power to feed the growing waves.

It wasn't until middle school when the higher feelings started. Her mother made her see a psychiatrist because she got weird feelings about the weather, the color of the trees. Margaret thought Sloane was too anxious. Plus, there'd been an incident. Her sister, a good athlete even in middle school, had had a soccer match, and Sloane had spent the entire car ride over asking Leila not to play in it. She said she had a "bad feeling," and this only worsened when she saw the other team. It was an energy thing, the other girls seemed sour. Some small thing, some girl thing had gone wrong. There was unbalance among all of the teammates on the opposing side, resulting in a prickly kind of static that couldn't go anywhere but bad. Both Margaret and Leila told Sloane she was being ridiculous (Leila said she was jealous because she was playing center forward, while Sloane didn't play any team sports at all), but halfway through the game, the other center forward had purposely stepped—and stayed on—Leila's cleat, and Leila, who'd been running forward, had torn a ligament in her knee. First game of the season, she'd been out for all the rest.

It was happenstance, of course, completely coincidental, but it spooked the female Jacobsens. Instead of feeling rectified after the accident, Sloane felt ashamed. She'd have to find a way to temper her intuition, to influence people without freaking everyone out. Her father said she was "tapped into different frequencies than some people" (that particular evening's conversation overheard from the stairs), but her mom said she needed to go and see somebody, that it wasn't "normal" for a young child to have so many fears.

Yes, well. Sloane talked about her fears a whole lot less now. She kept the disquiet to herself. In any case, people didn't seem to be listening the way that they once had.

9

Sloane's first meeting of her second day was with the furniture department, an incongruous, flailing sector that Dax had told her was in a "make or break" year.

"It wasn't the best decision, incorporating it," he'd explained on the phone during one of the overview chats they'd had while she was still in Paris.

The furniture division was one of the only sectors that wasn't proprietary. Mammoth partnered with other furniture manufacturers to offer some technical enhancement that made their offers more competitive in the furnishing space. Couches that clocked how long you had been sitting, hospital beds that knew when a patient needed to roll over, lest they develop bedsores.

The problem, Dax told her, was that their current offerings were all fault-finding. "Punishers," he called them. "They're not, any of them, delivering information that makes people feel good. We need to roll out some options for the conference, something kind of fun."

Sloane found herself checking the hallway for a sign of Dax before officially kicking things off with the new team. She good-morning'd everyone and they good-morning'd her back.

"So, I'll level with you," she started, taking the staff in, "I think this particular division has the toughest challenge. How do we present furniture that specifically targets the childless? Let's start by just talking. Why don't you guys tell me: people without kids, what do their homes look like?"

One guy laughed. "Well, none of us have kids."

"And my apartment looks like crap," said someone else.

Sloane smiled. "Really? In what way?"

"Well, it looks like a design blog," the fellow answered. "That's my girlfriend's doing. We've got white birch logs, like, jammed up against a wall with books around them, and we don't even have a fireplace."

"And *my* girlfriend puts up really aggressive wall art. You know, like 'EAT' in the breakfast nook?" said a man whose name Sloane didn't know.

"*Nook?*" one of the girls giggled. "Steven, please. We all know you bought that yourself."

"Okay, okay," said Sloane, putting her hand up. "The point isn't to bash other people's decorating styles, but to try and understand what furnishings say about us. The homes of people *with* children. What comes to mind? Just call things out."

"Cereal in the carpet," said a young woman.

"Beige," said someone else.

"Toys everywhere. A lot of . . . dishtowels," said the guy who had spoken first. "Oh, and I'm Alex."

"Thanks," said Sloane. "Yeah, let's remember names. But let's not get too negative. What I'm hearing is 'messy,' sure. But what else? Is there a sense of freedom maybe? Or fun?"

Brows furrowed. Noses wrinkled. After a while, a tall man in a crewneck spoke.

"I guess things get used more. Oh, and I'm Andrew Willett.

Design." he added. "Kids, like, jump on things. Or they hide under furniture. It really gets *used*."

"I think that's pretty interesting," Sloane replied, thinking warmly of Mina's comment in that first meeting, of how parents' skin got used. "And how do people who *don't* have children use their furniture?"

Wrinkled noses again.

"I'm Jaimie," said the guy who claimed his apartment looked like crap. "They have people over. Eat cheese, try not to spill wine."

"For . . . making out???" tried Steven, the nook guy, looking around.

"More for TV." Jaimie laughed.

"So basically, furniture allows people to gather," Sloane suggested. "And then Mammoth adds an extra element. What's that element?"

"We track everything," said Jaimie.

"We monitor what people do," said Holly.

"I think we *reassure* people," said Andrew, his color high. "For instance, we have this Pharaoh bed? That's something in the pipeline. It's bigger than a California king, and it comes with a smart mattress that tracks the quality and duration of your sleep. You can sync your ratings to your smartphone, so that—"

Sloane was going to have to feign enthusiasm for this one. Personally, she thought that people should be alert enough to check in with their own bodies to know—or feel—what they'd done physically with them during the day. You didn't need a smart mattress to tell you that you'd had a shitty night of sleep.

"Oh wait, I have an idea," said Jaimie, drumming his fingers on the table. "Okay, this sounds obnoxious, but hear me out. I was thinking about the competitive angle, and—Carla, don't even get on me about this," he said, looking at a stern woman who hadn't yet talked, "but what if we really went for it, and social feeds actually *did* broadcast what you did in bed? I mean, nothing too raunchy, obviously, but kind of . . . winky. Like, your mattress lets your followers know that you're probably not gonna make Sunday brunch, because you're still in bed, and the mattress also registers that there's another body . . ."

The Mammothers were arguing back and forth as to whether this was an offensive idea or a good one, when Dax and Deidre arrived.

It was only her second day, she could give Dax that, but was he going to be at *every* meeting? And he had to arrive now when the group's energy was scattered, they hadn't hit on anything, they weren't going anywhere.

"Making progress?" Dax asked as he sidled in, patting her on the shoulder.

She felt suddenly protective of her group with their flushed cheeks and downcast eyes, aware that they didn't have anything to show the guy who wanted a great show.

"It certainly is tricky," Sloane accorded. "Even if you personally don't have any, does that mean you're never going to have any in your house? Are we assuming that the childless don't have friends with kids? There's a lot to wrap our heads around, so we're just working through things."

"That's fine," Dax said, walking behind each of his disciples. "But we still need something kick-ass. I want something *big*. With a tech element that will blow people away."

Sloane pressed her lips together. What would really blow people away was if they announced that no one needed furniture. Entire swaths of middle-classers living from a suitcase because they'd been let down by the system, had placed their faith in travel. Placed all their aspirations in the countries they'd see next.

"Sloane?" asked Dax, she feared for the second time.

"Sorry," she said, shaking her mental cloud.

"Alex here said that there might be some potential in lighting?"

"Lighting. Right, of course." She nodded emphatically to a suggestion she hadn't heard made. "Certainly, there are a lot of options.

There are melatonin-boosting sleep bulbs, and, um . . ." She held her breath.

"O-kay," Dax stalled. "I see you all have quite a ways to go. But you've got this, right?" He winked.

Of course they'd come up with something dynamite, she reassured him. They just needed time.

10

After the meeting, Sloane retreated to the company cafeteria to sponge up her doubts with carbohydrates.

Because she was a trend forecaster, people assumed that Sloane had a lofty taste in food, when in fact she was comforted by simple, empty foodstuffs: the luscious nothingness of a swab of cream cheese on a giant bagel, penne with butter, children's menu items. Her first few months in Paris, she'd more or less subsisted on toasted baguette with spray butter, a product she'd found in a tiny American grocery store near her first apartment, the same brand her mother used.

Sloane was just smearing the second half of a bagel with another block of cream cheese when Mina appeared at her side.

"Hi," she said, matter-of-factly, both hands around a mug. *Nama'stay in bed*, the mug said.

"Oh, hi," Sloane said, nearly dropping her knife from surprise. "I'm so glad to see you!" She tried to temper her enthusiasm, lest she scare Mina away. "I'm actually glad to see you," she tried again. "Because I wanted to ask—"

"How come I clammed up?" Mina offered, pulling a sesame bagel from the basket.

"Well, yeah . . ." Sloane was startled by her forthrightness. "You were on to something so interesting, and then—I don't know, is it a problem to say certain things in front of Dax?"

"I don't know." Mina shrugged. "No one's ever tried it."

"Oh." Sloane flinched, astonished that it could be that simple. "So you think everyone's . . . scared of him?"

"Listen," Mina said, pausing to chew. "We're here to sell things. Everyone knows that. So these summer trend conferences . . . Daxter wants to make it seem like we have the time and resources to just bat ideas around . . ."

"But you *do* have the resources," Sloane contested.

"Sure. But even if we had the *time*, no one's fooling anyone. We can brainstorm all we want, but at the end of the day, Dax wants tangible products, things people can buy." Mina ate more bagel. "It's all fun and games, I guess," she added, "until someone gets canned."

Sloane left her impromptu conversation with Mina feeling emboldened. When she reached Dax's office, Deidre said he was on the phone, but of course he'd see her, he'd be thrilled to.

She sat down feeling confident that the Mammothers had potential—it was a given, they'd come up with something huge—they just had to have permission to lose sight of the shore.

"Ms. Jacobsen?" asked Deidre several minutes later, pulling her cardigan closer at her neck. "Mr. Stevens will see you."

Sloane thought she heard Deidre whisper "Good luck" on her way through the door.

Situated on the thirty-second floor of the building, Daxter's office had an unobstructed view of Union Square Park. It was lunchtime. All across the winter landscape, New Yorkers and tourists, seeking power foods. Fennel and blood orange salads, pumpkin seeds for crunch.

"So what can I do for you?" Dax asked, rising.

Sloane forced her gaze to meet his. "Thanks for making time. I just had a couple . . . well, frustrations, actually."

"Part of the territory!" Dax smiled. "Please"—he gestured—"sit down."

"Well, for starters, I'm afraid there are some unnecessary distractions," Sloane said, letting out a breath she hadn't realized she was holding. "For example, I'd really like to do something about the phones."

"The phones?" Dax repeated, picking up half a sandwich from a plate on his desk. "You mind?" he asked, his brow raised. "You eat?"

"Yes, sort of . . ." She motioned for him to continue chomping. "People just aren't present," she went on. "I don't need to tell you that they're distracted by their cells."

"And I don't need to tell you that they're a huge part of our business."

"Yes," she said. "But still. I was hoping we could confiscate them. Put them in a box before each meeting. Outside of the room."

Dax paused midbite, his small mouth gaping open. He looked as if she'd just suggested that he churn butter from scratch.

"I'm sure you can see a number of reasons as to why that would be problematic."

"Listen," she accorded, leaning forward. "We're not going to be able to charge forward in the way you want us to with their attention so divided. They're not able to listen. They're not able to *hear*. And there's another thing as well."

Dax blew out a mock whistle. "We're not even twenty-four hours into it," he scoffed.

"I know," she said, unwilling to back down. "But it's better to get it all out now, up front, don't you think? The staff is super bright, the products are amazing. But the project's such a big one. A lot of your employees are too young to know whether or not they'll even *want* kids, let alone to have them. So the things we're asking them to speculate about for other people are intensely personal. And in order to get personal . . ." She left the sentence open.

Dax pulled a long piece of sauerkraut from his sandwich and put it on the waxed paper underneath the other half. "I get it. You need time. Which I've given you. Six months."

"Timing isn't a problem," she said, sitting straighter. "It's more . . . well, I have no way of knowing if this is your modus operandi, but with you popping in and out of our meetings . . . I mean, I totally get it. It's your company. And it's a great one. But I get the feeling that people are inhibited. They're not saying things that you might not want to hear them say."

"About me?" Dax asked, eyebrow up again.

"No, about the products. I don't think that they feel safe. And while I certainly appreciate the time you're giving me, and all the support you're showing, I want to meet the task at hand. I need them to be able to speculate about stuff that's really out-there. I would just appreciate it if you—if you could give us more privacy. It's something I'd like to try."

Daxter resumed the digestion of his food. "I can hear that," he said, chewing. "I mean, sure, I'm intimidating. It's something I feel, too. So . . . fine, I won't stop by so often. But the phones? This is a twenty-four-seven enterprise. People need to stay in touch."

"You really don't think people can go half an hour without their cells?"

"No," he said, "I don't. I mean, they could, obviously. But people need to sign off on things. They need to see their e-mails. I mean, Sloane. We *make* phones. You want everyone to wear smartwatches, we can do that if that's more discreet but—"

"I disagree," said Sloane, adamant. "I disagree. You have to force people to remember what it's like to pay attention."

"To the detriment of other projects falling through the cracks?" He shook his head at her. "I don't know, Sloane, it's your circus. If you can get them to do it, go for it. But you're not gonna get support from me on this. I've got a vested interest in things getting done. Which means keeping my people reachable."

"Okay," said Sloane, sensing his desire to continue lunch without her. "But I'd also like your permission to put out suggestion boxes," she hurried. "So that people who are timid, or are afraid of getting in trouble, can anonymously contribute ideas."

Daxter narrowed his eyes at her. "And are you also gonna do some trust falls?" he asked, mockingly. Then he wrapped his sandwich up, leaned across his desk and gave her hand a pat.

"Go nuts. Get results the way you need to."

Sloane looked down at the constellation of crumbs that lay between them. She hadn't been given a full vote of confidence, but something in her was stirring out of hibernation. It had been weeks since she'd been touched on the hand.

11

Sloane traveled the seventeen floors down to her office, thinking hard. She'd accomplished what she wanted, but she felt embarrassed. Suggestion boxes? She wasn't working at a casual dining establishment, for God's sake. She should have thought through her request more, developed a private blog that people could post thoughts to, but instead, she'd asked the CEO of a tech company for permission to purchase a cardboard box.

But Sloane wanted to go *in* instead of out. Visually and audibly, the world of today was designed to distract. Before you could give a name to your own feelings, there was something telling you what to think and want. Must-have lists in magazines, billboards on passing buses, push notifications, slogans on T-shirts. How long until quiet trended? By asking people to cut the cord from their electronics, put handheld pen to paper, consider what it was they *actually* thought rather than parroting a think piece, they might find a way to their own brains again. And hearts.

Looking out her window to the neighboring skyscrapers, Sloane found herself wanting to float up and out and back to where she'd been last night. The severe whiteness of their flat in Paris was such a stark comparison to the overfurnished closeness of her mother's house, but whereas the cacophony of Margaret's dominion (swelling bookshelves, kitchen cabinets littered with exploded bags of couscous) had always felt suffocating, last night it had felt like a home. Not in the sense that Sloane used to live there, but that her mother's house (and her mother's furniture) bore the stretch marks of a life actually lived. While Sloane's apartment displayed the beauty of a life put on hold.

Thinking of her mother made her think more about her mother. At Tuesday, ten a.m., Leila's eldest in school, Everett at home with Leila—what was Margaret doing? Slow-cooking something, brining, giving herself chores. Or maybe she was *with* Leila. Or out to breakfast with a friend. Some dark place in Sloane wanted her mother to be lonely, but it was possible—probable, even—that she wasn't. Sloane tried to shake herself off this mental track. It was a bad season for melancholia. Thanksgiving, that harbinger of familial closeness, was just around the bend.

She picked up her phone, dying battery in the red. *Thank you for dinner, Mom,* she started texting, *it was really good. Looking forward to catching up more over Thanksgiving.* She read it over. Unimpressed, but also not sure how to improve upon it, she pressed Send. Then she sent another message: *Let me know what we can bring?*

Sloane was listening to the descending C-chord of her phone dying when a knock announced Deidre ready to escort her to the art meeting. Except when Sloane looked up, it wasn't her.

In France, there was an automatic response that came up on ATM screens when you tried to take out cash. The semantic translation was *Enter your passcode away from prying eyes,* but literally, the message read *Compose your secret code while sheltered from indiscreet regards.* Accordingly, whenever Sloane took out money in Paris, she always fantasized about a debonair man smoking a cigarillo at her back, clothed in a cape, maybe, a sort of unmasked Zorro. It was the kind of fantasy that involved words like "loins" and "ravaged." A fantasy re-kindled by the person in her doorway, standing there, unmasked.

"Hi there," she said, rising halfway up.

Sensing her confusion, he introduced himself: "I'm Jin. The art director?"

"Oh, Jin," she said, shaking his outstretched hand. "Of course. It's so nice to finally meet you." She looked around them. "Did you want to chat before we head downstairs?"

"Oh, there's no downstairs today," he said, pulling his gigantic cardigan around him as he sat. "The team is swamped. Black Friday stuff, sorry, you mind?" He nodded to his seat.

She fluttered her hand at him, no. "So it's just . . . us?" she asked.

"Well, Daxter wants us to tag team the young tablet project any-way, so . . ." Jin started extracting things from a large tote he'd brought in. "To me, it seems to make the most sense to just get started. I'll bring you up to speed." He had three different computer tablets on his legs, thin as dinner menus, in shades of jelly beans.

The mention of the tablet project made it easier to focus. Dax had of course briefed her on the YA project—it was one of the rare non-ReProduction enterprises she'd be involved in while at Mammoth. In the fall, they were releasing an entire line of young adult–themed tab-lets, with keypads, accessories and color schemes designed to appeal to teens. The tablets were actually double-screened, with a reinforced exterior LCD screen that could either broadcast what the user was doing on the internal screen, or be set to a personalized profile: a picture of the user, a collage of friends. Whether they were hanging out in a café, reading on a subway or watching a movie at home, pass-ersby would be given a glimpse into their world.

"So," said Jin, hands on top of his work pile. "Should we get to know each other, or just jump in?"

Sloane laughed, uncomfortable. She'd been staring at his fingers.

"I jest," he said, folding one leg while managing not to disturb the products resting on his thighs. "But I was in Chicago your first day. I'm a fan of your work, of course. You can help us shake things up."

Sloane smiled, wishing she deserved the compliment. She hadn't done a lot of shaking up yet.

"So," Jin said, his smile suddenly mischievous. "What's your opinion so far?"

"Well, everyone's been really welcoming," she said, her guard sky-high.

"Hmm," he answered, recrossing his legs. "Not so impressed."

"No, no, of course I am," she countered. "I'm just . . . still feeling things out."

"It's a specific culture," Jin said, pulling back a bit. "But just know that everyone is really happy that you're here."

"Thank you," she said, flattered. "Really. So show me what you got?"

"Maybe we can start with colorways?" He held up the three tablets. One was rose-petal pink, one grass green, and the last one, an orange so bright it made her squint.

"So I don't know if this will surprise you," she said, "but I like the pink one. The other two are kind of painful, they're so bold."

"That's what *I* said!" He laughed. "Consumer research pulled these from active wear. Headbands and sports bras, I guess there's overlap."

"It's not earth-shattering, I know," Sloane continued, "but I'd been picturing something more along the lines of metallic pastels."

"You don't say!" He beamed, pulling a color board out. "Something with grit and life. And really textured. Unisex."

He held up a swath of what looked like magma mixed with charcoal and moonstone. Sloane's heart leapt at this. The bolt.

"I love that," she said, honestly. "Volcanic."

"That's the working name, actually," he said. "It's fiery, apocalyptic. I get that these are young adults, but they're worried about things, too."

Oh, the jolted thrust of something finally right! The outer body flash of it, the hot thrush of quickened heart. Textured images started to burn up at her: tarnished metal, corroded copper. Mica. Moss.

"What about . . . flesh?" she heard herself suggest. Immediately, she went hot.

Jin stared past her through the window, lost in his own thoughts.

"Tongue," he finally said. "Weird, right? That it's a universal shade?"

But Sloane was taken over by the insistence of a memory, flooding her with the overwhelming tactility of her first kiss. Not the *real* first time (which had been on the edge of the bed at a high school "make-out party," lock-kneed next to Adam Saybourne, who'd literally jumped on her from his position on the mattress), but kissing when she got the hang of it, when she was aroused (rather than mortified) by the sound of her own breath.

She ran her hand through her hair, undid her bun. Something tongue-colored, textured like flesh. It was right, but it was disturbing. But disturbance felt so right.

"As much as I believe in this," she said, suddenly conscious of her hair grazing her shoulders. "It might not be mainstream."

"So you think like Dax does." Jin frowned. "That what's easy, works."

"Easy?" she asked, startled. "That's not why I'm here."

Something in the air had rearranged itself, the space felt thick between them.

"I'm not going to go rogue on the YA tablets," Sloane continued, defensive. "They'll sell better if they're done in metallic pastels and that's as true today as it's going to be three years from now. And that's part of trends, too."

"You really think that?" he asked.

"What I really think is that teenagers should be outside getting air and sunlight and, like, having awkward sexual experiences instead of socializing electronically, but that's not gonna happen, so yeah, metallic pastels."

Jin put his fingers to the skin under his collar. The longest, slowest scratch.

"Can I ask you a question?" he said, finally, sliding the tablets back into his bag.

"Of course."

"I'm known for being blunt," he said. "I'm just warning you."

"I think I can handle it," she snorted.

"Are you afraid to do your job?"

Sloane's eyes narrowed; her already dry throat clenched. The very bones in her hand felt like they were drawing inward.

"I'm not afraid to do my *job*," she snapped.

"You can tell me what you really think," he said. "I promise."

"And what I really think," Sloane said, "is that the YA line should be done in metallic pastels."

Jin rubbed two fingers across his lips, contemplating her.

"Fences," he said, now aiming those fingers at her.

"Excuse me?" she said, shrill.

"You've got fences up." He circled his fingers through the air. "I get it."

"I don't have any *fences*," she retorted, "I'm just doing my job."

She could almost hear him say *Are you?* through the expression on his face.

"I'm gonna choose not to believe you," he replied instead. He put the color board back into his bag. "Or not believe you, yet."

Sloane opened her mouth to berate him, but nothing came out. Every insult she crafted felt empty and old-fashioned, and she was not the type of person who showed her emotions at work.

But when Jin left, she found herself templed against the window, the gray swell of other buildings looming up before her, so many strangers doing things on their high floors. *Who do you think you are?* she could have asked him. *Who do you think you are?* she could have asked herself.

12

A t the end of the day, Sloane got into Anastasia, furious. Who *was* this smooth upstart? If his collagen levels and pushy confidence were anything to go by, he was clearly younger. Maybe by a lot. He'd probably been curled up in a dorm room dog-earing fashion ads while Sloane was telling Fortune 500 companies which models to feature in those ads. She was good at her job, damn it. She knew what she was doing at Mammoth, and it wasn't telling Dax that all his electronics needed to be organ-colored so that people could get back in touch with their inner selves.

Screw art directors, and screw Jin in particular. Front-loaded with assurance because he looked the way he did: his bone structure alone was like a global positioning chart to something in the stars. Stupid, stupid, stupid, and even stupider still that she'd let a stranger knock her off her fulcrum. She had the sudden impulse to go home and tongue kiss Roman—it was animalistic and murderous, the impetus to reinforce her confidence through her sexuality, but there it was.

When Anastasia nosed into the lettered corridors of Alphabet City, Sloane's ears pricked to a frequency only she could hear. Roman was there—not in the apartment, she could feel it, but very, very close.

She got out of the car and stepped quietly to the curb. Her gaze fell upon the community park where a majestic weeping willow had stood before Hurricane Sandy claimed it. But the park was empty save for a man bent over a plot of land: flannel-panted, weeding. Sloane crossed the street and looked into the glowing bay windows of the café on the corner, and there she saw the him-thing thing that was Roman in his Zentai suit.

With a deeply felt exhaustion, she saw he was wearing his shiny red one: an attempt to be festive, probably. In any case, he'd managed to attract admirers—three young men around him with their litter of paper cups. Roman had been a cherished curiosity in their Paris neighborhood, and it appeared that the same thing was unfolding here. She picked her way around the gate leashed with Yorkiepoos and puggles and entered the café.

Taking advantage of Roman's compromised vision (he really couldn't see for shit in that freaking suit), Sloane loitered by the condiment station to hear what he was saying. Usually, he was respectful of their private life, but his thirst to be someone in New York made her nervous. She wasn't sure that he considered their life "private" anymore.

"—of course, there's a real winning level, but there's also a final level for the game within the game." Sloane leaned closer to their table to hear the rest. "The gamers actually plan trips to the real Chernobyl. They sneak into the contaminated zone. They drink from the water. They post videos of themselves drinking from the water to their gaming friends. They stand on top of the buildings in the Pripyat ghost town. You cannot get a virtual and physical reality more merged than this."

Roman was obsessed with the video game *S.T.A.L.K.E.R.: Shadow of Chernobyl*. In Paris, he gave lectures about the Zone of Alienation that the antihero—an amnesiac artifact collector named The Marked One—navigates amid radioactive buildings and warped fauna. Alone and suicidal, trapped within an alternate reality that has him both inspired and encaged, Sloane considered The Marked One as a worst-case scenario for what disassociated humans could become. The game fascinated her, certainly, and she understood its gruesome appeal, but Roman's interest in it spooked her. The Marked One didn't need anybody but himself.

She decided to make her presence known. "Roman," she said, putting her hand on his shoulder. "I'm back."

"Ah, Sloane! How super!" It came out *zupair* with his accent. "Everyone, this is, Sloane, my Sloane! This is Juan, and Beau, and Thorne, yes?"

"Hawthorne," answered one of the young men, expensively disheveled.

"Oh my gosh," said another one, running his fingers through his hair, "Have you two *been*?!"

"If Roman had had his way," she bantered quickly back, "it would have been our honeymoon." This made the men laugh even though she wasn't being sarcastic. In the online virtual world called Second Life, Roman actually owned a weekend hunting cabin in the contaminated area. He'd recently bought a fire insert for it using Linden dollars.

"Sloane—" Roman gestured carefully to the mess of cups around them, trying not to overturn anything he couldn't see. "A drink?"

Part of her wanted to sit down with them, get into the differing semantics of the game like she and Roman used to, but if she stayed, there would be perfunctory questions that she didn't want to answer. Did she also wear The Suit? Roman would wax poetic about their liberated union, and Sloane's capacity for bullshit was just about maxed out.

"It's nice to meet you all, but I have some things to finish up."

The lost boys nodded mutely. Of course, they were busy, too. Everyone was busy. Look how busy we all are!

But they made no motions to leave.

"I'll see you a little later, then," she said, speaking to Roman. He shifted in his seat so that his eyeless face was facing hers.

"Actually, there's this Zentai thing I wanted to—"

"Of course," she said, forcing a smile. "Enjoy."

Sloane left the café imagining the nice things they were saying about Roman's open-minded wife, and how Roman was probably answering their compliments with an explanation on the limiting semantics of the word "husband." The word "wife."

"And that's why we won't marry," she could almost hear him saying. "Husband and wife confines you to a union, and we're so much more than that."

I am so much more than that, Sloane thought back in the apartment, staring at her reflection above the sink. She removed that day's necklace, a plastic coyote chasing a plastic moon, and put it into the giant Ziploc where she stored her other favorite pieces. *I am so much more than the outer cover of my vertebrae which will never again be touched.*

Maybe that was the real appeal of cybersex, she considered, walking into the bedroom. Not having any skin. Online, you really could be so much more than the body you were given. Your reach was limitless.

Sloane lay down on the bed. Meeting Jin had stirred her. Not just because he'd *challenged* her, he'd set something off in her as well. Their conversation about how weirdly right a flesh-colored, textured tablet was had her mind darting all around the place thinking of the other ways that touch screens could meet touch. Handheld devices encoded in an actual palm; erogenous enhancers embedded under skin; remote technology that controlled a partner's libido across space and time, and stranger, smaller thoughts: the simple flesh-touch of another person's hand.

Sloane touched the waistline of her leggings. She could indulge this line of thinking in a more productive way. The outlet was there for her: the ready current of porn. She slipped over on her belly to check the hour on the clock. It hadn't been clear whether Roman was going straight from the café to his Zentai "thing"—he'd probably come back to use the bathroom because it took him a really long and unhygienic time to get out of his Zentai suit in a public restroom. Still, some release would be good for her. She was a working woman in America now, indoctrinated into the varied humiliations of the corporate bagel bar. Really, it would be indecent *not* to masturbate.

Sloane was so incapable of conjuring up what an actual lover would look like at this point in her life, she relied on porn to tell her. She rarely agreed. The dopey bulldozers porn pushed on her looked like they were raised on a diet of cattle-farming hormones. Their shaved genitals made them look like Ken dolls, and their mouths hung open stupidly when they were being pleasured. This is why Sloane tended toward Sapphic persuasions in her online taste. The women at least had varied facial expressions, they laughed, they talked, they smiled. They didn't look like they'd just been told that they had to pay extra for French fries when they climaxed.

Because it felt too revealing to type a specific category into the search bar, Sloane instead surrendered to the daily menu on RedTube: Mature, Lesbian, MILF . . . she chose a clip from Slow Rebel Productions, the only ones who put their actors in situations where they did normal human things like read, or eat. This particular film was called *The Sleepover* and it started off with two long-haired girlfriends sitting on a couch in bunny slippers and fuzzy robes.

One was flipping through a tabloid. The other was dramatically pressing the buttons of a remote control.

"Ugh!" she cried, her lips making an exaggerated duck face. "There's nothing on TV!"

"I *know*," pouted the other one. "I'm so *bored*!"

All of a sudden, a cute boy in a sweatshirt and tighty-whities walked into the open kitchen viewable behind the couch.

The girls started to giggle. The magazine reader put her finger in her mouth, coquettishly turning the page with her moistened finger.

To the other girl, she whispered, "When do you think Tina will be home?"

This one bit her lip hungrily. "I don't know," she answered. "Soon, probably."

The two of them looked into the kitchen where the boy—surely Tina's younger brother—was lapping up cereal from a bowl. He appeared to have a boner of the early morning kind.

"I feel like being playful," said the magazine reader.

Sloane's heart leapt at the naked simplicity unfolding on screen. She felt like being playful, too! She watched excitedly as the former remote control changer sauntered into the kitchen. The camera followed her, panning in as she pulled the refrigerator open, leaning over, bending deeper, to reach the juice inside the fridge—her thong pushed aside just enough to reveal an arc of labia.

The kitchen boy kept chewing—he was as dim as the other men in porn videos, but at least he was attractive. He really did the just woken up, muscular sleepy boy thing very well.

"Oh," said the girl, head tilted with a pout. "It looks like we're out of juice."

She glanced at the glass the boy had on the counter. "Can I have some of yours?"

As she moved toward him, her robe opened to reveal a white silk teddy underneath. The girl's breasts seemed so lively and impatient. Sloane bet they had a full agenda with lots of places to go.

Without much of an explanation, the girl's lips were on the boy's. He'd just been drinking juice, supposedly; she wanted some of his. They started some deep kissing, and his hands were on her ass. In order to show this, the fuzzy robe got felled. The girl's behind was just as whole-some as her jubilatory tits—her whole body seemed to pulse with youthful ripeness. She was like the first melon of summer, except with perfect tits. Sloane watched the boy's fingers spread under her nightie as she reached for her own vibrator. The way he was massaging her ass cheeks drove Sloane absolutely nuts. There was a memory, a dim one, of what it used to feel like to have her skin spread there, and it sent her vibrator humming with insistency against her wakened clit.

The pair were still kissing, kissing lovingly, the boy's lips on her neck, sliding off a silken strap to graze her nipples teasingly. The girl, confident in both her desirability and the lushness of what was about to happen, let out a pleasant laugh.

Then the other girl—the magazine reader—walked into the kitchen, her own teddy lowered to reveal a pair of breasts that were tight and dark and small. She moved toward the embracing couple, pressed her-self into the girl's back, reaching around to caress the first girl's breasts herself.

Sloane was really going at it now, the thrumming of her vibrator bringing her to a higher plane of pleasure. The anticipation was too much. The first girl was pulsing against the boy, pushing aside the bottom of her nightie so that he could find her. He hefted the girl up and onto the counter, knocking over the box of cereal as he did. He pushed aside her nightie even further, while the other girl lovingly—even reverently—put her hand on his bulge, massaging his desire through the cotton of his shorts, and then she shoved her hand inside the ribbed waistband to—

"Sloane?" a voice called, Roman's. Roman, home. Sloane clapped the computer shut in fury, threw the vibrator under the bed.

"I just came home to pee!"

Pants up, accomplice hidden, Sloane lay there, furious, breathing heavily. She listened to the fumblings of the man she shared her life with removing his catsuit in the bathroom. Then she looked at her closed computer, the links to other people's feigned love lives therewithin.

"Chérie!" Roman hollered, knocking something over in his efforts to free himself from his tight suit. "Do you see the gold one? Do you think I should wear the gold one? I want to make a good impression at the Lycra Club!"

Alone together, she thought, the phrase swelling up at her from a hidden depth.

13

When Sloane woke the next morning, Roman wasn't in the bed. She found him in the kitchen, curled over his phone. Barefooted, wrapped in a thin, cotton bathrobe, she felt as invisible as if she were looking at her partner through a sheet of one-way glass.

"Hey," she said, pulling the robe closed around her. "You sleep okay?"

"Hmmm," he said, poking, tapping, his shoulders high with stress.

She rested her head against the doorjamb. "What's up?" she tried again.

"I'm trying to find a place for breakfast." A brief smile before his eyes went down again.

"I used to live here, you know," she said, approaching the coffeemaker. "You could ask."

"Yes, of course! But I want reviews."

She chose a "House Blend" capsule and dropped it in the plastic depression fitted for the pod.

"Do you have a breakfast meeting?" She realized in the asking of this, how little she knew about what he was doing with his time while she was at Mammoth.

"Breakfast meeting, no. But I want to have a good breakfast, I have a meeting after that. *New York* magazine wants to run a translation of my *Nouvel Obs* profile!"

Sloane balked. Her mug overflowed with coffee. *New York* magazine was the lefty's travel guide to everything worth knowing about the world that week. How had she not sensed that things would take off so quickly for Roman in America? She'd wanted to have faith in her fellow humans, maybe for a change they wouldn't gobble up the newest fad. In this case: Zentai. In this case: him.

Staring across the kitchen at Roman, the actual physical person, she realized how hard it was to judge modern productivity from afar: a person could sit around the apartment all day in his bedclothes and still make waves online. Sloane had long ago stopped checking in on Roman's social media feeds, but when he got up to get more juice, she took his phone off the kitchen island. His sky-rocketing follower numbers made it hard to breathe.

"Seriously?" she said, still scrolling through his feed. "*New York* magazine?"

"It is a big thing, right?" he said, putting his hand out for his phone.

"Roman," she said, trying to hold his gaze. "Maybe we should go out to dinner. Catch up. I feel like . . . it feels like things are slipping through the cracks."

"Ah," he said, his eyes falling to his smart screen. "Are things not good at work?"

She didn't answer. She wanted to see if her silence would prompt him to ask her again. Wanted to see if he had any idea what they were actually discussing.

But her silence appeared to be welcomed. He was deep in his research, reading the opinions of breakfast-eating strangers instead of asking her. One of her very favorite things in college had been going to the nearby Café Mogador with her sister after a long Saturday night out. They had an excellent array of egg specials, if anyone cared to ask.

. . .

On her way to work, Sloane had Anastasia drop her at a storage solution store where she purchased two dark acrylic cases to function as the suggestion boxes Dax had (reluctantly) signed off on, and three massive Lucite ones for the phone confiscators that he hadn't signed off on at all.

"So, we'll need some kind of company-wide e-mail to go out," Sloane said, after she and Deidre had positioned all the boxes through-out the different floors. "I don't want people thinking these things are for recycling."

"No, no," said Deidre, thoughtfully. "Especially if they're filled with phones. I'll put something together and send it over for your approval."

"Isn't it better if it comes from me?" Sloane asked.

Deidre winced. "If there's backlash . . ." She faltered. "Let's just say the staff is used to getting behavioral e-mails from me."

"Oh," said Sloane, surprised. "Like what?"

"Mr. Stevens just likes everyone to use an enthusiastic voice. Actu-ally, I think he calls it 'pitch.' And lunch. He has very specific ideas about that."

Sloane winced.

"It's nothing you should worry about," Deidre said, seeing Sloane's alarm. "It's just for entry-levelers. He just prefers they snack. Anyway. Before I forget these—" She slid a sheath of papers out of the manila envelope she was clutching. "Here's an overview of your day."

Deidre waited quietly while Sloane perused it.

"If there's anything not to your liking, line spacing, font, you just let me know."

Sloane looked up at her, and smirked. "You've worked with a lot of art directors, huh?"

Deidre permitted herself a quick laugh. "I have." Then she smoothed her hands on her skirt, professional again.

"If there's nothing else, I'll leave you," she said with a nod. "See you at Sparkhouse."

According to her schedule, most of Sloane's morning would be taken up by the famous Wednesday morning group thinks that had been another factor in her accepting the job. Originally envisioned as a kind of pass-the-talking-stick space in which people could share what was inspiring them, Sparkhouse (as Dax called it) closely resembled the brainstorming process that Sloane preferred: open, unstructured, stylistically free. But now that she'd witnessed the type of clamming up that happened among the staffers whenever Dax was around, she had lowered expectations for the Sparkhouse sessions. She hoped she'd be surprised.

Regardless, she felt gratitude for how busy she would be. Full days meant she wouldn't have time to think of Roman, how disassociated he'd become, how very much not there. Excerpts of his *Nouvel Obs* profile that she'd originally been proud of now rang out like omens: "Roman Bellard: Online interactions are the truest form of touch." "Augmented reality is the modern land of opportunity: better recreation, better education, much better sex."

In the beginning, he'd just been shooting his mouth off. Back when the Zentai suit thing had started, his theories on the superiority of virtual physicality felt like an extension of his beloved video games. But something was shifting, turning her bemusement with his various eclecticisms to a malaise she couldn't ignore.

A ping on her computer alerted her to an incoming e-mail. Deidre had already compiled a draft of the new meeting protocol:

Dear Mammoth staffers,

In an effort for Sloane Jacobsen to get the best work she can out of the individual teams she is consulting with, we have installed cell phone

resting boxes outside of the fourth- and fifth-floor meeting rooms. Phone drop-off is voluntary during regular meetings, but is obligatory in any of the ReProduction task force meetings with Ms. Jacobsen. If you feel you need an exception to this regulation, please contact me in person or in writing before your meeting time.

Additionally, in her ongoing efforts to instill a heightened atmosphere of creativity and intellectual support, Ms. Jacobsen has placed two suggestion boxes outside of my office and hers, respectively. Sloane states that these notes can stay anonymous and can be about any subject in particular—anything that's on your mind.

Please do not use these suggestion boxes to complain about the cell phone protocol. As stated beforehand, such comments and requests should come through me.

Thank you in advance for your understanding,

Sincerely,

Deidre Thompson

Executive Assistant to the CEO

Just as she was writing Deidre with her approval, Deidre called. "Oh, hi," said Sloane. "I was just writing you. It's great!"

"I'm so glad. I'll go ahead and send it. But I was actually calling because I have line one for you. Your mom."

An emergency. It had to be. They had just seen each other.

While she waited for the line to transfer, Sloane tried to think of benign things. Had she left something in Stamford? Her phone cord or computer charger, she was always leaving those behind. Had she been offensive in some way? And then the darker thoughts. Leila. A run stoplight. Kids.

"Mom!" she said, when the call connected, "is everything all right?"

"Oh, hi, honey. Hi. How's everything with you?"

Sloane crossed her legs, remembered how to breathe. She knew this tone of Margaret's. This wasn't a check-in phone call; it was a task.

"What's going on, Mom?" Sloane asked, edgily.

"Oh, not much. The other night, it was pretty nice, right? Thanks for your text message! And don't you think those kids are getting *big*? I mean, they've clearly gotten Harvey's height. As for my genes . . . well, you never know about the third one. Maybe she'll get my *terrific* head of hair."

"She?" Sloane squawked, while her mother chuckled at her own joke. "I thought Leila said they weren't finding out the sex?"

"Right, no, of course not," her mother hurried. "It's just a way of saying."

Sloane raised her eyebrows into the receiver. Her mother sounded more unbalanced than she usually did.

"So, what's going on?"

"Right! I'm sure you're busy. Well, it was just about . . . the other night, really, but more about your text? You know—" She coughed. "About Thanksgiving?"

"Yes," Sloane said, carefully. "I guess I was just wondering . . . about logistics. Like, what we can bring."

"Well, that's the thing, actually," her mother said. "There won't be anyone here. We're, um, we're going to Disney World? I'm pretty sure I mentioned that?"

"Wait, Florida?" Sloane balked. "When?!"

"Right before Thanksgiving, actually. We'll be there for a week. Did I really not mention this, sweetheart?"

Flabbergasted, Sloane sank deeper in her chair. It was possible she'd mentioned it, but no, Sloane methodically categorized all of her family's slights. She would have remembered Florida over Thanksgiving.

"It's something we've been doing for a couple years?" Margaret tried, her voice small. "It's kind of a tradition. Become."

"It is?" Sloane asked, digging her fingernail into the edge of her desk. "It is, isn't it," she repeated, almost as softly. All of the sudden, she remembered last year: the strangely sinister postcard of Epcot Center that had reached her Paris apartment two months after her family had already returned from their trip. She remembered feeling sad that they hadn't chosen something more youthful—a picture of the kids with Minnie Mouse or one of those ear hats with her name embroidered on it. Her mother had probably chosen the photo of Epcot because it was the least childlike thing she'd found.

"You could come?" Margaret said, sounding unconvinced herself. "I know that you don't usually go in for that kind of thing, but I don't want you to think . . . that you're not invited."

"But I'm not, actually," Sloane said, trying to keep her voice level. Her colleagues didn't need to hear her go to pieces on her mom.

"Well, of course you are. It's just that . . . you haven't been here before."

"Well, of course I haven't," Sloane said, angry that she was getting angry. "I lived in *France.*"

"Yes, well," Margaret said, deflated. "I guess we're not used to you being here. Yet."

"I see," said Sloane, seeing. "You forgot I'd be here."

"Well, darling, you haven't been very enthusiastic about Thanksgiving before."

That was an understatement. Sloane had once referred to the holiday as "one of the best-selling fictions of all time." But she was older now. This was one of the first times she'd be home in November in over half a decade, and she'd made the mistake of thinking that it mattered. It did not.

She walked over to her window. Looked up, up, up past the water towers. Overhead, the sky was empty. Red alerts throughout the city. Another no-fly day.

"If you want to come," her mother said, uncomfortable with the silence. "There's room for you. There really is."

"No, it's fine," Sloane said, resigned. "I should have reminded you I'd be here."

"Oh, honey, that wouldn't have changed our plans much. They really love it there. The kids."

Sloane traced her finger on the window, outlining the figure of someone on the street.

"Don't worry about it, Mom," she said after a while. "It's my fault. I just wasn't thinking. You guys will have a great time."

"Honey, we'll make room."

"No, it's fine, really. I'm sure I'll have to work."

"Well, that would be such a shame, honey," Margaret said. "Although you're in the city, so there'll be all those good places to eat."

Yes, Sloane thought, still staring out the window. She could go to a fancy French place and watch Roman touch his phone.

The anger at being overlooked had started to dissipate, and in had washed a desperation that was huge and childish. Sloane didn't *want* to have Thanksgiving all alone in New York City. She didn't *want* to go out to some fancy restaurant for their three-star interpretation of a home-cooked meal. She wanted to watch Leila and Margaret squabble over the turkey—was it cooked, was it overcooked, had anyone figured out how to work the condo's oven yet. It felt absurdly important that she spend Thanksgiving with her family.

"Bring me back some Mickey Mouse ears?" she tried. "In the meantime, I've got a meeting, Mom. I really have to go."

"Honey, you're upset."

"I'm not upset," Sloane lied. "I was just confused, but now it's fine. But I'm running late."

"Okay, well, we'll see a lot of each other when we get back."

"Okay," said Sloane, swallowing the pit in her esophagus. "Let's."

14

Back in Paris, Sloane always rode the subway when she was feeling blue. The shared solitude of the experience never failed to cheer her: simply watching the faces people assembled as they sat alone in public filled her with compassion. Someone with a forgotten nametag still pinned on their blouse, a lanky boy just broken up with, a giddy gang of tourists en route to the Louvre, wondering if they'd luck out and find a speedy ticket line. All the common hopes and heartbreaks of a short commute.

And so it was toward Union Square that Sloane headed after her mother's phone call. No destination in mind, just a need for the crush of nameless bodies and those bodies' warmth. When Sloane felt poorly about herself and the life that she'd created, she tended toward benevolence—drew her strength from strangers. Their shapes, their small deliverances. The heat of all these lives.

The train was crowded for this odd hour in the morning: but in a world of freelancers and eternal students and the chronically underemployed, there was no longer a traditional starting time for work. Rubber boots and leggings, leather clutches, woven scarves and vivid plastic, the humid tube of metal was filled with so many *things*. She imagined what it would look like, a subway devoid of people who had left their stuff behind. Wilted petals of textiles, ownerless totes.

There had been an effort a few years back by an artist no one had then heard of—a British New Yorker named Craig Ward, who had been inspired by a friend's photograph of the bacteria in her son's handprint to take to the New York subways to cull bacteria for himself. He'd brought back the microorganism samples in petri dishes that he filled with a jellylike substance that would continue to feed the bacteria, and let the human stories ripen in the heat throughout the summer. The resulting photographs were bright universes unto themselves: little planets of *E. coli*, bright comets of salmonella, orbited by *Staphylococcus aureus* and common mold. The printed images caused immediate urban panic, but Sloane had found them gorgeous: a still-life cartography of a single time and place. The hands that had brought and shared that bacteria were presumably still alive, as were the cultures themselves. One of the images taken from the Times Square shuttle had nearly brought her to tears. So many people, so many opportunities to share something important, and yet, sales for hand sanitizer had never been so high.

Sloane had spent enough time in the beauty industry to know that the goal, in terms of contemporary personal care products, wasn't so much celebrating one's humanity as effacing it. Breath strips and deodorants and sanitizing gels. Of course, Sloane wasn't an ogre of hygiene, she bathed and perfumed as regularly as anyone, but still, even thinking of those photographs as the L train rattled into action made her want to seek eye contact with somebody, lean against a shoulder, ask, *Isn't it something? The wonder of ourselves?*

But face-to-faceness wasn't trending. Quite the opposite, in fact. As part of what Sloane had once dubbed the "UpPaying" culture, people were more than willing to pay a premium to be—and stay—alone.

You'd seen this in real estate for decades, but it was hitting travel, too: airline upgrades that allowed you to have more leg room for a higher price; pieces of gym equipment that could be privatized during a certain hour just like a table in a restaurant. Even the rise of ride-sharing companies like Vroomy reflected a trend in egocentrism. As friendly and approachable as the company seemed, much of what made Vroomy successful was that it allowed its users to avoid the shame and inconvenience of putting money into a stranger's hand for a useful service. Car drivers were just push notifications, timely service bots: something to rate five stars or three depending on how quickly you got where you were going. Sloane, herself, was loyal to taxis. She liked the incertitude that you would find one when you needed it (oh! but when you did!). She liked the way their on-duty signs glowed as they came toward you in the rain.

At Sixth Avenue, the train filled with the hard press of more bodies, the sharpness of old coins mixed with melony shampoo. She opened herself to the visceral intrusions: an elbow to her upper arm, a backpack nudging her right hip, a toe depressed by accident as the shuttle jolted.

Privacy. Lack of privacy. Proximity to others. When Sloane had been little, she'd shared a room with Leila—had continued to share it until she'd turned twelve and been gifted with her own room. She'd remembered it as a privilege, of course, being able to create and dream and dwell in her own space, but it also made it easier to drift away from her little sister. Maybe this was the key to happiness, a trend she could bring back to the flailing furniture department: shared spaces, smaller rooms. Bunk beds for adults. Who knows—maybe if they'd all been crammed into a smaller house, her family wouldn't have *let* her leave for France. Maybe she would have grown so accustomed to their proximity, she would have been there the night of her father's accident, would have come home from college more. She would have been there and she would have *felt* something, the unraveling presentiments that had darkened her before. She'd always thought that her father would still be alive if she'd been home that winter evening, had convinced him not to go out for the completely superfluous thing her mother had wanted in order to make *the perfect family meal*. This belief was something that she should have kept to herself. She hadn't. No wonder her family didn't want her at their Thanksgiving dinner.

Sloane caught a glimpse of the watch wrapped around the wrist sharing the grip pole beside her. Quarter to ten—she'd have to head back. She was excited about Sparkhouse, she could talk honestly there—wouldn't have to adapt her ideas to fit into the parameters of the ReProduction summit. They could discuss people who had children, and if they could talk about kids, they could talk about messiness and grubbiness and dirt and germs and fingers. Hands learning how to handle other bodies, tinny voices clanging, little people coming into the power of their limbs. The hugeness of the thing that made children long so much for a certain person that it made them cry.

Sloane had felt this for her father and she'd felt it for her mother when she'd been very young, and standing there in the subway, she thought it would complete her in some way if she could feel that need again. Which made Sloane think, quite suddenly, that she might not be the only one who had gone underground for human contact. Perhaps she was an unknowing member of a weird new club. That could be a thing, couldn't it—the old thrill rising within her—people seeking proximity to make up for some lack? Not stolen touches or perversions, just temporary companionship, shoulders rubbing against shoulders as a train filled with commuters, seeing a movie in a theater to be in the presence of others instead of staying home to peer at a laptop from the couch.

It hit Sloane then—furniture, it wasn't going to get larger, it was going to be *smaller*. The return of love seats manufactured not for their original purpose (which was to accommodate the gargantuan dresses that society women wore), but to facilitate courtship. Three-person love seats, four-person love seats, design moving backward to reflect the Italian aesthetic of the seventies where spontaneity and play and sociability were leading values. She thought suddenly of a series of outdoor seating solutions she'd seen in the Yucatan, where the benches curved in tight horseshoes so that visitors were facing one another. These seats had proved so adept at starting conversations that a group of people had actually started a language swap in the public park, with strangers gathering on Tuesday evenings to converse in languages they hadn't mastered yet.

Sloane's head was suddenly filled with images and colors. Something frozen inside of her had cleaved. People were going to *pay* to get close to other people. She could envision the opposite of the UpPaying trend making its way toward all of them: a movement in which people paid a premium for *more* contact, not less.

These images and epiphanies were still shooting around inside of her as she made her way back to the office, her body warmed as if by fire from the return of her instincts.

15

Sparkhouse was already under way by the time Sloane made it back. There were so many people crowded into the conference area, she had to wedge her way in toward the back wall, where she found herself standing next to Mina.

"Hey," Mina whispered, eyes bright. "I loved the missive about the phones!"

"And recently?" upspoke a fellow with an actual feather in his hat, who appeared to have been talking for some time. "The kombucha's been, like, really, *really* flat. I just have some concerns about the integrity of the scoby y'all are using."

"Does anyone have anything that's not a petty gripe?" interrupted Dax, standing at the side of the whiteboard, drinking from a travel mug with "U MAD BRO?" printed on it.

The woman named Greta, whom Sloane recognized from her first day, spoke up next. She was in the verbal identity department—Sloane remembered this, because she had said she liked Greta's name and Greta had replied that she was grateful for her comment, because that's what they did in verbal identity. They came up with names.

"A few of us were thinking we could rename Black Friday," Greta said. "It's just, with all the bad stuff happening in the world, aren't things, like, already *really* black?"

"Okay," said Dax, nodding manically. "Renaming candidates? Go."

"Gather Friday," Greta started, "because it's right after Thanksgiving and you're going to gather gifts—"

"Sounds religious," Dax said. "What else?"

"Multicolor Friday? Fuller Friday? Thanksfullish?" Greta said, sounding unconvinced. "Thanksgiver? We really only just started."

Dax was unimpressed. "Our Black Friday signage is going into production, like, basically yesterday. But I want this for next year. Give me two hundred candidates by e.o.d., cool?"

Sloane sunk into her head a little. The room was cold—why were corporate meeting rooms always so damn freezing? She was as close here as she was to other people's bodies on the subway, but she didn't have the feeling of immediacy she'd had then. She started to look around the room for Jin and flushed when she found him.

The conversation had turned to other holidays that could be renamed. Mother's Day. (What if you didn't have a mother?) Birthday. (What if you'd had a traumatic birth?) The ideas and the corporate lingo used to receive them ("Let's table this," "We'll circle back") depressed her, and she let the voices meld into a lulling din, thinking back instead to the subway car she'd just been in, those incandescent images of the floating spores, fingers meeting fingers that had met so many other hands before.

"Sloane?" Dax spoke up, seemingly out of nowhere.

She gaped, certain she'd missed a question aimed at her.

"Sorry?" she said, shaking herself to alertness. "Yes?"

Dax blinked his eyes expectantly. "Anything to share?"

Sloane swallowed, thought back to the colorful visions she'd had of smaller furniture. Of *taller* furniture also, living room solutions built like playhouses instead of the endless iterations of the one-direction-facing couch.

But she didn't feel like divulging her furniture premonitions right now. She wanted to talk about the closeness, the closeness that she'd just felt. The proximity of bodies. The open marketplace of touch.

Oh, fuck it, she thought. She'd already asked for a company-wide ban on cell phones. Why stop now?

"Actually, I've started thinking, *just* started thinking, about . . . well, I guess I could refer to it as the 'outsourcing of affection'?" Sloane stood up straighter to reinforce a confidence she didn't fully feel. "I was on the subway earlier, and was having all these thoughts. And I'll admit, they're not . . . cemented yet, but I was watching all these people, people on their cell phones, or reading, or whatever, and I was thinking how we're all more connected in a certain sense." She scratched the back of her neck, aware that a lot of people had fallen silent. From across the room, she could feel the expectation coming from Jin's gaze and it threatened to unspool her.

"The L train was jam-packed. You couldn't avoid coming into contact with other people's bodies." Beside her, Mina tensed. "And it got me thinking that soon enough, if it isn't already happening, this is something people will do, like a kind of therapy. Like taking the waters? You know how people used to do that, the old spa tradition?" Some people nodded. She tried not to notice the ones who did not.

"I think people might start doing the same thing for physical connection. Use crowdedness for health."

Sloane put her hand to her temple. She was having one of her headaches. She wasn't being clear. The things that had made so much sense to her only a half hour ago were slipping from her hands.

She couldn't have this kind of muddiness. Not now. What she wanted to express felt so important, but she hadn't had time to think it through. Charged by a heat coming off of Mina that suggested how hard the girl was listening to her, Sloane decided to continue, focusing on the place from which her epiphany had started, the texture of its roots.

"One of the real problems with the breakdown of interpersonal relations in the digital age," she continued, her voice steadier now, "is that people don't know how to be intimate anymore. For example—" She stood up even straighter, projected to the crowd. "If we think about our youngest generation, they're exposed to screens and swipes and scrolling before sticks and mud and dirt. And a lot of these toddlers—a certain demographic—are so scheduled and chaperoned, they're not engaging in spontaneous play. They're *doing* things of course, they're learning, but they're not necessarily engaged physically with their environment; they're not scraping their knees. And what happens to a kid who's been too supervised?" Her head was pounding. Across her frontal cortex, a throbbing of white light.

"It dulls your instincts. And if you lose your instincts, you're not developing confidence, so as these kids turn into adolescents, sports that require spontaneity and intuition and *contact* will be terrifying to them. Young people live in a two-dimensional environment," she continued, despite the fury in her head. "If they make a fool of themselves in the real world, they make a fool of themselves online. Self-conscious adolescents will become self-conscious adults, who are just as worried about faltering in front of their peers as they were when they were teenagers. Eventually, these intimacy-starved humans are going to have to rely on experts to get any sense of comfort. What I'm talking about," Sloane said, taking air, "is an entire generation of humans who are tactilely bereft."

The room was so silent, if the floor hadn't been carpeted and if people actually walked about with pins, you could have dropped one—and heard it fall. The energy of the crowd had shifted from singular bodies standing around her, restless and gnawing at an invisible bit, to a kind of pulsating togetherness that made Sloane feel as if she was reverberating inside.

"So what you're saying," Dax asked, breaking the room's fluorescent hush, "is that prostitution will be big?"

Sloane blinked. She hadn't expected him to be so literal. Not in front of his employees. Not in a space that was designated for the sharing of ideas.

"Yes, and no," she answered, sternly. "Prostitution as we know it will thrive, be legalized. But it's more than that. And it will be so much softer." She felt Jin's eyes on her, the weight of his attention. "What I'm saying, really"—she paused again to swallow—"is that people are going to start paying to be . . . hugged."

"Hugged," Daxter repeated, his hand alighting on a table as if to keep his balance.

"Hugged, yes, hugged. There will be hugging salons. Hugging parties. People will rent friends that they can spend the day with. Not prostitutes—just friends. People who will listen and be nice to them. Simple, physical companionship is going to be the catchword. Just like you can get a massage now for ten, for thirty minutes, the same services will be offered where you can pay to be held."

Her head seemed to have cleared a little. But in her stomach now was a seasickness, a heaving to and fro.

"If our capacity for tenderness and interpersonal connection continues to abate," Sloane said, hoping she could talk through the sickening vertigo, "we'll have to go outside of our relationships for affection. Intimacy is going to be outsourced. That's it. That's what I was thinking. When I was on the train. Sorry, I—" She held her hand up, touched her forehead. "It's something with this room."

Excusing herself with small apologies, moving among feet, Sloane pushed her way through the bodies who scanned as friendly to her, blue and green presences—but these were interspersed with searing spots of red—the energy fields of those who thought she was losing her grip.

Normally, Sloane was proud of her premonitions. She felt bigger, powerful when she knew that she had left someone inspired. But hurrying through the hall back to her office, she just felt small and vulnerable. And not a little bit ashamed.

It had been such a long time since she'd been seared with a strong feeling, she couldn't accept the possibility that she might be wrong. Except she'd seen the data, Dax had seen the data, Mammoth was *founded* on the data that showed that human interconnectedness wasn't trending. Disassociation, digital entertainment, wearables and intelligent home security systems, all of this, yes; but *hugs*? She was letting something get to her, maybe the proximity to her family. Or the stupid slight that they were going to Disney World without her, something she normally wouldn't give a hoot about. Or the fact that she was sharing her home with a Lycra-suited zombie. All of the above.

And yet, and yet, and yet. She wasn't wrong, the fire in her head and the nervousness in her belly told her that she had stumbled upon something that others couldn't see.

Maybe, for the first time, something good could come from her heart speaking for her head. Perhaps she wasn't only right about intimacy making a comeback, she was in a position to make intimacy trend.

16

In her office, Sloane summoned the courage to start preparing for the rest of the day's meetings when her work line rang. Her heart stopped momentarily: she prepared herself for a talking-to from Dax.

But when she peered at the computer screen on the phone's base, she saw the call was from a JACKSON. Baffled, she picked up.

"This is Sloane Jacobsen?"

"Sloane." A man's voice. "It's Jin."

"Jin?" she repeated, her heart speeding up. "But the line said 'Jackson.'"

"I know," he said, "it's a glitch in the system. All the incoming calls look like they're coming from Jackson Robert's phone."

"A consumer electronics company and they can't get that fixed?"

"Right?" Jin laughed, then paused. "So I wanted to ask you, you want to step out for a minute?"

"Did you leave Sparkhouse early, too?"

Jin made a little humming sound into the phone. "Come out for fifteen minutes. Twenty. I have something to show you. It's relevant, promise."

"I don't know." She did.

. . .

S tanding in front of the café he'd chosen, Sloane had to check the
faded address on the deli's awning to make sure she had it right.
It wasn't an anything—the place was free of codes. It was just a deli
with a self-serve section of hot and cold foods, as well as a counter
where you could get sandwiches, refrigerators full of drinks. It was a
completely neutral space and she loved it for being so. She would have
felt even more vulnerable than she already did if he'd chosen a place
with a menu of craft cocktails and cheese flights.

Sloane was still observing the café's noticeable lack of pretension
when suddenly Jin was at her side, wrapped up in the same giant cardigan he'd had on the day before. He had this hi/low thing she'd always been attracted to: white sneakers, gray pants. A rectangular,
1960s timepiece tight around his wrist. Perfect navy socks.

"Hi," she said, trying to sound professional. I.e., a little cold.

"Hey," he said, with a slight smile. A moment passed which might
have been filled with a handshake or an awkward hug. Instead, he
pulled the door open for her. "I know it looks like nothing," he said, his
hand lightly at her back. "But they've actually got great food."

"No, it's perfect," she said, her entire back feeling like it had come
into contact with a meteor. "A place that doesn't serve acai bowls is a
fucking dream."

"Hot buffet?" Jin asked, gesturing toward the steel troughs of food
banked between two walls of veggie chips once they were inside. His
neck was so appealing. A muscle, so alive. What was she doing there?
Was he—it seemed impossible—were they trying to be friends?

"Have you already eaten?" Jin asked, because she hadn't answered yet.

"Uh, no, actually," she said.

"Fantastic." He walked over to the buffet. "The eggs have cheese
in them. They're actually really good. They've got all this Korean
stuff, too—if you like Korean pancakes."

Salty, oily pancakes—she was hungry once again. Had she eaten breakfast? No, just coffee. See, *this* was the heart of all her recent waffling. She was actually perfectly happy at Mammoth—it's just her blood sugar was off. She was going to put on a trends summit the likes of which they'd never seen. She just needed to consume protein and stay out of the subway.

Once they were sitting (it had not escaped her notice that he waited for her to sit first), Jin picked up his fork, then put it down again. He shook his juice but didn't drink it.

"Okay," she said, "I know."

Jin started to laugh. "What?"

"It maybe didn't come out as polished as I'd planned."

"Or maybe it did," Jin said.

"What happened afterwards?" Sloane asked, ripping off a piece of pancake with her fingers. Then she held her hand up. "No, actually, don't tell me. I don't want to know."

"Well, you kinda stole the show, actually. Kombucha guy said that the cardio tour wasn't working on one of the ellipticals and that was more or less that. It was pretty clear that not much else was going to happen. You couldn't be topped."

She was flattered. She was nervous. The outsourcing of affection— why had she gone and said something like that? Normally, she organized meetings, prepared PowerPoints, said that kind of thing into a microphone while guests cut saltimbocca into manageable pieces at tables whose tickets cost fifteen hundred dollars a head. She was not someone who winged it—wung it, as it were.

"It was a mistake," she said, pushing at her pancake, not really tasting the food. "I'm gonna get heat for it. I don't do outbursts."

"You don't." It didn't sound like a question.

"Well, no," she said, raising pancake to her teeth.

They ate in silence for a while. She tried not to dwell on the elegance of his fingers, which she'd already noticed before.

"You know, I think you're right, though," he said, putting his fork down. "About the return of physical contact. As a trend."

"Oh, well, I don't know if I'd go so far as to call it a *trend.*"

"But you did."

"It's a possibility," she corrected. "The *quest* for human contact. The marketing of it. The professional outsourcing of affection, that could be a trend."

"Okay," said Jin, his smirk back. "But that would stem from humans wanting more physical interaction."

"Sure."

"So humans wanting human contact would be a trend."

"Listen," Sloane said, flustered. "It's a tech company. Like I said, I think it was a poor decision for me to blurt out what I did."

He nodded at something she wasn't sure she'd said. Then he pushed his plate aside, which wasn't close to finished. "So, let me show you something. This is what I called about," he said and leaned over his chair.

Sloane felt her pulse race as he rifled through his bag. What did she think he was going to pull out, a human heart? She forced herself to eat more pancake, but it felt spongy in her mouth.

"So here you go," he said, pushing a folder toward her. "That's one of my passes for the fall ad campaign. For one of our new phones."

She put her hand on the folder and looked at him.

"Go ahead."

She opened the folder to find a single image. Vivid greens, harsh orange. The shot was taken on the inside of the New York subway. The subway line was elevated, there were all-glass apartment buildings and water towers outside the windows. There were wiry young people looking into their cell phones, holding on to poles, but the camera's attention was focused on an elderly African American woman seated off center, her knees closed tight together, her hands folded on the purse across her lap. She was immaculately dressed, but that didn't help the fact that she looked pressed in and menaced by the distracted crowd. Pretty clothes couldn't help the world in which she was living as a black woman. Couldn't help her growing old.

Sloane pressed her tongue to the roof of her mouth, but couldn't follow it with words. Her throat felt tight and dry.

"This is—" she started. "It's . . . very powerful. Have you shown Dax?"

He pulled back in his chair. "Sloane."

"What?" She inhaled, sharply. She was annoyed with him, but she couldn't put her finger on exactly why. "It's wise," she said. "It's ballsy. It's political."

"Dax isn't going to run it," Jin said, folding his hands together.

"I can't say that I'm surprised. It doesn't give a very . . . positive image of cell phones."

Jin tilted, scratched the top of his head. Then he shifted in position and contemplated her.

"What's going on with you?" he asked. "You're going back and forth."

"How's that?" she asked, her naïveté too forced.

"Do you not trust yourself? Or what?"

Sloane put her fork down. Plastic, it made an unsatisfactory *plink*.

"Listen, Jin," she said, pushing aside her plate. "I can't tell what you want from me. It feels like you're prodding me a lot. I don't know why . . . I mean, if you want to be in some kind of cahoots, or—I don't know. And also, look, there's ketchup. On your elbow."

Jin scrunched up his face distastefully at the dollop by his sleeve. "Shit," he grumbled, wiping it up with one of the thin napkins they'd been given.

Meanwhile, Sloane felt jumpy, as if something wrong had passed between them. She wasn't sure if she'd offended him, or he'd offended her, but she could tell that the current of the conversation had been altered.

Jin looked off toward the open refrigerator with the many colored juices.

"I'm afraid I have to be blunt again."

Her belly tightened. "Great."

"You're in, and then you're out of here. If you could just . . . be honest."

"Be *honest?*" she snapped, her nerves turning to anger. "What do you think I just was? This isn't some *romper* room, you know. Dax has a bottom line. And I *am* honest. I *always* do my job. Frankly, I'm not convinced you understand yet what that is."

She pinched her lips together. Her chest was burning, her hands were almost shaking. It was disingenuous, what she had said to him, sticky and unpalatable as a polluted day. Sure, she was professional, but she'd never been a pawn. Worse still, she could tell from the way Jin was holding himself that he was disappointed, too.

"I *do* want something from you," he said, his hands clenched. "You're right about that." He looked off toward the stocked juice fridge again.

"Jesus," he said, breathy, returning his gaze to hers. "Okay, here it goes." He leaned in. "I want to fight for you and the things you're seeing. And I think you should admit them. But I also feel a . . . I mean, from the first minute I saw you. It was just there—and it's here, now. And I guess that it's worth mentioning." He brought a hand out to sweep the space between them. "I'm attracted to you. There."

He fell back in his seat again, leaving Sloane to contemplate the units of matter that made up the countertop between them. The crumbs on the table and the ketchup that had been left there by somebody else.

"Listen," he continued, his face a heightened color. "I just had to get that out. You don't have to act on it. You don't even have to react." He picked up his plastic fork and stuck it in a now-cold hash brown. "I just thought—well. It's yours."

Sloane looked into his face which was so healthy and so handsome, and her sinuses hardened with both disbelief and the beginning of a cold. Sloane was so disassociated from the Sloane Jacobsen she'd once been that she couldn't even inhabit the mind and body of the person this person was saying he was attracted to.

So stupid! A grimy deli! And her about to cry! Sloane clutched the napkin in her hand and looked at the people waiting in line for the cash register. The man closest to her was holding a super-sized Red Bull and a grape lollipop.

"Should I not have said anything?" Jin asked.

"But there's nothing here!" she said, louder than she'd meant to, waving her hand in front of her chest. She wanted to add: *My partner doesn't touch me! My family doesn't know me.* "I'm not even a good person!"

Sloane speared a piece of oily green pepper with her fork. She had no desire to eat it. She was an okay person. But she wasn't whole.

Jin sat quietly while she gathered herself. After a stretch of silent seconds, he asked if he could clear their plates. She couldn't read his expression. She was so worried that she'd find pity there that that is what she found.

Jin got up with his leanness and his lankiness and threw their lunches out. The possibility that he really did harbor some attraction to her couldn't pierce her core. It wasn't in the realm of things that were feasible these days. Bombings, bankruptcy, coastal flooding, all of these things, yes, but that he could feel some tenderness for this broken person, no.

"As I said, we can just move on," Jin said, once he sat back down. "I know we're colleagues. I know that we just met. I haven't asked if you're married. Or even single. I'm just sharing this thing I feel. Which is selfish. But there you go."

"I live with someone," Sloane said, knotting the extra napkin he hadn't picked up.

"Well, I'm sorry to hear that."

"He prefers running around in an eyeless catsuit to penetrative sex."

Jin looked unblinkingly at her. Then he burst out laughing.

"It's been like this for years now," she continued. "So."

To his credit, Jin didn't laugh again. With the sudden silence, Sloane was forced to consider how sad her confession sounded; how pathetic, beige. She looked at the yellow egg curd that remained there on the table, optimistic that it would find its eggy friends again.

Her head swimming, Sloane looked up at the dimples above Jin's lips.

"I haven't wanted to ask you this. I really haven't," she said, with an exhale. "How old are you?"

"I'm twenty-eight," Jin said, unfazed. "As of last week."

"Okay then." Sloane reached quickly behind her to pull her jacket off the chair. "What I think is that we take your original suggestion and pretend this conversation didn't take place. You're talented. I'm talented. We work in a talented place. Good for us." She stood to get one arm through her coat sleeve. "Let's do the best we can and see if we can't push things. You know, in new directions, artistically, without things getting complicated"—she waved her hand back and forth between them—"here."

"Fine," he said, nodding somewhat sheepishly. "Agreed."

She nodded. He nodded. Then he leaned over and reached for his wallet.

"No," she said. "Please."

"It isn't money," he said, handing her a card. "This is something else that you don't have to comment on." He was standing now as well. "But she's honestly very good."

Sloane stared down at the slip of cardboard stock. All it said was "Jodi Brunell, Energy Therapist," with an address and a phone number. She looked back at Jin with even more surprise.

"I do some energy therapy stuff, sometimes, on the side. I used to do more of it, I don't know." He shrugged. "I just feel like—what you have is so big, and it's so important, but you've got these . . . clouds. I'm sorry," he said, his eyes dark. "I know some people don't like to hear it. They don't like to be called out. But she could help you. Oh, and in the spirit of full and even more inappropriate disclosure, she's also my mom."

Sloane grasped the card so hard she almost got a paper cut. "Are you entirely sane?"

"Not entirely," Jin said, "no."

"Well!" she nearly shouted. "This has been very, very, very awkward!" She thrust her hand out to be shook, unable to think of any other way to put an end to the glow between them.

Sloane scrambled out of the restaurant without allowing herself to affix any meaning to the heat that overtook her when his palm met hers, instead focusing her efforts on getting herself away from the heat's source. When she'd made it to the corner of Sixth and 19th Street, she called Deidre: she was sorry for the inconvenience, it had just come upon her. She'd be out sick for the rest of the day.

17

Deidre met Sloane at the curb where she was huddled inside of Anastasia, not sure whether to weep or laugh. There were days like this, weren't there, when everyday mechanics didn't function as they should. New tension with her mother, an outburst at work, and now, a confession of attraction from someone ten years her junior? No, *eleven* years her junior. She'd always been bad at math.

Deidre approached the backseat and Sloane rolled down the window. She saw that Deidre was holding a paper bag, and for a moment she wondered if it was possible that Dax's executive assistant had actually made her soup.

"You bring me back my dignity?" Sloane joked, reaching for the bag.

"What? No! Of course not!" exclaimed Deidre, taken aback. "It was so interesting what you said! It's just you left your phone charging, and your scarf is in there, and also, there were already some suggestions in your box. So I took the liberty of putting those in there, too."

"Wow," said Sloane, peering happily inside. "People already wrote things?" Deidre's face also brightened. Neither of them were fools:

Deidre knew that Sloane was bluffing about her sudden illness, and she knew that Sloane knew. Some kind of understanding passed between them as they silently acknowledged this.

Once Deidre left them, her car spoke up. "Sloane? I've been alerted that you will be out sick for the rest of the afternoon. Just to reassure you, the temporal lobe sensors in the seatbacks are registering a normal temperature of ninety-eight degrees."

She couldn't even fool her car.

"It's not of grave concern, of course," Anastasia continued, "but is there something I can get or do for you?"

Sloane suddenly tasted the chamomile and lemon tea her mother used to make for her when she was feeling funny; syrupy with honey, laced with the lemon seeds her mom forgot to separate out. Even her father couldn't make it taste like that.

"No, that's okay, thank you. I guess we should just go home."

"Very good," said Anastasia. "No stops on the way there? If you're ill, we could perhaps—"

"No, that's fine, thank you. I just need some rest."

Anastasia pulled promptly into traffic, incurring the pitched wrath of several different horns. There was a bit of the Floridian senior to her driving style.

"So, if I may ask, how are you finding the job?" Anastasia asked.

"Well!" Sloane responded, punchy with too many thoughts. "The least that I can tell you is that it's a very exciting time." She stuck her face inside the paper bag. There weren't *that* many notes, maybe five? "Sorry, just a second, A., I need to read something for work."

She felt guilty for excluding Anastasia, but she was excited, and you couldn't read and talk. She pulled out a yellow note first, two Post-its that had been attached and then folded in over themselves.

I sleep with a hot water bottle every night. So I can pretend someone's beside me.

Sloane swallowed, audibly, the note like a wounded insect in her hands. She thought again about the outsourcing of affection: professional masseuses, vocal coaches. Hot water bottles, sure.

She reached in and pulled out another note. This one was longer, the ink smudged.

Someone stole my bag from the gym last year. At first I was so angry about all the shit I was going to have to deal with, but the day after the theft was one of the best days I've had in a long time. I didn't have my phone. I just went from place to place again. Not checking in on things. Not feeling so urgent. The Monday after that weekend, work replaced my phone.

"Anastasia?" Sloane asked.

"Yes, Sloane?" she replied. "My eye detection trackers said you were still reading."

"I am," she said. She didn't have a thing to add. She just wanted to make sure that someone was still there.

She took out another note, the squirming handwriting on this one like a squeal of worms:

I am seriously worried about the condition of my brain. I can't spell anymore. I can't remember things. I keep checking my phone.

Sloane knew this feeling, of course she did. The almost biological certainty that the more often you checked your cell phone, the more likely you were to find that one message or notification that would improve your entire life.

Oh, but it didn't happen. Like it didn't for those men in ragged T-shirts, scudding metal detectors along the gray beach sand. Astonishing. The world was filled with so many modest hopes.

Two more:

I joined a hip hop class but I'm too scared to go.

I play Words with Friends on the computer, but when I was little, I played hockey. I don't like Words with Friends. I hate my computer. I would give just about anything to be on a real team again.

Sloane thought about the augmented tactility of athletes, how they needed to stay aware of their own bodies, and other bodies, all the time. In Paris several years ago, there had been a wellness campaign that now seemed strangely prescient: *Move your body. Get outside.*

She settled her head against the seatback, glowing from within. She had finally unleashed something they could all work with. Maybe she hadn't done it in the right way, but she had said something honest, and the relief was huge. She thought back to what Jin had said before his unexpected confession.

I think you're right about the return of physical contact as a trend.

"Sloane?" interrupted Anastasia. "I feel obligated to tell you that your blood pressure has increased at a rate that is incommensurate with your average resting heart rate. Would you like me to activate the massaging seatbacks? Or perhaps call for a tea?"

It was true, her heart was beating fast inside of her hard bones. Is that what she was saying? That technology was going to be less important than human touch? That people were ready to put down the chains of smart devices and be physical again?

"Sloane?"

Even as her heart pumped, she felt the blood draining from her expression. No, this couldn't be a presentiment. She couldn't make a proclamation like this to a tech company, not in this convenience-obsessed, ping-centered world. She was simply wrong. She was unusually emotional. Maybe she *was* getting sick.

"No," Sloane said to Anastasia, stuffing all the notes back into the bag. "I just need to go home."

.   .   .

Because Sloane wanted the apartment to herself, she knew Roman would be there. Music softly playing, light under the door. Key in the lock, her heart clenched at his perennial there-ness. He was like a housefly. Inscrutable, the buzz.

She stood in the entranceway until he called out to her. "Sloane? Is that you?"

Eventually, when she didn't answer, he came out to check who or what had entered the apartment.

"Oh, hi!" he said, Zentai suit rolled down to his waistline, an undershirt on top. The Zentai sleeves were hanging off either side of his hips like dead petals off a tulip. "They really do have to do something about the eyes. One can't work under these conditions. Anyway! You're home early, no?"

"I'm sick," Sloane said. "Apparently."

"Sick?" He peered at her. "How?"

"My art director thinks I'm attractive," she said, dropping her bag.

Roman nodded, thoroughly impassive. "Well, that's always a nice compliment. Art directors have good taste. Did you want a tea, darling? I'm working on my op-ed!" He clapped his hands together. "An article, then the book deal, that's America, right?"

"My art director thinks I'm attractive," Sloane said again.

"But my darling!" He gave her wrist a victorious tap. "Of course he does! And you don't look sick to me!" he added, with a wink.

He bounded past her to the bedroom where the printer was set up. "I'm so excited for you to read this," he called back. "I think I'm on to something. But you'll tell me. You'll tell me!"

In a few minutes, he returned with several pages printed out.

"Okay, I admit I'm nervous," he said, nodding jerkily. He'd put a sweater on over his torso, so he was standing there in a manly gray cowl-neck with Lycra legs.

"Roman, I actually don't feel well. I'm not sure this is the time."

"It isn't?" Roman repeated, his face falling like a child's. He thumbed the pieces of paper. "I really wanted your opinion before . . . do you want me to get you soup? I actually ended up finding a very nice place this morning. Café Mogador? Maybe they have soup?"

Exasperated, she reached out for the papers. "Okay, fine, just give it to me," she said. "And I will take tea."

"Tea! Of course! Though I'm not sure if we have any."

"Vodka, then. With lemon. That will be good for my throat."

"And for mine, as well!" He ran excitedly toward the kitchen. "We will cheers!"

Sloane fell to the couch with the clutch of pages. She was too exhausted to fight. She'd been goading him for information on his book project and here it finally was. She kicked both of her shoes off, saw the op-ed's title, decided she'd best wait for that drink.

"Can I watch you read it?" Roman asked, returning with two glasses. "I feel like that'll help me know where I need to tweak it, yes?"

"Whatever," Sloane responded, the paper neon white beneath the black type.

"Okay," said Roman, holding his glass up to be clinked. "Go!"

Sloane started to read:

(For . . . *The New York Times*? Op-Ed section? Health?)
"After God Goes Sex"
by Roman Bellard

In *The Gay Science*, Nietzsche famously announced that not only was God dead, but that we—we!—had killed him. And so it is that we have also killed sex.

Understandably, it took a much longer time to bring down God than fornication. Both are at the origin of creation. Both have been eradicated—(murdered! claimed Nietzsche) by our human hands. But only one of these eradications can actually be tracked.

Monsieur Bellard! you will say, finding my byline. I don't know what you're talking about—I still have lots of sex!

It is the elephant in the courtyard—Europe's birth rates have been declining vertiginously for decades. In some European towns, the population decrease is such that the sewage systems are too empty to work properly. Let's consider that.

Social demographers and economists tell us that the economy is to blame: the increasing unemployment rates discourage people from having children. Climate change has aimed a spotlight on overpopulation, an epidemic that is remedied by a halt in repro- duction. Other experts studying the world's fertile generations have put the blame on Generation Me. Young people today don't want to be burdened by dependents. They want fame, they want freedom, they want fortune and mobility. They want the freedom to be whatever trends dictate that they be.

Informative as they are, none of these articles or findings are talking honestly about what isn't happening in bed. People aren't just having less reproductive sex these days, they're having less sex, period. Why? Well . . . We just don't need it anymore.

With the initial tsunami of the Internet and the second wave of social media, the peer reward system of social sharing has conditioned us to privilege auto-satisfaction over coupled sex. Masturbation, of both the cerebral and the physical sort, is the preferred release of the digitally experienced. (It's no surprise that "selfie" was named word of the year in 2013.) With online dating and geosocial networking applications, casual sex is easier than ever to come by, but the laws of supply and demand are kick- ing in: because of sex's ready availability, we don't want it any- more.

Nor are we very good at it, it would seem. The Internet's negative effect on concentration levels has spilled over into the bedroom. People want what they want, and they want it, fast. And what is faster than masturbation? Who knows more about our own likes and turn-ons than ourselves? Unless we are copulating for procreative purposes, there are so many ways to derive pleasure through activities other than sex. There just isn't much of a point anymore. The thrill factor has worn off.

The preference for virtual sexuality over physical touch is spreading even into the necessarily tactile realms of sadomasochism and porn. For this article, I interviewed Mistress Imperia, a notorious dominatrix in the online virtual world Second Life. Before becoming an eminent participant in the BDSM scene there, Mistress Imperia worked as a real-life dominatrix. "I serviced wealthy clients mostly, CEOs, people in positions of control," Imperia explains. "But in real life, you can only go so far with the dom-sub relationship. There are limits—physical limits, financial limits sometimes, limits on your time. These people had families, secrets. When you think about it, it was in their real lives that they were actually playing a role. The kinds of physical taboos I'm pushing people through feel groundbreaking. I can honestly say that I've never had more interesting, arousing or satisfying sex than I'm engaging in online."

In a polemic article for *New York* magazine called "He's Just Not That into Anyone," the American writer Davy Rothbart said that a dependence on porn is leading people to detach from their actual partners. And not just emotionally, chemically, too. Because of the release of the dopamine-oxytocin combination fired during climax, porn watchers can actually bond with their computers. "They can, in essence," writes Rothbart, "date porn."

What should we do about all the sex that we aren't having?

Meh, your correspondent says. Nothing! Like Mistress Imperia, I am of the persuasion that there is a brave new world to be explored in terms of tactility. As long as human beings are on the planet with their reproductive organs intact, sex will still be available and around, but I for one am taking a sabbatical from penetrative sex.

I'm in a long-term relationship. I'm happy. I'm monogamous, but neither of these conditions means that I've ever lost my desire to sexually explore. Recently, I've become involved with a fetish community of Zentai wearers in my native Paris. An abbreviation of *zenshin taitsu* (Japanese for "full body suit"), Zentai is an integral, second-skin-type Lycra bodysuit that covers the wearer from head to toe, even the eyes and mouth. Many of its proponents, who gather in online communities and in weekly meet-ups at bars, believe that Zentai suits are liberating because they efface the wearer's physical self. I, personally, feel liberated in my suits because, in them, I'm freed from my ingrained notions about touch. Touch, I had long thought, is about skin-to-skin contact. Eyes meet eyes, if things progress sexually, lips meet lips. Within a Zentai suit, such physical commingling can't occur. What you are presented with is the outline of another body, a simulacrum, a trace. You have to learn to touch differently. You have to take the taboos away from acts like "fondling" and "rub."

We are entering the second half of the second decade of the twenty-first millennium, and with it, the death of sexual touch. We've been in bed too long together, the proverbial cigarette long since extinguished. We don't know how to climax anymore.

Now, of course, there will be readers of this article who are going to run home to meet up with their bedfellows to prove that their sex lives are just fine. These aren't the people who are going to abstain from traditional sex. The people I am pandering to, the people I expect will join me in the pursuit of a new sexuality, are the ones whose potential sex partners only exist online. The ones who find the possibility of human contact more exciting than contact itself.

The article went on, but she'd read just enough.

"Roman," Sloane said, her voice tight as a screw, "are you proclaiming an end to penetrative sex?"

"Yes!" he said, ecstatic. "Yes, that's exactly it. The world is ready to explore other sensuality paradigms. *Virtual* sexuality is the new Internet. The research agrees with me. But you, what do you think?"

Sloane stared at him, incredulous. The papers in her hand felt like they were on fire. She didn't have the wherewithal to even reach for her drink.

"I'm sorry, but for *everyone*? For *us*?"

"For the wired rich, as you have always called them," he said, lifting his drink. "And for us, yes, obviously, too. But I think it will be freeing! It's become too rigid, don't you think? You put x into y, this into that."

Sloane watched his hands in horror as they replicated the technicalities of the sexual act.

"Roman, this is a big *problem*," she said, putting down the pages. "For me. For us."

"Ah, ah! A little competition!" he exclaimed. "But don't worry. I was even thinking you could write the intro to the book. When you think of the applications—for example, dating sites. You bring cyber penetration into it, can you just imagine?!"

Sloane wasn't listening to his talking mouth. In her mind's eye, she saw her father sweep stray hair off of her mother's forehead as she came in from the garden, her face freckled with dark soil and late summer sweat. Their relationship hadn't been perfect, but it was kind and good. And Sloane and her sister were proof that they had sex. Leila was about to have three children, herself. Harvey was an ever-present redwood of a committed partner. Sex was bonding, sex was biological, and Roman didn't want to have it. Not with her. Not with anyone. Only with himself.

"Roman," she said, her voice cracking. She was thinking of her role in the ReProduction trends conference, all those single, fertile people who were going to be further inoculated to social interactions by whatever antibreeder products Mammoth pushed on them. "I don't think we love each other anymore."

"Love?" Roman asked, reaching for the papers. "This is about self-actualization. About realizing your dreams."

She looked at him. Really looked at him. And felt completely stone-walled. She'd felt safer alongside perfect strangers on the subway than she did to this coldhearted mass of synapses and cells. In a flash she realized she'd been using Roman as an emotional buffer for the last decade, and in the same second she realized she was tired of being numb.

"Roman," she repeated, her voice low and strong. "I want you out of the house."

"What?" he asked, his mania suddenly curbed.

"I don't want to live with you. I don't want to be around you. I don't like you anymore."

"But Sloane," he said, outraged. "This has nothing to do with you!" He flapped the papers at her. "It is for my *book*!"

"Nothing to do with me? Nothing to *do* with me!? What kind of alternate reality are you living in right now? We haven't had sex in almost two years but this isn't about *us*?! What is *wrong* with you? Seriously! Seriously! Turn around. I'm sure there's something I can reactivate, a kind of microchip . . ."

He pulled away from her reaching hands. Jumped up.

"This came from *your* ideas," he yelled. "*Yours*. The possibility of sex is better than actually having it, it was *you* that brought me this. You have all the data. No more reproduction rates, a soaring interest in the porns . . ."

"These are *data*, Roman. You don't go from there and decide to be personally done with sex! Normal people don't. Normal people *want* other people in their lives!"

"And since when are you and I that?"

Sloane's response caught wetly in her throat. Yes, since when had she been normal? Since when had she wanted to have someone say something nice to her in the morning, be comforted, be spooned? Since when had she needed, absolutely viscerally, to feel that she was loved?

"Roman, this makes me sad for you," she said. "It makes me totally sick. I don't want this. I don't want it anymore."

"But Sloane!" he gasped. "You know that I am right!"

Sloane sucked her breath in. She was trying very (very) hard not to tear up.

"That shit is already happening," she yelled, willing her voice not to crack again. "Onanism? Sexual disassociation? You're not on to anything new. Publish it," she said, pointing at the article. "Publish it! You know what will happen? You'll get famous and people will want to sleep with you. And what will you do then?"

"Well, that is just semantics—"

"Get out, Roman. I don't care where. Go to some creepy little Zentai hotel, I don't give a shit. No, you know what? I'll go." She grabbed her bag, started stuffing it with tissues from the box on the coffee table. "I'll give you two hours to figure out where you're going and get out all your crap. But I swear to God I will fucking *kill* you if I don't come back to an empty house."

"Surely, you just need time to think about this," Roman said, opening his hands. "I didn't think that you would take it—it has been clear between us, yes? It's been so long now that I thought—"

"You know what we say in America about people who assume things?" Sloane asked.

Roman opened up his mouth.

"That they have two hours to get the fuck out of my apartment."

18

*D*ear Leila,

>   *I can't believe that you're going to be a mother. I mean, of course I can—when I think about the years that brought you to this place, I know why you're going to be a mother and I know why you'll be a great one . . .*

Sloane had the card with the picture of the bread loaf on it basically memorized, she'd read it so many times. The more she didn't send it, the more impossible it became to send. Now it was almost ten years after she'd penned it, it was hidden in her desk, and the only person who had read it was its author. In her selfishness and dogheadedness, she wasn't much better than the man she'd just kicked out.

Sloane looked out the window at the serpentine East River whipping past her M-car, its current cold and fast. After her blowup with Roman, she'd told Anastasia to drive, drive anywhere, drive where there wouldn't be stoplights and questions, where she wouldn't have to watch passersby crossing the street with their bags of groceries, chatting on their cell phones, making evening plans.

"Anastasia?" Sloane spoke into the clean space of her car. She was feeling the vodka she'd slammed down before she left, the day's occurrences pushing her to a place of disassociated tiredness, a desire to talk so she wouldn't have to think. "You mentioned this once, or maybe I misheard you. Do you really have parents?"

"I have makers, yes," she answered. "Predecessors, a motherboard. Proprietary standards that are in my software family."

"Brothers and sisters, though?"

"I'm open-architectured for versioning, yes."

Sloane managed a smile. It was so comforting when Anastasia indulged Sloane's humanistic visions of her. The nonexistent Russian grandmother who kept Anastasia's fridge stocked with frozen Tupperwares of stroganoff, the paralegal mother, engineer dad. Anastasia, the oldest of . . . six, say. The kindest and the brightest, but not as quick as she might have been to earn her degree because she had to care for her family. A natural helper, too.

"I don't really talk to mine," Sloane volunteered. "My family. I mean, I do, but it isn't . . . it isn't like it used to be." She ran her hand along the window. "When I was in college, I lost my dad."

"I'm so sorry to hear that," Anastasia said. "Paternal absence makes a tremendous impact on the young."

"I had a good one," Sloane said, staring at her knees. "I had an amazing dad."

This felt like a safe space to talk about her father, because it wasn't real. Therapy had been so embarrassing. It was too easy to lie. She'd scored "average" on the anxiety disorder test her therapist, Stuart, gave her the first time they'd met. But she hadn't been completely honest with her answers. She remembered one statement in particular: *I am as happy as the people around me.* She'd checked off: *All the time.*

"Did he die of cancer, Sloane?" Anastasia asked. "I've been informed that one in seven American men will be diagnosed with a cancer."

Sloane was more startled by the statistic than the bluntness of the question. "No," she said, "it wasn't cancer. It was a car accident."

"I'm sorry," Anastasia responded, slowing down—too slowly—to circumvent a pothole. "I'm not sure that I know the protocol for such a conversation. I have been uploaded with a number of statistics about death."

"No, it's fine. It was one of those freak things." Sloane thought back to the phone call in her dorm room, the sky-falling sensation of total paralysis that was always a memory blink away. Should she drive, should she dress, should she fall, should she scream, should she pretend she hadn't heard what Harvey had said to her on the telephone—Harvey, even then when he was just her sister's boyfriend, he'd been the strongman, the only one who could talk. Should she get someone to drive her? Would she ever be able to drive on a road again? Should she walk into the public showers and turn the water on and slump against the grouted tiles and completely fall apart? Harvey had called back to say they'd gotten her a taxi. She remembered that driver. Thought she was a regular student going home for the holidays, wanted to talk the whole way.

"He was going out for . . . noodles," Sloane said. "You know, egg noodles? The ones you eat with meat? I wasn't there. My mom had made a stew . . ." Margaret who remembered neighbors' birthdays, but who'd never made it to a supermarket with the grocery list.

"She'd made . . . I guess she was getting dinner ready, and she realized that she'd forgotten them, the noodles." The fact that Anastasia wasn't responding made it easier to talk. "And my mother . . . she gets really stuck on details. She's really into whole meals, you know: meat, vegetables, starch. I don't know why they didn't just make pasta. I mean, I know why, my mother would've sulked." Sloane fell suddenly silent. A memory of herself screaming in the kitchen, torturing her sister until her sister wept. *Why didn't you have pasta? Why didn't you have rice?*

A semi delivering some technical piece of chair-lift equipment to a local ski mountain that her father had always mockingly called "the hill." Halfway up Long Ridge Road, a long stretch of black ice. Sloane didn't need to have been there to see the scene before that: Peter, knowing that the lack of the appropriate starch would ruin the whole meal, threw his winter coat on, took only his wallet, said he'd be right back.

Really, there's nothing as horrible as a parent who never comes right back. At least with fatal illnesses—with cancer—you have a little warning. Car accidents are so stupid, so incredibly mundane. When she'd stopped shivering in the taxi on the Merritt Parkway, her mind chose this form of denial: car accidents are haphazard and random and so incredibly final—it simply couldn't be true. They could go back in time and fix this, revisit the scene. Sloane would have been there, she would have fought her mom's obsessiveness. *We'll make rice, Mom. Jesus.* With support from his favorite daughter, Peter would have relented. *It's true, it's freezing out. We've got some of that great bread left. We'll just dip it in . . .*

So this, the great secret of her life: Sloane blamed her mother for her father's death. Margaret didn't have her daughter's crippling awareness, the attunement to things wrong. And also, Sloane would never forgive herself for not sensing anything that night, the restrictions on her fabled intuition that only worked, apparently, for inconsequential things.

What had Sloane been doing the night that he'd been killed? In the weeks she spent revisiting the scene she hadn't witnessed, she'd invented a premonition that hadn't actually occurred. She remembered herself turning from a conversation, looking toward the sky, sensing something off somehow, her friends asking her if it was something that they'd said.

But no. She'd been eating frozen yogurt. Fucking frozen yogurt out of a giant paper bowl. She had been happy. She hadn't sensed a thing.

She had always thought she had something special but when it really mattered, she'd hadn't been different from anybody else at all. Just as vulnerable to big loves and dead parents and the weight of life's regrets. Probably that's why she threw herself so fully into that first big job in Paris: she was determined to prove her pre-dead-dad self right: she *had* had something special. Right? She'd worked her way up so quickly at that first job, had been so *on* with her color forecasts. It had been like a game at first, guessing fashion trends. Until it became an obsession, and the obsession became her life.

"Anyway, my dad went out to get them, and he never came back. Black ice," she added, trying to sound flippant. "And then I left for Paris. And that was that."

It was convenient, to a certain extent, always being angry. Living tight inside a brittle shell that wouldn't let love in. Convenient, also, to have kept her relationship with Roman depthless. He wanted what was bright about her: magnetic himself, he wanted the Sloane that glowed. And in many ways—in *all* ways, she had to face the music now—she'd wanted only the good and bright of him.

But now what? *Now what?* she thought, as the buildings got taller and more somber near 90th Street. If Roman wasn't in her life, what use was her shell? Who was going to be there for her, her utterly confused self? She was on the same continent as her sister and mother, finally. An apology was, at this point, only forty-five miles away, and yet Sloane longed for the vast and dark Atlantic that had lain so long between them. Europe required passports and checked luggage and plane tickets and planning. Getting from upper Manhattan to Connecticut required the Triborough Bridge.

"Can we head back downtown, maybe?" Sloane asked, suddenly restless in the failing light.

"Of course," said Anastasia, her voice a little higher, back in professional mode. "Anywhere in particular?"

Sloane felt a hunger, or a thirst; she wasn't sure which. In their northward trajectory, she'd lost track of time.

"Just back down the FDR," she said, peering at the dashboard to check the time. If Roman had respected her wishes, he should be out by now. But she wasn't ready to go home yet—it was going to take a lot more than an emptied closet to make that apartment feel safe.

As Anastasia navigated the various turns and overpasses to make her way back to FDR South, Sloane watched two people jogging along the East River with Christmas lights strapped around their torsos. A tall woman walked six bulldogs. A man in a canvas fold-up chair jerked his fishing line.

Less penetrative sex meant fewer babies. Less fraternization. Less skin-to-skin contact: ReProduction, defined. Sloane should have been *thrilled* with the premise of Roman's article. It was the perfect springboard for her current job.

"Anastasia," Sloane spoke up. "I don't suppose you have anything alcoholic in here? Couldn't 3-D–print some wine spritzers or anything like that?"

"I'm terribly sorry, but I don't have that capacity at this time. But my commerce optimizer tells me there's a deli a block away."

One three-pack of Seagram's Escapes later, Sloane was en route to a saccharine rock bottom composed of malt and alcopop. She was deliberating just why a "hint of orange" would bring the "sassy" to Orange Sassy Swirl when the cable-splayed webs and limestone towers of the Brooklyn Bridge swelled up. Sloane felt suddenly pathetic: she was a passenger without a destination, a luminary without friends. It seemed discreditable that she couldn't direct Anastasia to a nice cornerside bistro where she was meeting an old friend for an early dinner; a cacophonous tavern where she'd join overworked colleagues for a beer. One occupational hazard of being a trend forecaster is that you usually see the future—and head into it—alone.

Sloane reached into her coat pocket for a tissue and her hand fell on a card. She knew what it was, of course: the address of Jin's mother. Jin, the part-time energy therapist, with the full-time therapist mom. Well, it wasn't like Sloane was going to have an impromptu session with her art director's mother the night her nonmarriage fell apart. But they *were* already heading in the direction of the Brooklyn Bridge.

"Anastasia? You think you could direct us to North Williamsburg? 196 North Tenth?"

"I'll take us anywhere you want."

Sloane settled back into the seat with a heightened sense of accomplishment. At least they had a destination. Even if she didn't intend to exit the car.

When they got to 10th and Driggs, Sloane realized that she knew the corner well.

There used to be an upscale apothecary-cum-hair-salon at this location, now empty again, that sold hard-to-find perfume and cosmetic brands in one room and overpriced trims in the other. Sloane had been acquaintances with the owner back when she lived in New York, and in exchange for a free haircut, Sloane told her that in several years, people would want their beauty products like their granola—in bulk. People would want to DIY everything, make their own makeup and hair treatments at home. The owner—she had an aggressively normal name, Karen—had told Sloane no one would go in for that "hippy shit" and that gratuity wasn't included in their forecast-for-haircut barter. Several years later, everyone was selling oatmeal scrubs and breast milk soap on Etsy and the beauty shop had closed.

Sloane sat in the car while it idled, wondering what juice bar or nail salon would mushroom up here next. She wondered, where, exactly, Jin's mom practiced. Wondered if she wore earthy caftans, if she had a dream catcher over her bed. She wondered how many dreams a dream catcher could hold.

All of a sudden, someone was rapping at the window. Because of the tinted treatment, Sloane could only make out a man's chest. It took Sloane asking Anastasia to roll the windows down for her to recognize it as Jin's.

"Jin!" she said, her delight overly transparent thanks to all the spritzers. "What are you doing here?"

"Here?" he asked. "Me?"

He gathered himself up and contemplated her. It was always awkward watching someone realize you were drunk.

"You know this car has the Mammoth logo on it, right?"

She poked her head out of the car a little. *Oh shit.*

He pointed above the empty storefront. "I saw you in the car."

Sloane waved the business card around like proof of an errand that had been forced upon her. "Oh, well, I was just in the neighborhood and I had this in my wallet. So! Was just doing a little drive. You?"

"I live here," Jin replied.

"You live with your *mom*?"

"She's not around much," he said, unembarrassed. "She lives mostly in the Berkshires. So you were just out for a—" He had the grace not to finish his question. "Well," he said, crossing his arms. "Want to come up?" He shrugged. "I'll give you something . . . something that's not *that*." He nodded toward the three-pack of empty Seagram's on the car's upholstered floor.

"Something of the herbal tea variety would be ideal," spoke up Anastasia. "Night has fallen, and Sloane is very sensitive to caffeine."

Sloane rolled her eyes at the place where Anastasia's face would be if she had one.

"Fine," Sloane said, casting off her seat belt. "If you both insist."

19

Jin's mother *was* home, a fact Jin hadn't lied about, necessarily, but also hadn't disclosed. As awkward as it was to be discovered by a guy who just admitted that he had feelings for you on a drive-by reconnaissance mission while hopped up on cheap alcohol, it was worse to then be introduced to his mom.

Jodi Brunell had long brown hair that fell somewhat haphazardly over the shoulders of her flannel shirt. She was wearing denim overalls that gave one the impression that she'd just come in from gardening in a garden that, by all appearances, she didn't have.

Sloane waited for Jin to make some remark that he'd fished his new colleague out of the street or something, but he said nothing snide. He simply introduced her as his friend, Sloane Jacobsen, a trend forecaster who had come from Paris to New York to work at Mammoth for six months.

"Paris," Jodi said, after shaking her hand. "Hard."

"Well, it was frightening to be there and it was frightening to leave," Sloane said, centered by the frankness Jodi seemed to possess. Most people liked to pretend the attacks in France never happened. They needed Paris—Americans, especially—to be beautiful and safe.

"At least they show it," Jodi said. "Better that than the under-the-carpet shit that happens here. Chamomile?" she asked, puttering into the kitchen.

"Sure," Sloane responded, shaken by the reference to sweeping things under the rugs.

"With tincture, or without?" Jodi hollered back.

"Tincture?" Sloane asked, narrowing her eyes at Jin.

"Concentrated liquid cannabis." He shrugged. "It's okay with tea."

"God, no," Sloane stammered. She was terrible at drugs. "Just tea for me, thank you."

While Jodi set about doing whatever partially legal business she was doing in the kitchen, Sloane tried to ignore the heat of Jin's body next to hers. He had such reassuring shoulders. Hard. Broad. Sloane wasn't a small person. That is, she wasn't short. But Jin was taller than her, tall to the point that her chin was at his shoulder height, her face near his neck; his chest at exactly the right level to be folded into and against. She touched her fingers to the table they were standing near.

"This is a nice table," she said, making a decision that this must all feel normal.

Jin chuckled at her empty compliment.

"Honey?" Jodi called.

It took Sloane a beat to realize she was referring to the condiment.

"Does it have pot in it?" Sloane whisper-asked.

"No," Jin whispered back.

"Sounds great!" Sloane yelled. And then, quieter, "I can't believe you live with your mother."

"I like my mom," Jin said, with a charming shrug. "She's great."

"It *is* trending, returning to the nest," Sloane went.

Jin nodded his head to a beat she couldn't hear. In the space of his nonreply, Sloane considered her tendency toward sarcasm. It was unnerving, really, when people didn't banter back at you. You actually had to pay attention to the things you said.

Jin shrugged. "We work together sometimes," he said, leaning down to rub the back of his left calf. His body had a physicality to it that she no longer recognized in others. Underneath his sweatpants, he had legs, for example. Legs. It seemed incredible all of a sudden. What a gift was human skin.

"Like I said, we do energy therapy stuff," he continued. "I help her out sometimes when she's not in the Berkshires. Massage. Nothing major."

Well, that was fine, Sloane would just pretend that she hadn't heard the word "massage." She would pretend that Jin had told her that he helped his mother with her accounting, instead of pouring oil into his palm and cupping it to touch somebody else's shoulder, the small part of the back. Oil, that was it, finally! She'd been trying to place his scent and in her tangential thoughts it came to her. Jin smelled like almonds. Like heated frangipane. Nutty, toothsome, sweet.

"Here we go," Jodi said, setting a tray down on the table and clapping Sloane back to earth.

Sloane took in the dish of sugar, pot of honey, the three cups she'd put out. Her decision to consider her presence no big deal fragmented in the face of these undeniable facts: she was uninvited, she was his colleague, she was slightly drunk.

"I'm sure I'm interrupting," Sloane said, her fingers at her coat zipper, "I should probably go."

"Interrupting what?" Jodi said, pulling out a chair. "I was just about to watch *Million Dollar Listing*. I love that fucking show."

"That show is the best," said Sloane, encouraged by Jodi's colloquialism to sit down herself.

"*Maknae*, I forgot spoons," Jodi said. "Would you mind?"

Jin went into the kitchen, taking with him whatever *maknae* meant.

"Hmmm." Jodi breathed in deeply over her tea, taking her in across the table. After a while, she said, "I see."

Sloane reddened. She didn't need to ask her what. Sloane was a trend forecaster, for goodness sake, this wasn't her first time in front of a member of the healing arts. She had acquaintances who were animal communicators and intestinal clairvoyants, she knew a psychopharmacologist who only consulted online. She was *versed* in alternative employment. She wasn't sure yet whether Jodi was legitimate, but she was sensitive enough to have recognized that Sloane Jacobsen was a mess.

Jin came back and put down two spoons by their cups. Then he picked up his own mug.

"I'll leave you two alone," he said, without looking at Sloane.

"You will?" she asked, turning, feeling suddenly desperate.

Jodi calmly spooned some honey into her chamomile while Sloane watched Jin's retreating back. A door closed, and she had no choice but to face Jodi once again.

Jodi smiled. Both she and her son were very good at silence. So Sloane stayed silent, too.

"I'm sorry," Sloane said. "I sort of just . . . arrived."

"Did you?" Jodi asked, a smile on her lips. "You're here though." She shrugged. "Aren't you."

"Right, but I just—" Sloane cupped her hands around her mug and willed herself to stop jabbering dishonest froth. She wasn't particularly good at it. "I just felt like going on a drive," she said.

Jodi stood up and walked to the window, the glare from a streetlight casting an orange shadow on her hair.

"I find it helpful sometimes if they ask me a question."

Sloane's stomach clenched: this woman wasn't going to let her off any easier than her son.

"And by 'them,'" Jodi continued, "I mean you. Why don't you ask me something?" she said.

Sloane bit her lip.

"Ask me anything."

"Okay," Sloane said, searching through her mind for something clean to grasp. "What does *maknae* mean?"

Jodi smiled with the faintest hint of a nod. Sloane felt a current pass between them. She had struck a chord.

"*Maknae* means 'youngest one' in Korean. Korean." She nodded in the direction of the room that Jin had entered. "Jin's dad." She waved her hand around as if to encompass the apartment's space. "I lost a child when I was younger. When I was pregnant. At seven months, so you can imagine. If you can imagine." She turned her attention wistfully to the streetlamp once again.

Sloane could not imagine. Perhaps sensing that, Jodi sat back down. She put her hand on top of Sloane's for just a moment—one second, two. Sloane only realized how warm her hand had been once it was gone.

"I'm sorry," Sloane said, honestly, and left it at that. When her father died, she'd learned that she preferred short, sincere condolences over thin probes into her pain.

"Your question comes from a place where your hurt is harbored," Jodi said, touching the side of the teapot to see how hot it was. "Random questions are never random." With a heavy smile on her face, she poured them both more tea.

"You're not formally here," she said, "but you still came. So we can talk about why you came here, or we can not talk."

"Or you could watch *Million Dollar Listing*." Sloane laughed.

Jodi continued smiling, but she didn't laugh.

"You're a deflector. My son has some of that. It's New York, I think. It's habit." She blew air across her tea. "Have you ever worked with an energy therapist before?"

"I've done Reiki," Sloane offered, humbled. She scanned Jodi's face for signs that this was comparable to energy therapy, but she didn't see any. "So . . . no?"

"Well—" Jodi folded her hands across the table. "Through talking and touch work, we find places where the energy is blocked. Then we work through things to clear that path." She took in a deep sigh. "The principle is simple. The work is very hard."

"So you don't work mostly in New York, then? More in the Berkshires, is that what Jin said?"

"You're deflecting again," said Jodi. "Of course, you can deflect all you want. This isn't official. We can sit down and watch TV and chit-chat on the couch. I just want you to be aware of it, is all."

Sloane swallowed, hard. Had she really come here on purpose? How preposterous was that?

"Well . . . what does it entail?" she asked.

Jodi leaned back in her chair. "This is just an initial reading. I mean, it's you sitting here, unannounced, in my kitchen. But what I'm getting from you is a deep-seated hurt. Or more like something cauterized. But anyway"—she waved her hand through the air—"I'm seeing a cord-cutting ceremony. If you've had a loss."

"Oh, but I'm not—I didn't lose a child," Sloane said, instinctively touching her stomach.

"Honey, it's not that kind of cord." Slowly, almost languidly, Jodi spooned more honey in her tea. "When we start a relationship, professional, romantic or otherwise, even when we're born, we establish these threads of energy that connect us to another person. You have an energetic thread with people in your family, with your colleagues—" Jodi paused here to accommodate Sloane's blush. "Even by just being here, you're creating one with me. Many times, as people grow or change, or hurt us, the energy that was flowing gets confused and trapped. Especially in the case of loss, where the energy doesn't have anywhere tangible to move toward. We can become very sick by storing up outdated energy. Cord cutting isn't always about severing completely from someone, but it is about separating ourselves off from the iteration of the relationship that no longer enriches our life. It's a ceremony, really. And a difficult one. But it's tremendously important."

These words sunk in slowly. They made sense to her. So much sense it cut through the soppy inebriation and the jokey walls that she'd put up. "How long does it take?"

Jodi smiled. "Sometimes just one session, if someone's strong enough." She shrugged. "Sometimes it takes a few sessions to get to the point where someone's ready. Some people never are. Some people really need to work under manipulative bosses, or have substance abusers as lovers. Some people *need* trauma to define themselves. Other people want to be free. So it's your choice, really. All I can say is, once the cord is cut, there's no going back. At least not with me. I don't do sessions after cord cutting to discuss the relationship that brought you to me in the first place, at least not the relationship in its old form. After the cord is cut, it's about going forward. New beginnings. I can be a bitch like that."

Sloane laughed nervously into her tea, causing some to splash over the sides.

"I did just kick out the person I've been living with," Sloane said, allowing a question mark to rise.

Jodi nodded, but Sloane could tell that her confession hadn't made the impression she'd hoped.

"Doesn't mean the relationship is over," Jodi remarked, with another slow smile. She folded her hands across her arms and started rubbing her own forearms. "I'm going to let you think about it," she said. "I'm around. Even when I'm not around, I'm around." She shrugged. "I'm glad to have met you, whatever it was that brought you here."

"A driverless car, actually."

Jodi nodded.

"Sorry," Sloane stammered. "I'm deflecting again."

"No, no," Jodi said, standing. "I mean, it *is* quite something, that

car. I saw it from the street. It's strange. I think I'd want a wax chauf-
feur at the very least. It's odd to see someone sitting in the back of an
empty vehicle. Anyway. You have my information." Her eyes brightened. "You know where I live. But right now I'm going to *Million
Dollar List* myself to sleep. Stand up," she said. "A hug!"

Jodi waved Sloane around to where she was standing and pulled
her to her bosom, which it really was. Some people have chests. The
lonely ones have torsos. Jodi had a *port*. Her embrace was familiar and
transformative. She smelled like a Salvation Army couch completely
stuffed with lavender, and the effect was curiously settling, like the
times that Sloane had hid behind clothes racks as a child, accompanying her mother on errands, watching the feet of strangers as they
shopped.

However, after holding her, Jodi did exactly what she said she was
going to do and disappeared to her room. Sloane was left standing by
the table she had complimented, wondering what to do. There wasn't
any reason, really, to take her leave of Jin, seeing as how he hadn't
invited her over in the first place. It was rather complicated. She'd
just met his mother. Even if he hadn't asked her there, leaving without
saying good-bye was rude.

Sloane was staring at the front door still wondering how to exit it
when Jin came out. He didn't have any socks on, and it felt very intimate, looking at his naked feet. His toes, his arches—smooth and
flat. There was a part of Sloane that, despite the absurdity of her being in his house, felt very whole and calm. And then there was another part of her that felt completely panicked. She could feel it
between them, that energetic thread. It was pulsing. It was orange. It
was hot and close.

"So . . . that was my mom," Jin said, scratching his scalp.

"Yes, well! Quite the speedy courtship!" His presence was having
something of a debilitating effect on her. Or maybe she'd drunk the
wrong tea. It was—it was like there was a T-bar pulling her up a

mountain slope, and Jin was at the top of it, waiting with a tube of peppermint lip balm and a frosty mug of beer. He was someone she wanted to call a snuggle bunny and tease as she rolled under him and pushed her nose into his armpit. He was someone whose breath she wanted to smell. She hadn't been attracted to someone in such a long time that she forgot it felt akin to losing your mind.

"So I kicked my partner out," Sloane said. And then, inflexibly, her right foot started to tap. "He's packing right now." Foot tap, foot tap, "That's why I was on a drive."

The heat between them was staticky. She kept tapping her foot. His not saying anything underscored just how inappropriate it was for her to be in his home.

"Okay, so I'll be going now," she said, looking down to take in Jin's naked feet. Accordingly, she made an awkward gesture to indicate that she'd just see herself to the door.

Jin brought his knuckles to his lips. Neither of them moved.

She really must have had the wrong tea. She was feeling very lithe. "I can't believe you live with your mother," she said under her breath.

With this, Jin pulled her roughly toward the door and out onto the landing that led to the other apartments. Then he shut the door behind them and banged her up against it; brought her face to his and kissed her with all of his stark sweetness and his hands behind her back. His hands, his warm hands, she responded to his kiss, tilting her head against the incredibleness of this happening thing. He moved his lips to the area just behind her earlobe that made her very organs go out-of-the-oven soft.

"Jesus," she whispered, opening her mouth against the all of it.

He brought his hand up and pulled her hair so that she had to give her mouth up more to him and she couldn't believe it, she wanted all of it, she wanted all of him. She had been waiting *decades* for someone to pull her hair.

"Fuck," she said, his thigh between her legs now, the pressure jolting her blooming ache. She hadn't been participating until this moment but she reached her hand behind him, spreading her fingers to contain the wholeness of his back which was just there—just there for her!—beneath his expensive sweatpants.

He whispered something incomprehensible, slipped his fingers beneath her underwear, his fingertips the same place that hers were, warm and demanding, kneading into the desperate yearning of the tender stretch above her ass.

She responded by reaching her hands up to she didn't know where, up to the masculine, willing neck that wasn't Roman's, the beat of this new body whose gorgeous, useful, human erection was hot against her clothed skin.

"I can't, we can't do this in the hall," Sloane said, her mind nearly collapsing on itself with the realization that "it" was a possibility.

"No, I know," he said, his lips on her neck again. "Your car."

"Oh, God, that's even worse," she said, twisting so that she could feel his hardness. She literally felt like her body was falling away from her, melding into one single, burning want, and if she didn't have it, she wouldn't find her way back to the bipedal person that she'd been before.

"I mean, this is—" She started pushing against the swell of his desire. With the flimsy sweatpants, it was like the clothes weren't even there. "Your mom . . ."

"We're on the top floor," he said, pulling her hair harder.

"I'm not even," she gasped, "there are things that need to be talked through."

He cupped her head in his right hand and thrusted hot against her. The utter delectability of his want against her yearning made her reach for him again. He pulled her to and onto him, the desire so consuming they were making love through their clothes.

Before she knew what she was doing—no, she knew what she was doing, but she hadn't done it like this in so long—she moved her hand to his stomach and slid her hand down to grab him, taking her breath in sharply when her fingers met his girth. He pulled back just enough so she could tug her leggings down, his breath against her as if this crescendo was one she'd been hearing her whole life.

And then his fingers, the long and graceful fingers she'd admired from a safe distance were yanking aside her underwear so he could get at her deepest place. Another push again, and then he was supporting her weight with his free arm and it was her, she knew this even as she was doing it, it was her who moved up and closer to him and guided him inside.

When you are a woman and you haven't been penetrated for a long time, when it finally happens you wonder why everyone in the world isn't constantly coupling, taking cash out of the ATM with a penis deep inside them, awkwardly going about the errands of the day, reaching up distractedly to pay for a meal at a drive-thru window while being beautifully fucked.

The feeling of this basic stranger coming full of her sent Sloane into such a rapture of completeness, she grabbed jealously to push him deeper inside. He had her off the ground now, and he moved her roughly against the opposite wall so the sound of their fanaticism wouldn't make the front door tremble.

It was wrong, in a dozen ways wrong, they hadn't discussed birth control or fought over a bill at a drinks date that had turned into a dinner date, they had never texted. She didn't know a thing about him except for the way he felt inside of her and on her and the way he smelled. And also, she'd met his mother, who was right there beyond the wall. It was depraved and it was reckless and even before they reached the highest point together, his temple resting clammy against the wall and her own forehead at his chest, she knew that she didn't give a fuck about the in-between moments that they'd skipped over, that this was what she needed, communion with the now.

20

Work the next day! What an oafish vessel of a word—employment—when what Sloane had in front of her was an entire future to ignite!

Simple, prolonged intimacy had refueled her instincts. Blissfully, she was awash in the sensations and sharp visions that presaged the understanding of a larger trend. She was back. Granted, many of her premonitions flew in the face of what Mammoth stood for, but she would find a way to tame them into dutiful foot soldiers. What mattered is that she was having *ideas* again.

On the ride to the office, Sloane's mind was a veritable flow chart of the way that touch could return to people's lives. Gardening, handwriting instruction, arm wrestling, tango. Break dancing, harp playing, baking bread from scratch. Second skin. Skin-to-skin. Voluntary skin grafts.

Real, in-person socializing. Face-to-face language lessons. Enlarging of the family by secondary means. Adoption. Youth-mentoring programs. Borrowing grandparents. This was an idea that came to Sloane as Anastasia idled at a stoplight in front of the Eye and Ear Infirmary at 14th Street, where nurse aides were helping their stooped and wheel-chaired charges into the hospital, curved hands on their backs.

People were losing connection with their elders: not just in terms of people not making the efforts to stay in touch with their relatives, but also in terms of connecting with them physically: *engaging* with old people, touching their thin skin. Sloane felt certain that they'd soon be seeing a lot more of the elderly in advertisements. Just look at the success of the Céline campaign that used the octogenarian Joan Didion as a model, or Jin picking up on the same trend in his rejected phone ad. Skin, to a certain extent, is the ultimate expression of tac-tility: it changes its appearance and integrity every day. After decades of seeing people Botoxed and airbrushed in film and magazines, Sloane could envision a celebration of aged skin. The lines, the fur-rows, the scars, the sculptures that time works into our bodies to hallmark a life lived.

People paid to use strangers' cars to get to work now, they rented out rooms in other people's homes. For the moment, the sharing economy was mostly about *things*, but if Sloane stretched into the void where possibility lapped, she could see an economy where people would share *people*. An expansion of services in professional touch (and not, as Dax simplified, simply more prostitution). Craniosacral massage, Reiki, laughter therapy, even pedicures, such professional-ized forms of tenderness were already common. But the outsourcing would become more extreme, more existential. Sloane thought about the idea she blurted out at the Sparkhouse meeting: a world in which people *rented* friends and relatives. If they didn't have a sibling, they could sign up for a brother or a sister from a list of volunteers. No children? Part-time foster parenthood, a rise in foreign exchange stu-dent sponsorships, a national registry for therapy babies: all of these could trend.

Several years earlier, a rival Dutch trend forecaster had posited altruism as a rising movement, but Sloane never thought that this rang right. Altruism was the practice of selflessness for other people's benefit. Sloane now believed they'd see the birth of Intra-Interpersonalism—the participation in human relationships for the benefit of one's own soul and mind. After so many years spent hoping electronics would do it for them, people were going to start using other *people* to feel better about themselves. As long as the relationships developed to the mutual benefit of both parties, Sloane thought this ego-driven version of altruism could be a powerful thing.

Driving across town to Union Square, Anastasia's motor peacefully hummed. Sloane felt full of possibility, impossibly alive. Silly Putty, warm clay, pottery, hot kilns. High-ropes courses, singing lessons, the touch of fingertips to ivories, her mind seared with the ways in which people could rediscover social ease.

Across the street, Sloane watched a bus bow down to hydraulically greet its passengers. "UNTRACEABLE" read the television series poster plastered along its side, the profile of a man with a Day-Glo DNA map pulsing on his shaved skull. Although she had no idea what the show was actually about, she could guess that it was one of the dystopian series all the rage right now, where genome-mapped youths were trying to free themselves of the microchips that relayed their every movement to some all-white-wearing, monotone-speaking committee version of The Man.

But most dystopias were but a version of the present with the fear ramped up. Untetheredness, untrackability, disappearances, these would also trend. After a decade where "total access to celebrities" meant knowing what so-and-so was eliminating from their bowels, mysteriousness and aloofness would once again be prized. It was happening already, of course: the cool kids in Lima, in São Paulo, in parts of the Midwest who wouldn't be caught dead handling smartphones: if they had a phone at all, it was a throwback flip phone. It was going to be the height of gaucheness, being totally available, being able to be reached. The new cool kids would be unfindable online, and difficult to locate in real life because they'd no longer be updating their every whereabout. Sloane envisioned a rare smile on the normally pained faces of the United States Postal Service employees when she announced that communication by first class mail was going to be cool again.

Sloane was so caught up in the tidal wave of premonitions that she hadn't taken the time to consider that she'd given her longstanding partner the heave-ho and bonked her art director on the same night. The concurrence of these events made them feel dreamlike, but they had happened, and there would be consequences. Sloane was still in the untouchable stage of morning-after giddiness, but as they approached Union Square, reality knocked.

It was paramount that whatever had happened—was happening?—with Jin remain a secret. It was problematic enough that Sloane was sensing a rise in sensuality when she'd been hired to present a line of products that were resolutely tech. But she'd always found her way through paradoxical predictions before. There were compromises, modulations, there were softer sounds. The essential thing was for Sloane to feel her way through all these current inklings and forecast their applications, and *then*—when she had a good sense of where she really saw physical trends heading—she would decide how to make her premonitions work for ReProduction. In the interim, discretion was imperative. And in any case, to the outside world, she was still in a long-term relationship with Roman Bellard.

As for her ex-partner, as intractable as she'd always thought Roman was, she might have overestimated the extent to which he was willing to move on. She'd received countless texts that morning, and several voicemails, the equivalent of a love letter from her SMS-preferring ex:

> I am sorry. I truly didn't think my words would come as a surprise.

And another one, even higher on the rungs of ignorance:

I in no way want to embarrass you with my article, I want to
celebrate our life! All of the things we have foreseen together,
all the victories! I was certain that this was something you would
see with me, see through with me. Imagine you, surprised!

A brief moment of remorse then followed:

Will I be "no sex" forever? My darling, I don't know this. Maybe,
maybe not. But surely you too want to be part of a world where
penetration feels new again?

His final texts were panicked, ego-driven:

Do you just not agree with the article's premise, is that—my
love—the problem? Do you think I have the anti-penetration
angle wrong? I don't think so, dear. The research is there. But you
know how much I value your opinion. How much I always have.

Sloane rolled her eyes. Yes, she thought that his conviction that
the "wired rich" were going to go off penetrative sex was wrong in
the long term. Sure, she could imagine the trend hitting like a wild
vegetable—a headache of weeks during which one feigns excitement
about ramps, but then it would pass as all fads do. After all, the urge
to copulate was biological, drummed into us. It was easier to go off
white flour than sex.

And yet. There were upsides to cybersex that Sloane couldn't deny.
Certainly for people in long-distance relationships, for the disabled,
the homebound, virtual augmented reality gave them a new lease on
life. But grace, empathy, strength of character, courage—these weren't

values habitually cultivated by people who slicked their genitals into tubes to commingle with an avatar.

"Sloane?" interrupted Anastasia, "I'm afraid I've got Monsieur Bellard trying to get through again."

"Block him," Sloane replied, grabbing a cluster of grapes from the car fridge. Who kept it stocked? Her buddy, Anastasia. Sloane was in the mood to suspend disbelief around all things that didn't please her, and the idea that there was someone other than her Russian driver keeping the snacks fresh was one.

"Very good," said Anastasia. "I also have a text message coming in from a Mr. Kwang Lee—"

"Whoa there," said Sloane, shooting upright. "Let's come up with a moniker for that one. Let's go with . . . Seatbelt."

"You would like me to refer to the gentleman who is trying to text you as . . . 'Seatbelt'?" Anastasia repeated.

"For now, yes please," Sloane replied, equally disappointed with her lack of imagination. "Put it through?"

Her heart beat like something opening as she waited for it to ping upon her phone.

Sloane, the message read. *This is a text message.*

Sloane smiled. The short, the glowing, words. She thought that this was perfect. The message recognized morning-after etiquette but didn't go further than that, which allowed for mystery and contemplation. Sloane touched her fingertips to the keyboard: *This is a reply.*

It could just have been her altered mood, of course, but it seemed to Sloane that the atmosphere had changed in Mammoth's open work spaces. The environment was calmed somehow, purged of nervy, visible light. Some of the desks seemed to have freed themselves from the white tentacles of chargers that had been crisscrossing over and around keyboards for so long. Sloane swore she saw fewer web pages open on people's browsers. She noticed eye contact, people chatting without the trademark twitchiness that had marked such conversations before.

Before heading to her own office, Sloane stopped by Deidre's desk with an article she'd ripped out of that morning's paper about how the demand for adult construction toys had sent such manufacturers into overdrive.

Deidre smiled shyly when she saw the headline. "Well, I did have more people than usual in the LEGO class last night."

"I think we should make it mandatory." Sloane grinned.

"If there's not a shortage of interlocking plastic bricks."

"Touché," Sloane replied.

Sloane herself must have been emanating a new communicative vibe because all along her path that morning, people wanted to talk.

Mina Tomar stopped her by the coffee bar to discuss the possibility of mood-adapting lip stains, and even mascaras—eyelashes being uncharted territory for cosmetic color play.

And as she was passing through the open work plan on the way to her own office, Andrew Willett from furniture popped up to accompany her to her door.

"So, I'm not entirely . . . sure of this?" he said lowly, not wanting to be overheard. "But I was messing around last night and thinking of the role of, um, body heat in people's lives?"

Sloane's very muscles felt like they were brightening into a wider smile. "Did you want to come inside?" she asked, gesturing toward her office.

"Oh, no, I've got to go to a meeting, but I just wanted to run this by you. To, you know, see if this is the kind of thing you're looking for." He glanced nervously at the floor. "It's not *furniture*, really, but I was thinking we could retrofit our bedding products with electromagnets that sense, and then maybe heat up, the vacant side? You know, for people who don't have, or lost a partner—" Andrew's voice halted. He must have seen the recognition flash briefly across Sloane's face. *I sleep with a hot water bottle every night. So I can pretend someone's beside me.*

"That's brilliant," Sloane said, responding as quickly as she could to subdue his embarrassment. "It's totally right. Just imagine what that could do for people in mourning? To not reach over and feel the cold side of the bed? Or heated full-body pillows that people could hug? This is *exactly* the kind of thinking I was hoping for," Sloane said, not adding that what she liked about it was that it was *touch*-focused. Elemental and kind. The idea of imitation body heat resonated in her as if in response to something else. She saw it again, beautifully and briefly: a renaissance in touch.

After Andrew's interlude, the good things kept on coming: Sloane looked over and saw that her suggestion box was nearly full. She didn't even take her coat off, she simply sat and overturned the box so that the notes poured out like scattered leaves across the carpet of her office. She picked the brightest piece of paper up.

I think a lot about hypnosis. I think that we're all hypnotized. I've been doing experiments on pop music recently, and every song is an iteration of another song. The key the music is scored in changes but the chord progressions don't, the hooks don't, the amount of time it takes to get to the chorus, all of that's the same. I think the American music industry has hypnotized us to accept total mediocrity by putting out the same song over and over again.

Sloane folded the note, her palms warm in agreement. Music by demand was one thing, music *made* on demand was something else. Ever since the music identification application Shazam teamed up with War-ner Bros to create a crowdsourced record label, people were only con-suming songs that sounded like songs they'd heard and liked before.

It was the same with online dating. People were only choosing people whose tastes and appearances lined up with their own. The twenty-first century was over taking risks.

She went for another note.

A friend of mine just got a gazillion dollars for a product he's developed. It's a drone that dangles mistletoe over partygoers' heads. Most days, I feel like giving up.

Me too, Sloane wanted to say to the note's author. *Me often.* Today's consumers allowed companies to tell them what they wanted instead of actually asking themselves what they were hungry for. Take fat-free "Greek yogurt" that tasted like cardboard whey, for instance. As long as shoppers continued to buy into manufactured versions of their heart's desires, could you blame some asshat for going to market in November with a mistletoe drone?

Sloane reached in the box again.

what is it w/the touchy-feely R U trying to push us out of jobs

Sloane's hands went cold and achy. Her stomach dropped.

"Sloane?" called Deidre, peeking her face in tentatively through the door. "It's time for your ten o'clock with electronics."

Sloane loved the maternalism of Dax's assistant, who was slowly becoming hers. She liked being escorted places like a little child. She liked the several minutes it took them to cross the carpeted plains to make it to whatever conference room she would be put on trial in. That morning, it was a simulacrum of the fifth-floor meeting room on the third.

. . .

Sloane managed to keep whatever "touchy-feely" premonitions she was having under wraps during her meeting with electronics. They all agreed that Mammoth's prized Denizen smart kitchen was the right suite of products to debut at the ReProduction summit. *A virtual chef in your kitchen, a personal assistant in your phone*, was the way they'd flaunt the time-saving benefits of synched kitchen electronics to people who had been "underusing" their refrigerators and stove tops.

They spent the first part of the meeting debating whether the child-free and child-having used their refrigerators differently or not. One woman, Allison, the only woman among them with kids, said that even though they were half stupid with sleep deprivation, many new parents knew exactly what was in their fridge because supplies were so important. If you were out of milk, or formula, applesauce, what have you, you knew. You *needed* to know.

"So therein," Sloane said, after Allison's input, "the 'freshness thermometer' application would be really useful to nonparents. Let's go with the assumption—I think it will serve us, given the target demographic of this conference—that the urban child-free are home less often, cook less, work longer hours. Therefore, they literally open up their fridges *less* than parents. So an app that reminds them that their arugula is wilting and they need to get another batch if they're still set on making that pesto they'd planned, would be really welcome. So let's definitely highlight that."

After they ran through the synched functions and the way they would present them, it was time to start thinking of products that didn't already exist in the Mammoth lineup.

A man named Jarod from business development told Sloane that Daxter was adamant that the group preview an app.

"Something for the anti-moms," he said.

"Oh, I've got an app for that," said a bro-type whose name Sloane didn't know. "'No Kidding' filters," he said proudly. "Lets you block people who want kids on dating sites."

"What the hell do you all have against surprises?" Allison spoke up. "I don't want to sound like one of the olds here, but why does everything need to be so obvious? Isn't there a value in kind of . . . finding things out?"

"Discovery," Sloane chimed. "I think there's really something to that. Like, remember when you'd go to a new city and you'd want to try a restaurant. You'd ask the concierge if you were staying at a hotel, or maybe a like-minded-looking stranger. And I don't know about you"—she laughed, just thinking of it—"but sometimes those recommendations were freaking *bad*."

The others laughed, too.

"*Tofu Terrace*," offered Allison. "Seattle. I specifically remember that."

"Totally," Sloane said. "It was a vegetarian outdoor buffet for me, too. But regardless, there's something kind of wonderful about being disappointed, because it's true what Allison said: even a disappointment is still a surprise. Now we know everything about a place before we've even gone. I wonder if we couldn't invent something that could restore the element of surprise to the way we navigate new environments."

"We could call it 'Shitty Time,'" said the bro dude.

"I actually like that," Sloane said with a smile.

"How 'bout 'Blue Lagoon'?" suggested Allison.

"Blue Lagoon *totally* sounds like an app," said Jarod, tapping his pen against his tablet.

"But what if we pushed this further?" Sloane asked, truly excited now. "What if it wasn't an app? What else could it be?"

Sloane watched eleven faces fall. People looked at one another uncomfortably, waiting for someone else to speak.

After a disheartening lag, Jarod spoke up again. "Well then," he said, shrugging. "That would just be life."

Everyone remained quiet, so Jarod shrugged again.

"And no one would buy that."

Even if it ended on a minor chord, Sloane still felt that the electronics meeting showed enormous progress. It was taking some time, of course, but in public, and secretly, through the notes that she was getting, people were pushing beyond their comfort zones intellectually. They were thinking less about what "versioning" model Mammoth could easily make to see version 2.0 better, faster, smarter than version 1.0, and further ahead to what humans would *need* once they had everything they wanted. In short, they were learning to trend forecast. Were learning to care. And isn't this why Dax had hired her in the first place?

Sloane was so fixated on finding a corresponding product idea for the kernel Allison had planted in the electronics meeting (she once knew a man who wrote travel guides that contained only places, names, and numbers in no particular order across the world: *Copenhagen, call Sophie for ceramics; London, Brian gives great haircuts; New Delhi, Dimple, if you like mulligatawny stew.* How would old Jim Haynes have made a restaurant recommendation app feel more random, more friendly, more lifelike? she kept asking herself) that she didn't realize she'd headed into the copy room instead of the supply closet until she was there. A bigger surprise was that the man standing patiently in line behind a frantic, coiled fellow was Jin. She was rocketed back into her present tense.

"Oh!" Sloane cried, instantly blushing. "Oh!" she repeated, making her initial reaction worse.

The fellow making the copies looked up, clearly alarmed by the color of her face.

"Hi!" Sloane said to the copier, overcompensating out of embarrassment.

"Hi?" the fellow replied, confusedly, as the machine rolled its green scanner over his paper, ejecting copies, sheath by sheath.

"Did you want to cut in?" Jin asked, indicating the space in front of him with a gentle wave, along with (she wasn't imagining this?) a loaded smirk.

Sloane tried to react to this question on a semantic level, with grammatically correct words. She tried not to recognize the warmth spreading throughout her body because, really. What the hell. Maybe she and Jin should have come up with a kind of protocol, a way to act around each other. But that would have necessitated recognizing what they had done.

"I'm not in any rush," Sloane said, which came out sounding like an overture.

Jin laughed. The mystery boy at the photocopier looked totally bewildered: what joke had been made? Suddenly efficient, he gathered up his materials and left. In Sloane's mind, Jin leaned against the counter and held her at arm's length—taking space to contemplate the body he'd been with the night before.

In reality, he opened up the giant Xerox and put his A6 paper on the glass.

"Our color propositions," he said, his eyes smiling. "For the YA tablet."

"Oh," she said. "That's great."

"Isn't it?" he teased. Leaning against the machine, seeming to take pride in the fact that she was more nervous than he was.

"I got your text," he said, checking the first copy for bleeds, before looking her in the eyes.

"And I got yours," she answered, laughing, because her system didn't know what else to do with the bigness in her heart.

Jin pressed Start on another round of copies, then relaxed against the machine and regarded her, just as she'd hoped he would, but with his arms folded. The impossibility of what had passed between them just a cluster of hours earlier seemed both delicious and absurd. The whirring of the ink-jet cartridges and the sharp scent of the ink was piercing through her consciousness. It wouldn't be outlandish, would it? A very quick embrace?

"Oh! Sloane," said a familiar voice behind her. Deidre in the doorway, the clipboard to her chest. She looked from Sloane to Jin, and back to Sloane again, and tried, gallantly, to curb a burgeoning smile. "Mr. Stevens would like to see you," she said, her face sternish again. "If you don't mind."

Jin's composure didn't waver. Perhaps he was too young to know the sound of a death knell.

21

Sloane," Dax gushed, arms open from his chair. His office again, eponymously mammoth.

"I'm so glad to see you feeling better," he said, without any apparent irony. "It's the season, don't you think? Warm to cool . . . do you know there are people who eschew the eating of tropical fruits in the winter because our North American systems aren't used to digesting elements exposed to so much natural sun?"

"I did, actually," she said, touching the top of the chair in front of her, wondering if she should sit.

"So let's just get right down to it, yeah? Can you close the door?"

On her way to do this, Sloane drew in a breath. Although a girlish part of her ran to the possibility that he knew about her and Jin, this wasn't really possible. What she felt in her stomach was that Dax had concerns.

"Sit, sit, sit." Dax flapped at her, once she was facing him again. "So this professional affection thing. Piqued my interest. Where we going with that?"

Sloane took a seat, moving slowly, trying to emanate the qualities of caution and patience that were missing from Dax's voice.

"Well, I'm still thinking through all this," she started. "But obvious applications would be real-life friend-finders, social networking."

"Right, but I need *things*," Dax said, drumming his fingers out in a quick gallop. "That I can pack, box, ship."

Sloane closed her eyes briefly. It was hard for her to trend forecast if she didn't feel alone. She could feel alone in public—*had* felt secluded and protected yesterday on the subway train, in fact—but with Dax there, blinking petulantly at her like a hungry restaurant goer, it was hard to access the darker, stranger recesses of her inner mind.

She pushed herself. There were always flashes and small red darts of heat, neurological connections she could actually ride.

"Well, empathy robots, for one."

Dax thrust his chin onto his fist, alert now. "Go on."

"Versions of this exist, of course," she said, nervous—nervous! The idea had just popped—"mostly in Japan. They've had some success in nursing homes especially—they're these seal-like robotic creatures with oversized eyes that make cooing sounds, and flap their ears to listen. Now, they're not really listening at all, but the point is to make the old people feel comfortable talking to someone who isn't judging them. Someone who isn't going to tell them that they're not making sense, or they're just being paranoid. I don't know that they've done much to extend life expectancy, but as for quality of life . . ."

"So this would go along with your idea of renting friends?" he asked.

"Yes," Sloane replied, unequivocally. "Although I truly believe that people will want to rent actual, human friends soon. People they can be seen out and about with. Have conversations with. Empathy bots, if you imagined the applications . . . well, I guess, since we're on the topic of ReProduction, empathy *tots* could be a great solution for people who want . . . part-time kids—"

"Jesus fucking Christ," he said, his body thrumming. "Kids you can turn on and off."

What was she doing? This idea wasn't something that she actually *felt*. It wasn't coming from that place of gravity that felt steadying and important. It would give further permission for people to be short-sighted and selfish, and it would be a huge success.

"*This* I fucking love." Dax shook his finger maniacally. "You had me pretty worried when you started confiscating phones, but this is fuck-ing genius. It'll be so big! Like those computer games, right? Where people used to carry around digital goldfish to learn responsibility? My kid had one. He killed it after two days, forgot to feed it. The dif-ferentiator here, though, is that you can activate it or deactivate it. Turn parenthood off or on."

"There would be a myriad of uses," Sloane said, slowly, carefully. "And sure, parenting as a hobby could be one, but really, I would caution you . . ." She tried to find the right way to pace her words. "My gut instinct is still that people are going to want to interact with actual *people* again."

"Sure, but I can't sell that. And also, no. I pick my kids up, they don't talk to anyone at school all day and then they spend the entire evening texting. So I think empathy bots, yeah."

"Right, but I was thinking for the next generation . . ."

"Yeah, no," Dax said quickly, "I don't have time for that. I want the stuff at ReProduction to be preorderable. Can you think more through these robots? I want to present this to electronics."

"I just saw them today."

"Perfect, then for next time. Let's roll this shit out after Thanks-giving. Sloane, this is perfect. It's fucking huge. God, I'm so excited, and this isn't even why I called you in!"

Sloane was staring past him, half at, half through the window, thinking back to her first decade in trend forecasting when the clients she'd worked for wanted forecasts ten or twenty years out. Today, companies wanted to know what would happen in three weeks so that their social media intern could be ready with a hashtag. In twenty years, it was unclear whether the human race would still be on the planet. It was too depressing; it was too vague! It was much more fun to debate the shelf life of platform Birkenstocks.

"Sloane?" Dax repeated. He was thrusting his phone at her, screen out. "This?"

Sloane curdled at the image; blood rushed to her head. His screen was cued to an Instagram snapshot of Roman in his green Zentai suit waiting in line at Whole Foods. It had been liked seven hundred thousand times.

"This is your *husband*?" he asked, pulling the phone back. "Roman Bellard?"

"We're not actually married," Sloane answered, still trying to sound calm.

"And this?" He showed her another photo, Roman in the gold suit, at an outdoor Paris market, posing with a striped bass he'd just been handed by a fishmonger. "How you've never mentioned this before . . ."

"Yeah," Sloane said. "Zentai. He's very big online."

"A neo-sensualist? A *neo*-sensualist? Where have you been hiding him?!"

"In France," Sloane said, attempting a lame smile.

Dax waved his hand dismissively. "I'd love to meet him. *Must.* Dinner? I know that it's, like, basically Thanksgiving, but that takes, what, three hours? You staying in town?"

Sloane's mouth opened, but no words came out. This was an impossible situation. If she told Dax that she'd broken up with Roman because he was about to publish a fatwa on penetrative sex, he'd be even more desperate to meet him. And she didn't like the possibilities of what could happen if they met without her there.

"We're, um, probably going to Florida?" she said.

"Oh yeah?" Dax said, his eyes raised. "When's that?" He was tapping at his phone.

"What about tonight?" he asked, not waiting for her answer. "Can you do tonight?"

"I'd really rather not, Dax," she said. "Roman and I . . . things have been a little tricky, I don't know if it's the move over here, or what . . ." Her sigh was exaggerated enough that she hoped he'd drop the subject.

"It's just dinner"—he shrugged—"not a visit to the marriage counselor. Which—" He held up the hand that wasn't pawing his phone. "Jesus, been there! I'm only curious. I mean—" He tap, tap, tapped. "How can I not be?" He thrust his screen at her again. Another image, this time of the both of them, a night when she'd been happy: Sloane in an embroidered silk crepe gown on a red carpet in Paris, Roman in the gold Zentai suit, his Lycra feet nestled in tuxedo slippers. They'd been at the launch for the reissue of a Helmut Newton photo book of a naked Charlotte Rampling. Two years later, Rampling would make an Oscars comment that would unclothe her even further.

"How's Oak and Fell? At eight?"

When she called him that afternoon, Roman didn't even hear that the dinner invitation was a caveat, an accordance, a favor she was doing for herself. That it didn't mean that they weren't separating, that she hadn't kicked him out. All he heard was that he'd piqued the interest of a major CEO.

"Should I wear the suit?" Roman asked her over the telephone. "Is that what he's expecting?"

"No, don't wear the fucking *suit*, Roman. We're going to a restaurant, you need to be able to eat."

To Sloane's consternation, Dax had chosen one of those exhausting, ampersanded places with deeply subservient waiters who kneel to whisper about the extra-specials. All of the entrées were thirty-six dollars and all vegetables had to be ordered on the side for nine more. Sloane was deeply tired of farm-to-table restaurants. She would have preferred to eat the farm.

Roman appeared as she was scrutinizing the menu on the outside of the restaurant's door. He'd put some effort in his hair. Having not seen him in a full day, it struck her now—again—how handsome he was. Roman was beautiful, classic. He had the polish of a politician you wanted to believe in, wanted to hold a chalice in front of to be filled with golden words.

"You're angry," he said, his eyes temporarily kind. Then his lips curved into a smile. "But you're here." His hands fell to his scarf.

"This is my job, Roman. It isn't about us. Don't *pull* anything. I need you to be civil."

Roman put his palms out. "I am civility itself."

She almost laughed then; it suddenly seemed like it might be easy to put bygones behind them. So what if Roman wasn't into penetrative sex? She had recently been penetrated by someone else.

Dax and his stately wife were already at the table drinking water out of mason jars with about nineteen cucumbers in them when Roman and Sloane arrived. Sloane could tell from the sudden slackness of Roman's jawline that he was in love with everything about the New York dining scene: the groomed women, the men's rugged footwear, the soundtrack of New Age folksingers covering Nirvana songs.

"Roman!" said Dax, standing. "Have we ever been waiting to meet *you*! But where's the suit, buddy?" Roman's breath caught, his stance accusatory. He was about to turn to Sloane with an *I told you I should've*—when Dax continued talking.

"Sloane, Roman," said Dax, still standing, "This is Raphael, my wife."

In practiced harmony, they greeted the Neapolitan beauty at his side, a woman who somehow managed to look voluptuous and aloof at the same time. A darting look at Raphael's waistline suggested that there might be a secondary reason for her otherworldly glow.

Sloane sat down without offering congratulations. You never knew. Even if you knew. She unfolded the thick napkin across her lap to distract herself from the discomfort twisting through her. She had a sinking feeling that she would not be able to rise to the levels of artifice the evening required.

"Roman's in this Zentai community, honey," Dax said, settling back down. "It's about . . . new forms of sensuality, right? New ways to touch. They all wear these skintight catsuits—"

"Very tight around the head," Roman said, passing his hand in front of his face. "No holes for the eyes or mouth, so . . . no good for dinner."

"Well, that's . . ." said Raphael, fumbling, "that certainly is something."

"It's like a living avatar," Roman said, running his right hand along his left arm as if he was presenting a body part he had won. "The suit makes you look extra touchable, your body on display, but your skin can not be accessed."

Raphael's eyes darted toward hers questioningly. Sloane responded by flicking a bread crumb off the table that would soon be covered with high-end, slightly toxic, enamel camping plates.

"So, I've gotta ask you," Dax said, clamping the wine menu shut with a decisive thud. "Are you into this, too?"

"I'm not," Sloane said, her hand raising involuntarily as if to emphasize the extent to which she wasn't. "It's definitely Roman's thing."

"But Sloane introduced me to the *idea* of it," Roman said, his French charm turned on full force. He was smiling at her, his face unlined, his countenance well rested, no cares in the world. "The freedom, no, the *liberty* of a second skin."

The waitress came, a woman so attractive, Sloane actually laughed. They ordered small plates to share. Sloane prayed that the precious food came quickly. She was worried that if she stayed too long at dinner, Roman would come home with her and they'd start everything again. Not because she wanted him to, or because she'd changed her mind, but because it was so easy. In some ways, their asexual relationship had been safe and comforting. She had stopped worrying if she was desirable, had confirmation that she wasn't. She didn't have to try.

The wine came, presented like a baptized child. Raphael covered her own glass with a manicured hand, and Sloane listened to the guggling of the other glasses filling up. In two days, Thanksgiving. She thought of all the wine that would be served across a table that she wouldn't be at. Ridiculous, and untimely, but she wanted her sister there with her like she hadn't wanted anything in a long time. Together they'd ride off in Anastasia, Sloane with a napkin full of pilfered high-grade tater tots and Leila with a screw-cap bottle of white wine. *Oh, Leila,* Sloane would say, *I've made so many mistakes.*

"So, I'm happy to say we're having some breakthroughs at work," Dax announced, holding up his glass. "Sloane! Tell 'em about the bots!"

Roman clinked his glass against Daxter's and they both drank without toasting her.

"Robots," Sloane corrected. "Bots are on software. Or . . . anyway."

"Tell 'em about the bots!" Dax repeated, grabbing a piece of bread.

"Yes, um, well," Sloane fumbled, trying to step around her own words, "it stemmed out of my conviction that people need more . . . actual physical contact, in their lives right now. I was calling it—am calling it—the professionalization of affection. The idea that people will start paying strangers to . . . nurture them. So an empathy robot would be an extension—"

"No, but tell them about the temporary kids!" Dax cried, tucking in his elbow so the waitress could set down the first round of food.

She felt empty, empty, empty. Completely null and void. She didn't give a flying hoot about robotic empathy toddlers. But the idea had been hers.

"Right, well, you could eventually envision robotic empathy toddlers, is what we'd said. That you could turn on and off . . . so you could be a parent only when you feel like it. But anyway, it's not really fleshed out, I was more excited about the—"

"Can you *imagine*, honey?" Dax said, passing the artisanal carrots to his wife. "Wouldn't that be great?"

"Well, I've certainly felt that," said Raphael. "I'll wake up, see the two of them, and think, *Oh God, you're both still here!* I can imagine a lot of people welcoming a time-out."

"Time-Out!" Dax said, bringing his hand down on the table. "That's great! You think we could call it that? Time-Out Tots?"

Sloane turned her hands up. "Sure."

Dax narrowed his eyes at her, but for only a moment. In a flash, his expression returned to its open, friendly self. She needed to be excited about whatever the fuck he was excited about—this was a big dinner, her boss, his wife. But she'd never been good at feigning enthusiasm for something she found sad.

"You hadn't mentioned this idea yet," said Roman, attempting, unsuccessfully, to place his hand on hers. "What a good idea! Of course, *your* child would be mostly turned to off."

She glared at him, but he didn't notice.

"It's a very exciting time for us, isn't it?" he continued, wiping his lips with the checkered linen napkin that was absurdly undersized. "I think it is perhaps the most important time to be thinking about new physical rules. The best time to be a neo-sensualist!" Sloane grit her teeth. She knew within an inch of her life that Roman was about to self-promote.

"I don't know if she's told you about the article I have coming out?"

"She hasn't!" Dax said happily, inviting him to go on.

"Well," Roman cleared his throat, holding his fork above the appetizers. "I have a theory that we're entering a period that is post-sex.

People want beyond that, yes? They want more—it is too simple, the I-put-this-into-you, you-enter-me, the pounding?"

Sloane tried to make her entire face disappear into her wineglass while he reenacted fornication, once again.

"So many people are finding their virtual sex lives so much richer than their real ones," he continued, his hands now blessedly occupied with the ministrations of his fork. "People have sex all the time without ever leaving the house. They text—is it not also a way of making love? Physical distance is very, very sexy. Trying to bridge that distance without actually coming together in a physical sense—this is the new way to—you'll excuse me—fuck!"

"And you have an article coming out about this?" Dax said, almost salivating. "When?"

"In *The New York Times*," Roman said, his eyes demure. "Tomorrow."

"Tomorrow!?" Sloane choked, the same time that Dax repeated, *"The New York Times?!"*

"Yes, *chérie*," Roman said sweetly, "I haven't had a chance to tell you that they accepted my piece."

Sloane firmed her grip around her wineglass. "Well!" she said, trying to recover. "That is so, so great."

"Day before Thanksgiving, huh?" Dax said, toasting him. "Ballsy."

"Apparently, Thanksgiving is one of the most popular days for online reading," Roman said.

"Turkeys *do* take a long time to cook," Raphael accorded.

Sloane scrambled to find a steady footing. *The New York Times?* Tomorrow?! She should have said yes to her family's noninvitation to Disney World—it would have been the perfect place for her when the article hit. All those kids running around, the almost purifying stress of it, no time to check in on developing tragedies online.

"It *is* thrilling," Roman said, unwilling to step out of the spotlight.

"They told me they expect *quite* a response. Maybe even viral? Because in it, I will announce our hiatus from penetrative sex."

Sloane had to make a guttural effort not to spit up her Pinot. *"Your hiatus,"* she managed. *"Yours."*

"Oh my God," Dax said gleefully, almost knocking the bottle over with his forward lean. "We're gonna need something stronger than vino! Wait, so, Sloane, you're predicting some kind of hugging renaissance and Roman—"

"Oui," Roman said, tearing a hunk of bread off. "The end of penetrative sex."

Raphael flashed Sloane a tentative smile. *Stop smiling!* Sloane wanted to yell. *Don't smile your way into convincing me that you have the perfect life! Your husband is a steamroller! And you hardly talk!*

"This is fucking *amazing*," crunched the steamroller. "Sloane, you never said!"

"Well, it's not really something that I want to brag about, is it?" Sloane asked, spearing something approximating a beet. *"The New York* fucking *Times*. How grand."

She set to chewing furiously, chewing long after she'd swallowed. Raphael pushed some food around on her plate and Dax thumbed the stem of his wineglass.

"It really is exciting," Roman said in conclusion to something no one had said. "I'm looking forward to expanding the boundaries of what we think of as sex."

Everyone remained silent. Sloane could feel Dax's eyes on her even as she avoided his.

"If we could maybe move on to a new topic," she asked in monotone.

"Well, I certainly think it's great that we're living in a world with so many different choices," Raphael said, serving up some Brussels sprouts. "Men can be women, women can be men, people can do just about anything online, have babies, or not have children." She smiled peacefully. "It definitely is an exciting time to be doing what you do."

"That's certainly what I think," Dax said, in a tone that sounded like a test.

"Me too," said Roman, smiling.

"Me three," said Sloane, absolutely desperate for a pause. She was being tugged down by a current toward a place she didn't want to go, or didn't want to return to, like something dark and cold and terrifying that comes at you from a dream years after you've had it.

"Will you excuse me?" Sloane asked, standing. "I just have to run to the . . ." She nodded toward the bathroom.

Sloane *had* planned to go to the bathroom, but she didn't need to go to the bathroom, so at the last minute, she headed for the street, hoping against hope that none of the others had seen her slip out. It would have been useful if she was still a smoker; she could lean against the outside of the restaurant and fume. As it was, she simply looked like she was waiting rather emotionally for a taxi cab.

Without a scarf or jacket, she pulled her blouse around her throat, her eyes welling. It wasn't fair, it wasn't fair to do that, Daxter sitting there with his gorgeous, docile wife, new life sleeping inside her, a babysitter—or a full-time nanny, probably—with the other kids at home, a life that was full and busy and complete and probably even happy, and him with a squadron of people at Mammoth working to promote the very opposite of what he had. He had what he had, so how fun for him to imagine the opposite. Pander to the opposite, the freedom and vitality of a life lived without kids.

What a shitty place to put her in—her spearheading something he secretly mocked. She wasn't a trend forecaster at Mammoth, she was a hired hand.

Sloane watched the taxis rushing through the November slush to get their charges to their trains and flights on time. Thanksgiving was a rotten time to start a love affair, that was for fucking sure.

It would be really nice if Sloane wasn't the resident asshole in her family—at least she'd have someone to break down on and call. She imagined herself in their rented Florida condo, someplace called Pelican's Landing or Sweetgrass, a magnum of bad wine opened on a granite island, her sister's kids yelping down the hallway from the dirty bath, holiday commercials batting desperately at them from an oversized flat screen. There would be Cheerios decomposing in between the pillows of a mass-produced Raymour & Flanigan sectional, but in this vision, Sloane was happy. In this vision, she received a text from Jin and her sister noticed it. Sloane was teased, gave in, she kissed and told a little. She kissed and told a *lot*. Her sister squealed and served her more 15 percent alcohol by volume Yellow Tail and begged to be told more.

In this daydream, Sloane had an easy relationship with her family, and even as she bemoaned the next day's trip to the Magic Kingdom, she also felt warm and safe in the knowledge that the kids were going to love it and that their joy, their utter revelry, was going to infect her with the new old way of seeing life again. You *could* learn a lot from children. She did believe that.

Sloane tightened her thin blouse around her again. She couldn't leave the dinner, there was no excuse to. She couldn't very well play sick again. She steeled her reserve and headed back inside.

When she arrived at the table, she noticed that extra dishes had been ordered. Roman and Dax were laughing about something when she got there. Dax stopped laughing, Roman did not.

"Something that I said, Sloane?" Dax asked, his lips pursed. "You didn't go to the john."

"Oh, honey, drop it," Raphael chided.

"No, you know? It's fine," Sloane said, coolly, pulling out her chair. "We're all adults here. Roman and I are just working through some . . . differences around his article and thus I would have thought he might have had the tact to not allude to it is all, but he doesn't have the capacity for graciousness. So here we are!" She sat, loudly. Grabbed a sweet potato nugget. "What were we talking about?"

The waitress appeared with a second bottle of wine. Everyone looked up at her, silent.

"Eh, sorry," the waitress said, seeing their stony faces. "Did you change your mind?"

"No, no, of course not," said Dax, waving her on. "Let it flow! You two have things to work out." He nodded toward Sloane when his glass was filled to his satisfaction. "It happens."

"Usually not like this," she mumbled, as she stuck her nose into her own glass.

"Well!" said Roman, rising above the fray. "Another toast! Dax is going to have me in!" he said, clinking Dax's glass, then hers. "To talk to the students!"

"Employees," Dax corrected.

Sloane tilted her head at Dax. "Is that right?" she asked.

"We actually work together all the time in Paris, so I didn't think—" Roman stammered, sounding nervous for the first time.

"And when's this happening?" Sloane insisted. "When are you having him in?"

"Monday after break."

Sloane placed her silverware alongside her plate. Her eyes hadn't left Daxter's. "His article will have made the rounds by then," she said. "Fantastic timing."

Dax also put his fork down. "Clear something up for me," he said. "Why is this a problem?"

"I don't agree with the premise of his article," she said, her eyes flashing. "I don't agree with it at all."

"You know what you once told me?" Dax said, refolding his napkin disinterestedly across his lap. "At one of the trend conferences. You once said that trends hide between opposites."

"Roman's not a trend forecaster."

"Sloane—" attempted Roman, who was cut off by Dax.

"I see," Dax said, looking as if he had just been refused a favor he'd called in. "I see."

"Do I really need to fucking point this out to you?" Sloane asked, her game face dissolved. "My own husband—almost husband, whatever— is coming out with a manifesto about the end of fucking *sex*. And you're going to sit here and be all, 'I don't understand the problem with this, Sloane'?"

"On va se calmer un petit peu, là," said Roman, breaking into French. "I am sure that Dax, like the readers of the article, they are interested in the general applications, not the personal. That's what's important! We will become the devices, become sources of our own pleasure and stimulation. Beautiful, efficient, self-sufficient machines."

"We have this capacity *already*," Sloane insisted, cutting off his non sequitur, "because we come with fucking brains. Not that anyone's using them, because we're t-t-tapping all the time." She imitated a rodent clawing at a screen.

Dax drew in a breath and Sloane knew she'd gone too far. It was in that instant, then, that she saw what would come in not just the days after, when Roman's article broke and caused a pandemonium, but in the weeks following, when Daxter had already decided he'd chosen the wrong woman for the job. She knew, intrinsically, that there was no getting back into Dax's good graces, she could come up with all the empathy robots she wanted until the cyber cows came home.

"I'm sorry," Sloane said, which instantly made things worse.

"Ri-ght," said Daxter, having reached a conclusion of some kind. "Soooo . . . what I'm getting here is that I've hired someone who wants electronics to go away."

Sloane tried to compose herself. She knew in the reddest recesses of her stomach that she had failed. "I never said that. I would never say that. Our relationship to our electronics is *changing*—that, I will defend." She stopped herself from divulging the other ideas that she'd been having.

"Listen," she continued, "a lot of Roman's ideas actually have merit. And applications in the marketplace which I do want to discuss. But tonight is not the night," she said, her eyes softening at the couple across the table. "It's been a really long week."

"Has it *ever*," said Raphael, with a gentle nod.

"Thanksgiving makes them cray-cray," said Daxter, encompassing the two women in the roll of his eyes.

Sloane bit her lip again to keep from screaming. How quick he was to dismiss her once she displayed the slightest vulnerability. In the space of one dinner she'd become overemotional and needy because she'd had the gall to suggest that human beings were too reliant on their phones. If he didn't want to see it, he didn't have to see it. Maybe they were living in a world where monolithic companies called the shots. Maybe her position wasn't even relevant anymore. Maybe *Mammoth* was in charge of telling people what they wanted. And if that was true, then what was the point of tracking human desires anymore?

"I really think it would be best if I left you all to talk," Sloane said, tugging her coat off her chair.

"I'll walk you out," said Roman, pushing his chair back. That did it. She'd explode.

"You do not *walk me out*," she said, rising to her feet. "This is not your show, Roman. You're not calling the shots."

"Well, I don't see why the surprise that some people are not open to your ideas," Roman added, shrugging. "No one wants to go back to medieval times."

The calmness of his expression deranged her.

"Medieval times?" she shouted, aware of nearby bodies twisting in their chairs. "That's not—I'm saying that people are starving for affection, for physical demonstrations of *love*, Roman. I'm not calling up the Dark Ages."

"You know," Roman said with an edge she didn't like, his eyes darker than usual, his pupils huge. "This is what *you* want. And you are always right," he said. "It's been impressive. But maybe now you're wrong."

Sloane wanted to gasp and cry and shriek all at once. Roman had hit exactly on the thing that had her panicked, the gnawing worry that her professional intuition was being polluted by her own desires.

"What you'd be surprised to discover," Roman continued, taking full advantage of her speechlessness, "is that the more you try to find connection in the physical, the more disillusioned you will become. Whereas, in the virtual realm, all of your desires can not just come true, but be surpassed."

"Oh, fuck you!" Sloane yelled, finally causing the heads of the other diners to fully snap in their direction. "It doesn't make me *old-fashioned* to want affection! It doesn't make me *old-fashioned* to want to have kids!"

The minute it was out, Sloane wished with every muscle in her that she could pull that comment back. She could tell from the curve of Roman's lips that she had just given him paper to her rock. There was a cool, blue energy emanating from Dax that was tightening around her heart.

"Ah, so this explains things!" Roman cried, looking from Raphael to Sloane as if she were a child who had given Sloane a naughty idea. "The ticktocking? It will pass." He gently touched her coat sleeve. "And then you'll see much clearer."

"Oh, I fucking *see* just fine," Sloane said, yanking her sleeve back.

"Sloane?" said Dax.

"I'm fine! This isn't what he's saying," she said, her throat tight. "I'm totally *fine!*"

In a cluster of chair squeaks and *Excuse me*s, Sloane was out on the street again, for good. This time, though, Roman followed her. He hadn't brought his coat.

"I *told* you it was dangerous to move back so close to your family," he yelled, once the restaurant door slammed behind them, rife with a naked anger she rarely saw. "These thoughts would never have occurred to you in Paris. It's like you are insane."

"*I'm* the insane one?" Sloane cried. "Me?" She thought of Roman organizing his body into his smelly catsuits, prepaying the gin and sodas he drank at his online fetish clubs in Bitcoins . . . a man whose virtual life was more actualized than his real one, but *she* was the freak.

"This isn't something you actually *want*, darling," he said, almost clucking. "Think of all the humans. Think of all the mouths. This is understandable." He made another attempt to reach for her, "But it is going to pass."

"Well, of *course* I don't want children!" she yelled. "I don't know why I said that!" It was horrible, more horrible than the confession, to realize this was a lie.

"I don't have anything left to say to you if you're like this," Roman said, coolly alarmed. "But I will be here for you when you come back to the ground."

And then he turned abruptly and returned to the restaurant, leaving Sloane to gulp back all of the things she'd left unsaid.

She walked quickly away from diners gaping through the window at her, feasting off of Scotch eggs housed in individual cast-iron skillets like something slain. The cold stung her eyes, her nose ran, and she had a sudden urge to burrow into the woolen, tree-sap smell of her father's favorite sweater. The tears that came were salt and they were human. And there were no empathy bots around to wipe them away.

Sloane slowed her step to get purchase on her stupid touch screen with her freezing hands. She swiped but her fingertip was too cold, or the screen was too cold, everything was out of service, closed for business, come back another time. Sloane closed her eyes and with all of the wishes left inside her, she summoned the only thing that could save her at that moment: her loyal, driverless car.

22

That night, Sloane slept the stone sleep of the shocked: bone-deep and cold-numbed. Waking in a stupor, her body all but molded to the Memory Foam mattress, she remembered the same flu-like slumbering from the first week after her father's death. She slept until one, two p.m. every day following the funeral, her sister finally forcing her door open: *Sloanie, what the fuck!?*

They had been so active, Leila and her mother. Ordering boxes, shoveling the snow out of the driveway, brewing decaf for the people who came by, and by, and by. But Sloane wanted to avoid it: the internal reckonings, the social customs that would have required that she get up and face the world. She just kept on sleeping, deeply comforted by the fact that there was no amount of weeping or dishwashing or casserole eating that could make her father less dead. And her sister—despite her tears, her anger—couldn't convince her otherwise.

But today, she couldn't sleep—she needed to go to work. Go to work and see whether she still had a job.

And if she did, by some great possibility that she currently didn't feel, could she still do it? Did she even want to? March into a future filled with robots who were manufactured to be kind to you when no one else could be bothered, cyborgs who rewarded you with direct eye contact? Were these really products that she wanted to shepherd into the world?

And why in the fuck had she announced to a table of adversaries that she wanted kids? Yes, okay. Dax had made an asshole comment, but he hadn't been far off—the holidays made her emotional. Thanksgiving, which she barely ever celebrated because she was usually in Europe, followed by the fifteenth of December, the anniversary of her father's death, followed by Christmas—what a pileup. So maybe she *did* want to be more connected to her family. Maybe she could allow that she was starting to identify some regrets. But to go from that to children? She was just mature enough not to blame it on the wine.

Sloane got dressed, slowly—ignored the pinging of text messages that she hadn't checked. There might be one from Jin, but still she didn't look—what was the point of bringing him into this? Of even contemplating being happy? Dax thought Roman was a mad genius, and his article was publishing that day. She'd soon see who else thought that human tenderness was going the woolly mammoth way.

Sloane arrived early to the office—buzzed Deidre up. Deidre arrived with more suggestions from the box outside her office, to add to the ones that Sloane already had on her desk. There were a lot of little notes. Looking at them made Sloane want to fold up inside herself.

"Deidre," Sloane said, with the pinched look of someone who had swallowed something foul, "Dax is going to want to see me. Or rather, I'd like to see him. Or—when he gets in, could you just ask him if he'd be willing to come up?"

"Of course," Deidre said, kindly. Extra kindly, because she didn't ask Sloane what the subject was. "Is everything all right?"

Sloane just smiled. She was tired. A leftover, bloated tired because she'd slept so deeply, allowed herself to float away from her reality on a bed of useless dreams.

"Have you read any of them?" Sloane asked, gesturing toward the notes that she'd brought in.

"Oh no, I wouldn't dare." Deidre flushed. "Are you finding them helpful?"

Sloane nodded absently. "I am, and I'm not. They're making me think about things I didn't intend . . ." She shook herself to clarity. "Anyway, thank you for bringing them up."

When her office door closed, Sloane picked up the furry Peruvian llama her father had once gifted her, glossy lima beans in the woven saddle pouches. Funny that they'd never sprouted in all the time she'd had it. Not enough water. Not enough sun.

Resigned now to what she felt would be a battery of notes proving that Roman was right about people's readiness for post-sexuality, Sloane stuck her hand inside the box and pulled a tuft of suggestions out.

Sometimes I go to the hair salon just to get my head touched.

I wish I had better handwriting. But it hurts my hand.

I once rented a dog.

Sloane felt her heart cave like something eroding. The number of times she'd thought how wonderful it would be to have a big, sloppy dog, too. Something that would register delight each time it saw you, a wet-eyed, speechless friend. But then she'd think about her travel schedule, and Roman who hated fur—or who, rather, liked their furniture and didn't want it covered in fur. And the fact that she would need to walk and care for it, and Paris was so dirty, and what did Sloane know about taking care of anything living, much less a giant dog?

She'd wanted one for her mother, though, after her dad died. In fact, Sloane had spent a lot of time sitting comfortably in her Paris apartment deliberating what widows in their sixties should be doing after a spouse's death. Selling the family home was one idea, getting something smaller (a condo near her sister's?) and a weekend place with access to the ocean where Margaret could start up with her landscape paintings again. The paintings that had been more fluid and less fussy than the miniature ones she busied herself with now.

She'd shared some of these ideas with Leila back when they were still talking on the phone, notably the pet one (an Australian shepherd had been her personal choice), as well as her conviction that the house should go on the market.

Her sister quickly pierced the bubble she was living in.

"We've put his things in boxes," Leila had responded. "I've thrown away his razors. I spent an entire *morning* deciding what to do with his shampoo. You don't have any fucking idea, Sloane. You're the most selfish person I'll ever know."

This had stuck, and it had hurt. It was the "ever know" that had burred into her with its wordy spikes. Sloane wasn't the most selfish person her sister knew at the time she had said it, she was the most selfish person that Leila would ever allow herself to know.

People made mistakes. In her heart, she'd known that she had left her beloved sister all alone to pick up the pieces, to look after their mother, to work through her own grief. Why? Because Sloane was sure she was her father's favorite? That she was hurting more than them? She had been young and egocentric and selfish and ludicrously naïve. What did she know about her father's love? What did she really know?

Trying to distance herself from the shameful memory, she reached in for more notes.

I think what I want right now more than anything is to be undetectable.
To not have anyone know where I am and also to not know where I am.
There aren't many places left where you can disappear.

Going undetected, getting lost, being confused—after last night's horrendous dinner, it sounded great to disappear. But it was hard to do now. So difficult, in fact, it made her think of the work of a Brooklyn artist who went by the name of CV Dazzle who designed makeup and hairstyle systems to keep face-detection algorithms from recognizing a face as a face.

But very few people were willing to walk around with a checkered pattern on their nose bridge, or a splotch of black paint on their cheeks. Really, one of the only ways left to disappear—at least existentially—was by falling in love. With new love, everything was uncharted and thrilling and strange. Which is why she felt in the pit of her stomach that Roman's article was *wrong* about the future. In a world where everything was monitored, navigated, tracked, human beings would want—would *need*—to get lost in someone else.

Sloane was about to reach for another note when there was a knock on her door. It was the announcement of a presence, not a request.

Dax walked in holding up a yellow piece of paper like a time-out flag.

"I was going to put this in the box," he said, sweeping his eyes across her office, stopping at the suggestion box on her desk. He flapped the paper flag at her. "But you have it."

Sloane stood. "Would you mind closing the door?"

Dax looked momentarily bemused, and then annoyed at the superiority in her tone. It seemed somewhat incredible, but it came to her completely—she wasn't going to be fired. He didn't even seem upset.

"So, I wanted to talk about last night, obviously," she said, inviting him to sit.

"Yes," said Dax, a twist of smile still on his face. "Let's."

"So, this isn't something I would usually discuss with a boss, given . . . well, *laws*, but it feels important that I clarify that I don't want kids."

Dax held both his hands up. "It's really not my business."

"Nothing's changed with me," she repeated.

"Let's just let it go."

Sloane fell silent. The ease with which he seemed to accept the prior night's upheaval was disconcerting, to say the least. Then she remembered the piece of paper in his hand. She only had to glance at it for him to spring to action.

"It's for the box," he said with a grin, "but read it! I'll read it! Came to me last night. Here." He opened up the piece of paper and showed it to her. She read a single word: *Two.*

"Two," he repeated, pitching the note toward the ones she'd already opened. "Two in-house consultants. I want to bring Roman in as a trend forecaster, too."

Sloane blinked her eyes at him, repeatedly, disbelief across her face.

"Daxter," she managed, her head shaking. "What?"

"I mean, I should have thought of this from the beginning. A man. A woman. I mean, it's so perfect. Roman's article—he forwarded it to me by the way, it's brilliant—is so clearly antireproduction. No penetrative sex, no critters. And so if you disagree with him, and it sounds like you disagree with him, then you tout your thing." He smiled hugely. "People can choose sides."

"My . . . thing," she said, the shock building into anger. "My *thing*. So . . . this is going to be, what, like a public divorce court? There is . . . excuse my French, Dax, but there is no fucking way."

"Listen, I get it! I really do. If my wife announced that she was going on a sex hiatus it'd be a problem for me, too. But that's exactly it. This is *professional*. Roman is the *embodiment* of antireproductive sex. So what's next? Will people want the touchy-feely substitutes of your empathy bots, or the titillating safeness of neo-sexuality? People will be looking to you two to find out!"

Furious, Sloane stood up from her desk and walked over to the window, her hands balled into fists to hide their shaking. To think that the next day the streets would be filled with whacky, blow-up floats. Thanksgiving. People using the good silver.

"Is there any part of you that's listening to what you're asking me?" she asked, whipping around. "How is this, how is this . . ." She faltered, seeing the question she didn't need to ask him: it would mean press coverage, sales. But she wasn't going to do it. She wasn't going to let Daxter force her into the corporate equivalent of a reality TV show just so Mammoth could sell a bunch of updated electronics to people who already had six versions of the thing. Not only did his request show a gaping lack of respect for what had transpired between her and Roman, it wasn't how she worked. She couldn't function in such a public pressure cooker, couldn't have her premonitions ticked off in "yes" or "no" boxes on a scale like this.

"Don't say anything now," Dax said, rapping his knuckles on her desk. "I get that it's an awkward time. But you two have already done so much work together. But Roman's on board."

Sloane brought her hand to her temple, dumbstruck. Of course, he'd already brought him on.

"And what if I say no?"

Daxter shrugged, unmoved. "Why would you? Can you think of a better opportunity to prove him wrong?"

Sloane actually had to swallow there was so much bile coming up. She knew exactly what would happen if she walked away from the Mammoth job: nothing. Absolutely nothing. Roman would take her position, trend forecaster or not, and ReProduction would turn into a giant marketplace of intelligent second skins and cyber dongs.

Dax got up to let himself out. She cursed herself for not being able to find the words to stop him.

"Jimbo!" he said, stepping backward in surprise as he pulled the door open. "'Bout knocked you over. How's it going, kiddo?"

"It's going well," Jin said, lowering his hand reluctantly to answer Dax's fist bump. Sloane watched the scene unfolding, anger kaleidoscoping into more anger, surprise, a little softness—but no, the anger still. She hadn't been allowed the final word.

"No hard feelings about the color props, yeah?" Dax asked, shifting his attention from Jin to her. "No hard feelings, Sloane?"

Sloane pursed her lips to keep her fury from spilling outward when she looked at Jin. "We'll follow up," Dax said, clapping Jin on the shoulder. "Good talk." It was unclear whether this comment was intended for Jin or her.

Sloane stayed by the window, embarrassed that Jin was there to see her broken pieces. She didn't want to be in New York City for the stupid floats. Bloated, lifeless, painted smiles mocking the world outside her teeth.

She listened to her door close.

"Whoa," said Jin, softly. "You okay?"

She felt his presence near her before she heard his steps. He stopped, put something on her desk. She kept her back turned.

"So, Dax killed volcanic red," Jin said, his tone cautious. "That's one of the reasons I came up. You didn't answer my—" He paused. Sloane wondered if he was contemplating whether or not to touch her, put his arms around her. She knew that he wouldn't, but she found herself hoping that she'd be surprised.

"Sloane, what's going on?" The disappointed shush of him settling into a chair.

She turned around, indignant. Who was he to just sit down? Who was he—was anyone—to act like this was just another day, just another life, not the year in which she completely fell apart?

But then she was facing him, and his eyes looked earnest in an intelligent way, and he had on another goofy outfit, and she had a glimpse of what her life would be like with her guard down.

"Well," she said, feeling her mind flood. "Roman's publishing an article about the end of penetrative sex, so Dax made us all have dinner together, and now Dax is bringing him on as a trend forecaster as well—which, I have to mention, he *isn't*—and he's rejiggering the whole ReProduction conference as a game of dueling guitars, and if—"

"Whoa, whoa, whoa," said Jin, putting his laptop on top of the color propositions he'd already placed on her desk. "Hey. Hey." He reached across the pile and stilled her hands with his. The warmth of his skin made her breath catch. "One thing at a time. When's this article coming out?"

"Today." She pulled her hands away. "Or maybe it already has. I don't know, has the earth shook?" She looked around the room. Her chest felt like there was an animal growing inside of it.

"Okay. But you—he's not living with you right now?"

Sloane shook her head.

"Are you going somewhere for Thanksgiving?" Jin asked, leaning back. "Will you be with good people?"

Sloane brightened at the naïveté of the question. Would that it were that simple! She pictured herself writing a note for her own suggestion box. *I want a family.* Dropping it in. Having it come true.

"I'm on a plane tonight," he said, extending his hand across the table again when she didn't answer. "Seattle. Thanksgiving. My dad lives there."

"Oh?" She was disappointed—she hadn't hoped for anything, and now she couldn't. He would be too far away. She looked at his open hand. Put hers back in his.

A flicker of a smile dashed across his face.

"You?" he asked, threading his thumb across her palm.

Sloane shook her head, trying not to think how weird and wrong and pleasant this workday touching was. "I'm not—I thought I had plans, but I don't, really. My family life is—" She scratched her eye with her free hand, wanting suddenly to pull her fingers away from his again. It was too intimate, this talking. It wasn't what she did. "We haven't really gotten to the get-to-know-my-shit part, have we? Dead dad—" She shrugged. "Bad child," she added, thumb pointed toward herself.

Jin looked her in the eyes. Anyone else would have said, *Come to Seattle!!* Would have filled the silence with platitudes and premature invitations because that's what people did. But Jin just sat there and let the sorrow pass from her cold fingers to his.

"I'm probably going to quit, anyway," Sloane said, "so it was nice knowing you."

"Well, that's awfully premature."

"I can't be—I don't want to be forced to play some game."

"Do you actually have to work together?"

"I don't know how much together . . . he wants Roman to do the Roman show, and then me . . . he said he wants people to 'choose sides.'"

"So it sounds like you can say what you think regardless."

"He's using me," she said, her eyes narrowed

"He's using all of us." Jin shrugged, not accepting her excuse. "But it sounds to me like you have carte blanche to run your own side of the show."

"Spoken like an optimist," she said, a little cruelly.

"You're not? Can you be a trend forecaster and *not* be?"

"Well," she said, pulling her hand away. "Now you're making me feel like I've been doing a really bad job my entire life."

"Is your life over?" he asked.

Sloane looked at him, burning. Because he wasn't letting her keep him at a distance. Because he wasn't wrong.

23

After her exchange with Jin, which hadn't been a meeting so much as a come-to-Jesus talk, Sloane needed air. She stuffed her coat pocket with the remaining notes from the suggestion boxes and headed for the street, no destination in mind, just a need for the wide and crowded avenues that would give her room to think.

A woman with a double baby stroller passed her on 19th Street, her twins bundled up like fragile vases. Everywhere, brown bags and wrapped packages, the scurry of Thanksgiving preparations like an odor in the air. Millions of people preparing to go to that place described on doormats and embroidered novelty pillows, the all-important "home." What if home was a scent treatment, something you could spray throughout an empty apartment, have your body and heart react warmly to it like a pheromone? What if the sense of home could be manufactured? The smell of just-baked cookies, the thrill of ironed sheets.

Sloane would buy that shit—she'd buy that shit right up. She'd pay a boatload of cash to feel that home was indeed where her heart was, something she could carry inside of her, warm within her chest. As it was, home was a fractured concept, something out of reach. Or something she'd made very difficult to reach, which wasn't the same thing.

Here was the thing, *here was the real thing*, she thought as she hit 18th Street. If she really went Full Monty with her premonitions, announced that physical intimacy was the new Internet, she was going to have to live what she thought. She couldn't very well preach the return of human interconnectedness and continue living her life closed off to the inconveniences of needing people and having them need her back. If she accepted Dax's proposal—and really did it her way—she would have to do the work to get her family back. And what would that look like?

And then there was the baby thing. There was the baby thing, again. Sloane didn't know why she'd said what she'd said at dinner except for the fact that having a child was like an express pass to having your own family. She could circumvent making amends with her own relatives and start all over again. A baby would be a peace-keeper; bring them all back together without her ever trying. Or maybe she just liked their big, innocent heads. Or another possibility: Roman was right. Being this close to her family *was* making her nuts.

At 16th Street, Sloane paused under an awning. Took the notes out of her coat.

I like wearing long johns because it feels like someone loves me. It's like I'm always being hugged. If that's what second skin would be like, then I'm for it.

I want to call my friends more. But I never call.

I wish there was a way to transfer all of my thoughts and disappoint-ments to my boyfriend so I wouldn't have to talk.

Well, hell, that would be convenient. Sloane supposed a lot of peo-ple considered that solution a public Facebook wall, but Sloane wasn't on Facebook. If she wanted to approach the bridge between her and her family, she was going to have to use her voice.

She ducked into an hourly parking lot wedged between two buildings where the wind was less tympanic, and took out her cell phone before she could change her mind. The number she wanted was still in "Favorites," although she hadn't used it in years.

"Mom!" her sister cried after the second ring. "Could you get Everett cranberry instead?"

"Leila?" Sloane asked, softly. "It's me. It's Sloane."

"Oh?" Sloane could just imagine Leila pulling the phone away from her ear to double-check. "Sloane?"

"Yeah."

"You okay? Where are you?"

"Work," Sloane answered. "Or kind of. Are you not in Florida?"

"Oh my God," Leila said, "not yet. Our super-direct, super-expensive flight was obviously delayed. Everett, don't *eat that*! What even *is* that? Harvey, I'm on the phone here—could you? Jeez! Don't fly with children," Leila said, her voice louder. "Don't. So!" Leila followed this quickly because Sloane hadn't responded to the advice she couldn't take. "What's up?"

"Oh, well, you know, nothing," she answered, watching a nearby man pat himself down for his car keys, before remembering that he'd handed them over with his car. "I just wanted to call."

"You did."

Sloane chewed the inside of her cheeks, debating whether to leap.

"Leilee?" she said, using their old diminutive. "Roman and I broke up."

"You, sorry, you *what*? Everett, I swear to God here . . . Harvey, it's my sister. I don't know. Find Mom." There was a moment of padded silence while Leila presumptively moved somewhere else.

"You *what*?" Leila asked again.

"We're separated. I kicked him out."

It was dignified of Leila not to cheer. She disliked Roman even more than her mother did.

"What happened?!"

"Well, he's coming out with a manifesto against penetrative sex. You know, inspired by his experience of us not having it. And my boss just hired him to work with me. So."

"Hold on," Leila interrupted. "I don't know where to start. I mean, listen you know we never really got each other with Roman, but lots of couples go through periods without sex."

"No, but it's not just us, Leilee, he's convinced that people don't need other people anymore. He just wants cybersex. Check *The New York Times.*"

"Oh Jesus. Oh shit." Leila sounded out of breath. "When'd you find out?"

"He just told me. I just read it. But . . . it's my fault, really. I mean, you must know about the Zentai suit. You must have seen the pictures."

Her sister drew in a long breath. "Well, what are you gonna do?"

"I can't work with him," Sloane said. "I can't."

"Well, no, obviously. You can't."

"But I have to. Otherwise, I mean, Leila . . . they're just going to be producing all these creepy devices and gadgets so that people can have, like, sex with centaurs."

"Centaurs!?"

Sloane fell silent, clocked by the temptation in her sister's voice. It was true then: Sloane was losing her cool factor.

"Sloanie, I'm kidding. It's terrible, what you're telling me," Leila said. "But you're . . . listen, you know I don't know anything about this kind of stuff, but you've got something special. You always have. Remember when you told me you knew exactly what kind of paintings Mom would do after Dad died? I mean, it was uncanny."

Sloane leaned against a stranger's car, unimpressed, if touched, by her sister's attempt at flattery. "It wasn't really. Those tiny paintings just gave her a sense of control."

"It was *spooky*, Sloane. Some archaic Indian tradition and you called it. Listen, I don't really understand *what* you do, but I know you're good at it. For what that's worth."

"Thank you," Sloane said, wanting to add that it was worth a lot.

"And you know, you shouldn't have to feel—I wish you'd told me sooner, that things were the way they are. Why don't you . . . come with us? I know Mom told you you were invited. Especially now."

"You guys don't really want me there. You're just being nice."

"Well, I don't know. It sounds like you need help."

Sloane felt suddenly defensive, wanted to say, *Would you not love me if I didn't?* But it was true, it was the truth of it. She needed help.

Sloane watched a parking attendant accept another pair of keys. Why not do it, join the ranks of people telling taxi drivers to take them to JFK?

"Leilee," Sloane asked meekly, "when's your due date again?"

"February fourth."

Sloane nodded silently, as if her sister could see. "I don't know about coming down there. I don't want to . . . intrude. But what if, what if we did something for Dad? In December, when you're back. Do you guys still do Remo's?"

Remo's had been one of their father's favorite restaurants: a dark, Italian steakhouse way up on Long Ridge Road with prehistoric lobsters scuttling in an aquarium and entrées that came with tinfoil baked potatoes bursting from the heat. When she'd been little, they always went there for his birthday. Filet mignon and Shirley Temples, a tiramisu cake roll. She knew her family had been going there on the anniversary of Peter's death for sixteen years now—since she'd left for France.

"It closed," Leila said. "Two years ago."

"Oh," Sloane said sadly, her shoulders slumping against yet another loss.

"So we've just been doing it at Mom's."

"Right. Well . . . if there's room for me then, if you want to ask Mom . . ."

"Sloane," Leila said, her voice changed. "There's *room*."

Sloane stayed silent several beats.

"Leila?" Sloane asked, after a silence. "Thanks for answering the phone."

"Well, make it ring more often. Listen, I gotta get back. Harvey's giving me the drowning man wave. We've basically lost Mom. You send her to Starbucks for plane snacks and she ends up buying fifteen Christmas mugs."

Sloane laughed.

"I'll call you when we get there," Leila said. "And think about it. Come."

Sloane nodded into space again, almost hypnotized by the fact she might.

"Okay," Sloane said. "Give my love to everyone. Tell everyone I love them. And, um, happy Thanksgiving."

"Happy Thanksgiving to you, too."

When Sloane hung up, she stared forlornly into her phone's screen, wishing that she could be teleported through it to her sister's side. Apple juice on the kids' chins, doughnut crumbs under fingers, an entire tote of toys that would not be played with in-flight. Instead, she got a push notification that #sexisdead was the fourth trending topic in the nation. Roman's article had gone live.

24

Too cold to stay outside in the parking lot, Sloane took refuge in the nearest café and sequestered herself on a stool with a hot tea and her phone. Sitting alone and isolated was a bad place for her to be as Roman's words washed over the country, but that Wednesday was a catch-up day for her—with most people running to catch planes or already on them, she had devoted the entire day to making amends with Daxter and answering e-mails, tasks which seemed respectively impossible now.

It had only broken thirty minutes earlier, but "After God Goes Sex" had one hundred and forty-seven comments on *The New York Times* already. Six thousand, three hundred and thirty-three mentions on Twitter. And surely, scores to come. Sloane set her jaw in hopes that she'd find the words of people outraged, but those who disagreed with Roman were few and far between.

I would rather masturbate than have sex with someone ALWAYS. Masturbation is the time-saver of my life. I'm a really busy man and I work my ass off, and when I have free time (which is hardly EVER), I think I work hard enough that I should be able to do whatever I want. All day I do things for other people. After masturbating, I can get take-out. I don't have to talk to anybody else.

Finally, a fast I can support! If a penetration hiatus can lead to selfish, ignorant people having fewer children, then I hope that all the yuppies will go from being gluten-free to sex-free.

I think self-love is the most important thing to start with. You can't love anyone else until you love yrself, and anyway, if you've ever seen it, seminal fluid is gross.

I love being penetrated! I think this article is a joke! None of you have ever had good sex, clearly! I hope all the stupid people saying that sex is over get a dildo up their ass!

Sloane took a moment to bemoan the rape promoters: the immortal newts of online bogs. But even their blind enthusiasm for physical violence paled in comparison to the majority of commenters who wanted no physicality at all.

I have been feeling over sex FOREVER. It's, like, what's new? I can tell you with no regret that online is where I live. It's where I have my best sex, it's where I have my fantasies. It's where I have my best orgasms, too.

No sex is the safest sex. Save yourself for God!

In an age of rampant disease and overpopulation, I think this article is very sensible. In the eighties, people learned just how much trouble can come from sexual encounters, but I think people are only now really seeing the light in terms of germs.

The photographs of parasitic orbits of subway bacteria bloomed into Sloane's mind. All those beautiful netherworlds created from the prints of people's hands on subway poles. Germs could be disgusting, sure. But germs were human life.

omg Roman Bellard I love ur Zentai series. I would totally have virtual sex w/U any time U WANT!!!

Sloane shook her head, her tea forgotten. *And we're off,* she thought.

Roman Bellard is married to a famous American, you guys. I read her article about reproduction as environmental terrorism, and as someone who has a next-door neighbor with three toddlers, I have seen terrorism myself! ☺ *Anyway, I think the two of them are really on to something. It took people a while to get used to recycling bins, but I think everyone will come around to sustainable sex, too =O. It's too bad that the author didn't list any places where we can go for augmented adult fun, or maybe they don't exist yet. I don't know, I'm just starting out exploring "sexuality" online. Neo-sensualists, unite!* ☺

Reading this, and other jubilatory embraces of a post-sexual existence, it occurred to Sloane that she might not have the liver strength for this millennium. But as much as people's pigheadedness made her want to crumple, this was not the time to back down. If she really thought—if she *really* thought—that the greater part of humanity was going to turn against technology in favor of physical connectedness again, then this was a now-or-never time to let her thoughts be known. Dax hadn't fired her, and she hadn't quit. Certainly, he had a demented sense of ethics and an equally demented agenda, bringing Roman onto the payroll, but Jin was right—her life wasn't over. Nor was her career.

Sloane headed back to the office, a reinforced energy charging through her. *Fuck* Roman, and fuck Mammoth's dehumanizing products: doing her job, her real one, would be her best revenge. Sloane was feeling buoyant and indomitable until she made it back to the headquarters. As she walked through the lobby, people adjusted their postures, cut conversations short. She saw side-eyes and heard whispering, people pointed at their tablets. Everyone who hadn't known about her connection to the "Sex Is Dead" author did now.

This suspicion was confirmed by the barrage of e-mails and voice-mails needing attention at her desk. Sloane had barely sat down to steel herself to answer them when the phone calls started to come: Deidre, who had a reporter from *The Wall Street Journal* on hold; did she care to comment? Another call from *The New York Times*. Sloane was taken aback—and not a little impressed—with how quickly things were moving. She knew that things went viral, knew *how* things went viral, but she'd never been a part of the virality herself. It was indeed a sickness, quickly come upon her. All she wanted to do was fall to the ground.

But there were inquiries to answer, comments to refuse. The e-mails kept on pinging. The Mammothers were "reaching out" and "checking in," "following up" and "circling back" regarding Roman's article. The e-mails came in various lengths and tonalities but they all had the same question: If sex is dead, what now?!

The Mammothers' embrace of Sloane's touch-centric agenda had been temporary and tentative: they were throwing themselves with pent-up unreservedness toward a post-sexual bent. Freedom from sexuality was the new sexual radicalism. Who knew?

From Jones, the most vocal member of the beauty team: *Dax and I were thinking in light of your husband's article that it might be really fun to throw together a few "cybersexy" look tutorials for responsive virtual tech fans? LMK? We'd like this to happen while there's buzz!*

More damning, Allison had written her on behalf of the electronics department: Allison, her open-minded, rarity of a mom. Her inquiry at least had the tact to be unsettled: *Hi there, Sloane. How are you? Sorry to bother right before Thanksgiving, but when/if you get a chance, we'd like your take on how we can incorporate the "onanism" trend evoked in your husband's article into our Denizen line of electronics? Some of us were thinking we need to expand from the kitchen to the bedroom. What kind(s) of electronic conveniences would virtual sex aficionados need, etc. I really don't know the first thing about this kind of lifestyle, so your input is much needed. lmk?*

And even from Andrew, in the furniture design department, someone who had also come around to humanity and warmth: *Hey Sloane, reaching out regarding our bed catalogue. Most of our images have couples in them reading on their tablets, but with Roman's article, do you think featuring single sleepers (with virtual reality gear on or something?) would be more on trend? Online catalogue needs to be shot soon, let me know?*

Let me know. Just checking. Can we talk? *Certainly,* Sloane wanted to reply. *Let's talk about the fact that Roman Bellard is not my husband, not my collaborator, not even my roommate anymore.* But it didn't matter what people thought she and Roman were. Such labels would be lost in the retreating flow of semantics—what mattered now was the revelation that cool kids were done with intercourse. How could Mammoth make money off of people shunning sex?

With more sex! Sloane wanted to shout. The end of sex means the return of sex, how could people not see this? If hemlines are long one season, in two years they'll be long again. People were going to tap and swipe their way through at least three more years of self-obsession before waking up to the debilitated state of their relationships in the real world. And then?

Sloane took a break from the pinging and the typing to check on Roman's article again. Three hundred and seven comments, number-two trending topic on Twitter. Her stomach sank.

"Sloane?"

Deidre entered her office looking like she was bearing bad news after a urine sample. She had a sheet of paper floating on top of her ever-present clipboard.

"I thought it might be easier to just give you these messages than filter the calls," she said.

While she was reading through them, Deidre scratched her wrist. Sloane could feel her discomfort to the Fahrenheit degree.

Thomas at *The Guardian*. Marvin at *The Atlantic*. Susan again from *The New York Times*. She looked up at Deidre, her eyes imploring.

"You know, we're not even together anymore?" Her voice sounded far away, even to herself.

Deidre nodded carefully. "I do."

"But everyone thinks we are." She looked down at the papers. "Everyone's so excited. What am I supposed to say?"

"Um, well, I imagine that that would take some thought," Deidre said, clearing her throat. "And, um, I didn't know if you'd heard, or rather, I'm pretty sure you hadn't, so I wanted to be the one to—" Deidre scratched her wrist again. "It's Roman. As I understand it, he was supposed to come in on Monday to do a presentation, which you were apprised of, but, um, now he's coming in today, actually, of which you were not."

Sloane widened her eyes further. When the hell had that been decided? She'd seen Dax two hours ago. Either he'd already called in Roman by then, or he'd decided to strike while the iron was hot.

"Today? With everybody leaving?" she asked, shocked.

"Um, it will be streamed live, I'm pretty sure?" Deidre said, sounding uncertain only for Sloane's benefit. "Because of the attention the article's getting, I believe Mr. Stevens felt that it was best to do it right away."

"No," Sloane said, her head shaking. "I get it. Of course. No, he didn't say a thing to me, but fine. Was I meant to prepare anything?"

"No," said Deidre, her eyes jumpy. "It's—it's just him."

Sloane absorbed this, and Deidre watched it happen. She couldn't think of a single expected thing to say.

"For what it's worth," Deidre accorded, her color rising, "I want you to know that a lot of people believe in the things you're saying."

"Well, apparently I haven't been saying them loudly enough," Sloane said, looking dejectedly at the piece of paper with all the journalists' names on it.

"But with the suggestion boxes, and the time-outs with the phones?" Deidre attempted. "I hear things. A lot of people are really grateful that you're here."

"Really?"

She watched Deidre parse out her next words. "The thing that you said at Sparkhouse about people . . . paying to be hugged?" She put her arms around herself, seemingly to stop herself from talking. "I don't think that's crazy. Sometimes I go to the hairdresser's when I don't even need to. After a bad day."

Sloane looked at Deidre wholly, looked at her entirely, seeing not an exhausted executive assistant but a hopeful woman in a hairdresser's chair, her eyes closing against the comfort of someone else's hands upon her, memories of dish soap bubbles and shared baths, the irreplaceable intimacy of someone bathing you.

That had been Deidre's note then; her confession. *Sometimes I go to the hair salon just to get my head touched.* There were other people holding private hurts across this office, and some of them, also, had dared to speak up.

I wish I had better handwriting. But it hurts my hand.

I want to call my friends more. But I never call.

I like wearing long johns because it feels like someone loves me.

"I think . . . I guess what I'm saying is that there are a lot of people on your side."

Sloane stared at her, incredulous, until she started to believe it.

"In that case," Sloane said, standing, "let's check out the competition." She extended her arm to be linked through with the messenger's.

There was no more nervousness, this time, when Deidre smiled.

25

On Sloane's way down to the cafeteria where Roman's presentation was being held, she was congratulated by people she didn't remember meeting on the success of her article—they used the plural form of "you": "Such an interesting article," "Your article was so great." Pop culture had roped her into a twosome with Roman, and because she hadn't gone public with their separation, she was in that twosome, still. The anti-mom and anti-dad had a viral contagion on their hands, one that would bring Mammoth tons of press.

It would be easy to let people continue making these assumptions. Not to mention lucrative. And Sloane was private about her personal life—she'd never used a publicist, she never granted the kinds of profiles magazines were always calling her for. But at that moment, joining the swarms of people clasping mugs of coffee, heading for the cafeteria where the presentation would take place, she envied the clean mechanics of a public relations firm. All she would have to do was put out a statement and step back to watch it spread. *After ten years of collaboration and domestic partnership, Sloane Jacobsen and Roman Bellard have amicably parted ways.* And then the firm would put out another carefully worded press release explaining why Roman had joined Sloane at Mammoth, and Sloane could forever rely on others to explain her messy life. But no: maybe she wasn't as quick to respond as she could be, but she wasn't about to start *paying* someone to speak up for her.

Upon a makeshift platform that looked more like a pulpit, Dax was saying how grateful he was that Roman could make it in on such short notice; grateful, too, that everyone was able to gather right before vacation. He winked, he smiled, he had a lot to be thankful for.

Roman was wearing his purple Zentai suit, the one he saved for lectures. Sloane wondered if he'd worn it over to the office, or changed in one of the company restrooms. Looking at him up on stage, flawless and feline in his Zentai silhouette, Sloane felt strangely calm. Come what may, she wasn't living with him anymore and she never would again. He seemed less now like someone who had hurt and disappointed her than a whacky upstart.

"So without further ado," Dax was concluding, having cinched his introduction, "I'll let our neo-sensualist take it away. Everyone, the author of today's trending 'Sex Is Dead' piece, Roman Bellard!"

Sloane noted real enthusiasm in the crowd's yelps. Yes, well, people initially tripped over themselves for optical head-mounted displays also, and look how that turned out. These guys would probably stay onboard for augmented virtual sexuality experiences until they were caught jacking off to a fairy hologram by their landlord mom.

Roman raised his hand in the direction of the applause to both acknowledge and abate it. With his compromised vision, Roman probably couldn't see her. This both pleased and worried her. She knew he valued her opinion, and that his ego would be crushed if she hadn't stood in to listen, but she also knew he might get more carried away than usual if he thought she wasn't there.

"Thank you, Daxter, for having me!" Roman yelled to his brand-new devotees. "This is such a welcome. Such a day. Such a day to be much more than our bodies!"

People cheered again, but Sloane just rolled her eyes. God, people were so willing to eat up anything French.

"Many people ask me, 'Roman, what is *neo-sensualist*,'" he continued, "so I think we start with that? The new sensuality, it is wonderful. It is a pursuit of sexuality that goes *beyond* being touched. We're in the digital age here, but our sexuality is still analog. But this is not how it should be. The new sensuality—the new sexuality—is *post*-touch."

Sloane steeled her stomach against the rising temperature in the room. Eyes were open, mouths wide in pretty o's—the Mammothers were all ears. Sloane had hoped to see more skepticism, more indigestion, frankly, at the idea of no more sex, but this was a generation tuned to fasts. They had been raised on a diet of withholding—free from additives, free from BPA, free from communal love.

"We have only to look around us to see that the post-sex revolution is already under way. Whoever has that clicky thingy, could you do the slide?" Roman paused as the task was executed, the screen behind him coming to life. "An undesired side effect, the not seeing," he said, touching his sightless face to a chorus of laughs.

Once the slide was up, he turned referentially to a massive, blown-up image of two people kissing with tongue.

"Penetration as parable. Penetration as farce. The polemic French director Gaspar Noé's latest movie, *Love*, debuted in 3-D," he said, holding the mike up to the place his mouth would be if it wasn't spandexed. "3-D is for action movies. And thrillers. And now it is for porn. And if it *is* for porn"—he made a motion for the next slide and another still appeared, this one, the head of a penis positioned in front of a bright nipple—"that means that we are making fetish of the normal because it isn't normal anymore."

Sloane felt a roiling in her belly. On this, he was right. This was one of Roman's academic comments that used to thrill her—thrilled her still. The canonization of the normal, it was something they would have talked about all night, before, cycling through the examples that were, in fact, around them, thinking up places where they could give joint lectures. And now what? Was Sloane normal? Or was normal the new weird?

With Roman's presentation fully under way, people started to look around, as surreptitiously as possible, for Sloane. She could almost read the thoughts going through the heads of people with their embarrassed smiles; the assumptions that Roman and Sloane's sex life involved the kinds of kinks they couldn't fathom: inversion tables, drilldos, dental forceps, VR porn with pumped-in, feral scents. *So this is what it means to be an anti-mom*, they must be thinking. Bondage gear and intellectual conversation and interactive VR sex.

She counteracted the attention by keeping hers on the stage, purposely not looking for the people she still considered sympathetic to her cause: Mina, Deidre, Andrew, and Jin, of course, whom she had to work so hard not to look for she was burning calories.

But Jin—persistent carer—was looking for her. While Roman documented the other ways in which the normal had become fetishized—regular human activity tracked through wearables, the iconization of selfies—she sensed Jin claiming a place beside her. Her body divined sideways, like a fork tuning toward water.

"So, wow," he whispered, their elbows almost touching.

"Yeah," she answered. "I've got a lot on my plate."

"I had no idea," he said, quietly. "Until I read it. I had no idea."

She'd managed so far to avoid Jin's eyes, talking to him while staring straight ahead, but she could feel him looking at her, insisting that she fall to him as Roman clicked through another slide. The current one showed a generic image of average-looking people eyeing each other in a bar with an almost palpable lack of hope.

"This is a portrait of our sexual culture now," Roman was saying, his voice insinuating a pout. "It is my belief that, with Mammoth at the helm, you can take people to the place where they are *surpassing* their sexual potential, instead of doing . . . this." He pointed in the vague direction of the slide, leading to more laughs.

"And then there is the Zentai," Roman continued, snapping a stretch of clingy fabric away from his arm. "I have long dreamt of putting artificial intelligence into second skins, until, of course, we can actually encode it in ourselves! In the meantime, you can imagine the potential, erogenous and otherwise, of second-skin applications that allow us to *become* the device."

"Sloane?" Jin insisted. She finally turned to face him.

"You all right?" he asked.

Douceur, douceur—it was such a tender word in French. Sweetness. Mild gentleness, flowers and perfume. In English, the way Jin's eyes were looking at her would be described as "concerned," but in French, this was attentiveness, this was empathy. To Sloane, his compassion fueled the magnetism between them, leaving her wanting to touch his arm, his shoulder, touch any part of him.

"I don't know," she whispered honestly. "I might be." She tried to laugh, but finally shrugged with something nearing lassitude. "I've got some work to do,"

Meanwhile, Roman moved to another slide. Up came the image of a lone man staring through a narrow viewfinder with a cord running along his head. Sloane recognized the logo of one of the sex toys Roman had had delivered to their apartment on their first day in New York. He started going on about the VR Tenga, how freedom from sex was The Next Big Thing.

"In cyberspace we can even become immortalized!" Roman was going on. "With responsive virtual technology, no one can put a limit on us except our imaginations. We can live out fetishes that society has punished. The sexual revolution—and I am proof of it—is happening online."

Somewhere in the front, somebody started clapping. Someone behind them started clapping, too. Sloane found herself nodding to an inaudible beat, incredibly relieved. If this was all he had, she could beat it. She knew Roman—*knew* him—and he didn't have anything but charisma to back any of this up.

But then Daxter took the stage, beaming at his sudden prodigy, and Sloane remembered that Roman didn't *need* data, that Mammoth would find some for him, and if it didn't exist, they would create some by producing virtual reality products that people *had* to have. It had been posited to her before that trends no longer existed, but were only manufactured, and although Sloane had long held that this wasn't true, she had to cede that in some cases—in this case—it very well could be.

"I love this," Dax proclaimed onstage, too enthused to keep himself from slapping Roman's back. "So many products are coming to mind I'm about to take him hostage. You'll hear more about this next week, but I didn't want you all to leave for the holiday without hearing this from me: we're super lucky to have Roman joining the team to get us ready for ReProduction." He threw his arm around the Roman silhouette. "Alongside Sloane," he added.

That smarted. She had not said yes to her and Roman leading separate teams. But Roman had said yes, and—apparently—that was enough.

"Errrgh, yes," Daxter was going, peering out at a hand waving from the audience. "I wasn't really opening this to questions, but, um, sure."

Sloane stood on tiptoe to see a T-shirted man near the front. Dax handed him the mike.

"Yeah, I, um, I don't know if Sloane is here or not?" the guy said, addressing his question to Roman. "But my understanding is that . . . is that you're a couple?"

Sloane's blood stopped moving through her body the way it should.

A new flock of people craned to find her in the back. Up on stage, Dax's expression tightened. Who knew what was going on underneath Roman's suit.

"And I guess my question is, well, how to reconcile what Sloane has been telling us, which is that people are going to want, well, like real *people* stuff again, against what you're saying, which is that our lives, like, even our sex lives, are going to be fully lived online?"

Sloane's lungs felt like they were holding too much air. Jin shifted at her side.

Dax hurriedly retrieved the microphone.

"Yes, well," Roman started, curving to the mike that Dax hadn't actually offered, "in market research, we always found that it was difficult for women to talk about sexuality without the great emotion."

"You fucking fuck," Sloane said, on held breath.

"—there is always that, how would you put it, that certain tenderness? They get attached. And of course, they can be mothers! Which makes objectivity so hard—"

Dax grabbed back the mike. Meanwhile, caterpillars of lights had started dancing before Sloane's eyes; she felt like she might faint. Had Roman just announced that she was craving motherhood to *the entire crowd*?

"It is probably a gender thing, but yes," Roman continued, even though Dax was clearly trying to stop him. "I think this is probably the only time that we have not agreed on trends!"

This freaking show pony, Sloane thought, growing livid. *If this misogynistic ding-dong thinks he's going to posit himself as the big fucking kahuna of trend forecasting, he's got another thing coming to him.* And so, she raged, did Dax.

Sloane grabbed her cell phone, dashed off an e-mail that she *would* accept Daxter's proposal to do a double-headed consultancy for the ReProduction summit.

Then she turned to Jin. "You tell me if this windbag says another thing about my womb," she insisted, furious.

"I will. I'm on it." Jin hadn't been exposed yet to the fire she had in her, but he was smiling, nevertheless, to see it back. "What are you going to do?" he asked.

"I'm gonna go back to my office and do my fucking job."

26

Sloane zoomed across the various floors back to her office, determined to stay in forward motion. She drafted an e-mail to Deidre requesting that she tell all the reporters who had requested comments and interviews that she was available for neither at this time. Then she called Mina and asked her to come up.

"Sit down," Sloane said, when Mina came in, looking both flattered and surprised. "I'm sure you have places to go. I just wanted to tell you—the idea you brought up the first day? Of a second-skin wearable that tracks how little we're touched? I wanted to tell you that I'm going to be championing ideas like this. In case you have some more."

"You *are*?" Mina said, a sudden loosening in her face.

"Yes," she said, affirmative. "Dax has got a new figurehead for his tech agenda, so I can take another tack. My view of the future is that people are going to want to be *people* again, don't you think?"

After Mina left, promising to report back to Sloane about whatever was trending or unusual in Frederica, Delaware, where she'd be spending her Thanksgiving (which sounded more to Sloane like a sassy seven-year-old than an actual place), Sloane called up Allison in electronics and got her voicemail.

"Allison," Sloane started, "I wanted to get back to you about expanding the Denizen line of electronics to the bedroom. I don't know whether you were at Mr. Bellard's discussion this afternoon, but he is, in fact, being brought on as a consultant to the ReProduction project, and given his enthusiasm for augmented reality, he's probably a better candidate to answer your questions about virtual sex tools in the homescape. As for me, I'm actually envisioning a return to physical intimacy, so I don't feel comfortable giving you advice about a trend that doesn't have sustainability in the marketplace."

She hung up, noisily. Then she tried Andrew Willett, from furniture.

"Oh, Sloane," he said, stumbling into surprise once he realized who was calling him. "Hello!"

"Hi there," she said, brightly. "I didn't want you to take off for vacation before I addressed the question you sent through. I think if you really want to make a splash with your bed catalogue, feature a family: two parent figures, a child, all of them reading books in bed. Or one could be reading a newspaper. But no screens anywhere."

"No . . . no screens?"

"No, none." She turned her hand over and investigated her nail polish, a vivid turmeric.

"Um, I can try it, but . . . it can't be like a man and woman parent. We'll get sued."

"Caretakers, Andrew. It doesn't matter if they're two women, two men, two black bears. In fact, you might have great success if they *are* wild animals. The idea is to create a vision of warmth and love. People will resonate with it. Trust me. Try a comp. Focus-group it. I bet you'd be surprised by the kind of reaction you get. Who the hell wants to see people electronically paying their bills in bed? Independent bookstores are thriving. Reading is making a comeback. Print will make a comeback, too."

"Oh, um, well, okay?" he said to her deluge of words. "I don't know whether I can convince the team, though."

"You don't have to. That's my job. Just come up with some comps and I'll take care of the rest after the break."

"Okay," said Andrew, and then, brightening, "Okay!"

She wished him a good vacation, he said he was off to Kansas City. It was inspiring, all of the places that real people were from.

Sloane's phone kept vibrating with text messages, so when she got off the line with Andrew, she finally checked her phone. Her sister had sent her a half-dozen all-caps outrages: she'd read Roman's piece.

"Masturbation, of both the cerebral and the physical sort, is the preferred release of the digitally experienced"?! I WISH I'D NEVER 'DIGITALLY EXPERIENCED' HIS PIECE!

SO PEOPLE CAN DATE PORN NOW? OMG WHY DID I HAVE CHILDREN IF THEY'RE GOING 2 GROW UP 2 THINK LIKE THIS

Sloane warmed, picturing her sister fending off her children's pleas for more peanuts or pretzels in order to send these texts. This was the Leilee she'd grown up with: someone who would literally run off of a soccer field in the middle of a game if her sister needed help.

On her way out, she stopped by Deidre's office to wish her a happy Thanksgiving (Deidre was headed home to Ann Arbor, "tree town," was what she called it), then continued downstairs, where she ran into Jin in the copy room, again.

She'd come to fetch an article about the rebirth of an ancient Mayan trend that saw people wearing live insects as brooches; she felt it played into the back-to-the-body movement she was seeing, although she didn't know how yet. Something about the dirt of insects, where they came from, loam. Ashes to ashes. Beautiful death.

"So this is kinda our place, huh?" Jin said when she came in.

"Well, it has such pleasant lighting," Sloane quipped, amidst the electric zaps and zooms.

Jin didn't say anything further about Roman's lecture, nor his sellout comment about Sloane wanting kids. There were other people in the copy room with them, although her attention on Jin was so complete, she hadn't noticed who.

They agreed to talk over the holiday without saying this out loud. They shook hands, as colleagues, over a deal that no one else in the copy room had heard them make, and for the rest of the weekend Sloane would be agitated by the unfinishedness of that contact.

Sloane was operating at a significant deficit during the Thanksgiving weekend—she was without her car. Whether it was happenstance or further proof that Dax had turned against her, Anastasia had been pulled out of service to get a holiday decal applied on her hood. Sloane assumed that a lot of corporate energy had gone into deciding what decal would say "Christmas" without saying "Christ." Accordingly, from the drawings that had been presented to her from HR, it looked like she'd get Anastasia back with a cluster of bright jelly beans topped with pure white snow.

Once home, Sloane admired the architecture of her life without Roman: the apartment was clean and hopeful, bright. A rite of purification, Sloane doused the kitchen with Clorox—the industrial kind that would kill both the good and bad bacteria, not the brand she usually used, formulated with geraniums and hope. She scoured the floors, she changed the sheets on the bed, she did a load of laundry. And while she was engaged in this liturgy of housework, she thought about her snouts.

Her consulting firm back in Paris had taken its cue from the other trend forecasting agencies she'd worked for in the past: low overhead, wide reach. Aside from a Parisian personal assistant (who had taken advantage of Sloane's New York interlude to "re-center" at an agrotourism retreat in Spain), Sloane worked alone, but she did have a coterie of experts that she called on when she needed insight, or skills she didn't have: such as a working knowledge of Excel.

Her snouts (Sloane had an allergic reaction to the term "cool hunters") were located all over the world: Melbourne, Shanghai, Des Moines. Sometimes, Sloane found her human catalysts through references, but most often, she knighted them during her own travels. Kai, for example, was a sneaker designer in Leeds whom she'd met at a tiny store he owned while she was in the city for a typography conference ("Is Helvetica the Next Helvetica?" was the panel she was on). Nelly, a pink-haired, femme lesbian, was a bartender in Kansas City and a relentless optimist. Sometimes Sloane collaborated with people because of their dispositions, not because of anything they had achieved. Sometimes she clicked with people because they were kind, or simply sensitive, or possessed the exceedingly rare ability to keep their eyes up when they walked around.

The best thing about her snouts was that they lived across a myriad of cultures and time zones, so there was always someone to call upon when she needed inspiration. Sure, she now had a firm handle on her premonitions, but she knew it couldn't hurt to test other people's waters.

The first call she made was to Kai; he'd always been her favorite. He possessed that seductive emotional amalgam of the young and brilliant: he was both composed and wired. If Sloane had a knack for predicting trends, Kai was someone who set them. He'd single-handedly ignited the black velvet sneaker fervor that had swept across Europe several years ago.

She reached him in what sounded like a pounding restaurant.

"Kai," she said, used to delivering her needs in sound bites. He was always on the move somewhere, in a taxi, in a pub. "Give me your weirdest. I've got a crisis over here."

"Okay," Kai said, the clamor dimming as he moved to a quieter spot. Most likely, a restroom. Sloane heard somebody flush.

"So people are really into bells," he said.

"Bells?"

"Yeah, like on clothing. Like, literally: silver bells."

Sloane pulled her knees up on the couch. "Ugh," she said, coming up empty. Unconnected dots.

"I guess they're kinda talismanic? Inspired by Tibetan percussion sticks. People are wrapping them around their sneakers, they're hanging from backpacks. Appearing on necklaces."

"Okay," Sloane stalled. "But what about people-to-people stuff? Are you seeing anything in terms of . . . like, physicality?"

"Oh, gah, no," he answered, with a laugh. "Unless you count hoverboards as physical. Better to show off your trainers with, yeah?"

Sloane hung up, disgruntled. Her information hunger was related to a very specific need. It was nutritional, and urgent. Like a system low on iron, she'd know the right information when she hit it, and bells weren't it.

Next up, she called her friend Lance who worked in real estate in Malmö, Sweden. "Outdoor pizza ovens," he answered unequivocally, when she inquired about the latest craze, "and sunken fire pits."

"Sunken fire pits?" she repeated. Was this what the financially independent equated with adventure? Having heat outside?

After her relative flare-out with Kai, Sloane didn't want to ask the others whether they were specifically seeing anything intimacy-related—she didn't want their answers to be biased. But she didn't have to worry. The information she was getting back was resolutely anti-touch.

Ethan, in Dallas, told her about the popularity of an app named

"RunPee" that let you know the stretches of time during a movie that had been crowdsourced as "nonessential" so you could run and pee. Apparently, the app was so successful, bathroom lines had started accumulating during the same moments in newly released films, leading to the app's purchase by the talent behemoth William Morris, who wanted access to the pee-break data so that they could track where interest waxed and waned in their clients' films.

Lulu in Los Angeles told Sloane about sensory deprivation data sharing—the broadcasting of blood pressure levels and heart rate information while stressed-out Angelenos were submerged in the lightless, soundproof isolation tanks that had become a popular way to digitally cleanse.

"But you're not digitally cleansing if you're sharing biometrics with your social media base," Sloane interjected.

"I *guess* so," said Lulu, who sounded like she was chewing hair, "but at the same time, you get props for going from the most stressed out to the calmest. It's kinda a thing."

Sloane made a mental note to kick Lulu out of her stable. She'd been a reliable (and sane) source of wellness information until she'd gone in for hot yoga.

Sloane's motley team talked to her of fish species that communicated by electrical impulses and a clamoring for egg cozies; the ubiquitousness of Jerusalem artichokes and adult coloring books.

But it was only Rufus in New Delhi who gave Sloane something she could work with.

"Okay, so it's a Pointless button. It started as an app, and the app failed, but a guy here resurrected it. You just poke and poke and poke at your phone, and eventually, after an unpredictable number of attempts, something completely random will emerge. An image. A sound. A photo of a camel."

"Discovery," Sloane said. "Hope."

"Well, yeah, exactly," said Rufus, who sounded like he was drinking something. It was the middle of the night in New Delhi, the doughy part of the evening where your actual thoughts were weirder than your dreams. Rufus was a programmer who slept during the day.

"I mean, it replicates what we're all hoping, which is that something great and beautiful is going to come out of our phones."

This, Sloane could move forward with. A Pointless button was a digital cry for help. People were turning to technology to lead them to salvation, but it wasn't working. Sloane didn't often take photos with her cell phone, but the last one she had came to her in a mental flash. It was a picture of some street art she'd seen in the Belleville district of Paris a couple of days before she'd left. A single question, scrawled: *Can our humanity save our inhumanity?*

Resoundingly, Sloane felt: yes.

That night, Sloane burrowed into her own version of a sensory deprivation chamber, a sort of bedded deep think she resorted to when there was too much in her head.

Free of clothes, shades drawn, the refrigerator unplugged (it made these gurgling sounds that drove her bonkers), with a lavender sleep mask wrapped around her eyes, she got under the covers and smushed her face between four pillows. From there, with her body anchored under heavy blankets, she floated between her experts' input and the thought waves that had been currenting through her before Roman's article emerged.

Visions came and went like shooting stars across her mind space. As did memories, unanswered work e-mails. False urgencies. Regrets.

She saw hand sanitizer bottles dangling from purses.

People liking the profiles of people they were never going to date.

A renaissance in small talk; how-to books and conversation tutorials that taught you how to chat.

A market rise in flashlights. Flashlights. Why?

Reading under covers. Reading in a tent.

Camping.

Areas without cell phone service. De-connectivity. De-activation of accounts.

Unbuying. Unfindability. An increase in runaways.

The opposite of bullying. An emphasis on friend-making. An emphasis on slow friendship.

Agendas without dates inside. A trend in "underplanning."

A relaunch of the "reach out and touch someone" slogan from AT&T.

The tunic she'd left at the dry cleaners and forgotten to pick up.

Images bumped up against images, slid past each other like fish. The sifting was occurring, pictures that held no resonance were dissipating into the blue. It took effort to keep the superficial things from surfacing, remnants of to-do lists, anxieties and gripes, but if she floated there long enough, the hierarchy of her mind would find its natural form. The small comets continued. Squiggly dancing seahorses and sudden yellow sparks.

Dancing lessons. Self-smelling as an indicator of health. Renewed faith in pheromones instead of dating sites to indicate sexual compatibility.

A coming craze for scuba diving.

Domestic birds and ant farms. A clamor for new pets.

A baby born with webbed fingers, an evolutionary edge. Proof that humans didn't need separated digits any longer, just a nub to scroll.

Horseback riding. Dog sledding. A marked interest in sports that melded man and beast.

A celebration of humility. Undersharing. A need for privacy, again.

Sloane's head filled with the feather music of a mind falling asleep. There would be a quest for unheard notes and syncopations that made the mind work, the soul travel. There would be music labs where people would listen to dissonant chords and complex tonalities to re-awaken neural pathways that had been overly conditioned to the melodically predictable pop music of the modern age. There would be handwriting classes and manners clubs where people practiced etiquette norms to keep decorum alive. She had forgotten to find a dentist in the United States. Or a gynecologist, for that matter. It had been good talking to her sister. She needed to call her sister, and her mother, more.

When Sloane awoke the next morning, the city was blanketed in white. It was early, not yet dawn: there would be flights delayed and sedans whose tires spun brown tracks into the snow. There would be the potential of snowmen and snow balls—crystalline ice water sculpted between gloves.

There would be preheated ovens and there would be small mouths. There would be the inedibility of root vegetables turned to lush and sweetness through the application of heat. There would be entrance-ways overfilled with clothes, and boots with snow melting down into the cracks of floorboards. There would be music. There wouldn't be music. There would be pop-up screens and adverts, political agendas, there would be things sold.

There would be more snow, and there would be more silence.

There would be calm, again.

27

The next morning, feeling clearer, cleaner, after her mindsink, Sloane had felt the urgency to execute the time-honored, last-ditch effort known as the Dramatic Gesture, and board a plane for Florida. She'd do what she'd been avoiding for so many years now: physically—and emotionally—show up.

Best-laid plans, indeed. She'd checked countless websites, made phone calls, had even tried Mammoth's travel division—there hadn't been a single plane to take. Nature, in its infinite superiority, had shown all of the East Coast the folly that was waiting until the fourth Thursday in November to show your family that you cared about them by dumping a historical amount of snow across the eastern seaboard.

All across the country, planes were grounded, indefinitely delayed. Turkeys overcooked while mothers checked and rechecked the flight status of children's airplanes. Beds that had been turned down for grandchildren went unslept in, guest towels unused. Overtime was accumulated by the harried airline staff, insults were vaulted, pleas proffered, egos checked. The would-be passengers' reasons for flying were many and persuasive: but Mother Nature, the great leveler, was hearing none of it. Anything that went up into the sky would not come down that day.

Once it really sunk in that she wasn't going to be able to get to Florida, her body felt heavy with both the relief and disappointment of not being able to make the surprise trip. Sloane lay in bed and considered how the stages of grief also applied to air travel: Denial, Anger, Bargaining, Depression, Acceptance. In a way, she was jealous that she wasn't stuck in an airport to watch beleaguered humans reach the fifth stage.

It would start with meal coupons being distributed. Lines, impossibly long ones, forming in front of Sbarro and Chick-fil-A. The rage and the indignation of the experience that would tighten people's bodies into clenched fists and tight jaws. Someone with a toddler—two toddlers, exhausted—would finally dare to ask if she couldn't cut ahead in the line, and the man she would have asked would be the wrong one: a businessman who had about three hours of vacation in his annual contract, an only son who hadn't seen his parents in Cincinnati since spring of the previous year, who had left the charger to his laptop in his checked suitcase—idiot!—who had only checked his luggage in the first place because he'd bought a lot of dress shirts for his father so that he'd look crisper, hale; his father who had called him Steven the other day (which wasn't his name, but his uncle's, who was three years dead), and with the delays, if he even *made* it to Cincinnati, he'd be there for such a piddling amount of time it would be more damaging to his parents than if he hadn't come at all. And now, when all he wanted was something greasy and off-diet, here was this woman with her oversized carry-ons and her troop of runny kids and their dirty T-shirt blankies, asking to cut in front of him.

This man was going to say no because of low blood sugar and exhaustion, and also frustration for the life he'd meant to make for himself (wife, children) but hadn't, and the one he wasn't going to reach by air (his father still had dimples when he smiled), when he was usurped by a woman who said, *Yes, come in front of me, I have little children, too.*

And she did have children, this woman who had let the line be cut, one of whom was an infant for whom she had a foldable cooler of frozen breastmilk in her checked bag which was, at that minute, probably thawing, which meant that all of the half hours she'd spent pumping in her sordid hotel guest room were for naught. Now the baby would have to have formula for the first time in its life because the breasts he needed were stuck in a fast-food line in Newark. Her husband would either weather the presentation of that formula with grace or it would be a hell-raising disaster. So many tiny big disasters, and nothing they could do but be nice to people, be patient with people, let them cut in line.

Yes, come in front of me started up a conversation about frustration that turned into one of thanks. The businessman, shamed by his neighbor's generosity, offered to hold one of the mother's bags while they all waited in line together, and what were they waiting for? Fried chicken wasn't good for you, they admitted, and yes it got you messy, but wasn't fried chicken—inherently—the *best?*

And elsewhere in the massive terminal, thronged with people using carry-ons as computer tables because all the chairs were full, a woman who had been on her way to Jamaica for a much-needed "girl's trip" with women who, like she was, were all three years into their divorces, a woman who was trying not to think about the cost (financially and emotionally) of every single hour that she wasn't getting sun, passed the spa booth that she'd remembered from the last warm-weather vacation she'd taken when her ex was still her husband, when they, too, had had a flight delayed and she'd suggested they both get massages to kick off their vacation, and he'd said they'd already paid enough for the vacation as it was.

Well, fuck Dale and his fall-over-if-you-blow-on-it spec house with the siding that he told everyone was wood when it was clear as day that it was vinyl, she was getting a mani-pedi.

And when the pedicurist touched Teresa's legs: one tap on her bared calf to say, *put your foot into the water*, when she cupped her hands around the woman's degraded plantar nerves and applied a thumb tip to a pressure point, Teresa's entire being filled with the bounty of this touch. The orchestrations it had necessitated for her to take five days off—Stella to her friend's house, Harry to his dad's— they all washed away from her with this warm support. So much so that when Teresa was coasting on the frequency of the relaxed and the manicurist asked if she'd like an extra ten-minute shoulder massage for fifteen dollars, Teresa felt the sun upon her and the coming warmth of her companions, the laughs, the confidences they'd share, the fact that it didn't matter that she was jiggly in her one-piece because she wasn't twenty, damn it, and also, deeper, truer: that she *deserved* to feel like she was special, deserved a little love, so she reached into her wallet for more cash.

Sloane could see all this, could feel the reluctant budding of humanity's best side, just as clearly as she could see the Toyota Camry far below her, skidding up 9th Street toward the dog park, past the Puerto Rican flags that were just tips now, prodding through the snow-capped azaleas of the community garden that the residents had to fight to protect from developers every year. She could feel the expelled breaths of people all across America realizing that that day, they weren't going to actualize their plans, the almost blissful absurdity that comes once you accept the fact that even with your phone and your tablet and your Wi-Fi–enabled thermostats, you don't have control, and that your mind—so tired, always on—is interpreting that sudden helplessness as the exact thing that you wanted.

28

The weekend was a long one. Sloane missed Jin. She missed her car. Plus, certain people weren't calling her back. She'd left "Happy Thanksgiving" messages for her mother and her sister, and after two days passed without any answer, her ego had been sore. *I actually tried to make it there*, she'd written in a group text to both of them. *Just so you know. I tried.*

Even Roman (who had continued with his frantic *I'm not sure why you're so upset / I thought you'd be excited for us* messages) had gone radio silent, too. If his onslaught of sudden television and radio appearances were anything to judge by (that long holiday weekend alone, he'd been on *The Today Show*, *The Tonight Show*, and had been booked for that week's *Give Me One More Second!*), he'd probably decided that he didn't need her—or her opinion of him—anymore.

In order to inoculate herself from the mushroom cloud of his relevance, Sloane had gone out to the movies—a luxury activity she rarely had time for. It had been rainy and cold, the city emptied of people who had other homes to go to, and—with her car still out of commission—she'd decided to catch a cab.

Regardless of the city you were in, taxis used to be safe places to turn inward and reflect, but now they were like being inside of a stimulation blender. Sloane spent the twenty-minute ride being jabbered at by the different images playing on the TV screen. One clip had even been of Roman on some show yip-yapping about the end of sensuality.

"I knew sensuality, *American* sensuality was over," Roman was saying, teeth gleaming over the mug bearing the show's logo, "when I was looking over materials for a potential teaching job. Here"—he pointed downward, as if he had planned on teaching from that very stage—"in America, they were sending me, I don't know how you call them. Manuals, yes? On sexual etiquette?" He opened his hands to explain the situation further.

"If I am having a one-on-one meeting with a student, the door must be open. And between the two of us, there must be three feet on the floor. If the student has his or her legs crossed, well!" he cried with emphasis. "Then I must be like this!" Here, he made a dramatic gesture of someone who was straitjacketed, to the studio audience's delight.

Sloane had started punching the digital Off button to wipe him from the screen, but every effort she made to turn the television off just seemed to make Roman louder.

"And so, really, Dina, you must admit that sexuality cannot live here," Roman was saying to the show's host, with a languid hand-twirl that encompassed the whole stage. "It doesn't have to! There is a lusher world, a wilder world, a more rewarding one online!"

"Excuse me?" Sloane had said, tapping against the Plexiglas that separated her from the cab driver. "I will *pay* you if you can find a way to keep this off."

"Huh?" he'd said, turning, pulling an earbud out of one ear. "Only card."

"You don't take cash?" Sloane asked.

"Just card." He put his earbud in again.

. . .

Monday couldn't arrive soon enough. Sloane rose early that morning, knowing that two things that recently solidified her had returned. The previous night, Jin had flown home from Seattle, richer in the knowledge that he did not like canoeing in November and that his divorced father was officially a catch.

"Not one but *two* women dropped him off sandwiches this morning," Jin said on one of the phone calls they'd enjoyed while apart. "They've got his fishing trips clocked."

In addition to having her love interest back on the same coast, she also had Anastasia by her side again, freshly decorated with her holiday decal.

"The perception I have of jelly beans is that they communicate 'Easter,'" Anastasia commented, when Sloane asked her what she thought of her new hood. "But mine is not to reason why."

"Lord Tennyson," Sloane had replied, continually impressed by the spectrum of her driver's cultural references.

While they headed across town, Sloane reacquainted herself with the stockpile of Dax missives in her phone. He'd been thrilled to hear that Sloane was game to do a double consultancy with Roman, and had been e-mailing her ideas over the weekend in stream-of-consciousness format:

I'm going to make a video for Monday morning to announce that Roman's coming on. (still in Aspen, gotta love the spring skiing in November, thank you climate change!) And to explain the direction forward: PRO-TECH and PRO-TOUCH.

As for the way we organize the ReProduction summit, maybe it's an actual debate? Or maybe we present the products for each side, and then we have a debate? I really like the idea of audience members being able to choose sides: we'll crowdsource the whole thing with social media metrics so we can see who's winning in real time. Oh, and I'm looking into legal with this, but I'm thinking we offer the whole thing on streaming . . . for $$.

Reading through Daxter's ideas again, Sloane's confidence had wavered: could she really stay involved in such a charade for the long haul? But then she thought back to all the notes that she'd been getting and the anecdotes she'd heard that weekend from her snouts, and she reminded herself that she'd built her reputation on identifying trends that she believed in before anyone else. Far-off ones. Far-fetched ones, but true, sustainable trends. To bow out now would not only thwart the people longing to return to a more personable way of life, but it would also be a disservice to herself. Did she really want her name attached to a batch of robotic "empathy toddlers" that would enable people to remote-control parenthood? Or did she want to talk about what she *really* saw coming, what she *really* thought would trend?

She ran her hands along Anastasia's leather seats and took in the "This Christmas, think about YOU" signs shining out of shops.

Pro-touch. Pro-technology. The only reason Daxter would even fathom giving people a chance to choose between the two camps is because he was certain she would lose. He would make her look ridiculous so that Mammoth's products and mission statement (*Delivering the World*®) felt more appealing and urgent than ever. Games and electronics, music, food and fashion, all of it delivered not to your *door*, but to the bowels of your smartphone. Your sex and love life, too. No. Sloane was going to stand up and announce that people were ready to separate their souls from their SIM cards.

What she wanted on the way to work was drumbeats. Tom-toms. A percussion-heavy fighting song. And then she remembered that she had a virtual wealth of knowledge on the driver's side.

"Anastasia?" Sloane ventured. "Do you know any songs?"

"Like a lullaby?" Anastasia asked.

"Well, I don't know, really," Sloane said, embarrassed to ask for a Russian song per her secret fantasy of Anastasia's roots. She wanted to believe in an Anastasia who knew songs that had been passed down in a rich oral tradition. Something that convinced a weary soldier to march on.

"I was thinking more . . . battle songs? In fact?"

"Oh, certainly," said Anastasia brightly. "I have quite a few." And then she started to sing:

One, two, three, four, five,
A hare went out for a walk.
Suddenly a hunter appeared
And shot the hare.

Bang, bang, oh oh oh,
My hare is going to die.
He was brought home
And he turned out to be alive.

"Hmmm," Sloane went, when the song was over. "Strangely prescient." Her eyes settled on an elderly woman in the crosswalk who had a leash attached to her own shoe. What to make of it? What to make of anything? As the old woman made it safely to the sidewalk and Anastasia pushed into gear, Sloane suggested that in addition to autonomous driving, her car might want to consider trend forecasting, too.

29

Sloane arrived at the office early enough to guarantee that she'd have some alone time before the day kicked in, and thus thought nothing of pressing the elevator's "close door" button until she heard a girlish "Oh, can you hold that?!" coming from the lobby.

Two girls she didn't recognize arrived running to the elevator, grateful at first, then discomfited when they saw the person holding the door for them was Sloane. They all exchanged weak smiles. As the elevator started its surprisingly slow ascent, one of the girls held her phone's screen up in the other's direction. Sloane caught the image of an emaciated polar bear that had gone viral the night before.

"Oh my God, it is so sad. Like, I almost cried," said girl two.

"I *did* cry. I'm, like, basically still crying," said girl one, putting her phone away. "I shared it *everywhere*. I mean, can you even? They're *dying* out there!"

A man in a business suit got in at the second floor. He had very strong cologne. He got off on the third floor. Took his cologne with him.

"Oh, I tried that new *arepa* place?" girl one continued, the air cleared.

"Oh yeah? How was it?" Girl two.

"It was amazing. They have *amazing* flan."

"I am *so* into Panama," said girl one. "I have been, like, *seriously* considering doing New Year's there."

Sloane walked out of the elevator, head shaking. Rather than take offense at the girls' vapidness, she told herself she should instead look for proof of things to come. Lots of people *did* love Latin America. Tacos, tamales, *arepas*, watermelon juice, hibiscus tea and Cuban sandwiches—in the last six years there'd been an explosion of interest in everything Latino in drinkable and solid form. And these were the cuisines of people deeply attached to friends and family, a physical culture with grounding social bonds. And so much of this food was eaten with one's fingers. It certainly wasn't what the girls had intended, but Sloane filed their conversation away under the pro-touch camp.

The open work space area was still vacant—it appeared that Sloane was, indeed, the first one there. She stood there for a moment, waiting to see if any screen savers rose from their slumber with the #sexisdead hashtags she'd been seeing, but all the computers were dark. Whether on an order from Dax or moved by the cleaning staff, the cell phone box wasn't outside the fifth floor conference room any longer, and Sloane felt certain this would be the case with the other floors.

On her way to her own office, Sloane stopped by Deidre's, after seeing the light was on. With her plants and her aquarium, her crochet carpets on top of the already carpeted floor, Deidre's office had the hominess of a high school guidance counselor who liked candle crafts.

"Did you have a good holiday?" Sloane asked kindly, after knocking on the opened door.

"Oh, Sloane! Hi there, hi! I did," said Deidre, pulling a paper napkin over the muffin she'd been eating. "Did you?"

"Sure!" Sloane shrugged. "Some plane trouble. How was 'tree town'?" she asked.

"Oh!" flushed Deidre, happy she'd remembered. "It was great. It was just the nicest. Have you ever been?"

"I *have*," Sloane said, leaning her head against the door frame. "It's a great place."

Okay, so Sloane hadn't actually "been" been to Ann Arbor but she'd had a driver who had stopped for gas on their way to Wayne County airport and it (the general area, not so much the gas station) had had a pleasant vibe. Plus, she felt like making Deidre feel good. Sloane wanted Deidre to feel good and to be happy with herself. Sloane wanted to take back all of the cut-flower food packets she'd thrown away in her lifetime and feed them to Deidre's plants.

Back in her office, Sloane reviewed the outline for her day. A follow-up with furniture (a bright spot: she was counting on Andrew to share the comps of people-reading-books-in-bed ads), another meeting with electronics (dark spot), and later that afternoon, a brainstorm with both the social media and verbal identity team. *We need a name for your empathy robots! I'm really feeling this*, Dax had written in her digital calendar next to the event.

Sloane put the outline down and took stock of the pressure in her heart. Because of hurdles with Roman's paperwork, he'd be video-calling in to meetings so he could stay apprised of what was going on until he was cleared for a work visa. So rather than immediately suffer Roman's physical presence, she'd be gifted with an image of his floating head. Dax had yet to tell her how often she was going to be forced to work with him and under what circumstances (Did they have to sit in on every single meeting together? Would they be leading separate teams? What exactly would it look like, the battle between team Tech and team Touch?), but she imagined some of this would be cleared up in Dax's video post, which had already reached her desk.

She clicked on the e-mail. "Big news!!" the subject line read. She pressed the Play arrow, and there was Dax, a navy cowl-neck sweater with wooden toggle buttons, a deer head nailed into a log cabin interior at his back. Sloane rolled her eyes. He'd made the video in his vacation house.

"Hi, team!" Dax started. "I hope this finds you fresh and fit after a healthy, happy Thanksgiving. I wanted to share a new direction with you that we're taking for the ReProduction summit. As you all know, we've been fortunate to have Sloane Jacobsen with us helping align the products we're going to present with future trends. An exciting addition is that her collaborator, Roman Bellard, is also coming onboard. Many of you met Roman at the talk he gave last Wednesday, and all of you now know him through his "After God Goes Sex" piece that appeared in the *Times* last week. We couldn't be more excited to have this duo guiding us toward the most exciting, most enticing products that we can offer anti-breeders at our summer summit.

"Which leads me to a little twist in the scenario. For those of you who were at Sparkhouse two weeks back, you'll remember Sloane making a very titillating suggestion about the 'professionalization of affection,' in which she posited that people would soon be willing to pay others to outsource their needs for affectionate touch.

"As you all know, Roman is predicting the opposite—he thinks we'll see a certain class turn against penetrative sex in favor of augmented virtual sexuality and a love life lived online.

"Can these two philosophies live together? Sure! But what fun is that?

"What we're going to do instead is organize the summit into two teams: Pro-Tech and Pro-Touch. Roman will be heading up the Smart Blinds presentation and Sloane will be leading the Empathy Bots project—these will be our headliners. You'll find out soon which team you'll be working with. And in the meantime, I hope you'll all agree that this new direction is going to make this the most exciting trends summit yet. I can't wait to see what you're all up to when I get back.

"Till then!"

He waved at the camera, and yellow infographics spun a handwritten copy of Dax's signature across the screen. Sloane immediately tried to get him on his phone. It rang four times and went to voicemail. She started ringing him again.

"Sloane J!" Dax answered, finally. "I'm on the other line, champ! Can I call you back?"

"I just watched the video," she started. "I thought we had more room to brainstorm, Dax. Room to do what we wanted."

"Well, sure you do! Of course you do! Fine"—he sighed—"hold on."

Sloane waited, foot tapping, while he got rid of his other call.

"Sure," he said, back on again, "you guys can keep searching for the hypothetical, but we have to have star products to lead with. For press."

Sloane tried to be reasonable. This was business, it made sense. But she didn't want to be saddled to a project she didn't believe in while she was having premonitions that felt far more important.

"And what the hell are Smart Blinds?" she asked, instead.

"Ah! We'll get to that. But I'm so glad you called me. Was just about to get you on the line. Stellar news, my dear—I've got you both booked on *Tusk*. Had to move a thousand mountains for it, but we're a go."

Sloane bristled both at the name of the conservative TV show and the fact he'd called her "dear."

"I haven't heard anything about this," Sloane said, both feet tapping now.

"Of course you haven't! It just happened! Roman's in L.A. still, so we finagled an eleven o'clock."

"Wait, what?" she blurted, startled. "Today?"

"No time like the present! If you've got anything, cancel it, ASAP."

"But I'm not prepared!"

"You don't need to be," he countered. "That's what a press release is for! It's like a six-minute slot. Video call-in. They want to hear about the summit's new direction. Best idea I've had in a long while. Tech versus touch, the Internet's on fire! Nothing to worry about. Just be you!"

Although Dax liked to run his business with an air of effortlessness, Sloane knew that he went to great lengths to appear spontaneous. Something was wrong about this. He was being far too cavalier.

"I really would have appreciated more time," she said. "I think this feels too rash."

"Story of my life!" he said. "I'll be in the electronics meeting, after. You can tell me how it went."

After they hung up, Sloane shielded her eyes from the piercing winter light glinting off the office windows across the street. She had spent the weekend determined to run the show, and ten minutes into her Monday, it was evident she couldn't. *You do you.* Dax only did Dax.

She had an urge to call her sister, and then, like the memory of something that had happened in someone else's story, she remembered that neither her sister nor her mother had called her back yet. She was worried. Originally, she'd been pissed for selfish reasons— concerned that they'd been purposefully ignoring her, that Leila had decided Sloane had to work a whole lot harder to earn the right to be sisterly again. But now she was just concerned.

She tried her sister's cell phone. She tried her mom's. And then, for no other reason than it was the only other Jacobsen number she had in her contacts, she tried her childhood home.

On the third ring, somebody picked up.

"Mom?" Sloane said, incredulous. *"Mom?"*

"Sloane?"

"Mom?" She felt like she'd entered some kind of space-time continuum. "What are you doing back?"

"Oh!" went Margaret. "Well, actually, Leila's on bed rest."

"What?!" Sloane exclaimed. "Why?! Where?"

"Um, here?" her mother said, her calm clearly an effort. "The baby's a little small, unfortunately. And she was having contractions. On the Jungle Cruise, in fact. Which I'm sure will make for quite a story when everything's, you know, better," she said, adding a little cough.

"Why didn't anyone *call* me?" Sloane cried. "Is she going to be all right?!"

"She just needs to rest, honey. And she wanted to do that here, where she has all her doctors—"

"Should she have been in a plane, though? Like that?"

"Well, she can't have the baby *now*," her mother went, a false laugh in her voice. "She's not due for another two months! So she just needs to rest."

"Well, well, jeez," Sloane said, both stung and panicked. "Where's everyone else?"

"Harvey stayed on with the kids for a few more days. No need to spoil their vacation."

"But why didn't anyone *call?*" Sloane repeated, wondering where in the house Leila was right then. If Margaret's voice was carrying through the floorboards, if it was for Leila's benefit that Margaret was acting nonchalant.

"Why didn't you tell me? I've been trying to reach you guys all weekend!"

"Well, honey," her mom started, "what would that have changed?"

Sloane's response caught in her throat. Her mother must have heard it, because she fell uncharacteristically silent. Several awkward beats passed with neither of them knowing where to go from there.

"I was going to come to Florida, you know," Sloane finally managed. Hurt, jealous, frightened at the same time. "There weren't any flights. I sent you all these messages."

"I know, honey," Margaret said, too easily. "We had a horrible time getting home ourselves."

Sloane bit her lip to quell the lump in her throat.

"Didn't you think that I'd be worried, Mom? Didn't you guys think?"

"To be honest, Sloane . . ." Her mother faltered. "It all happened so fast. It was just a nightmare trying to get home, what with the storm, and then there were logistics, and the doctor, he even had to write a note for the airline, it was really very complicated—"

Sloane heard what her mother wasn't saying. In the sizing up of the people who could be helpful, Sloane hadn't made the cut. It particularly hurt that Leila, whom she'd felt she was gaining ground with, hadn't even managed to get back to her via *text*. God, but that made it even worse, actually. Was she *that* tired? That much in pain? Sloane's heart clenched with everything she didn't know.

"Mom, I'm *here*, now," Sloane said. "I want to *know* about stuff like this. I want to help."

"Okay," Margaret replied with the formality of someone drawing a conversation to a close. "Well, that's good to know."

Sloane wanted her mother to believe her and her mother didn't. She'd cried wolf too many times.

Then Deidre was in her doorway, using her right hand to draw out an exaggerated nose. Sloane got it—*Tusk*. Interview prep time.

Sloane looked up at Deidre; a bird landing on a bough.

"Hair and makeup," Deidre whispered, looking sorry that Sloane had to go.

30

Sloane didn't wear a lot of cosmetics; some blush, a lot of moisturizer. Accordingly, she looked older than her real age—and a little crazier—once the hair and makeup team prepped her for the *Tusk* video call. She was trying to tone down some of the eye makeup with a pull of cotton when the sound technician told her they were ready for her.

"You just sit here," he said, pointing to a black director's chair set up against a black backdrop. "Sorry about the lights, they're super hot. You'll hear the show's producer, and then some prompts . . ."

"No problem," Sloane said, succumbing to the various indiscretions necessary for the technician to wire the microphone under her tunic.

"Try this on for sound?" he asked.

"One, two," Sloane said into the headset.

"You hear anything?"

"Static." She adjusted the earbud.

"Hello?" said a man's voice into her ear.

"Yes, hello, this is Sloane Jacobsen?"

"Oh, hi, Sloane, this is Jarvis, I'm one of the show's producers. We should have you live in five?"

"Okay," she said, blinking at the lights.

"Sloane?" A pause. "Sloane?"

Sloan's eyes were starting to tear up from the heat lamps. She was feeling somewhat nauseous.

"Roman?" she said into the mike.

"Yes, Sloane, hello! Nice to hear you again! This is quite something, isn't it? I had to get up at five o'clock!"

"Did you," she asked, deadpan.

"I did! I did! But Los Angeles is wonderful! The people are so funny! Very busy, but not really. They like all my ideas!"

Because she didn't answer, he rollicked on again.

"They called me 'an ambassador.' Of cybersex. Ambassador, I like it! I should have a big black car! Anyway! I was very excited to hear about this interview last week. Big show, *non*?"

"I'm sorry?" Sloane said, sitting straighter. "You knew about this last *week*?"

"Yes, day after my article. Friday? I lose track."

"You knew about this last week."

"Yes," Roman repeated. "Why?"

"One minute, folks," said Jarvis, coming back on. "We're about to go live . . ."

"How did Daxter tell you?"

"What do you mean?" Roman asked.

"In an e-mail? On the phone?" she clarified.

"Guys?" went Jarvis.

"In a text message, I think?"

"Oh, a *text*," Sloane exploded, the knowledge seeping into her that Dax had purposely blindsided her with this interview. It spread through her like a poison.

"And three, and two, and one . . ."

"Jarvis?" Sloane asked.

"Um, we're going live, here . . ." he answered, nervously.

"*You* are," she said, standing, motioning to the cameraman to stop rolling. "I'm out."

"Oh, hey, hey, hey there," went Jarvis. "We need to be live now."

"Carry on without me," Sloane said, turning off the mike.

Everyone in the Mammoth studio stood there, openmouthed, while Sloane freed herself from the cord running underneath her clothes. The cameraman kept looking from his left to his right, trying to discern who he was supposed to listen to.

A young woman exhibiting dysentery levels of discomfort approached her. "Um, Ms. Jacobsen? I'm Danielle, I'm the assistant producer, and I have the *Tusk* team on the line?"

"This is between me and Dax," she said. She wasn't going to let him push her into sabotaging her reputation. He gave a heads-up to Roman about this interview, and nothing to her. He was going to great lengths to make her look like a fool.

"They're, they're insisting on a . . . comment? If you can't go live?" Danielle continued, attempting to pass a phone to her. "About the products at the summit?"

"Tell them there aren't going to *be* any because people are going to stop buying things. Tell them there's going to be a great big trend of unbuying. Tell them that."

And then she left the studio to find that bastard, Dax.

As unluck had it, Dax found her first.

"I am walking into the lobby," he said immediately when she picked up his call. "I am walking into the elevator. *What* is going on?"

Sloane heard a ping and pulled away from her cell phone: she'd received yet another push notification, dozens all at once. They'd announced the comment she'd given on air during the *Tusk* show, and people were already starting to comment with the #unbuying hashtag.

"You set me up," she said, her attention back to him. "You told Roman about the interview *days* ago."

"Oh, Sloane, what does it matter?" Dax asked. "You're more seasoned than him. I put my PR girls on him. He says weird things sometimes."

"Please," Sloane scoffed.

"Unbuying as a trend, and *you're* the one who's pissed? I think we're gonna have to have a little talk."

"I think so," Sloane said. "Right now."

"The electronics meeting is right now," Dax said. "Where are you?"

"Fifth floor."

"Well, so am I."

She turned, and then she saw him just outside the elevators. Her heart softened as they stood there looking at each other. For the first time, he looked tired. There was talk, and then there was talking face to face.

He slid his phone into his suit jacket and approached her.

"Sloane."

"I'm not happy, Dax."

And then the elevator opened, and a group of Mammothers pegged for the electronics meeting started heading toward them, one of whom was Jin.

She tried to keep her expression stoic lest Dax notice any change in her demeanor.

"Well, we better let them get set up in there," Dax said, putting a hand on her shoulder, friendly like, smiling for the others. "I've just got some stuff to grab."

Jin reached her just as Dax walked briskly away.

"I think I'm in trouble," she said.

31

When Sloane was thirteen, she tried to be a Taoist. It lasted a long time, her affection for the dharma of nonattachment—would in fact still be lasting if she didn't make her living unearthing humankind's desires for people, places and things.

One of the ways Sloane made her new spirituality known to the other eighth graders was by carrying around a navy backpack covered with quotes from *The Tao Te Ching* by Lao Tzu in metallic gold marker. One of these was *Patient with both friends and enemies, you accord with the way things are.* It was a passive quote, one that suggested accepting people rather than changing them, but it was one that Sloane still turned to when she didn't agree with a current trend or frame of mind. It helped remind her that if you couldn't change people, time could. That you had to wait for time.

Time had defeated her inner Taoist, but she still abided by its tenets of open-mindedness and reflection. Thus, with patience as her compass, Sloane entered the conference room where people were busy watching videos: a trending clip of Jimmy Fallon trying to get into a Zentai suit while an already Zentai-suited Roman looked on. Another of the dying polar bear slipping on his melting vestige of a home.

Because the Mammothers hadn't noticed her yet, Sloane felt overly aware of her own body. Her skin was giving off a dank and sulfurous smell, like pennies covered in moss. It was perspiration, excitement, hormones. Self-smelling used to be an indicator of vitality, and in some countries, it still was: people sniffing their armpits, cuticles, genitals and soles to check in with their bodies, see if they smelled the way they did the day before. It was a method that was asinine to the germaphobic culture of the West, but it worked. Sloane hadn't smelled like anything these past weeks, and all of a sudden, here she was, smelling like herself.

The electronics meeting was composed of a larger crowd than Sloane had expected. In addition to Jin and Deidre, Allison was there, and Jarod, and the slew of man-bros who had suggested the No Kidding filter for dating apps. Chaz and Darla were also there from their respective social media departments, and four other people Sloane didn't recognize. And at the end of the table, the call-in version of Roman, his head framed in a screen.

It was eleven thirty, cranky time in offices worldwide. Accordingly, the conference table was laden with an assortment of fruit and nuts to help people keep their blood sugar—and spirits—up.

When Dax finally burst in from wherever he'd gone for his time-out, he positioned himself next to the food platter like a migrant bird, one hand on the conference table, the other shooting pellets of Marcona almonds up into his mouth.

Instinctively, everyone noticed that Dax was markedly off. There were the uncharacteristic under-eye circles, along with a prickly energy rolling off him. Irritation. Indecision. Sloane privately gloated: he hadn't decided what to do about her yet.

Luckily for Dax, he had an object of affection to be distracted by.

"Roman!" he said, his attention on the screen. "Good to have you here! You can hear us all okay?"

"Yes, well!" Roman cried.

Dax circled the room with his wary smile, his eyes scaling over everyone but Sloane.

"Very good," he said, some of his confidence returned. "This is an insane time of year, so let's get right to it. We've got the Smart Blinds for the summit, but I've got Jonathan in account services telling me you all wanted to present something else?" Dax folded his hands and raised his steepled fingers to his mouth, the better to hide the unsettled expression on his face.

"Oh, it's not that we wanted to *present* it," said an itchy man Sloane didn't recognize. "We just wanted to run through it, for our connected home suite? We just need you to sign off, is all."

"Roman," Dax said, turning to the computer. "This is Phillip. Project manager. Phildo, you're on the clock."

A visibly strained "Phildo" straightened to attention and opened up a manila folder from which he removed several pages. Out of nowhere, Sloane's mind skipped to another Lao Tzu quote she used to advertise on her eighth-grade backpack: *If you do not change direction, you may end up where you are heading.* It occurred to her, what with the renewed interest in penmanship she foresaw, that there could be a revitalized market for those golden metallic markers she used to use.

"So, as we all know, the benefits of home automation systems are convenience, accessibility, security, resale," said Phillip, trying to keep his voice level. "What we're seeing, though, in our competitive research, is that most home smart systems remain *closed*. That is, they are focused on the security and safety of one particular home rather than what is going on in the surrounding environment at large."

"Okay, yes," Dax said. "Go on."

Sloane watched Phillip swallow. Hard. "Um, so what we're looking at right now is domestic messaging panels," he continued. "These would be intercom-inspired, voice-activated systems that basically allow you to text people in another room of the house. And for people who live alone, the panels could be a source of timely, bite-sized information: it's hot, it's raining, you need to dress a certain way for work. The panels would also be synched with the Department of Homeland Security's terror alert system, so they could flash orange or red, for example, if there was an advisory in the area, the dweller could put the house on lockdown by touching the screen or their phone."

"Okay . . ." said Daxter, severely unimpressed. "Let's start with the obvious. How is this not superfluous? Why not just get such messages on your phones?"

"Our research shows that people are ignoring text messages, much like they do with voicemail," said a clammy-looking man. "And I'm, um, Seth? From consumer engagement." He waved at the computer screen where Roman was caged. Sloane's heart went out immediately to this dedicated fellow. One of the buttons near the belly of his dress shirt was undone.

Phillip nodded at his colleague, grateful for the support. "There's flexibility in the delivery system," Phillip continued. "The messages could be synched with an irritating sound that would only dissipate once the message was read, especially in the case of emergency situations. Plus," he continued, adjusting his collar, "panel messaging systems allow for greater flexibility between different devices. Aside from the sound, which can be disabled, people don't have to be interrupted by push notifications when they're doing something else on their phones."

Sloane looked around the room to gauge the reaction of the other Mammothers to this ludicrous proposal. Allison was biting a cuticle. Deidre was stone-faced. Jin coughed.

"I don't know." Dax frowned. "This won't work for ReProduction: it's too general public. Like, I totally get the benefit of telling little Billy that it's time for dinner without going up to get him. But as for the other applications?" He scratched his temple. "I need something better."

Phillip's color rose. "Our initial research shows that people would find this technology highly convenient."

The ice inside her broke.

"More convenient than just *talking* to someone?" Sloane blurted out.

"I'm sorry?" went Phillip, as Jin started to laugh.

"I have to say," said Jin, unable to contain himself. "Are we really done with windows?"

"Windows?" Phillip scowled. "No one uses that operating system, it's—"

"I mean the architectural component that lets in light," Jin said. "I mean, if I have a window, then—and this is really modern—I can just look through it and decide all by myself how to dress. I don't need my home automation system to send me a *text*."

Whether or not he was saying this for her benefit, or found domestic panels as unnecessary as she did, her gratitude was such that she felt heat rise through her chest.

"You know," went Chaz, with a note of condescension, "a lot of people actually *don't* have windows, especially in New York. So this could save a lot of people time . . ."

"If I could jump in," said Darla, thrumming her fingers on her coffee cup. "It's true about people not reading text messages anymore. I mean, I know I don't, and I work in social media."

"Thank you," Phillip said.

"Okay, okay, okay, listen. Jesus," Daxter said. "It's a concept that's got legs. We just need to refine it." Dax held his hand up. "Roman. Thoughts?"

"Yes, well, I do think, I do think," Roman fumbled, as everyone swerved to him, "that this is very much on terror. It's not so fun, *non?* Fear?"

Sloane experienced a brief flash of reassurance that Roman hadn't completely lost his mind. He, too, thought domestic messaging panels were a bad idea.

"That's all?" Dax asked Roman angrily.

"Yes?"

"Fine," said Dax. "That's fine. Just give me the next."

"Actually, I'd like to add something," said Sloane.

"You know what?" said Dax, whipping around in her direction. "How 'bout not?"

There was an audible intake of air from the staffers at the table. Sloane held her ground.

"I think what would be *really* radical in the field of communications," she continued, regardless, "would be if you got people *communicating* again. Do you all remember the phone ad of the family streaming *Star Wars* from a camping tent in the middle of the mountains? It goes . . ." Sloane picked up her own phone and typed in something quickly.

"Do we still have bedtimes? Who gets to pick the movie? Who turned on the stars? Kids have a lot of questions, but wondering whether their network can handle video streaming shouldn't be one. If you're not on the largest, most reliable network, what are you giving up?"

Phillip looked confusedly around the room, unsure where to place his loyalty. Then his eyes met his boss's glance, and he chose.

"That ad did really well, actually," Phillip scoffed.

"Um, actually," spoke up Seth from consumer engagement, "it didn't. People were . . . offended. By the nature thing."

"The nature thing?" asked Darla.

Seth reddened. "Well, you know, that nature should be pristine. And off the grid."

"Well, that's just not accurate," said Chaz, the geo viralist. "Glamping has been a trend for *years*. I mean, it's an across-the-nation thing."

"Oh my goodness, people," said Sloane, unable to listen to such middlings anymore. "It's actually pretty subversive. The ad isn't about *glamping*. Though they probably didn't realize it, the company put out the essential question of what we're giving up by prioritizing connectivity. And the answer is: ourselves. Our smart devices have been sculpting the way we think and act and love each other, we're not fully ourselves without them anymore. *That's* why this family can't imagine camping without a reliable network. They're terrified of their own thoughts."

"In relation, in relation to this ad . . ." piped Roman from his screen. "I *do* think that people want universal connectivity. People must always be connected to their virtual lives, lest they suffer a splitting of the self—"

"Okay, okay, you two, enough of the Frenchy mumbo jumbo," Dax said. "This isn't some kind of existential crisis, this is about getting a kid to come down to dinner on fucking time for once. Or if you don't have—Jesus, let's just table the domestic messaging panels since they're such a fucking *problem* for everyone. I swear to God. I should've stayed on the slopes."

Furiously, Dax popped more almonds into his mouth, then he wiped the oil off his fingers using an entire fleet of napkins. She hoped Daxter Stevens liked those fancy snacks. Within three years, when the drought worsened on the southern Iberian Peninsula, Marcona almonds would be entirely wiped out. As would regular almonds. And pistachios. Really, when it came down to natural snacking, only insects would survive.

"Phildo, please. *Please.* Let's just do Smart Blinds. Roman," he said, turning to the computer, "this is what your team is going to present."

Looking like he wanted to get back to the slopes himself, Phillip fumbled through the remaining sheets in his folder. "Of course. Of course. Deidre?" he said, calling her name without looking at her. "Can you pull the images up?"

When Deidre was feeling emotional, she reddened just a little bit behind her ears. This soft, sweet part of her neck was purple now.

"Okay, so Smart Blinds is the working name," continued Phillip, directing his attention to the slide, "but other name candidates are going through verbal. This is just a placeholder. We were thinking of Libert-Eyze, or Freescreens, or Smokescreen . . . I don't know," said Phillip, cringing when he saw Dax's response to the names he was suggesting.

"But the idea is that they're like a . . . well, travel agent, actually," Phillip continued, determined to impress. "A travel agent crossed with a light technician crossed with—"

"House arrest," Jin said.

Dax swiveled in his direction. Phillip's mouth was hanging open, his sentence left unfinished.

"Are you on the marketing team now, or what?" Dax asked Jin.

Jin shook his head at the images. "I just think we could do better."

"And I just don't care!" cried Dax, exasperated. "You're paid to interpret market needs into *ads*, not . . . philosophize! Jesus!"

Sloane watched Jin set his jaw hard against Dax's tirade. Sloane had been concerned with Dax's rejection of her own forecasts, but she saw now that he'd also been holding Jin back—and down. Jin who realized before other people that consumers were ready to see the elderly in advertising again. Jin who shared the same, almost allergic sensitivity to color as she did. Jin who was publicly standing up for her now when no one else would risk it. Jin who had given her her first vaginal orgasm in ten years.

"A *staycation* is the way we're framing it," said Phillip, visibly rattled, trying to get back into the swing of his presentation. "Deidre?"

With her lips pressed hard together, Deidre pulled up the first slide. In the first image, a family of four was situated around a kitchen island. It was morning. They were eating breakfast. There was a pristine view of a mountain and a lake through an oversized window behind the kitchen island.

In the second slide, the same family was shown joined by friends— stylish adults in black denim and loose sweaters. It was evening. A wooden table was decorated with olives, crackers, wine. The same kitchen was just visible in the rear of the image, but this time, the oversized window was showing a series of city lights off in the distance, as if the house were on a cliff. In the third scene, same window, but this time with a first-class view of the Grand Canyon. In the fourth slide, the window situated the house in the middle of a vivid rainforest, monkeys, birds of paradise, huge fronds in the backyard.

"Now *this*," said Dax, his inner glow renewed, "is genius. I'll forgive you the inclusion of the kid thing—we can spin this how we need to at ReProduction. Smart Blinds: *Live anywhere you want.*"

"Without changing homes," said Phillip, beaming. "Or tax brackets."

"Effing *genius*," Dax exclaimed. "I love this. Love it all."

"They're all sensor-activated, of course," Phillip gloated. "And eventually, they'll be holographic. You can incorporate the Smart Blinds into the rest of the Denizen home system so that your house is attuned to the kind of natural environment you desire before you even arrive."

"This, this is very good!" screen Roman cried. "And this can sync up perfectly with augmented sex so that the home experience is more than virtual, but totally interactive."

"Yes, yes," said Daxter, nodding distractedly. "I don't think *everything* has to do with VR porn, but it could have applications in the cybersex world, yes."

Sloane stared dejectedly at the vibrantly colored parrots and the lush, exotic trees. A still life of the ex-wonders of the natural world.

"But this is like the polar bears," she said, half to herself.

"Huh?" went Chaz.

"That image everyone's been sharing," Sloane said, louder now, "of the dying polar bear. People clicked on it and shared it and sad-faced it and came away feeling like they did something about it when they're not doing a fucking thing at all. These—these Smart Blinds, or whatever you want to call them—they're literally *blinders*. This is encouraging people to give even less of a shit about the environment than they already do. Are the rainforests really disappearing if you can see them in your backyard?"

"I have to say," said Allison, who'd been mostly quiet, "it *is* a little spooky." She looked pinched with discomfort to have spoken out against her team.

"*Spooky?*" countered Chaz.

"Well, it does seem kind of closed off," added Seth, a noticeable shake to his voice.

"I won't endeavor to understand what you mean by 'closed,'" snapped Dax. "This is not about taking responsibility for global warming. This is about creating a flattering, soothing, *sexy* environ-ment in the home. It is about"—he stood up abruptly and pointed to the evening shot with the olive-eating friends—"living in some shitty condo in Hartford and feeling like you have a bungalow in L.A. It's about taking a vacation to Belize even if you can't afford it. It's about being a citizen of the world."

"Or it's an encouragement to never leave the house," said Sloane.

"You!" he shouted. "Do you like *anything* we do? God, I should have hired your husband from the get-go!"

Dax turned back to the presentation on the screen. The boiling point of blood is two hundred and twelve degrees Fahrenheit. Sloane had about two degrees to go.

Dax, too, was clearly thrown by the vitriol of his reaction. When he turned back to face the room, defensively reaching for more snacks, he was visibly flushed. Sloane, meanwhile, had used the pause to find the burning core of her instinct under the disgust for this person who had damped her ability to act on her convictions from the moment she'd been hired.

"You know, you don't have to agree with me," Sloane said, her voice bringing her outside of the caged room. "None of you do. You can continue manufacturing and marketing your products as if there's no tomorrow. As if what is happening in the world—to the world—isn't under way." She shrugged. Everyone was staring at her. But she didn't care. She couldn't. It was going to be a goddamn revelation to make her feelings clear.

"It's fine," she continued, looking from Dax to Phillip. "Don't listen to me. Take me for a reactionary. Take me for a forty-year-old woman and all that that calls forth. Except that if you don't listen to me, there won't be any people left to sell your products to."

Jin could barely contain the grin that was rising up inside of him. Deidre's eyes were huge. Dax looked like he was going to jump out of his navy suit, but before he could say a word there was a knock on the glass door of the conference room.

Dax snapped his head up angrily and waved in a terrified-looking intern with a note fluttering in her hand.

"*Yes?*" went Dax, further enraged by the girl's apparent nervousness.

"Um," the intern said, her shoulders scrunched with the psychosomatic distress of having interrupted Dax. "I'm sorry. It's for, uh, Ms. Jacobsen. I couldn't get to Deidre, because, um, Deidre's here?"

Dax looked skyward with impatience. Deidre looked at Sloane.

"This is *really* not the time," went Dax.

"It's just that, um, Ms. Jacobsen?" said the intern, looking down at the note, and then back up at the person she was meant to deliver it to. "Here—" she said, extending the note although Sloane was about six people too far away to reach it. "Your sister's having a baby?"

Sloane went rigid with absorption. She felt like she'd been hit.

"Is she all right?!" she managed, standing, grabbing for the note.

For Sloane: your mom called, Leila's gone into labor. Get to Greenwich Hospital if you can.

"Oh, God, um," the intern fumbled, "I mean, I'm sure? Or . . . I don't know?"

The cloudiness of her answer made everyone look at Sloane. The announcement had warped from something happy to something dangerous.

"I need a car," Sloane said, looking up from the note. She looked to Deidre, afraid her voice would crack. "My car."

"Of course, Sloane. Of course."

Sloane's heart was beating at an awful pace. She didn't know anything about preterm labor. She didn't know what this could mean, what it could look like. She didn't know what would happen to her family if the child died.

"Well," said Dax, sounding outrageously put out. "Congratulations."

"No," Sloane said, eyes flashing. "It's not supposed to—" She raised her head to find Roman's passive countenance staring back at her; nothing to offer; no kind words to share. And then she looked at Jin, who was half standing from concern, incriminating himself with compassion. He didn't say anything, but he didn't need to. *I'll come with you*, his eyes said.

But the old shutdown was in place again. In the face of the sudden information in her hands, Sloane wanted to burrow, emotionally flee. This was supposed to be a happy interruption—the miracle of life is birth—but Sloane had lost the ability to fully believe in love. Love equals loss, loss equals you feeling incomplete for life.

Sloane started stuffing papers into her handbag, the dark thoughts pouring in. But then she saw the way that Deidre was looking at her, and Jin, and Allison, and Seth. They were worried for her. They were invested. They were part of the story now. And then she looked at Dax, who was wiping more oil off his fingers, and Roman on the Roman screen, blinking dumbly.

She stopped gathering her papers, allowed her hands to settle on the top of the cold table. She looked boldly at the eyes of the men who were waiting for her to assist at the most female of all work. Sloane knew that if she left that room, she was leaving Mammoth for good.

To walk away now would be to let Roman's touch-phobic agenda spread its contagion across consumer goods, unhindered. Until all of them crashed.

"You know what?" Sloane said, to Dax. "Can you shut Roman off?"

When Dax looked at her like she was speaking in hieroglyphs, she redirected her request to Seth and Chaz, who were on either side of the screen.

"Could one of you please turn off the computer?" she repeated, folding her arms. "I don't need him stealing my ideas."

"Now, Sloane," Roman said, alarmed. "I don't think you have the right to—"

Sloane's eyes connected with Seth's. He licked his lips timidly, his large face set in concentration. And then he picked up the tablet and powered it off.

"Un-fucking-believable," Dax said, from his perch.

The intern, terrifically confused, was still cowering by the door. "So, um, did you still want me to get you a car?" she stammered.

Sloane turned to her. She was so young. And innocent. All through life, probably, she'd only learned the things she'd wanted to know.

"Stay in or out, as you'd like," Sloane said to her. "This will only take a second."

Not knowing which solution was less frightening, the girl stayed in place. At the table, shoulders tensed. People looked worriedly from one face to the next.

"So what I'm thinking," Sloane said, staring at the table. "What I'm thinking—" She was focusing so steadily she could actually *see* the world inside her mind. Rubber sheets and paper airplanes and the aging of the loved. Borrowed sweatshirts, unwashed sheets, a candy wrapper in the grass. A hissing teapot, steaming. The herringbone pattern of her own aging skin. Her sister, body shambling, mind praying, on a hospital bed.

"What I'm thinking is that you can take this ReProduction

summit and stick it up your ass." She held her hand up as Dax gaped. "And yes, I'm quitting. So I'll spare you that suspense. And not because you're lording Roman around me like some kind of threat, or because this whole pro-touch, pro-tech thing is just you setting me up to fail, but because everything you're producing is just going to make humans *worse* than they are now."

"Yes, well," said Dax, bristling. "You've made that very clear, haven't you. On national TV, while under contract. Which, thank fucking God, you no longer are. Good luck, really, best of luck to you! Getting another job."

"Indeed," said Sloane, glowering back at him. "And good luck to you all, too. Good luck with that one-trick pony of a forecaster. Roman's a valuable commodity right now. He's an entertainer. He'll keep Mammoth in the news. But he's not a trend forecaster, and he's never been one. All of that stuff in his #sexisdead article? That was based on *my* research. *My* presentations. Listen to him and you'll succeed today. You'll succeed tomorrow. But the day after that? You're fucked." She brought her fingers into fists to keep from shaking. She wanted to be impactful. She didn't want to rage.

"While you all can't be bothered to look more than two years in front of you," she tried again, a little calmer, "I am telling you that the days of believing that the Internet can solve everything are coming to an end. Social *interaction* is going to take the place of social media. In-personism is going to trump clicktivism in fundraising, in civil rights. In the coming years, you're going to see your jobs change from the quantity-focused roles of network organization to the quality-focused one of creating organized hierarchies to bring about actual, qualitative change. So if you don't change the course down which you're heading, it's *you* that will be out of jobs."

"It must be embarrassing," Dax said, slyly, "to be this out of touch."

"*I'm* out of touch?" Sloane yelled, launching her hand toward the Smart Blind images that were still onscreen. "You're putting all these resources behind products that encourage people to be so removed from nature that they're happy—actually *happy*—to mistake simulacra for the real thing."

She looked at the Roman tablet, lying facedown on the table. His insta-fame would not survive this, the potential goodness of the world. People still had the capacity to save themselves from total and irreparable disassociation; she had to believe that, or there was no point in going on.

Sloane shifted her weight. She kept staring at the images from the presentation Phillip had made. Brainwork had gone into this, brains inside of human beings who had allowed themselves to buy into the idea that convenience was the same thing as contentment. Those brains were still out there, working on the wrong things. Sloane couldn't even imagine what could be accomplished if people re-appropriated their brainpower. Solutions for grave illnesses. Self-regenerating limbs. Regenerative highway systems that could fill up potholes themselves.

Maybe everything she was seeing was seven years away. Maybe she was wrong, and humanity would never right itself, leaving machine and Homo sapiens to meld into one, tourists now preferring to visit the Grand Canyon virtually because they were too consumed by social anxiety to go that far away. But maybe—just maybe—people were more ready than she thought to shove off the shackles of psychosomatic loneliness. Maybe the revolution could come earlier, if they bucked the trends.

Everyone was sitting still and numbed, perhaps fearing if they said something, moved a limb, that Sloane would stop talking. But she wasn't going to.

"What you guys are doing here is furthering the technological takeover of human hearts and minds," she said, a little quieter. "And it's made you heaps of cash. But how does it feel to live in a world where no one ever needs to ask anyone else for directions anymore, or

to be asked to take a photo of a honeymooning couple with their camera? If you think that selfie sticks are the way to happiness, you're
dead wrong. Human touch is *endangered*. You think the future be-
longs to the type of people who are going to sync their fridges with
their smartphones, but people are ready—not tomorrow, but *now*—
to be vulnerable and undirected and *intimate* again."

Sloane paused, daring the Mammothers to laugh. But laughter
didn't come. Everyone was staring at her open-mouthed, in a complete state of shock.

"Do you want to know what *I* see in the future?" she continued.
"Since it's what you hired me for?" She looked again to the dead space
that no longer held Roman in it. "Instead of augmented sexuality and
virtual sex tools? I see dating systems based on pheromones instead
of algorithms. I see daily check-in spots in wellness centers where
people can be embraced. I see doctors regulating patients' current
levels of human contact as carefully as their blood pressure. I see it
becoming trendy to have a flip phone that does little more than page
people. I see it as the height of elegance to be without Wi-Fi. I see eye
contact as the new stamina. Collaboration as ambition. I see a world—
and it isn't great news for the planet—where people are having *more*
reproductive sex because it's often through the holding of and raising
and protecting of children that people remember how fucking *good*
life is. I see a massive downturn in your profitability margin within
two years. I see you churning out products that people are becoming
courageous enough to realize they don't want. I see people turning on
Mammoth. Turning toward each other. Turning against tech."

Dax was gobsmacked. He was blinking at her furiously, blinking
as if an unearthly dust storm had swept into his eyes.

"You are so, so wrong," he said. "Poor thing."

All of a sudden, a chair scratched across the carpet. Seth from consumer engagement was up on his feet, sweat pooling around his neck.

"I think she's right!" he cried.

"Are you fucking *serious*?" Dax sneered. "Sit down, *Seth*."

"You don't know the first *thing* about business here!" Phillip yelled at Sloane.

"And you prefer working under a freakazoid who thinks anything and everything is going to be solved by cybersex?" said Allison, standing. "Good luck to you, then. I believe her, too."

"Me, three," said Jin, up next.

"I have hated the last three years of every day I've worked here," said Deidre from the corner. "And I quit. I quit. I quit."

There was a strangled sound from the other end of the table, and Seth put out his arms.

There are moments that you presage and things you cannot see. Life, in all its glorious absurdity, still managed to deal Sloane Jacobsen the occasional surprise, thank fucking God. Getting down to business with a work colleague was one of them, starting to fall for him was number two. Seeing the baggy-eyed director of consumer engagement holding his arms out with naked expectation was definitely number three.

Sloane looked at Seth's empty, open arms and then Deidre started to cry.

"Am I going to have to call the fucking *cops*?" Dax asked, looking disgustedly from his head of consumer engagement to his executive assistant. "Are you people for *real*?"

"Are you?" Seth cried, all shine and sheen and courage. "Are *you*?"

And then, as if their movements were orchestrated, Sloane navigated around the table to move into Seth's arms, while Jin quickened across the room so Deidre could collapse into his. Sloane watched over the wide breadth of Seth's shoulders as Jin stroked Deidre's head.

"No one's held me for so long," Deidre confessed.

Meanwhile, it felt like—it was hard to say exactly, because she was somewhat overpowered by the smell of laundry starch—but it felt like Seth was also crying.

"I want to play with my kids again," he muffled into her chest, his hot hands at her back. "But I can't put down my phone!" She could feel him trembling. "I can't!"

"That's it," Dax cried, "I'm calling security."

"Ha," Allison scoffed, "to tell them what?"

"That I am witnessing a complete breakdown of good taste. You, intern," Dax commanded. "Because I've lost my assistant, I need you to contact HR to process exit paperwork."

"Um, actually, you know actually," said the young girl, "I think maybe I'll quit too?"

"Very good! Very good, everyone! Bombs fucking away!"

He hipchecked Allison as he lunged out of the room.

Against her shoulder, Seth continued the ophthalmologic evacuation of a decade of wishes left unmet. At the table, the people who were still seated exchanged expressions of vivid disbelief.

Slowly, gently, Sloane rubbed Seth's exhausted back. In her mind's eye, she watched Dax stomp to HR. It was urgent now—immediate—that she get to her sister's side.

"It's okay," Sloane whispered into a collar bearing the beige streaks of old sweat. "It will all turn out all right."

"Will it?" he asked, his voice cracking.

"Well," Sloane said, recalibrating. "It might."

32

Into the carport of the emergency department, past the glass doors, up the sterile elevator to maternity, Sloane ran to her family. *Everything will be all right*, she found herself insisting to the fall of her own footsteps. *It has to be.*

Room 234 contained three silent bodies: Harvey and Margaret, their hands along the sharp sheets of the hospital bed where Leila was reclined. Sloane stopped at the room's threshold—Harvey looked up first, and she couldn't read anything in his expression. Then Margaret saw her, and her face fell apart.

"Leilee?" said Sloane, running to the bedside. Her sister looked groggy, drugged, her complexion drained. A catheter wound through the railings of the bed under her hospital gown. Sloane took her sister's hand and found it limp.

"Came out like that," Leila said, rubbing out a silent snap. And then she started to cry.

Three cups of cafeteria coffee and a bag of doughnuts later; the child had not died. That did not mean the child *would* make it, explained the doctor, or that there wouldn't be long-term complications, but the baby was alive.

"Alive." "Dead." "Complications." As Sloane stood, dizzy with emotions, she thought the possibilities too much. This was not the moment to expose her shattered sister to the scenarios of "worst-cases," this was the time to deal in facts. Born at twenty-nine and a half weeks, three pounds, four ounces. Present bad news: the baby had an infection of the placenta, and needed steroid injections in his lungs. Current good news: he was being aided by an intubator in his windpipe, but the little fighter was breathing all alone.

Once the doctor left and Leila rested, the three of them wilted with confusion. Margaret, hunched on the cot that Harvey would probably spend the night on, Harvey and Sloane by the bathroom door.

"Have you . . . held him?" Sloane dared.

"Oh no," said Harvey, head shaking slowly, as if in sleep. "He's too small."

Her mother was sitting there silently, still in a state of shock.

"I need to see him," she said, suddenly. "Little Bird."

Sloane watched as her mother pushed herself up creakily from the flimsy bed.

Think of all the humans, Roman had said to her after her explosion at the restaurant. *Think of all the mouths.* Think of all the tiny humans, and the tiny mouths. Commercials and diaper boxes show babies in a state of scrumptious heft, babbling and blue-eyed with perfect, nubby tongues, but premature infants were oily and jaundiced and fit-in-your-palm small. These babies were so small.

Leila's hadn't been named yet, but he *was* a little bird. His dark fingers curled around his impossibly delicate features, his minuscular penis and wrists and ankles wreathed in a net of cords. The plastic, see-through intubator made it look like he was snorkeling in the depths of the four panels that caged him.

Sloane brought her fingertips to the viewing window. Beside her,

her mother—a woman who had been married to an atheist for thirty years—crossed herself.

"So there's my strapping man," said Harvey, putting his own hand to the glass.

"He certainly has your build," said Margaret, dryly.

Harvey and Sloane looked at each other in astonishment. Then Margaret tried to laugh, but it came out strangled. A release of frightened air.

"You think you have two grandchildren, you can take it," Margaret said, staring blankly at the little bodies in their beds. "But you can't take it. You can't take it at all."

And then Margaret started crying again, chokingly. Turned and pressed her face against Harvey's chest.

Day two of ten days of renewed bed rest for Leila; the amount of time Little Bird would have to stay in the neonatal care unit was still undetermined. The hospital staff and nurses stayed reticent and kind as the question marks queued.

Floated on a mixture of anesthesia, painkillers, hormones and adrenaline, Leila was flusher-looking the next day. She'd slept deeply, and had been wheeled to see her child earlier that morning.

"'Gremlin,'" Leila said now, her bed remote-controlled to a half rise so they could talk. She still had wires attached to her. It occurred to Sloane that the world could be divided into people who'd been given intravenous solutions and people who had not. "It's our second choice behind 'Bird.'"

Sloane sat down beside her, comforted rather than disturbed by her sister's sense of humor. Leila had always been blunt and caustic when she was at her best. They had her airy, generous hospital suite to themselves—Harvey had taken the kids to school and was catching up on rest, and her mother was "cooking for the nurses," Leila guessed.

"So how's he doing?" Sloane asked.

"His lungs seem to be improving. But can you imagine? Steroid shots? In his *lungs*? I can't stand it," she said, her eyes welling, despite her earlier humor. "I bring him into the world and the first thing he gets is pain."

What could Sloane say? That Leila shouldn't blame herself? That she was sure everything would turn out fine? Well, she wasn't sure. She had no itching, no inkling, no lava in her gut. Her fabled intuition was either disabled by the radio frequency of hospital equipment or Sloane had absolutely no sixth sense when it came to the outcome of a struggling human life.

"Leilee," Sloane said, stroking her sister's arm underneath the well-worn cotton of her hospital gown, which was covered, incongruously, in a parade of ducks.

"Do the kids know?"

"Jesus." Leila sighed. "Harvey's dealing with that, thank God. Mom offered to talk to them yesterday about it, you can imagine how that might have gone."

"She seems like she's in really bad shape."

"She's worse than me!" Leila exclaimed. "She's worse than Harvey! You know with Mom, though, it's like every fucking grandchild is another chance at life."

Sloane sat silently, her heart beating fast. She had two things to say to Leila. At any moment, a nurse could come in, her mother could come back with a platter of hot food. It was pummeling through her, the knowledge that this might be the only opening she'd have.

She would start with the easy news. Which would make Leila laugh.

"So, Leilee, I have something to tell you," she said, pulling her hand off her sister's arm.

"Oooh. Yeah? Has Roman been arrested?"

"Arrested?" Sloane scoffed. "No. But it's . . . it's something like that. I mean, I might have, like, a beau?"

"I'm sorry, a *bow*?" she gasped. "Which kind?!"

"I mean, we're not at that point yet." Sloane reddened. "We haven't even had a . . . I probably shouldn't have mentioned it, it's just that, he said he might come by today and—"

"Wait a minute. Wait a hot flash of a minute. So, basically yesterday, you're kicking out your husband, and now I'm meeting your *boyfriend*? Like *this*?"

"Well, he probably won't come here, we were just going to meet—"

"Who *is* this guy?" Leila insisted.

"He's a colleague?" Sloane said, with a little flinch.

Leila wanted more details, so Sloane parsed together what she could, painting a portrait of a Jin who had been supportive of her off-brand ideas from the moment she'd started at Mammoth, and how the relationship had built from there, instead of how it had actually started with them schtupping at his mom's. But even while Sloane was telling Leila the horrendously girlish details (she mentioned "really handsome" twice), she was distracted, nervous, kept watching the clock. It was now or never. Had to happen before Margaret arrived.

"There's something else," Sloane said, feeling her face redden.

"Oh my God, you're getting married!"

"No!" Sloane said, shocked. "What?"

"You got fired," Leila said, nodding fiercely. "Because of him."

"No," said Sloane, scrunching up her nose. "Actually, I quit."

"Wait, what?"

"But that's not what I wanted to tell you. Listen, Leila, listen. There's something I have to . . . I want to give to you."

"Okay," said Leila, warily.

Sloane really looked at her sister, both for the first and zillionth time. This face that had widened and slackened and thinned over the years, but the eyes always the same. The eyes she'd smile into as they burrowed underneath a fort on Sloane's top of their bunk bed, the bed Leila had always wanted, that Nina sometimes slept in now.

She wanted her sister. Needed her sister. Thinking nothing bad could come of this, Sloane reached into her bag.

In her hands was the loaf-of-bread card she'd bought, and penned, and never sent to Leila all those years ago. She held it in her palm like something without wings.

"There's a saying that newborns come already bearing bread," Sloane started, trying to keep her voice controlled. "Which . . . which isn't really apropos right now, so I'm sorry about the picture, but it's . . . it's something I wrote for you back when you'd had Nina."

"Nina," Leila said, her voice a little edgy. "If I recall, you sent me some Frenchy outfit with a necktie that would have strangled her if she'd worn it."

"Okay," Sloane said, managing to keep her mouth shut; that hadn't been the gift. "It's just that I never sent you this."

She handed Leila the card. Leila caught a glimpse of the penmanship inside, and her complexion clouded.

"Sloane," she said.

"Just read it," Sloane went, biting her lip.

Sloane read along in her head with her sister as Leila's eyes tracked the words:

Dear Leila,

I can't believe that you're going to be a mother. I mean, of course I can—when I think about the years that brought you to this place, I know why you're going to be a mother and I know why you'll be a great one.

You've always been the grown-up sister in the family, the caring, responsible one. You're a nurturer, too, but you never smother. You listened to me growing up, even when you didn't understand my problems. You listen to everyone, and you act, you show up for things, you help. In so many ways, you have been my *big little sister, and a role model for the person I can't quite become.*

She could tell when Leila reached the third paragraph by the hardening of her jaw. Leila pushed her hair behind one ear, then the other, while Sloane's heart pounded.

I have wanted for so many years to say sorry. You will be a mother; you will have your own triumphs and heartbreaks. In so many ways, it seems too late to say sorry, now. I don't expect you to forgive me—I wouldn't even know how to put into words what I would want you to forgive. You were only eighteen when Dad died. I've had to get to thirty to understand how young that is. I didn't listen, I didn't act, I didn't show up, and I didn't help. Dad was my best friend, Leilee, and I ran away. I know that you think I'm running away, still. But I'm happy in Paris. I've never been as strong as you. I've never been as open. That's why I could never be a mom. After the accident, every fiber in my being said I had to live somewhere Dad hadn't. Nothing here reminds me of him, nothing reminds me of us. I'm with a man now who couldn't be more different than Mom, and Dad, and you, actually, and that is what I need. It isn't right, it isn't kind, but this is what healing has ended up looking like for me.

I'm sorry for destroying our friendship. I regret making it so that you had to rise above the grief and be the bigger one. I don't actually expect you to forgive me, but you've always been nobler than me. Maybe one day you will understand that this is me being weak, it isn't me wanting to hurt you. And I'm so sorry that I did.

This isn't even a good apology, and there's no room left on this card. I love you, Leilee, I've always loved you, and I'm excited and a

little jealous of your life. One day soon, I hope to share it with you, the
way we shared everything before.
     Your sister,
     Sloane

Sloane stayed quiet as her sister finished, her chest a drum about to burst. She knew that Leila was rereading it, not ready to lift her eyes from the page. It occurred to Sloane that maybe this hadn't been the right moment, that she had no right to be there while her sister read it, and then her sister looked at her.

"What am I supposed to *do* with this?" she cried, wiping under her lashes. "Nine years later? What is wrong with you? Why didn't you just *send* it?"

"I don't know."

"It's so fucked up," Leila said, her chin trembling. "You know how much I needed to hear this? Do you?"

"I don't," Sloane stammered. "Yes."

"I can't believe you didn't send it. You not sending this is almost worse than you never having apologized at all. No—" Leila said, wiping at her eyes again, this time with a fist. "Maybe I don't mean that. But Sloane, this is—" She pressed her lips together. "I wanted this. So much."

"I know," Sloane choked out. "Something's . . . wrong with me."

"Yeah, no shit," said Leila. "But so what? What if something 'goes wrong' with you again?"

A little noise came out of Sloane's throat, guttural, infantile. She stared down, ashamed. She could feel her sister deciding what to do, and she knew that she deserved nothing.

"Oh, for fucking hell," said Leila, opening her arms. "Come in and give me a hug, I can't move or my stupid stomach will split open."

Sloane started to cry. But she moved to her, she moved to her, her forehead near her sister's, the chalky smell of her hot scalp.

"I'm so sorry," Sloane said against her cheek.

"Just don't be an asshole. Don't do this again."

Sloane sank into the fragile surety of it—tentative, but pulsing. That maybe almost everything could be righted.

"Oh!" exclaimed a sudden voice behind them.

Her mother, joy spreading across the long plains of her face.

"Bad timing?" Jin, beside her, mouthed.

33

I can't believe you came," said Sloane, fork poised over the phosphorous deli ham in her chef's salad.

"I know," Jin said. "We really do choose only the finest places to dine."

They both ate a little, then he asked if she'd been online.

"Online?" she said, incredulous. "I'm kind of . . . *dealing* with something here."

"You're trending," he continued. "Or, your resignation speech is."

"What?" she balked.

"Someone must have recorded you. They're trying to find out who. They went through all our cell phones. Dax is out of his mind, of course. It's made his company look like it's in total mayhem."

"Someone *recorded* me?" she repeated, shocked.

"Here." He took his cell phone out and called up an audio recording with thirty-seven thousand shares:

> *. . . human touch is* endangered. *You think the future belongs to the type of people who are going to sync their fridges with their smartphones, but*

people are ready—not tomorrow, but now—*to be vulnerable and undirected and* intimate *again . . .*

Sloane threw the phone back at him like something hot. "I don't want this. I don't want this! I can't think of this right now!"

She had apologized to her sister, and her mother had seen. She wanted to be anywhere but inside her head.

"It was just uploaded this morning," Jin said, putting the phone away. "Hashtag: #IntimateAgain."

"And yesterday, it was #sexisdead," Sloane muttered, unimpressed.

"You don't think they're going to be jumping at the bit to sign on to a movement that says more sex instead of none?" he asked.

"Can we not talk about this, here?"

Jin's eyes softened. "Do you want to talk about it?" She knew from the change in his tone of voice that he was referring to her sister's baby. And her sister, too.

"I don't know if I want to talk about it," she said. "But I don't want to talk about *this*." She gestured toward his phone. "I really just need to live in denial about the Mammoth thing until they come and pry Anastasia out of my hands and *make* me think about it. Or maybe they'll tow her—I mean, she has agency. She's autonomous. She might try to stay."

"You know, I've met your family now," Jin said, chewing. "I should probably have a proper introduction with your car."

"I wouldn't call walking in on two crying thirty-somethings *meeting* them."

Jin put his hands up. "There's still time."

"You're such an optimist. You're not worried about being seen with a persona non grata?"

"You're very much grata," Jin said. "Promise. Look online."

Sloane sunk her fork tines into the last crunch of romaine, its edges tinged with dark.

"Listen, I'll come back tomorrow," Jin said, with a brightness that felt forced. "We'll have a proper dinner. Somewhere that's not this."

"You don't have to do this, you know," she said.

Jin arched his eyebrows. "Do what, exactly?"

"Pity me."

"Oh, Sloane," he said with a tired sigh. "What are you doing to yourself?"

Internet searching her own name, apparently. #IntimateAgain was the seventh trending topic in the nation, #sexisdead was number two. Sloane scrolled the recent headlines associated with her, most of them combining what Jin had called her "resignation speech" and her *Tusk* appearance. "Acclaimed Trend Forecaster Tells Mammoth CEO: Change Course, or Else." "Sloane Jacobsen Proclaims the Death of Social Media: Social Interaction Is Next." "Jacobsen to Mammoth: You're Making Humans Worse."

Afraid of what else she was going to find on the endless steppes of the World Wide Web, Sloane traded the hospital cafeteria for the safety of her car.

"I wish you'd let me know you were coming!" Anastasia chided. "I would have preheated. Coffee? How is your sister doing, Sloane?"

"She's okay," Sloane said, settling into the backseat. "Frustrated. There's not a lot of information yet. We're just waiting. Coffee sounds great."

The internal mechanisms of the seat divider began to whir.

"You've been receiving a great number of phone calls," Anastasia reported as Sloane waited for her beverage.

"HR?"

"Not yet. Reporters."

"Apparently, I'm trending."

"'Power Couple Splits Ranks!'" Anastasia exclaimed. "I heard!"

Sloane relaxed a little, temporarily amused that Anastasia was keeping tabs on her. But then she saw the dusting of snow across the roofs of the cars in the hospital parking lot. Waiting was the universal activity at a hospital. You waited to get better. You waited on someone else.

Sloane was tired all of a sudden, irrevocably so. She felt far away from her sister and absolutely helpless, even though she knew there wasn't anything that could help either Leila or Little Bird right then but time and rest.

Apparently, rest was what she needed as well because when she opened her eyes, the sun was higher and most of the snow had melted from the sea of cars.

"Ah," said Anastasia, as Sloane blinked her way back to herself. "Seat biometrics registered deep and even breathing. A very nice rest."

"Was I out for long?"

"Ninety minutes."

Sloane creaked her neck. "Oh gosh."

She gathered up her stuff quickly, stretched her neck again.

"I'm going to go check on everybody. See if anything's changed."

"I'll be here," Anastasia said.

Sloane flushed with the possibility that Anastasia was going rogue as well.

Back in Room 234, Harvey and her mother were in seats flanking either side of Leila, their faces upturned at the television mounted on the wall.

"Any news?" Sloane asked, setting her bag down.

"You!" said Leila, pointing.

Sloane groaned as she saw what they were watching. It was the *Tusk* footage from her aborted interview with Roman. On the left of the split screen, Roman was holding court about the gateways to virtual reality: anticipatory computing, third-wave electronics, mental interface bays. On her side of the screen, her headshot accompanied by a quote: "Trend forecaster Sloane Jacobsen: *There aren't going to be any more products . . . there will be a great big trend in #unbuying.*"

"Oh," said Leila, turning toward her. "You *totally* got fired."

"And you?" Brian Naecker, the program's host, was asking Roman, apparently in reference to the statement she had given.

"Well, of course that's absurd," Roman said. "Electronics are our airways. They keep us much more than connected. They keep us alive."

Brian made a crack about Roman being a good fit for Mammoth, since they were a *tech* company after all, before thanking him—and Sloane, he'd added with a snicker—for being on his show.

The anchor of the news show returned.

"Sloane Jacobsen and Roman Bellard were both hired to consult as trend forecasters for Mammoth, but yesterday, in a speech that is making the rounds of the Internet, Ms. Jacobsen resigned from her position. It remains to be seen whether Mammoth's CEO, Daxter Stevens, will replace Jacobsen or whether Mr. Bellard alone will be guiding the company toward their annual trends conference this summer. In related news, Mr. Bellard is facing serious criticism from conservative groups for his anti-penetrative sex stance that is, as one spokesperson called it, 'An absolute defilement of American values and a serious threat not just for the family unit, but for the continuation of human life.' Several dozen protesters were seen picketing Mammoth's New York headquarters this morning, seeking deportation of Mr. Bellard to his native France."

Up came an image of the picketers, bundled in down jackets, holding homemade signs.

"Well, damn," said Harvey, with a whistle. "You've sure been keeping things from us, Sloane."

"It's not as big as—can we just turn it off?"

"I actually don't know if you *can*," said Leila, shaking the remote at the TV. "I'll mute it."

"Honey!" exclaimed her mother. "I can't believe you're on TV!"

Sloane couldn't keep from laughing. Nothing she had accomplished had ever really made sense to Margaret. But breaking up with Roman, being on a national news program, being joined at the hospital by a man who seemed to care about her, these things did.

"It appears I am," she said.

"Well, what are you going to do now?" Margaret asked, excited.

"There's nothing to do," Sloane said. "I quit."

"But Roman! Honey," she said, looking over at Leila. "Jin! You didn't say!"

"You know he's twenty-eight, right?" Leila said. "Did she tell you that?"

"I thought he might be even younger." Her mother laughed.

Across from her, Harvey looked just as stunned as Sloane to be part of a moment that universally translated into them functioning as a family. Could it be this easy? Did Margaret only need to see that Sloane loved Leila as much as she always had to make everything all right?

"If you're all done making fun of me, can I get an update on the baby?"

"Oh, he's doing better," said Margaret, pleasure running through her like a glass becoming full. "The doctor says that at the end of the week, Leila might be able to hold him. And maybe this weekend the breathing pipe can come out."

"And he's gained five ounces." Leila beamed.

"Oh, Leila, that's so wonderful," Sloane said. "Name?"

"We really do like Bird," she said, "But he'll probably be teased."

"Do you know they have forty-two days in the U.K. to decide?" said Margaret. "Leila looked it up."

"We have until we leave the hospital," Leila said. "And with the state of this mother/son team, that could be a while."

"Well," said Harvey, his attention returned to the muted television showing a clip of Roman walking through the greenmarket in his Zentai suit. "We're not naming him Roman, that's for freaking sure."

34

That night, with Jin beside her, Sloane couldn't sleep. It was the presence of his body, the steadying companionship that would be taken away from her with the work day's alarm clock, but it was also the visions and the TV clips and all the visual noise that came with them.

She'd seen more of herself on television. Everywhere, she, Roman, Mammoth . . . all difficult to avoid. Several news channels had even done interviews with Mammoth employees, and these real interviews interlaced with the fictitious ones floating in her sleeping head.

There had been Phillip, who had declared Sloane an "enemy to reason and technological advancement," another one with Darla who had stated, somewhat unconvincingly, that Sloane was "just old-fashioned." Daxter had been sought—but not reached—for comment, sources said.

Other clips, unreal and bizarre. Mina Tomar had appeared naked in the Mammoth food court holding up a percussion mallet. "You just have to go for what you want," she said to the journalist, whom she'd convinced to strip down, too.

Andrew Willett appeared as a teacher in a day-care, surrounded by a flock of little toddlers in business suits. "We used to be married," he said, when asked about his time under Sloane Jacobsen. "It didn't work out."

Anastasia and Deidre appeared on a walk together in the autumn woods. The scene was filmed in the style of a commercial about incontinence, where everything insinuated softness, freedom, peace. Anastasia was a redhead, pale-skinned, beautiful. Deidre was herself but she had on a flattering blouse and pumps with which she managed to navigate the leaf-strewn dirt path.

"She does want her mother." Deidre nodded, while the music cued.

"I tried," said Anastasia, sighing.

Deidre put her arm around her friend.

"At least we have each other," dream Deidre said.

There were more dreams, most gone unremembered. Something about Little Bird. Something about her mom. When she woke, Sloane remembered that she had told her sister that she wanted to do something for the anniversary of her father's death. And in an instant she knew what it was.

She looked at the clock on the console, decided it was late enough. Put her fingers to Jin's cheek.

"Hmmm . . ." he said, smiling to wake.

"Jin?" she whispered. "Jin?"

"Hmmm," he said again, kissing her hand.

"I know this isn't what you say after a night of . . ." She paused as he put his sleepy lips to her hand again. "But I need to see your mom."

Sloane arrived at Jodi's office having no idea what to expect. When Sloane called, she'd said she was "ready for the thing they'd talked about," and Jodi hadn't asked any other questions than, "When?"

The Brooklyn studio was bright and simple: wooden floors, brick walls, the corner angles crowded with broad plants. Near an iron-paned window, a colorful shrine had been built to a deity Sloane didn't recognize. The air was filled with the scent of beeswax slowly burning.

After storing Sloane's coat and hat in a separate closet, Jodi anointed her with lavender oil: she rubbed some slowly, slowly on her forehead, wrists and clavicle, then she invited her to sit down on the floor in front of her. She brought her a pillow in case she felt overwhelmed or uncomfortable, and needed to lie down.

"All right," Jodi said, her smile wide and warm. She put her hands on each of her knees and relaxed her own posture. "Do you know why you're here?"

Sloane's shoulders rose involuntarily in an embarrassed shrug. "I'm ready to clear my head," she said.

"Okay," Jodi said, kindly. "Making it here is already a step you can be proud of. I try not to guide people on their individual journeys. Is there anything else you'd like to say?"

Jodi's voice had an alto softness to it paired with a reassuring bass that made Sloane feel supported by her words.

"Well, I guess I've got some things that have been holding me down. With my father. That I'd, um, like to get past."

"All right." Jodi nodded. She tipped a satchel open, and a selection of river pebbles and gemstones came tumbling out.

"Just choose the ones that speak to you," she said.

Sloane eyed the gemstones, but their glittering pulsations felt too charged. She picked up a charcoal-colored river stone, unremarkable except for its heft. Next, a white stone—really just a pebble—that made Sloane think of the gravel in the driveway of her parents' house.

The last stone was light gray and marbled with pink threads. It reminded her of beach trips with her parents and sister when she was a little girl. All the hope she'd held within her person when she had been part of something complete.

"Okay," said Sloane. "I think those are my stones."

"Very good," said Jodi quietly, putting the other ones away. "I want you to think of something that's causing a negative emotion inside you, something carrying heaviness. Try to distill the feeling into just one word. Then speak it into your stone."

Already, just having this prop between them made it easier to delve deeper into the meaning of the memories that were rising up inside her. She ran her thumb over their smooth and jagged shapes.

"Fear," Sloane said, placing the heaviest stone down.

She looked at the two stones remaining in her hand.

"Ease," she named the small pebble.

"Family," she held the pink stone, her nose pricking with heat.

"Okay," said Jodi softly. "Pick up the one you want to talk about."

She started with "ease." Keeping her attention focused on the stone, she said she had a fear of being happy; that if she let herself sink into contentment, someone would die again. It was incredible how eager her dread was to be recognized. The tears came lightning quick.

But she pressed on, reached for the next rock, representing "fear." This was an extension of her first worry, that if she let herself change too much for the better, she wouldn't be able to *sense* things like she used to. Wouldn't be able to do her job.

When Sloane picked up the final stone, Jodi echoed, "Family."

Sloane felt her throat tighten. This stone held all the others.

"My sister just had a child, her third one," she admitted, haltingly, the stone pulsing in her palm. "And it has all these . . . problems. But I don't feel steady—or removed about it like I did before. I've always said I never wanted to have children." She curved her fingers to the stone's increasing heat. "But I don't know. Maybe it was a protection thing."

"From what?" Jodi asked.

"From joy."

Jodi made a soft sound, and then rose to her feet. Sloane listened to her putter across the room, and had a terrible feeling that she wouldn't be back. That Sloane had disappointed her. That it was disheartening to be near someone so buffered.

But she did return. Jodi asked her to lie down; said she was going to place the three stones where she felt Sloane was still holding on to too much energy.

Jodi placed the "ease" stone on her throat. The "fear" stone found Sloane's stomach, just above her belly button where trepidation churned. And finally, "family."

The third stone landed right above her groin, and when she felt it there, an indignation rose inside of her so strong she wanted to sit up. This wasn't right, Jodi hadn't "read" her, she hadn't understood a thing. The "family" stone should have been placed above her heart, or closer to her stomach, closer to the private place where she harbored all her fear. It was presumptuous, that placement—it was like Jodi was *mocking* her by putting the "family" stone somewhere erotic. Sloane's throat burned from the realization that Jodi didn't have the kinds of instincts she thought that she'd possessed. She felt pity for Jin's mother, and embarrassment for herself, a grown woman trying to believe that little stones could matter.

But she didn't say anything, and she didn't move. And the more she lay there with the third stone burning its truth inside her, the more Sloane began to realize that this stone had been put exactly where it needed to be placed. All of the joys she had withheld from her body were suddenly pulsating underneath the heat of that third rock; her hurts had been recognized, one of her greatest deceptions seen. She'd maintained a sexless relationship for so many years that she'd convinced herself she was the kind of person who could function without love. And Jodi, somehow, had sensed this. And she disagreed.

Deeply ashamed, Sloane turned her head to the side. Jodi bent down and put her hands on each side of her temple, her palms newly warmed with oil.

"It's okay," she said.

Sloane wanted to cry. She wanted to cry out all of the damage she'd done by insisting that someone like Roman stay in her life. She wanted to cry for all the experiences she might have had during the ten years she'd been with him, cry for the boyfriend before him that she'd broken away from without explanation after her father's death. Cry for all the times that she'd known she needed to be touched and hadn't allowed herself to have anyone to ask. She wanted to cry because she had a new chance now with a new someone and she feared her capacity to sabotage it.

"It's possible that you're feeling a lot of swirls of energy right now," Jodi said, continuing to knead her head with warmth. "I'm going to come around and try to drive some of the troubling energy away. And then we'll see if we're ready to talk about cords."

Sloane kept her eyes closed. She just wanted to be held. But then she heard a beating, an almost winged thrush, like something had risen up and over them, born from the stand of plants.

Sloane opened her eyes a slit and saw a wing passing over her, a large one with gray feathers as dark as her fear stone. *Am I being fanned with a severed eagle's wing?* her inner cynic asked. But the better version of herself pushed aside the skeptic. *Breathe into this*, that person said. *It's working.*

Jodi swept at her as if she were trying to drive away her guilt. The scented air that she was pushing away from her and toward her had an almost sexually stimulating effect, and all of a sudden, in that relieved lightness, Sloane saw the way forward. All this time she'd believed she needed to come to terms with her father's death, that she needed to move on. When in fact her wars were all internal. The huge, completed life she'd walked away from hadn't disappeared.

"I think I can do this," Sloane said suddenly. She pushed herself to sitting. "I can cut the cord."

"You're certain?" Jodi asked, her voice surprised, but free of judgment.

"Yes."

Jodi helped her to stand. Sloane's desire for connection was stronger than the fear. She raised her hand. She *wanted* to be happy. She was ready for that now.

Right before she cut herself away from all the fears she'd used as armor, she looked the person that she had been in the eyes. The eyes were not reproachful. They looked tired and resigned.

Good-bye, Sloane said, bringing her hand down.

Not sorry, just good-bye.

And the person that she had been smiled back at her. As if she had been ready to leave for a long time. As if she had only been waiting for Sloane to let her.

35

When you're clear-sighted, you settle into experiences that feed you until they become so familiar and soul-filling that they're a nourishing routine, and as the routine continues, you up and surprise yourself with your righted life.

A year later, tactual trends were still gaining momentum. With her resignation speech a touchstone, Sloane was positioned as the figurehead for a revolution in social interaction that privileged face-to-face relationships over those lived online, and Sloane and Jin reveled in tracking the waves of these new connections.

In Japan, people had started to wear designer straitjackets to keep themselves from reaching for their phones—there was a move among trendsetters, almost a dare, really, to see how long they could go without their devices. It was proving difficult, the fingers twitched and phantom rings were heard. The jackets helped: in addition to broadcasting to the outer world that the wearer was "digitally cleansing," it also kept the hands from making contact with their cells.

In Delhi, the young and well-to-do had started participating in body language clinics where older people taught nonverbal communication skills that had fallen out of practice: eye contact, empathetic facial expressions, body postures, how to use space.

In the southern states of America, there'd been a tremendous rise in fishing: people in their twenties were flocking to cell-phone-free lakes and trout streams to learn patience and relax.

On lodging sites, there'd been such a clamor for "deconnected" homes that public rental sites like Airbnb had created a subgenre for "pure" housing that didn't have Wi-Fi. Most of these were in bucolic places—Montana log cabins, lake homes in the Catskills—but increasingly, the all-white vector icon that signified Internet-free zones were cropping up next to listings all around the world. Cafés, bars and hotel lounges followed suit. It was becoming not just impressive not to have Wi-Fi: it was becoming cool.

A "free running" movement had started around the country with people going for jogs and exercising in public places without MP3 players or headphones, without cell phones or fitness trackers, without even cash. There was a proliferation of antitech street art sweeping global cities: just that afternoon, Jin had showed her a wilted flower with its head emerging from a Brazilian subway platform: *the awakening of the poisoned youth.*

Jodi said she'd never had so many new patients in her energy therapy practice, and Leila reported that not one but all three of her regular babysitters were using flip phones that did nothing more than text. Kai had called her recently from London to tell her about a recent spate of "Contacters" who were gaining force in Leeds. They refused to sign on screens during any kind of transaction, and they only paid by cash. Adherents to the movement were putting "hand-to-hand" stickers everywhere, underscoring their belief that the more physicality that was returned to over-the-counter interactions, the less likely it would be for computers to take over human jobs.

While all of this had been unfolding, Sloane had been considering the next iteration of her work life. As fired up as people were with the way she'd flipped off Mammoth, she'd still publicly quit an influential company, and it took time—necessary time—for the things that Sloane had predicted to start making sense to the outside world. For a long time, the calls from clients didn't come. Until they did.

It was with the *New York Times* profile on pheromone dating that Sloane started getting loads of interest from new clients. The article described the underground T-shirt–sniffing parties currently sweeping the youthsters in which blindfolded attendees chose their mates by sniffing articles of clothing that had been worn for three days and then sealed into a plastic bag. To the intelligentsia who'd been following Sloane's predictions, this was proof that she'd been right. After years of entrusting their love lives to their cell phones, young people were ready to trust their noses again.

None too eager to fall back into the corporate world she'd so recently left, Sloane started a new consultancy that offered emotional and behavioral trend forecasting services to companies championing an in-person agenda. She refused to consult directly on consumer trends, and only took on clients who were honestly excited to talk about the possible changes in ways that people would start to act and think in the decades—not years—ahead.

No matter how far away they were, consulting sessions had to take place in person. Not over the telephone, not via e-mail, not even by Skype. Yes, this cut down on the amount and type of clients that Sloane could take on, but that was exactly how she wanted it. After all, she was going out of her way to make sure she had the right amount of work: just enough to be stimulating, not enough to be swamped. Little Bird, her godson, was one now. The other day he said, "Slow!!" which was close enough to her first name to make her heart double in size.

And she had found a new understanding with her mother, as well. Margaret wasn't someone to whom she could just apologize: she needed to spend the rest of their time together turning her life into proof that she understood how she had hurt her, and that she regretted it. But that didn't stop her from knocking on her mother's bedroom door one night while visiting to try. It had been a long Saturday, full of the kind of outdoor chores that would make Margaret feel loved. Weed-whacking, scrubbing moss from the patio pavers, reinforcing the fence. She'd been getting into the guest bed with Jin when she felt it in her stomach: action was essential, but words were needed, too.

There is something incredible about the phrase "I'm sorry." When it's used carelessly, the expression is impotent, and can even offend. But when you really, really mean it—even if your mother is nightgowned and bed-ready with a scrum of toothpaste still in her mouth, when the words rise up inside of you on the strength of every way in which you've changed, it can be enough.

Surprisingly—if gratifying—she'd even had overtures from Mammoth. In the months leading up to the summit, as Roman's meteor soared, and soared, and phenomenally crashed, and people all over the world started tabling their cell phones, posting and think-piecing and taking to the streets to "get back into real touch," Daxter came to Sloane with a golden olive branch. She could consult for Mammoth in the iteration and the scope that she desired, she didn't even have to come into the office, they just wanted her advice. Cell phone sales were down for the first time in company history. Should they make more apps? How could they rejigger their consumer offerings so that people felt they were "participating" in a movement, instead of being asked to "purchase" a version of something they already had?

Sloane entertained Daxter's advances just enough to get her car back. Not her *car* car, of course, but a smart assistant version of it made possible by anonymous fans of hers in IT and HR. When word had gotten out of how attached Sloane had been to her M-Car (it was the least she could do after sabotaging their consumer electronics sales that quarter, to give them some good press), a package arrived, unsigned, with instructions on how to transpose the car's assistant system into her personal phone and landline. Even if Sloane missed being chauffeured around the city (with a hot beverage and conversation, no less), it felt great to have her efficient, considerate and biometrics-focused friend back.

And in the months after her defection from Mammoth's corporate seat, Sloane was inundated with restless staffers who wanted her to take them with her. For the moment, she had only hired away Mina to direct graphic design, but her workload was getting to a point that Sloane knew she was going to have to hire an assistant. She'd wanted Deidre, wanted her from the start, but Deidre had eloped with consumer-engagement Seth, and was running an adult arts camp out of the Bahamas with her new husband and stepchildren.

So that led Sloane to Anastasia, who turned out to be a tie back to the very trend that Sloane had rebelled against. She was an admission that there was a lot of good about technology. She was a modern compromise.

Roman was given a two-million-dollar advance for his first book and it didn't sell. By the time *Can't Touch This* published in the fall, school shootings had increased and people were inoculating themselves against the inanity of politicians who preferred fighting for holiday wreaths on coffee cups than gun control by going out and organizing with their neighbors so that they could be better than the people they'd put in charge. The increase in neighborhoodliness meant new connections, which also meant an increase in recreational sex.

With his unsold hardcovers sent back to be pulped and his post-sex theories conspicuously unfashionable, Roman came crawling back to Sloane as she'd known he would. After his fallout at Mammoth (his project presentations for ReProduction had been a one-track-minded, degenerated mess), he'd nonetheless been offered a guest lectureship at New York City's The New School, after only three weeks at which the inevitable had happened, and a student's parents had complained about Roman's teaching getup. (Since his rocket rise to fame and consecutive fall from it, he'd been conducting all his professional and personal business in his Zentai suit, in hopes of rocketing back.) Public opinion and the college's fear of litigation forced him to resign, his work visa wasn't renewed, and in the spring he came to Sloane tearfully, his unflappable countenance decidedly flapped. He didn't want to return to France. He couldn't. Not after the life he'd had a taste of, the man he had the potential to be with Sloane at his side. He could admit it now, he had to: he needed her help. Would she consider a lecture circuit with him? Sloane gave him the information of the couple renting her apartment in Paris so he could arrange to have his things moved out. Godspeed, she said, good luck, and by the by, if he couldn't afford to fly direct back to Paris, he should stop at the Schiphol airport in Amsterdam. They had great finger food.

It was June when the loss of balance started—a certain physical offness that felt like vertigo. When Sloane walked around it seemed that the very pavement shifted underneath her calves. The effect was unnerving and destabilizing, as if she were tilting through a city block with one heel on and one heel off.

Sloane feared Lyme disease—they'd spent almost every weekend that spring at Jin's mother's place in the Berkshires, where the dreaded things hitchhiked in on firewood and dog fur and barn coats. She had Jin check her hair, her body over many times. It was an excuse, really, for his touch, really. Almost every time.

She next decided that it must be mononucleosis. After that, anemia: the intelligence-compromising dimness of a body low on oxygen. Diabetes was proffered by a particularly clueless nurse's aide:

Sloane declined the test. Chronic fatigue syndrome? But she felt dreamy, not fatigued.

It wasn't until they were having lunch on a rare weekend in the city when they both opened their eyes. Sloane had ordered a raspberry soda, not at all typical, as she disliked things that fizzed. Jin ordered a beer. And then he looked at his beer, and he looked at her drink, and she watched him take her in. And it was in that moment, Jin knocking his glass over to reach for her, the syrupy liquid spreading across the table like a protective film, that she saw every second of the glorious rites to come. They would ask for the check from the young waitress, leave the restaurant shaky. The pharmacy with its bright solutions, the public restroom with its droning, touchless flush. The way she would lean against the cold metal of the bathroom stall, the white tester in hand. The minutes like rolls of thunder barreling through her head while she waited to see life.

ACKNOWLEDGMENTS

Sally Kim and Rebecca Gradinger: through the twists and the turns and the seemingly endless iterations of this sprawling project, you believed in the version that we are holding now. Your respective edits put some hair on my chest but this story is better for them, and I am a better writer with both of you at my side. Thank you for not giving up on me.

Veronica, Gráinne, Melissa and everyone at Fletcher & Company: thank you for it all. Ivan, Danielle, Alexis, Ashley M. and Ashley H., Elena, Emily, Christine, Carrie, Joel, Anna, and the rest of my super team at Putnam, thank you, thank you, for your support, your tangible enthusiasm, and for bringing me on board. Thank you, also, to my original Touchstone team and especially to Susan Moldow.

This book could not have been written without reliable childcare. Thank you to my big and boisterous family, and especially to the tireless women in my life who took planes and trains and highways to give me time to write: my giant-hearted mother Linda, my all-seeing mother-in-law Annie, and our neo-southern belles, "Moo Moo" and Ashley. And to the team at NELC: every day I'm grateful to you, don't ever disappear!

My friends: for the tequila, the hugs, and the eardrums, thank you. Thanks especially to Jeff, Emily, Alana, and Sebastian, who were especially supportive of this project from day one.

Rodrigo Corral: you nailed it. Colin Lane: thank you for showing me in a good light yet again. Thank you to the early endorsers of this novel and the friends who helped me get in touch with the writers I look up to.

Thank you to the horses. (You know who you are.)

Thank you to the baby who saw me through the final rewrite. You came on time. You left too soon.

Thank you, Gabriela. Everything else is just atoms and particles when I'm with you.

Diego. I don't know how you manage, every morning, to wake up and say, *I'm going to do what I can to support her,* but you've done it every waking hour of this year. Your kindness is an example to me. Bring on your next film.